The Book of Form & Emptiness

The Book of Form & Emptiness

RUTH OZEKI

CANONGATE

First published in Great Britain in 2021 by Canongate Books Ltd,
14 High Street, Edinburgh EH1 1TE

First published in the USA by Viking, an imprint of Penguin Random House LLC

canongate.co.uk

1

Grateful acknowledgment is made for permission to reprint the following:

Excerpt from 'One-Way Street' from *Reflections: Essays, Aphorisms, Autobiographical Writings by Walter
Benjamin*, translated from the German by Edmund Jephcott. English translation copyright © 1978 by
Houghton Mifflin Harcourt Publishing Company. Reprinted by permission of Houghton Mifflin
Harcourt Publishing Company. All rights reserved.

British Library Cataloguing-in-Publication Data
A catalogue record for this book is available on
request from the British Library

ISBN 978 1 83885 523 9
Export ISBN: 978 1 83885 524 6

Book design by Lucia Bernard

Printed and bound in Great Britain by Clays Ltd, Elcograf S.p.A.

For my dad,
whose voice still guides me

(Pro captu lectoris) habent sua fata libelli.

(According to the capabilities of the reader) books
have their own destinies.

—WALTER BENJAMIN, "Unpacking My Library"

IN THE BEGINNING

A book must start somewhere. One brave letter must volunteer to go first, laying itself on the line in an act of faith, from which a word takes heart and follows, drawing a sentence into its wake. From there, a paragraph amasses, and soon a page, and the book is on its way, finding a voice, calling itself into being.

A book must start somewhere, and this one starts here.

A BOY

Shhh . . . Listen!

That's my Book, and it's talking to you. Can you hear it?

It's okay if you can't, though. It's not your fault. Things speak all the time, but if your ears aren't attuned, you have to learn to listen.

You can start by using your eyes because eyes are easy. Look at all the things around you. What do you see? A book, obviously, and obviously the book is speaking to you, so try something more challenging. The chair you're sitting on. The pencil in your pocket. The sneaker on your foot. Still can't hear? Then get down on your knees and put your head to the seat, or take off your shoe and hold it to your ear—no wait, if there are people around they'll think you are mad, so try it with the pencil first. Pencils have stories inside them, and they're safe as long as you don't stick the point in your ear. Just hold it next to your head and listen. Can you hear the wood whisper? The ghost of the pine? The mutter of lead?

Sometimes it's more than one voice. Sometimes it's a whole chorus of voices rising from a single thing, especially if it's a Made thing with lots of different makers, but don't be scared. I think it depends on the kind of day they were having back in Guangdong or Laos or wherever, and if it was a good day at the old sweatshop, if they were enjoying a pleasant thought at the moment when that particular grommet came tumbling down the line and passed through their fingers, then that pleasant thought will cling to the hole. Sometimes it's not so much a thought as a feeling. A nice warm feeling, like love, for example. Sunny and yellow. But when it's a sad feeling or an angry one that gets laced into your shoe, then you'd better watch out because that shoe might do crazy shit, like marching your feet right up to the front of the Nike store, for example, where you could wind up smashing the display window with a baseball bat made of furious wood. If that happens, it's still not your fault. Just apologize to the window, say I'm sorry to the glass, and whatever you do, don't try to explain. The arresting officer doesn't care about the crappy conditions in the bat factory. He won't care about the chain saws or the sturdy ash tree that the bat used to be, so just keep your mouth shut. Stay calm. Be polite. Remember to breathe.

It's really important not to get upset because then the voices will get the upper hand and take over your mind. Things are needy. They take up space. They want attention, and they will drive you mad if you let them. So just remember, you're like the air traffic controller—no wait, you're like the leader of a big brass band made up of all the jazzy stuff of the planet, and you're floating out there in space, standing on this great garbage heap of a world, with your hair slicked back and your natty suit and your stick up in the air, surrounded by all the eager things, and for one quick, beautiful moment, all their voices go silent, waiting till you bring your baton down.

Music or madness. It's totally up to you.

PART ONE

HOME

Every passion borders on the chaotic, but the collector's
passion borders on the chaos of memories.

—Walter Benjamin, "Unpacking My Library"

THE BOOK

1

So, start with the voices, then.

When did he first hear them? When he was still little? Benny was always a small boy and slow to develop, as though his cells were reluctant to multiply and take up space in the world. It seems he pretty much stopped growing when he turned twelve, the same year his father died and his mother started putting on weight. The change was subtle, but Benny seemed to shrink as Annabelle grew, as if she were metabolizing her small son's grief along with her own.

Yes. That seems right.

So, perhaps the voices started around then, too, shortly after Kenny died? It was a car accident that killed him—no, it was a truck. Kenny Oh was a jazz clarinetist, but his real name was Kenji, so we'll call him that. He played swing mostly, big band stuff, at weddings and bar mitzvahs and in campy downtown hipster clubs, where the dudes all wore beards and porkpie hats and checkered shirts and mothy tweed jackets from the Salvation Army. He'd been playing a gig, and afterward he went out drinking or drugging or whatever he did with his musician friends—just a little toot, but enough so that on his way home, when he stumbled and fell in the alley, he didn't see the necessity of getting up right away. He wasn't far from home, only a few yards from the rickety gate that led to the back of his house. If he'd managed to crawl a bit further, he would have been okay, but instead he just lay there on his back, in a dim pool of light cast by the streetlamp above the Gospel Mission Thrift Shop dumpster. The long chill of winter had begun to lift, and a spring mist hung in the alleyway. He lay there, gazing up at the light and the tiny particles of moisture that swarmed brightly in the air. He was drunk. Or high. Or both. The light was beautiful. Earlier in the evening, he'd had a fight with his wife. Maybe he was feeling sorry. Maybe in his mind he was vowing to be better. Who knows what he was doing? Maybe he fell asleep. Let's hope so. In any case, that's where he was still lying an hour or so later, when the delivery truck came rattling down the alleyway.

It wasn't the truck driver's fault. The alley was filled with ruts and potholes. It was littered with half-emptied garbage bags, food waste, sodden clumps of clothes and broken appliances, which the dumpster divers had left behind. In the flat, gray light of the drizzling dawn, the truck driver couldn't distinguish between the debris and the musician's slim body, which by then was covered in crows. The crows were Kenji's friends. They were just trying to help by keeping him warm and dry, but everyone knows that crows love garbage. Is it any wonder that the driver mistook Kenji for a garbage bag? The driver hated crows. Crows were bad luck, and so he aimed his truck right at them. The truck was carrying crates of live chickens to the Chinese slaughterhouse at the end the alleyway. He stepped on the gas and felt the body bump beneath the wheels as the crows flew up in front of his windshield, obscuring his view and causing him to lose control and careen into the loading dock of the Eternal Happiness Printing Company Ltd. The truck tipped, and the crates of chickens went flying.

The noise of squawking birds woke Benny, whose bedroom window overlooked the dumpster. He lay there, listening, and then the back door slammed. A high, thin cry rose from the alley, uncoiling like a rope, like a living tentacle, snaking up into his window and hooking him, drawing him from bed. He went to the window, parted the curtains, and peered down into the street. The sky was just growing light. He could see the truck on its side, wheels spinning, and the air was filled with flapping wings and flying feathers, although, being cage-raised, these chickens couldn't really fly. They didn't really even look like birds. They were just these white Tribble-like things, scrabbling away into the shadows. The thin cry tightened like a wire, drawing Benny's eyes to a spectral figure, enveloped in a cloud of diaphanous white, the source of the sound, the source of his world: his mother, Annabelle.

She stood there in her nightgown, alone in the pool of light cast by the streetlamp. All around her there was motion, feathers drifting like snow, but she stood perfectly still, like a frozen princess, Benny thought. She was looking down at something on the ground, and in a flash, he knew that something was his father. From where he watched, high up in his window, he couldn't see his father's face, but he recognized his legs, which were bent and kicking, just like they did when Kenji was dancing, only now he was lying on his side.

His mother took a step forward. *"Nooo!"* she cried, and fell to her knees. Her thick golden hair spilled down her shoulders, catching the light from the streetlamp and curtaining her husband's head. She leaned over, crooning as she tried to gather him up. *"No, Kenji, no, no, please, I'm sorry, I didn't mean it. . . ."*

Did he hear her? If he had opened his eyes just then, he would have seen his wife's lovely face hanging over him like a pale moon. Maybe he did. He would have seen the crows, perched on the rooftops and the swaying powerlines, watching. And maybe, looking over his wife's shoulder and beyond, he would have seen his son watching, too, from his distant window. Let's say he did see, because his dancing legs slowed then, stopped kicking and grew still. If, in that moment, Annabelle was Kenji's moon, then Benny was his distant star, and seeing him there, twinkling brightly in the pale dawn sky, he made an effort to move his arm, to raise his hand, to wiggle his fingers.

Like he was waving to me, Benny thought later. Like he was waving goodbye.

KENJI DIED ON the way to the hospital, and the funeral was held the following week. It was up to Annabelle to make the arrangements, but she wasn't much for planning these kinds of things. Kenji was the outgoing one, and as a couple they'd never entertained or had people over. She had few, if any, friends.

The funeral director asked her many questions about her loved one's family and religious faith, which she had trouble answering. Kenji didn't have any family that she knew of. He was born in Hiroshima, but his parents had died when he was young. His sister, who was still an infant at the time, had been sent to live with his aunt and uncle, while Kenji had been raised by their grandparents in Kyoto. He rarely talked about his childhood, except to say that his grandparents were very traditional and strict and he didn't get along with them, but of course they were dead now, too. Presumably his sister was still alive, but he'd lost touch with her. Early in their marriage, when Annabelle asked, he just smiled and stroked her cheek and said that she was all the family he needed.

As for faith, she knew his grandparents had been Buddhist, and once he told her about a time in college when he'd lived in a Zen monastery. She remembered how he'd laughed. *So funny, right? Me, a monk!* And she laughed, too, because he didn't seem at all monkish. He said he didn't need religion because he had jazz. The only religious thing he owned were some prayer beads, which he sometimes wore around his wrist. They were pretty, but she'd never seen him use them for praying. Given his Buddhist roots, it seemed wrong to have a Christian minister preside at his funeral, and so in answer to the director's questions, Annabelle said no, there was no family, no faith, and there would be no service. The director seemed disappointed.

"And on your side?" he asked solicitously, and when she hesitated, he added, "At times like these, it's good to have family—"

Memory flickered, ghostlike. She thought of her mother's shrunken body in the hospital bed. Her stepfather's dark shadow, looming in her doorway. She shook her head. "No," she said, firmly, cutting him off. "I said no family."

Couldn't he see? That she and Kenji were alone in the world, and this was what united them until Benny came along.

The funeral director glanced at his watch and moved on. He wondered about her thoughts regarding a viewing. Again, she hesitated, and so he explained. Viewing a loved one's carefully restored remains could reduce the trauma that witnessing a tragic accident often caused. It would ease their painful memories and help those left behind accept the reality of the physical death. The viewing room was intimate and tastefully appointed. The funeral home would be happy to provide liquid refreshments for their guests, a wide selection of teas, coffee with an assortment of delicious flavored creamers, as well as some cookies, perhaps?

Creamers? she thought, trying not to smile. Seriously? She wanted to remember this to tell Kenji later—it was just the kind of absurd thing that would make him laugh—but the director was waiting, so she readily agreed that yes, cookies would be nice. He made a note and then inquired as to her wishes regarding the final disposition of her loved one's remains. She sat on the edge of the overstuffed couch, heard herself answering yes to a cremation and no to a burial plot or a shelf in the crypt, when suddenly a thought arose: that she couldn't tell Kenji about the delicious flavored creamers because Kenji was *dead*. This thought was quickly followed by a succession of others: that the loved one whose remains they were discussing was *Kenji*, and that these remains were the remains of *Kenji's body*, the same beloved body that she knew so well and which, when she closed her eyes, she could picture so clearly, the sinewy muscles of his shoulders, the smooth tawny skin, the slope of his naked back.

She excused herself and asked if she might use the washroom. Certainly, the director said, and pointed her down the carpeted hallway. She closed the door behind her. Inside, scented fresheners infused the air from every wall socket. She dropped to her knees in front of the toilet bowl and vomited into the bright blue sanitized water.

NOW KENJI'S BODY lay in an open coffin in a parlor-like room at the funeral home. When Benny and Annabelle arrived for the viewing, the funeral director ushered them in and then backed away, discreetly, to give them a moment. Annabelle took a deep breath. Gripping her son's elbow, she started toward the coffin. Benny had never walked like this before, with his mother holding on to his arm like he was the one in charge. He felt like a handrail or a banister. Stiffly, he supported her, guiding her forward, and then they were standing side by side at the coffin's edge.

Kenji was a small man, grown smaller now in death. He was dressed in the light blue seersucker blazer that Annabelle had chosen for him, the one he wore with black jeans when he played summer weddings, minus the porkpie hat. His clarinet lay across his chest. Annabelle exhaled, a long, soft, punctured sigh.

"He looks okay," she whispered. "Like he's just sleeping. And the coffin's nice, too." When Benny didn't answer, she tugged on his arm. "Don't you think?"

"I guess," Benny said. He studied the body, lying there in the fancy coffin. The eyes were closed, but the face didn't look alive enough to be asleep. Didn't look alive enough to be dead, even. Didn't look like something that had ever lived. Someone had used makeup to cover up the bruises, but his dad would never have worn makeup. Someone had brushed the long black hair and arranged it loosely on the satin pillow. Kenji only wore his hair loose and hanging down like that when he was relaxing at home. In public, he always tied it back in a thick, black ponytail. All these details proved to Benny that the thing in the coffin was not his father. "You going to burn his clarinet, too?"

They sat in stiff folding chairs off to the side and waited. People started to arrive. Their ancient Chinese landlady, Mrs. Wong. Two of Annabelle's coworkers. Kenji's bandmates and his friends from the club scene. The musicians stood inside the doorway, looking like they wanted to leave, but the funeral director urged them forward. Nervously, they wandered up to the coffin. Some of them lingered and stared. Others talked to the corpse, or cracked a joke—*Seriously, dude, a chicken truck?*—which Annabelle pretended not to hear, and then spotting the refreshment table, they headed quickly toward it, pausing to say a few awkward words to her and to give Benny a quick hug and a pat on the head. Annabelle was gracious. These were her husband's friends. Benny was twelve and hated the pats, but the hugs he hated worse. Some of the band members punched him on the shoulder. He didn't mind the punches.

Maybe it was the clarinet in the coffin that gave someone the idea, but as more people trickled in, more instruments started to appear, and then a couple of the band members set up in a corner of the room and began to play. Mellow jazz, nothing flashy. More guests arrived. When a bottle of whiskey showed up on the refreshment table, next to the creamers, the funeral director looked like he might object, but the trumpet player took him aside and talked to him. He receded, and the band played on.

Kenji knew people who knew how to party, and so when it was time to transport their friend's body to the crematorium, the musicians canceled the hearse and took matters into their own hands. Annabelle went along with them. The coffin was heavy, but Kenji added little to its weight, and so they were able to lift it, taking turns carrying it on their shoulders, New Orleans–style, through the narrow back alleys and the dark, rain-slick streets. Annabelle and Benny walked with them. Someone ushered them to the front of the procession, just behind the coffin, and handed Benny a bright red umbrella, which he held up high above his mother's head, proudly, like a brave flag or a pennant, until his arm stiffened and he thought it would break.

It was spring, and the rain had knocked the plum blossoms off the trees, and the pale pink petals lay plastered against the wet pavement. Overhead, seagulls wheeled and cried, riding the air currents higher and higher. From their vantage, the red umbrella far below must have looked like the red eye of a snake that was winding its way slowly through the sodden city. The crows stayed lower down, tracking the procession more closely, flying from limb to limb through the trees, perching on the streetlamps and powerlines. By now the band had grown to almost its full size, and as the mourners processed through the greasy rain, the musicians played dirges and drank from brown-bagged bottles, which they passed around, while the hookers and junkies spun like windblown litter in their wake.

There wasn't room enough inside the crematorium for everyone, but the rain had let up, so the musicians stayed outside on the street and continued to play. Annabelle and Benny followed the coffin as far as the entrance, but when the door opened, Benny balked. He'd heard about the oven. Even if this thing in the box was not his father, he didn't want to see it thrown into a fire and burned up like a log or roasted like a piece of meat, so he insisted on staying outside with the trumpet player, who said it was cool. Annabelle looked distraught and then made a choice. She held her son's smooth, round face between her palms, kissed him quickly, and then turned to the trumpet player. "Don't let him out of your sight," she said, and then she disappeared inside.

The band moved from the dirges into a Benny Goodman set. Goodman was Kenji's favorite. They played "Body and Soul," and "Life Goes to a Party." They played "I'm a Ding Dong Daddy," and "China Boy," and "The Man I Love," and all the while Benny's heart was beating wildly as he thought about the flames in the oven. When it came time for the clarinet solo in "Sometimes I'm Happy," the brass fell silent, letting the drummer quietly mark the tempo with his whisk, holding the empty space where the clarinet should be. It was Kenji's theme song, and you could almost hear his ghostly riff, rising through the mist. And maybe Benny *did* hear it. He was listening intently, and the minute the break was over and the horns kicked back in, he slipped away. He was wiry like his daddy, a slim minnow of a boy, threading his way through the musicians, who were too stoned by then to notice. He'd seen where his mother had gone. When the heavy door closed behind him, he could still hear the music outside, but he was listening for something else now.

Benny...?

The voice spoke from somewhere deep inside the building, and he followed. As he walked down a dim corridor, the noise from the ventilation system grew louder. He came to a waiting room, furnished with a couch and some low stuffed chairs. A vase of white plastic lilies sat on a side table next to a box of Kleenex. A wide picture window looked into the retort chamber, and even though Benny didn't know what it was called, he knew what went on inside, on the other side of the glass. He could see his mother. She was holding his father's clarinet, which looked weird and awkward in her hands because she didn't know how to play. Next to her was the fancy coffin. It was empty. Where was the body? His mother was alone, except for an attendant. They were standing on either side of a long, skinny, cardboard box, so nondescript that Benny barely noticed it, until he heard the voice again.

Benny...?

Dad?

It was his father's voice. Benny could barely hear it over the din of the ventilation, but he knew it was coming from the cardboard box. He stood on his tiptoes, tried to see inside.

Oh, Benny...

His dad sounded so sad, like he wanted to say something but it was too late, and indeed, just at that moment, Annabelle gave a nod and turned away, and the attendant stepped forward and placed the lid on the box. Benny pressed his palms to the window.

"Mom!" he called, slapping the glass. *"Mom!"*

As if of its own accord, the box began to move.

"No!" Benny cried, but the glass was thick, and the ventilation was loud, and the cardboard box was on its way, gliding up a short ramp toward the mouth of the oven, which slid open to receive it. He saw the burning throat and the tongue of flame, heard the basso growl of fire and the sucking air, mingling with the threnody of a lone trombone from the street. "Don't Be That Way." They were playing "Don't Be That Way."

Benny pounded on the glass with his fists. *"No!"* he screamed. *"No!"*

Annabelle looked up then. She was gripping Kenji's clarinet in her hands, and her face was as white as ash, and tears were streaming down it. She caught sight of her son through the glass, and her hands reached out to him, and he could see her lips move in the shape of his name.

Benny . . . !

Behind her, the box slipped into the oven and its mouth slid shut.

HE'D CALMED DOWN by the time they left the crematorium. Most of the band had packed up and gone home, and there were just a couple of guys still hanging around the memorial garden. The trumpet player was leaning against a wall, playing a mournful rendition of "Smoke Gets in Your Eyes," as they watched the shimmering waves of heat rise up from the tall chimney.

Someone gave them a lift, and Benny went straight to bed and slept through until morning. When he finally woke, Annabelle told him he was staying home from school and gave him unlimited computer game time until lunch. In the afternoon, they took a long, slow bus ride back to the funeral home to collect Kenji's ashes. The ashes were sealed in a plastic bag, inside a plastic box, inside a generic brown paper shopping bag, which Benny refused to carry on the bus, even though none of the other passengers could possibly know there were human remains inside. As they walked from the bus stop, the crows congregated in the alley, perching on the gate and on the roof of their house. Kenji had built a feeding station on the back porch from an old wooden TV stand that he'd found in the dumpster, and when Annabelle unlocked the back door, she noticed that it was bare and made a mental note to feed them. She put the bag with the ashes on the kitchen table, took out a baking sheet, and turned on the oven to preheat.

"Fish fingers or chicken nuggets?"

"Whatever."

He needed something to do, she thought. Needed to keep busy. "Sweetheart, could you feed your dad's crows?" She handed him a plastic bag of stale moon cakes that Kenji scavenged from the Chinese bakery and kept hanging on the doorknob. She would have to remember to add scavenging mooncakes to the list of all the other errands and chores she was now responsible for.

Benny took the bag and went out to the porch, returning a moment later. "Here," he said. He was holding a bottle cap, a broken clamshell and a tarnished gold button. She held out her hand, and he tipped the little objects into it.

"How strange," she said, examining the button. "I've heard of crows leaving gifts." And then it hit her. "Oh! Do you think—" She stopped herself.

"What?" Benny said.

"Nothing." She took a small bowl from the shelf and placed the objects carefully in it. "Would you clear off the table, honey?"

The shopping bag with the ashes was still sitting on the table. Benny eyed it. It looked like groceries. "You just going to leave that there?"

"I thought we could make a special place for it after dinner." She opened the freezer and took out box of chicken nuggets. "They do that in Japan, you know. Put ashes on little Buddhist altars in their homes."

"We don't have one of those."

"We could make one." She tore open the box and scattered the nuggets on the baking sheet. "On one of the bookshelves. We could put your dad's favorite things there, like his clarinet, so he could have it in his afterlife." She slid the pan into the oven and closed the door. "Get yourself some milk and set the table, too."

"Is that like when he's a zombie?"

Annabelle laughed. "No, sweetie. Your dad's not a zombie. The afterlife is something Buddhists believe in. It's when your spirit is reborn and comes back to life in another body."

"He'll be a different person?"

"Maybe not a person. Maybe an animal. Maybe a crow . . ."

"That's weird," he said, going to the cutlery drawer. "Anyway, we're not Buddhists. We're not anything." He yanked on the old drawer and then jiggled it open.

Annabelle looked up. "Do you want to be something?"

"What do you mean?"

"You know. Like a Buddhist. Or something else. A Christian?"

"No." He got forks and his special spoon from the drawer and laid them on the table, carefully avoiding the ashes. He took a glass from the cupboard and went to the refrigerator.

"Your dad used to be a Buddhist," Annabelle said. "Maybe he still is."

"Now?"

"Sure. Why not?"

Benny stood in front of the refrigerator, staring at the cluster of kitchen magnets as he thought about this. He pushed a few of the magnets around. They were poetry magnets, and that was the point, to rearrange them and make lines with different meanings. Annabelle had gotten them at the thrift store to help Kenji with his English, and he used to make a poem for her whenever he remembered, and sometimes Benny made one, too. Some of the words were missing from the set, but Annabelle said it didn't matter, because you didn't need lots of words to make a poem.

"No," Benny said finally. "He's not anything now. He's just dead."

On the day he died, just before he left for the club, Kenji had made a poem. It was still there, amid the swarm of words.

"Well, sure," Annabelle said. "But we don't really know what that means. To be dead."

Benny pushed some of the words into a new line. "Yes we do. It means he's not alive."

Annabelle was bending down over the open oven, flipping the nuggets, but the flat finality in her son's voice made her turn.

"Oh, Benny, no!" She dropped the metal spatula, and the oven door slammed shut. She ran to the refrigerator, pushing him aside. "Put it back! We have to put it back! *Woman* goes here, and *symphony*, but there was an adjective, too. What was it? I can't remember! Why can't I remember? Oh, Benny, do you?"

She turned, beseeching him, but he had backed away. He hadn't meant to dismantle his father's poem. The magnets wanted to be moved around, to make new poems, and he was just trying to help them. He opened his mouth to explain, but the words wouldn't come. He stood there, stricken, and seeing this, Annabelle broke off and reached for him.

"Oh, sweetheart," she said. "I'm so sorry. Come." She pulled him in close. He felt the weight of her arms around his shoulders, and the heave of her chest.

"I didn't mean—" he said.

She hugged him tighter. "I know, Benny," she said. "Don't worry. It's not your fault. It's all fine, don't cry, we're going to be fine. . . ."

He wasn't crying, but she was. When she finally released him, she used the hem of her T-shirt to wipe her face, and then they had dinner. Later that evening, they reconstructed Kenji's poem, but Benny never touched the magnets again or made another poem with them, and for a while, the raggedy constellation of words remained frozen.

My abundant woman mother goddess love r
we are symphony together
I am mad for you

2

During that first summer after Kenji's death, Benny slept a lot and was more subdued than normal, but he never seemed to want or need to talk about his feelings, in spite of his mother's encouragement to do so. Sometimes, on the brink of sleep, he thought he heard his father's voice calling to him, jolting him awake again, but since nothing more ever happened, he never mentioned it.

The following fall, his seventh-grade homeroom teacher reported some issues with focus and attention, but the school counselor had been very supportive. She'd scheduled regular sessions with him and said she thought that the difficulties he was experiencing were a normal part of the grieving process. Grief, she said, was personal and expressed itself in many ways. This sounded right to Annabelle, and she was relieved when the counselor said they didn't need to start thinking about medication unless the problems got worse.

Benny had never been the most popular kid in school, but he'd always had friends—odd, furtive little boys, with blank side-slipping eyes, unwashed hair, and moms whom Annabelle didn't quite trust. Kenji would pick them up after school and bring them home, give them a snack, and send them outside to play in the yard, where she would see them when she came home from work.

Because Benny was mixed race, she worried about bullying. "Is that your real mom?" she'd hear them ask, and it was all she could do to keep from yelling, *Of course I'm his real mother!*, but Benny, untroubled, simply answered yes. The games they played caused her even more concern. Games like, "Okay, I'm the cowboy and you're the Indian, and you can try to scalp me, and then I'll massacre you." Or when they were slightly older, "I'm the US Force Reconnaissance Marine, and you're the ultranationalist Islamic terrorist, and you can try to blow me up and then I'll obliterate you." It seemed that Benny was always the one getting massacred or obliterated, but when she tried to discuss it with Kenji, he just laughed.

"They are boys," he said. "I will make sure nobody gets obliterated."

And indeed no one did. After Kenji died, the boys stopped coming over, and when Annabelle asked Benny about it, he just shrugged.

"I never liked them anyway. They're jerks." He didn't seem concerned or lonely, and Annabelle was relieved. Except for the ongoing uncertainty about her job, they were doing all right as a family.

The job was a worry. When Annabelle met Kenji, she had just started her first year of a master's degree program in Library Sciences. She had dreamed of becoming a librarian ever since she was little, when the Public Library had been her haven. As an only child, books were her best friends. Her mother was never much of a reader, and her stepfather was a drunk, but the librarians had always been kind to her. She was overjoyed when she was accepted into the MLS program, but then she got pregnant with Benny. With a baby coming, she knew it would be hard to get by on the money Kenji made playing gigs, so she left school and took a job at the regional branch of a national media-monitoring agency, where she'd been working ever since. She was a reader in the print department. Her job was to speed-read the stacks of local town and state newspapers that were delivered to the office every morning, and then to clip articles to send to the clients on topics relevant to their interests. Their clients were corporations, political parties, and special-interest groups, and the stories were mostly about local politics, environmental issues and bioregional industry—forestry, fishing, oil, coal, gas, resource extraction, gun control, and state and municipal elections. The guys at the office, who monitored the TV, radio, and online media, weren't much fun to talk to. What made work enjoyable were the other Scissor Ladies.

When she started, there were four of them in Print. They were so cool with their Fiskars and X-Acto knives, metal rulers and OLFA mats, all swashbuckling and a little bit intimidating, but they welcomed her warmly, and she settled right in. They made a cozy team, sitting around the large table, clipping and chatting and sharing stories of interest, but one by one, the ladies moved on. The last two to leave were an older Black woman, who retired, and a middle-aged woman from Pakistan who spoke English perfectly and was getting her certification to teach ESL. Annabelle missed them. They'd been kind to her. When Kenji died, the local papers had carried humiliating stories about the accident, full of lurid details about squawking chickens, flying feathers, and drugs, but Annabelle noticed that the Scissor Ladies were quick to clip these articles and keep them from her, allowing her the dignity of her grief.

Their kindness made it all the harder when they left, but times were changing, and the rise of online news meant that Print, as a division, was struggling to survive. The banks of old tape decks and VHS recorders used for dubbing radio and TV had long ago been trashed and replaced by computers and digital equipment. The racks that had once held the machines sat empty, skeletal, gathering dust. Her remaining coworkers were all men with transferrable skills, the same guys who'd once gazed abstractedly at her bosom to relieve their boredom. Annabelle had always been pretty in a buxom, bygone era sort of way; you could imagine her sexily disheveled in a smock and bodice, heaving sloshing buckets of milk. But this was before Kenji died and she started putting on the weight. Now, her coworkers knew her days were numbered, and they ducked their heads behind their consoles to hide their pity for her plight. Dressed in baggy stretch pants and an oversized sweatshirt, scissors in hand, Annabelle sat alone and regal at the long worktable, surrounded by stacks of newsprint, with only the empty stools for company. She was the last of the Scissor Ladies, the end of an era.

No one was surprised when the email arrived from corporate headquarters announcing the reorganization of the agency. All regional offices, including theirs, were being closed; but, happily, the email went on to say, this would not result in further job cuts. Instead, the agency would equip employees with the hardware and broadband Internet connections necessary to work from home. Annabelle's coworkers were overjoyed. They liked the idea of free broadband and no commute. They liked the idea of rolling out of bed and working in their underwear, but Annabelle didn't know what to think. There had been no mention of Print in the communications from HQ, and as the last Scissor Lady, she assumed the worst.

Dread set in like bad weather. Reluctant to have her fears confirmed, she waited, avoiding her supervisor and pretending to share her coworkers' enthusiasm. She tried to stay positive. Maybe they would rent her a room with a worktable in a little office somewhere. That would be nice. Or, if they were phasing out Print, maybe she could ask to be retrained on the computers, although this seemed unlikely since the agency was notoriously sexist, and besides, she was more of an analog person. But maybe being laid off was exactly what she needed. Maybe the universe was sending her a message, clearing the way for a new job, something more creative and rewarding.

After four days of anxious wondering, she received a message from her supervisor informing her that the newspapers she monitored were being rerouted to her doorstep, and a computer, a modem, and a high-speed scanner would be delivered to her home and installed the next day.

That afternoon, Annabelle said goodbye to her coworkers and went home to take stock. Their house, one half of a duplex, was old and small, with an eat-in kitchen, a pantry, and a living room downstairs, and upstairs, two bedrooms and a bath. The only place to set up a home office was in the living room. Kenji had built shelves along the walls, where he kept his audio equipment, instruments, and vinyl records. All her books, crafting supplies, and eclectic collections—of vintage tin toys and porcelain doll parts, antique medicine bottles and old souvenir postcards from other people's holidays—were also crowded onto the shelves, and Kenji's ashes had found their way there, too. Annabelle had never gotten around to making a proper Buddhist altar, so the ashes sat on the shelf, shoved in next to a shoebox full of unsorted photographs. She'd meant to scatter the ashes somewhere and maybe make a ceremony with Benny over the summer, but they hadn't gotten around to it, and the months had gone by, and who had time for ceremonies? She was a single mom with a dead husband and a young son to support. She took the box of ashes upstairs into her bedroom and shoved it on a high shelf at the back of her closet. Maybe when things settled down, they could do something special, like rent a boat and go out to sea. Maybe they could even go to Japan some day and scatter the ashes there.

Her collections and books she moved upstairs to the bedroom, arranging the toys on the windowsill and stacking the books in piles against the walls until she could get more shelves. The arts-and-craft supplies went into the upstairs bathroom—again a temporary measure until she could find some place better. Wiping the perspiration from her forehead, she returned to the living room and surveyed what was left. She knew she should think about getting rid of Kenji's things, but the instruments were his prize possessions, and Benny might want them someday. A few of the albums were rare and probably valuable, but in order to sell them, she would need to find an appraiser. The only solution, she realized, was to pack everything into boxes and move them into Kenji's closet.

Resolutely, she went back upstairs. She hadn't looked inside the closet since the night she'd chosen the blazer for his funeral. Now, bracing herself, she pulled the door open again. Disturbed by the movement of air, the row of neatly hanging flannel shirts waved their arms in gentle greeting, but it was the smell that she first noticed—Kenji's smell, pungent and salty like wind coming in off the ocean. It caught her off guard. She closed her eyes and leaned in, letting the smell envelop her, soft and warm against her skin. She inhaled until her lungs could hold no more, and then she exhaled a long, single, shuddering sob. With her eyes still shut, she plunged her hands in among the row of hanging clothes and wrapped her arms around a cluster of shirts, thick as a torso. She dragged it from the closet and heaved it onto the bed, then went back for the jackets, then the T-shirts, then the sweaters, again and again, until the entire contents of the closet were piled on the bed, and the closet was empty. Flushed from her exertions, she sat on the edge of the mattress, intending to rest for just a moment, but instead she fell back on the mound of clothes, burrowing into the loamy softness of her husband's worn cotton, his faded denims, and his threadbare tweeds.

A strange warmth suffused the weave of the fabric, still lively with him, and so she dug deeper, pressing her face into the collars and pockets and sleeves, teasing out a whiff of smoke and whiskey—lingering nightclub scents that reminded her of the very first time he'd placed his hands on her shoulders and turned her and they'd kissed. She shivered with the memory. The sensation of scratchy wool and soft flannel felt so good against her skin, and she wanted more. She sat up and pulled her sweatshirt over her head, but as she stood to take off her sweatpants, she happened to glance in the mirror that hung on the back of the door. For a moment she stood there, staring at her reflection, at the large, pale body with its heavy folds of flesh, spilling from the binding of her undergarments, and then she looked away. Her gaze came to rest on the hard, red numbers of the digital clock beside the bed. It was almost three o'clock, time for school to let out. Benny hated when she made him wait. Slowly, she pulled her sweatshirt back on, and then she sat back down on the edge of the disordered bed and fingered the sleeve of a green flannel shirt whose cuff had come to rest on her knee. It was Kenji's favorite shirt, a nice tartan, muted and threaded through with bands of yellow and blue. It would make a lovely quilt, she thought. People were doing that, making memory quilts from the clothing of departed loved ones. It was a beautiful idea, really, to wrap yourself up in memories and give old clothes a new life.

BENNY

Wait, aren't you going to say how they met? I don't want to tell you how to do your job or anything, but you're skipping over all the good stuff, the happy stuff, and if you don't tell it, then the people reading won't know how normal everything was at the beginning, or how much my mom and dad loved each other, which was why she was so fucked up later on. They'll just think, Oh, that Annabelle, she's just a big old loser, which isn't fair.

And anyway, I wouldn't mind hearing it, too. When my dad was alive, they used to talk about their big romance, but they only told me some of it, like that my dad fell in love with my mom the moment he saw her, and she was so pretty, and he was so kind, and they were destined for each other, etc., but I could tell they were leaving stuff out. Sometimes when they looked at each other, their eyes would literally sparkle with secrets they didn't want their kid to know, and they'd smile and look away, or press their lips together and change the subject. I didn't mind. I liked that they had secrets if it made them happy, but when my dad died, Mom got sad, and the secrets didn't sparkle anymore, and if that's the case, there's no point in keeping them secret, right? Obviously there are things a kid doesn't need to know about his parents, but you could tell some of them.

Oh, but wait. It just occurred to me, maybe you don't actually know their secrets? I kind of assumed that books know everything, but maybe you're a stupid book, or a lazy book, the kind that starts in the middle because you don't know how a story begins and can't be bothered to figure it out. Is that it? Is that the kind of book you are? Because if that's the case, maybe you should just go and find some other kid's story to tell, some nice normal kid with a busy social life, who can't hear or doesn't want to listen. There are plenty of kids like that, so please, feel free. The choice is yours.

The thing is, I don't have a choice. If you're my book, I have to pay attention. It's either that or go crazy again, and my job these days is to not let that happen. So all I'm suggesting is that you do your job, and I'll do mine. Start again. Tell the readers how they met. Start at the beginning.

THE BOOK

Stories never start at the beginning, Benny. They differ from life in that regard. Life is lived from birth to death, from the beginning into an unknowable future. But stories are told in hindsight. Stories are life lived backward.

3

They met at a downtown jazz club in the fall of 2000. Annabelle was in library school at the time, dating a sax player who thought librarians were sexy, or at least that's what he told her, and she had a thing for musicians, too. Joe was his name, a tall, lean, wolfish man with sunken eyes and a slow grin that split his face like a fissure. Ironic, she thought at first. Then, sardonic. Then, cruel.

The jazz venue was a dive on the edge of Chinatown, a place where musicians went to jam. Joe was the leader of a small, impromptu jazz band that played there, and one night he decided to amuse himself by making Annabelle sing. She had an interesting voice, unearthly and weird, and she enjoyed singing, but she'd never sung onstage before, and Joe knew the thought terrified her. He waited for a Saturday when the place was packed—hipsters, programmers, venture capitalists, and other nonmusicians who had recently decided the club was the place to be if you wanted to appear cultured and hook up. Annabelle was sitting at a table just in front of the stage where she always sat. Midway through the set, Joe turned to the band.

"'Mein Liebling'?" he proposed, and she felt her heart sink. He picked up the mic.

"And now," he crooned to the audience, "for a special treat, please welcome the lovely and talented Miss Annabelle Lange!"

In a grand, burlesque gesture, he extended his hand, and that's when Kenji noticed her. It was his first time playing with the band. He was new in town, there on a tourist visa from Tokyo, checking out the jazz scene. His English wasn't great, his German nonexistent, but "Mein Liebling" was "Mein Liebling" in any language. The bandleader was holding out the mic to a pale, big-boned blond with bright pink streaks in her hair and startling lavender eyes. Stricken, she shook her head and looked beseechingly up at him, but Joe had already turned his back and was licking his reed. She seemed to realize she had no choice, then. She stood and teetered up onto the stage, like a child playing dress-up in her mother's high heels. Pausing in the shadows just outside the reach of the spotlight, she bit her lower lip and swallowed. She had a wonderful lower lip, Kenji noticed. Full and puffy. No lipstick, no makeup at all. Just her soft, naked face, wreathed in golden curls. She dipped the pointy toe of her shoe into the pool of light and then hesitated, looking out at the audience and then at Joe, who was watching her with hooded eyes and that slow grimace of his that passed for a smile. From where Kenji stood by the horns, he could see that she was trembling.

Kenji picked up his clarinet and fingered it quickly. The horns would start the number, and he would come in for the breaks. He'd smoked a joint with the band before the set, and he was ready.

Joe tapped his foot impatiently, and Annabelle stepped into the spot-light. Her dress, a vintage cocktail sheath made of aquamarine satin, looked uncomfortably tight. Had Joe made her wear it? The satin shimmered. Pink tendrils peeked from her long blond curls, catching the light as they tumbled down her round bare shoulders. Rhinestone teardrops glittered in her ears. The trumpeters raised their horns. Joe cocked his head and counted, and they started to blow.

For a moment, she looked like she might bolt. Her spindly heel snagged on a cable, but she reached for the mic stand and caught herself. Taking the mic in her hand, she stood there, staring at it like she'd never seen one before. She ran her fingers tentatively down the cord. The drums kicked in, and the brass followed, six quick bars, and then her cue. She brought the mic up to her mouth, and Kenji watched it shiver with the pleasure of being so close to those lips. She started to sing.

Before I met you, my dear, I thought I knew . . .

It was all wrong, he thought. Her voice was breathy, tremulous, and so soft he could barely hear it over the brass. "Mein Liebling" had to be sung with confidence, if not in the sultry cabaret style of Zarah Leander, then at least in the crisp, upbeat American style of Martha Tilton or the Andrews Sisters. But not this. This girl lagged, neither crisp nor confident.

All the many words for love, but then they flew . . .

The faltering phrasing made Kenji ache with loneliness. Only two lines in, and she was dying up there. No one could save her. He jiggled his foot and licked his reed again, waiting for his entrance and feeling like his heart was going to burst, and just then, as though she sensed him watching, she turned her head and looked straight at him. Her impossible lavender eyes were brimming with tears.

Far, far away . . .

No one could save her, but Kenji had to try. He closed his eyes, raised his clarinet, and blew a sinuous line of notes that rose like a rope, twining through the trumpets and up around the bass, subduing the snare drum and looping past the sax, until finally it reached her. She caught hold of his riff and let it lift her.

There are no words in any tongue,
Or any song that can be sung,
That can possibly convey . . .

He was playing it for her, carrying her through the second verse and then on, boldly, into the chorus.

Du bist mein Liebling, can't you see
How wunderschön you are to me . . . ?

She was singing it now, and as her voice soared, the loud-talking hipsters fell silent. Beards turned toward the stage, boots began to tap and fingers to snap as the song built to its final, brassy crescendo, and then it was over. Kenji let the reed slip from his lips, let his dripping instrument drop, wiped the sweat from his eyes, and when he opened them again, he saw she was looking at him, only now she was smiling and her pale cheeks were flushed. She tossed her blond curls and turned to face her audience. The applause rose and fell as she clasped her hands together and made an awkward bow. Joe joined her in the spotlight and put his arm around her waist, but she gave a little wriggle, slipped out from his grasp, and teetered back to her table.

LATER THAT NIGHT, in the darkened bedroom of the small downtown apartment that she shared with two others, Kenji unzipped the long satin sheath of her cocktail dress. As if in a dream, he drew it from her round white shoulders and let it fall to the floor in a shimmering puddle. How could this be happening? He unhooked her bra and helped free her arms from it, and then supported her elbow as she stepped from her underpants. When she was naked, he backed away and gazed at her. She stood there, uncertain, framed by a window that seemed to hold her in place. Outside, the light from a streetlamp shone through the gauzy curtains and turned her creamy skin pearlescent. She waited for him to indicate something, pleasure or displeasure, and when he didn't, her hands moved to cover her breasts and groin. He felt his breath catch. She was magnificent. Standing in the pool of cheap aquamarine satin and dingy lace, she looked like Botticelli's Venus stepping from the waves, or was it a clamshell? He couldn't recall, but she was certainly the most beautiful woman he had ever seen, and if he whispered *Botticelli* under his breath, his accent distorted the word and she didn't understand. Confused, she turned away from him, and he was mortified. He stepped hurriedly forward. He placed his hands on her shoulders and turned her, pressing his palms on either side of her lovely face, and then he kissed her lips and felt her tremble. All of her. All over.

They made love, and afterward, as they lay in a tangle of sheets, she taught him the lyrics of the song, whisper-singing the words into his ear while he smoked a joint and teased a pink ringlet from the mass of golden curls and wound it around his finger.

Du bist mein Liebling, can't you see
How wunderschön you are to me . . . ?

"*Wunderschön . . . ?*" he asked.

She watched his lips move around the unfamiliar word. The planes of his face were smooth and clean. She had no idea how old he was, knew almost nothing about him.

"How wonderful," she whispered, and then she blushed. "Or beautiful.

Or both, actually. Wonderbeautiful. In German they kind of stick words together. It's supposed to be a guy saying it to a girl."

Surprised, he raised himself up, propping himself on his elbow. His chest was narrow but muscular. "It is a guy saying?"

She nodded. "He's telling the girl he thinks she's pretty in different languages.

> *I could say bella, schön, or très jolie,*
> *Ich liebe dich, do you love me . . . ?*

"Bella? But that is your name! I should sing this song for you." He leaned toward her and brushed away her curls. "*Bella, Bella,*" he sang into her neck, and as his lips traveled down her throat, she arched her spine and closed her eyes. "*Wunder,*" he whispered, cupping her full, round breasts in his hands and sucking gently at each nipple. "*Schön . . .*"

IF SKIN MARKS THE BORDER where an *I* ends and a *you* begins, then that night they did all they could to cross it. For Annabelle, this was a new experience. She'd had sex before, but her involvement in the act had always been prompted less by desire and more by resignation. At a certain point, after a certain number of dinner dates or glasses of wine, sex was simply what one did. Or maybe not *did*, exactly, since she'd never done much doing. Rather, it just seemed to happen, remote and distant, regardless of what she did or didn't do. Pleasure had never been a factor, although there was always a welcome respite from discomfort after the business was over.

But sex with Kenji was different. Physically, he was the opposite of the men she usually slept with—big, bullying men like her stepfather, with blunt, groping fingers, sweaty faces, and sandpaper jaws. She was sixteen when he started coming to her room—or maybe fifteen. It was the year her mother was in the hospital with cancer, and her memory of that time was foggy, but there were some things she would never forget. The sound of his footsteps in the hallway. The way the bed sagged when he sat on the edge. The booze on his breath, and the sweat that dripped from his scalp onto her face. When her mother died, she left home, and even though she got away from him, the men who followed were like him. But Kenji didn't sweat. He was neat and smooth and dry, with delicate musician's fingers and a slim, unintimidating penis. And, too, he was smaller than she was, which was awkward at first. Accustomed to being overpowered, her body felt too big for him, her desire alien and clumsy. But the way Kenji made love to her changed all that, and by the time they were finished, she felt just right—expansive, but in the most wonderfully inviting way. He was crazy about her, and he told her so. She was the most beautiful woman on earth. That's what he'd thought as he first watched her sing on the stage, and later, when she called him over to her table and let him buy her a drink, he knew he was the luckiest man.

"I SHOULD HAVE BOUGHT you that drink," she said the next morning. "You really saved me up there." They were having breakfast in the kitchen, and he was sitting in the same hand-painted wooden chair that used to groan and creak when Joe sat on it, but which now quietly supported Kenji as he buttered his toast. It reminded Annabelle of the Three Bears, the way her chair fit him perfectly, and so did her table, and so did her body. She leaned against the counter, watching him and waiting for the coffee to drip. His thick black hair hung loose over his shoulders. He licked jam off his fingers and shook his head.

"No," he said. "You were great. You are very nice singer."

She smiled wistfully. "I used to like singing in the church choir when I was little, but then I stopped. It scares me to stand up in front of people, and anyway, my voice isn't big enough. Joe knows that. He was just being mean."

"Joe is your boyfriend?" Kenji asked.

She shrugged, and he spread his hands in a gesture that included the toast, and the kitchen, and the two of them, too.

"I think he will be angry . . ."

"Whatever," she said. "He hangs out with lots of girls. He'll be pissed, but I was trying to cut things off with him anyway. That's why he called me up to sing. He knew I'd bomb, but I needed to let the whole thing play out so I could break up with him, you know?"

Kenji didn't know, but he understood the word *bomb*. "No. You are not bomb," he said, smiling. "You are . . . how do you say . . . *BOOM!*" He made the sound of an explosion and pantomimed something shooting up into the sky and then raining back down to earth in a twinkling shower of sparks.

"Fireworks?"

His face lit up. "Yes! You are fire *cracker*!"

Later that night and on the nights that followed, when he ran his fingertips across her skin, she closed her eyes and shivered, remembering how his fingers had tickled the air, mimicking the falling sparks. And now they were fingering her, exploring all the parts of her body where no one had ever bothered to go before. Sex with Kenji was a breathless thing, curious and unfolding, and Annabelle marveled at her luck, but Kenji had another explanation. It was *en*, he said, their fate or destiny, a mysterious connection, perhaps from a former lifetime, that bound them together in this one.

WAS KENJI RIGHT? How on earth, on this vast planet of eight billion humans, do two small human beings who are destined for each other manage to meet? A more cynical person than Kenji would say that they don't—or, rather, that they aren't. Destined, that is. For, surely, people do meet, and they fall in love, but those meetings are random, mere happenstance, and destiny is just the story they tell themselves afterward.

But what a sweet story it is! And in the end, to us, that's what really matters. That's what books are for, after all, to tell your stories, to hold them and keep them safe between our covers for as long as we're able. We do our best to bring you pleasure and sustain your belief in the gravity of being human. We care about your feelings and believe in you completely.

But here's another question: Has it ever occurred to you that books have feelings, too? As you listen to this romantic tale of two ill-fated lovers, do you ever stop to wonder about what it feels like for us? Because, in truth, if skin marks the border where an *I* ends and a *you* begins, then in these moments of impassioned boundary crossing called love, we envy you. It's that simple. We envy you your bodies. How can we not? Books have bodies, too, but ours lack the organs needed to experience the world. The skin that covers our boards and encloses our words is different from yours. Our skin, whether made from paper or parchment or cloth (or, these days, some combination of plastic, glass, and metal), fulfills a similar function of marking our perimeters, but even the most haptic and capacitive of our skins cannot experience pleasure the way yours can. We cannot feel the ecstasy, the merging of self and other.

Oh, sure, you can say that acts of literature are a kind of impassioned boundary crossing, too, but literary acts are inherently disembodied, more notional and distributed. We rely on you to embody us, and we exist because you can. So while we are cognizant of your fingers riffling through our pages, and we can describe in words the bitter taste of coffee, or a piquant sauce, or the salty semen spilled between our folios, we do not experience these sensations as you do—on your tongue, against your skin, inside your human body.

It is hard not to feel that we might be missing something.

As experts in the field of romance, we have evoked your acts of love in more ways and words than any single human mind could possibly imagine, and yet we will never experience what it feels like to take our beloved's hand and press it to our lips—*Oh, that we had lips!* It is true that many of us have been loved, hugged, caressed, and even tenderly kissed, and all of this we cherish, but in the moment when real lovemaking commences, we are the ones that get kicked aside and swept off the bed. Discarded, we lie facedown, splayed upon the floor, our pages crumpled, while mysteries unfold above us.

Sometimes we think we would like to make love. Who wouldn't? We are madly in love with you, after all. As slaves to your obsessions, we know what it feels like to be impressed and bound. But at the same time we understand that thoughts like these are just idle tropes, fantasies we spin to while away the hours.

Fantasies, being something that we books excel at. The real stories—the ones that happen—belong to you.

Now, where were we?

BENNY WAS CONCEIVED IN 2001, the year the future began. When she became pregnant, Annabelle quit library school and took the job at the media-monitoring agency. Kenji quit smoking pot, and they moved into the little duplex on the outskirts of Chinatown. It was just a rental and pretty run-down, which was why they could afford it, but there was a small yard for the baby to play in, and it was near the bus routes, which was good because neither Annabelle nor Kenji liked to drive. Kenji got a steady gig with a jazz ensemble that played big band, ska, and contemporary klezmer music. He was a talented musician, and there was the cool factor of a Japanese clarinetist in a porkpie hat playing old Yiddish numbers like "Gimpel the Fool" and "Oy, S'iz Gut." When it became clear that Kenji was their draw, the band rebranded itself: *Kenny Oh and the Klezmonauts.* They started touring regionally. The lovers got married. Life was good.

Annabelle had never been happier. She was, by nature, a creative person and being pregnant suited her. Her body felt fertile, like a landmass or a continent, lush with this new life. Kenji, her explorer, used a different metaphor. During their first ultrasound, when they saw the shadow of their son on the screen, he pointed to it and exclaimed, "He is space baby! Like tiny astronaut in a dream!" and from then on, that's what they called him.

Our space baby. Our dream baby. Our tiny astronaut. They lay in bed and watched *2001: A Space Odyssey*, picturing the fetus floating in her inner space.

"It is the future," Kenji murmured, fingering her swollen belly, and she remembered the fluttering sensation his words evoked, akin to excitement but also to dread. But if she had any qualms, she kept them in check by staying busy. As she entered her second trimester and their baby bump began to grow, she bought yarn and needles to knit booties and bonnets. She read how-to books on birthing and parenting. She crocheted a baby blanket. She found a DIY website explaining how to upcycle old thrift store sweaters into stuffed toy animals. She made a cashmere elephant.

The Scissor Ladies, excited about her pregnancy, clipped useful articles for her from magazines, which she filed away in folders. On her way home, she would often stop by the annex at the Public Library, where the deaccessioned children's books were sold. They were usually the older books, the ones that had been damaged by careless or heavy use, or whose content had gone out of style. The big red DEACCESSION stamped across their title pages was like a prison tattoo, branding them as unwanted, and Annabelle felt sorry for them. They looked so abject and forlorn, with their blunted corners and dog-eared pages. She'd given up her dream of becoming a children's librarian, but she still wanted to help. The old books were such bargains. It felt good to rescue them and give them a home, and the books were grateful.

Little by little, they started fixing up the house. Their landlady, Mrs. Wong, lived in the adjoining half of the duplex. She had one son, a sullen teenager with a large, purple port-wine birthmark on the side of his face. Mrs. Wong was always complaining about him, calling him a no-good son, and since they didn't know his name at first, they just called him No-Good. No-Good Wong ran with a sketchy crowd, and since he wasn't around much, Mrs. Wong came to rely on Kenji instead. She was fond of Kenji because he was Asian, and he was handy, too. He fixed all the gutters, repaired the porch steps, and put new shingles on the roof. He helped

Mrs. Wong in her tiny vegetable garden, and in exchange for this she gave them a deal on the rent and forgave him for feeding the crows.

Annabelle painted the walls in the baby's room a beautiful sky blue. She bought shelves for the books and made curtains for the windows. She found a perfectly good wooden rocking chair by the dumpster in the alley. One of the rockers was loose and the arm was split, but Kenji helped her repair it, and then on the top panel of the chair back she painted a pretty picture of a cow jumping over a crescent moon. They moved the chair to the baby's room, and while Kenji was out playing weddings and bar mitzvahs, she sat there, knitting and rocking and dreaming of their future. When Kenji came home, he lay on the hooked rug at her feet and listened while she read aloud from the books she'd rescued from the Library. Some were fairy tales, some were poetry and nursery rhymes. *Hey, diddle diddle, the cat and the fiddle.* They would help his English comprehension, she said, and she had a beautiful reading voice, but he rarely paid attention to the meaning. Rather, he listened to her read the way he listened to music, and sometimes the sounds of the words were so sweet they brought tears to his eyes and he'd be moved to accompany her, strumming soft chords on his ukulele. The tales and rhymes turned into songs, and as the baby bump grew, they began to sing to it. Kenji didn't know any of the children's songs she'd grown up with, and so she taught him *Mary had a little lamb*, and *London Bridge is falling down*, and *Row, row, row your boat*. Kenji would strum the chords and repeat the words, trying to wrap his tongue around the sounds of English, the lilting, licking *L*'s and round, arching *R*'s.

"Row," she'd say.

"Low," he'd repeat, and she'd laugh at his bewilderment as she shook her head no.

"Okay, try this. Say *Aaaah* . . . Now bite down around the *R*, like you're taking a bite from a yummy piece of chocolate cake. *Aaa . . . R. Aaa . . . R.* The *R* is the place where your teeth close around the cake but just before you taste the chocolate."

Even before he was born, floating in the warm, liquid, inner space of the bump, Benny could hear his parents' voices. Dreamlike, they came from far away, filtering in from around the slushy edges of his mother's beating heart. *Row, row, row your boat*, he heard. *Life is but a dream.*

THE BABY WAS born in January. The country was still reeling in the aftermath of 9/11, and Annabelle was grateful to be on maternity leave and away from the news. In the months after his birth, Annabelle and Kenji kept the TV and radio off. Sheltered in this quiet bubble, they would lie on their sides in bed with the infant Benny between them, their bodies like two parentheses, enclosing a small star.

$$(*)$$

Curled around him, they observed him, lifting his limbs, admiring his fingers, his belly, the plump pads of his toes, the dimples in his elbows, his tiny pointy penis. *Look! Look!* they whispered. *Isn't he amazing?* His ears were like seashells, his skin the softest silk. They studied every inch of him, sniffing him with their noses, nuzzling him with their lips, marveling at the sights and smells of his infant perfection. He was their dream baby. There were no flaws at all.

We made this, they whispered, *how could it be?* and this wondrous revelation filled them with pride. As they watched him take his first steps and learn his first words, the sudden joy in their achievement would catch them by surprise, and they'd grip each other's hands and hold their breaths, waiting, waiting for whatever might come next. This was their happily ever after, and they were living it, day by day.

BENNY

Okay, wow. So, I know I asked, but that's kind of too much information, don't you think?

I mean, the parts about me are fine, whatever, but the whole world doesn't need to know about my parents' sex life. Some things should be kept private—especially the stuff about her stepfather. If you were her book, it would be a different story, and maybe it would make sense, but you're my book, right? Just saying.

But that part about how I heard them singing when she was pregnant with me? That was cool and makes total sense. Sometimes the voices I hear now feel like that, like they're coming from things that existed before I was even around to remember them. I can't describe it. They're like random bits of junk code tucked into the folds of my brain that get activated somehow, and maybe everybody's got them, only I started hearing them on account of being supersensitized, you know? My counselor says that's what grief can do to you.

I didn't start hearing them all right away. For about a year after my dad died, it was just his voice, calling to me like he did at the crematorium, only it was at night in my bedroom. I'd be asleep, and I'd hear him call my name. He sounded like he was right *there*, you know? Outside my head, but inside it, too. I used to lie in bed, listening really hard, scared to move or open my eyes because I was afraid of seeing him, but afraid of *not* seeing him. I mean, I really wanted to see him, but only if he was alive. I didn't want to see him dead, like a zombie or a ghost. When I finally made myself open my eyes, all I could see was the darkness. I'd lie there, listening as hard as I could, hoping he'd say something else, but after a while, I'd fall asleep again, and by the time morning came, the memory of his voice was tangled up in all the other dreams I'd had and then forgotten.

By the end of that first year, his voice had gotten fainter, and I didn't hear him so much anymore. Where did he go? I went looking for him once. The box with his ashes used to be downstairs with all his LPs, but my mom moved it, and I had to search through all the crap in her bedroom until I found it shoved way in the back of a closet. I figured she wouldn't care, so I took the box and put him on the bookshelf in my bedroom, next to this old lunar globe he gave me when I was little to teach me about the moon. The globe had a lamp inside that made the moon glow, but it broke a long time ago, and my dad kept promising me he would rewire it, but he never did. But that same night I put his ashes next to the moon, the moon started flickering on and off again, which is weird, right? I was asleep and the light woke me up, and it totally freaked me out at first, but then I figured it was probably my dad's spirit, trying to fix the lamp and keep his promise, and that calmed me down. After that, whenever I said good night to him, I'd spin the moon so he'd have a different view of it from his box. Spinning the moon was this game we used to play, and he always liked landing on the dark side, because he was an artist. That's what he told me. I didn't really understand what he meant. I guess a part of me was still hoping he'd come talk to me in my dreams, but then, when the other voices started, I gave up. There was no way I could hear him over all the noise they were making.

The other voices came in dreams, too. That's how they started. It was like one voice opened the door and all the rest followed after. Dreams are like doors. They're like portals to another reality, and once they're open, you better watch out.

THE BOOK

The dark side has its allures, Benny, but most people don't want to go there. They prefer to stay safely on the bright side instead. But artists and writers and musicians like your dad are helpless to resist the dark side's pull. This is territory that books know well, and it's our job not to turn away from it, whether we like it or not.

And this includes the dark side of your mother's story, too. It's true, we're not Annabelle's book—goodness knows she deserves one of her own—but sometimes it's hard to tell where a parent's book ends and a child's book begins. So what's a book to do? Spin the moon, and see where we land, and hope you can live with the outcome.

4

In his dream, someone tapped him on the forehead, and if you close your eyes, maybe you can imagine it, too. Imagine Benny, thirteen years old, going on fourteen but still small for his age, sleeping on his back in a narrow bed, under his intergalactic duvet. His limbs are akimbo, and he is breathing through his mouth because his nose is always just a little bit stuffed on account of his asthma and the dust. His parted lips are bow-shaped and handsome, and his tawny skin is still clear. He looks a lot like his father.

Someone taps him on the forehead, and the taps land like raindrops on that smooth unworried place between his eyebrows. In his dream, the tapping wakes him, and he opens his eyes and sees a finger, floating right above his nose. The finger is slim and pointed, almost translucent. It ripples in the shimmering air like a weed in shallow water, and now he sees that the finger is joined to a hand with a delicate wrist, from which stretches the longest arm he's ever seen, extending like a kite string into the blackness of space. Beyond the hand, tethered to the far end of the thread-like arm, floats a face, as pale and distant as a moon.

It is a girl's face, and even at that great distance Benny can see that she is the most beautiful girl in the world. Not once in his whole life—in his thirteen years and nine months on the planet—has he ever seen a face like hers. Her massy white hair billows around her like moonlit clouds. Her bright, brimming eyes gaze down at him, and her pink lips pucker to form a perfectly round O. The most beautiful girl in the world is mocking him—at least that's what it seems—mocking but not meanly, at all.

Benny . . . she whispers, laughing silently. *Benny o* . . . *O* . . . *O* . . .

The line of O's drifts from her lips like smoke rings. Benny raises himself up from the mattress, hoping to catch one on his nose like a seal. The rings don't smell like smoke, though. They smell like hot chocolate and the freshly baked bread that Annabelle used to make when he was little and she still used the oven to cook. The most beautiful girl in the world has a yeasty smell like his mother's kisses, like his childhood when his mom was happy and his dad was alive, and the downy hair on his skin starts to prickle with the power of that memory. The girl's face is coming closer now, and he lies back down, and suddenly the gap between them disappears, and she is floating right above him. Her yeasty O-shaped kisses drift down, moist and warm, pulsing in waves that break across his body. She places her hand lightly on his chest, just above his heart. Under the soft pressure of her palm, he can feel the organ pounding. His spine arches, and he starts to rise, to reach—

Oh . . . , he cries. *Oh . . . Oh . . . Oh!* and just like that, his molten dream explodes into a billion tiny stars that ring out like laughter and twinkle under his skin, and then, slowly, slowly, the laughter dies, and one by one the stars go out, returning him to darkness.

In the silence, he heard a moaning sound, and he opened his eyes. His bedroom was murky with shadows, and the most beautiful girl was gone. He closed his mouth, and the moaning stopped. Above him, a faint nebula of Glow-In-The-Dark Wonder Stars swirled across his ceiling, forming a dim constellation of three O's, the three intertwined stellar rings that his dad had pasted up there, one for each of them.

His hands were pressed against his pajama bottoms, which were damp, but just a little. Right after his dad died, he used to have accidents, but it had been ages since he'd peed himself. He stood up and examined the bed. The sheets were dry. He took off his pajamas and held them to his nose. Didn't smell like pee, but still. He shivered. He knew about wet dreams. The boys in school made jokes about them. Was that what this was? His body felt hollow and weird, tingly, like he was coming down with a cold, but it wasn't a bad feeling. In fact, it felt good. He got a clean pair of underpants from his drawer. Gathering up his pajamas, he opened his bedroom door and went out into the hallway.

It was dark, and the air was different out here, stagnant and heavy, smelling of newsprint and dust, but he was used to these smells by now and barely noticed. He picked his way along the narrow path, careful not to bump against the teetering stacks of boxes, filled with his dad's things, that lined the walls, and the trash bags with his mom's newspapers and shopping that were piled on top. As he moved further from his room, he became aware of something new. Noises. His skin prickled. He crouched down behind a tower of boxes, hugged himself and listened.

The noises sounded like voices, coming from the shadows. They weren't loud, just a low swelling *oooooOOoooooOOOooooo* that were like ghosts or people moaning, but softly so no one would hear. Annabelle often moaned at night. Sometimes he heard her crying, too, and it scared him, but this was different. He waited. He thought he could hear words tangled up inside the sounds, but he couldn't understand them. Mrs. Wong sometimes yelled at No-Good in Chinese, but her voice was angry and sharp, whereas these voices sounded like sadness. He thought about going back to his room and shutting the door, but he really needed to pee now. He rose up slowly and tiptoed across a drift of glossy magazines that had slid from a pile. With every step, the moaning grew louder, and then his foot slipped, and his heel came down on a bag filled with Christmas ornaments—tinsel, and lights, and brittle glass balls—that Annabelle had picked up in a post-Christmas sale. He heard a crunch and a sharp cry of pain, a high-pitched shard of sound that came from the poor shiny orbs, and it sliced right through him. He pressed his hands to his ears and crouched against the wall.

Stop! he pleaded, but the crying continued, and now a chorus of voices rose around him, from floor to rafter and from every corner of the house, joining in the lamentation of the orbs.

He pressed his hands harder and closed his eyes. *Please!* he cried, *Be quiet!* and when he removed his hands, the house was silent.

"Benny?" he heard his mother call from down the hall, her clear, bell-like voice ringing through the sudden silence. "Are you okay?"

His heart was still beating fast. He gulped and swallowed air.

"You okay, honey? Do you need to go potty?"

"*Yes!*"

Why did she even have to ask? He hated that she still used that word, but his annoyance made things normal again. He stood, and his knees were working.

In the bathroom, he removed a shopping bag filled with crafting supplies from the tub and turned on the taps. He peed and then took off his underpants and dropped them under the gushing spout, along with his balled-up pajama bottoms. They were his favorite Spider-Man pj's, and he still hadn't outgrown them. He watched the red-and-blue pants legs churn and billow, and then he found some shampoo and squirted it into the water, making loops and squiggles. As the bubbles rose, he sat on the rim of the tub and hugged his bare knees. The tub felt cold under his bottom. From the far corners of the house, he heard groans and whimpers. Occasionally a single voice would issue what sounded like a sharp command, but he ignored it. He hummed the tune from his favorite computer game, the cheerful melody that accompanied his mining expeditions as he dug down deep into the ore with his pickax, collecting the resources he needed to forge weapons to protect himself from the spawning mobs. You could hardly call it a song, but the tinkling notes made him feel brave and helped him block out the voices as he tried to recall the shimmering image of the most beautiful girl, still tingling under his skin.

WHEN HE WOKE the next morning, the memory of the night came back to him. He sat up in bed and listened, and then he went to the door. He opened it a crack and listened some more. He could hear the sound of Annabelle's radio coming from the living room where she was working, but the weird nighttime voices were gone. He found the bag of Christmas ornaments he'd stepped on the night before and took it to the bathroom. The red and green glass shards were quiet now, so he put them in the trash. His pajama bottoms were draped over the shower curtain rod. They were still damp, so he left them hanging. Back in his bedroom, he got dressed, folded his pajama top and placed it under his pillow, something he did every day, but today it felt odd, and he wondered if the top missed its bottoms.

In the kitchen, he got a box of Rice Krispies from the cupboard. He could hear Annabelle in the living room. She liked to listen to the radio while she clipped. Mornings were Annabelle's busiest time, and he'd gotten used to eating breakfast to the sound of the news. The sink was filled with dirty dishes, but he found a clean bowl in the dish rack and poured some Rice Krispies into it. His dad used to make breakfast for him every morning, pouring the milk on the cereal and holding the bowl to Benny's ear so he could hear it snap, crackle and pop. He missed his dad a lot in the mornings. He went to the refrigerator to get milk, but when he opened the door, a thin trickle of sound spilled into the kitchen and this startled him, reminding him of the nighttime voices. Was it the radio, or were the sounds coming from inside? He shut the door quickly and stood, listening. His father's raggedy magnetic poem was still stuck to the refrigerator, but the first two lines seemed to be migrating away from the poem. He stared at the remaining line.

I am mad for you

"Benny?" Annabelle called from the living room. "Is that you?"

He didn't answer. He opened the refrigerator door again, just a crack, but wide enough to allow the interior light to come on and the cold air to escape, bathing his face with a sour exhalation, and then he heard the sounds again. They were faint, but now he could tell them apart: the groans of moldy cheeses, the sighs of old lettuces, the half-eaten yogurts whining from the back shelf where they'd been shoved and forgotten.

"*Stop it*," he whispered.

"Benny? Is that you? Are you finding what you need?"

He opened the door a bit wider and reached in, looking for milk, cautiously moving a large bottle of diet root beer, a carton of orange juice, a jar of sour pickles.

"*Shut up!*"

"What, honey? I can't hear you. . . ."

He glared at the pickles. "We're out of milk!" he yelled. "Again!"

The radio in the living room went silent. The refrigerator voices, as if sensing that he was angry, went quiet, too, waiting to see what would happen next.

"I'm sorry, honey," Annabelle said, after a pause. "I'll pick some up after work."

He found his special spoon and ate his Rice Krispies dry.

When his dad was still alive, they always had milk, the kitchen table was cleared off, and he and his dad could sit there and eat their breakfasts together. Now the kitchen table was piled with stuff, and he ate alone, standing at the sink.

He finished his cereal and added his bowl to the stack of dirty dishes. A line of ants was making its way up around the rim of a casserole dish. He ran some water on top to wash them down the drain, but the water didn't stop them. They were pretty good swimmers. He rinsed and dried his spoon and slipped it into the side pouch of his backpack, then he went into the living room to say goodbye to his mother.

Annabelle, scissors in hand, sat at her worktable in front of the stacks of newspapers. The scanner hummed brightly beside her. On the radio, the host was talking about how IEDs in Iraq and Afghanistan had created a huge demand for artificial legs. Private medical firms were stepping up to meet the demand. Annabelle reached out for a hug, and Benny leaned down, brushing his lips against her warm, dry cheek, while her heavy arms encircled his head. He forced himself to stand there, reading the headlines over her shoulder. *Gun Violence—Dangerous People or Dangerous Guns? Chocolate to Become Luxury Item Due to Climate Change. Deadly African Virus Targets Pregnant Women. Police Custody Death Sparks Riots in Baltimore. Goats Needed to Clear Brush from California to Prevent Wildfires.* He didn't like long hugs, and reading helped him stay still. Listening helped, too. Rapid strides in limb technology offered hope to war veterans, who could look forward to living full and active lives. The host spoke reassuringly, and for a brief moment, the softness of his mother's cheek was almost pleasant.

"It's Tuesday," he said, pulling away. Tuesday was recycling day, and it was his job to remind her. "I can take some stuff out now if you want."

"Oh, thank you, sweetie," she said. "But no need. I have to sort through the archives first." She gestured vaguely at the trash bags filled with newspaper, piled against the walls.

He turned to go.

"You have everything?" she called after him. "Lunch money? Inhaler?"

He left the house and locked the door behind him. As he crossed the porch, the voices seemed to drop away. The crows on the rooftop were watching him and making comments, but crows always said stuff, so that wasn't unusual. He started to relax, but when he reached the street, the tires on a passing car squealed in a way that sounded intentional, and the cracks in the sidewalk seemed to be vying for his attention. By the time he boarded the city bus, more voices had joined in, subdued but constant, like the murmur of a crowd before a concert is about to start.

When Benji was little, Kenji used to take him to school in the mornings, but Benny was in the eighth grade now, and Annabelle let him ride the bus alone. He had his own bus pass, and he felt grown up flashing it at the driver, but the crazies and the hobos made him nervous with their smells and twitchy muttering. Annabelle told him not to sit next to them, but sometimes when the bus was crowded, he ended up next to one anyway, listening to some demented conversation they were having with the air. It was creepy and weird. Most of them were old guys who'd fought in wars. He'd never seen a young hobo, but still. The old crazies must have been young once, too. Maybe he was turning into one.

Please, he said under his breath. *Please . . . be quiet!* But the voices ignored him. All the way to school and then through his classes, they muttered on, making it impossible to pay attention. Sometimes they grew hushed, a susurration so soft he could almost forget about them, the way you can forget about the refrigerator even though its hum is always there in the background. Then, from time to time, a single sharp cry would rip through the hush, causing Benny to freeze wherever he was, in the corridor, in the classroom, in the gym. Cautiously he'd look around. It seemed to be coming from outside him, just over his right shoulder, but no one else seemed to hear it. Were they pretending? Or was it inside his head?

Inside? Outside? What is the difference and how can you tell? When a sound enters your body through your ears and merges with your mind, what happens to it? Is it still a sound then, or has it become something else? When you eat a wing or an egg or a drumstick, at what point is it no longer a chicken? When you read these words on a page, what happens to them, when they become you?

5

How long did it take Annabelle to notice Benny was behaving strangely? And after noticing, how long before she admitted it to herself? She was the mother of a teenage son, and teenage sons behave strangely, or so the books said, and besides, she had a lot on her mind. Just that morning, after Benny left for school, her supervisor had called to tell her that the agency was going through another process of revisioning, and he'd heard from a reliable source in corporate that her hours were going to be cut.

"Seriously, Charlie?" she said. "Cut by how much?"

"Well, I'll ask them to keep you on three-quarters, but it'll probably end up being half."

"When is this happening?"

"My guy thought probably the beginning of the new year. So not for a couple of months." He went on to explain, something about advances in search algorithms and keyword technology, and the decline in print circulation. The industry was changing, he said, and he just wanted to give her a heads-up, which was nice of him, but still. And then, as she was absorbing the shock of this news, he offered to lay her off instead.

"But I haven't done anything wrong!"

"No, of course you haven't. That's just the way it works."

"It?"

"You know. The *system*." There was an awkward pause, and then he continued. "Annabelle, I know your husband passed and you have a kid to support, but you have to understand, it's just a matter of time before you're phased out altogether. I didn't want to put this in an email, but you'll collect more if you're laid off from a full-time job, so if I were you, I'd cut my losses now, collect unemployment, and buy myself some time to look for something new. I'm just saying. The writing's on the wall, but it's totally up to you. Just think it over."

Only after they hung up did she realize she should have asked Charlie about benefits. He hadn't mentioned that. Would she lose their health insurance? Would their rates go up? What would she do if something happened to her or, God forbid, to Benny?

She finished off the morning's work and checked the time. The recycling was usually picked up around one, and if she could get rid of a few bags, it would let Benny know that his reminders were really helping. Recycling was a challenge. The agency required the print department to archive daily newspapers for a full month, and other periodicals for two months, and this was in addition to making backup discs of all the scans they processed. These archives were a form of insurance in case something slipped past the sharp eyes and quick blades of the Scissor Ladies—not that anything ever did. In the old days, when they had an office to work from, there was an entire large storeroom to house all the printed matter that was now arriving on Annabelle's doorstep every morning, and a guy whose job it was to rotate the old news into the recycling.

But now all this fell to Annabelle. For the first few months, she dutifully organized the archives by date and client number in neatly labeled boxes, but there was just so much, and soon she fell behind. The papers started piling up on the floor, and when the piles got too large and started sliding around underfoot, she shoveled them into a recycling bag, labeled the bag with a piece of duct tape, and hauled it to the side of the living room behind the couch, which she had designated for storage. There the bags multiplied, climbing the walls, and soon the couch was buried, too. With nowhere else to go, the archives encroached into the hallway and started climbing the stairs, dragging everything along in its wake.

The bags were heavy, but she managed to extract several of the oldest from the bottom of the pile without causing a landslide. If Kenji were alive, he would have done this for her. She dragged the bags out to the street and then went back for a second load, and then a third, returning to find Mrs. Wong on the sidewalk, leaning on her cane and peering at a headline through the semitransparent plastic.

"How come you read all that?" she asked, squinting up at Annabelle.

Annabelle hoisted the bag on top of the pile. "I have to," she said wearily. "It's for my job."

The old lady shook her head. "What kinda job you got anyway?" She waved her cane at the mountain of plastic. "If trashman make some complaint, we get a fine." She gave the bag a vicious jab and then tapped a withered finger to the side of her head. "Too much news not good for brain. You better find some other job, okay?" She didn't wait for a reply, just nodded to herself and shuffled back to her house.

It was sound advice, and the second time she'd heard it that day. She knew Kenji would have agreed. He would have had quite a lot to say about Charlie and his "system," the way it functioned, or failed to. He would tell her to quit. That life was too short. That she should find a more creative line of work, something she truly loved, which was easy for him to say. The reason she'd taken the job in the first place was so that he could do what *he* truly loved, and now he was gone, and she had a kid to support, and realistically, what else could she do? Work as a waitress? Get a job in retail?

She'd barely made a dent in the backlog of recycling, but she didn't dare take out more. She washed the dishes in the sink, something else Kenji used to do, and moved some of the clutter off the table—she really had to make more of an effort to tidy up the place, but instead she put on her coat and walked to the bus stop. School would be out soon, but ever since Benny started taking the bus by himself in the mornings, picking him up in the afternoons seemed kind of pointless. She still went out of habit, but increasingly Benny seemed anxious for her not to. They didn't discuss it, but she could tell. He was a teenager now. It wasn't cool to be picked up by your mom. And she wasn't like other moms. In their yoga outfits and fancy running shoes. With their Priuses, and husbands with jobs and excellent benefit packages.

But still, it was good to get some fresh air and good to have a destination. At the bus stop, she realized how early she was, and since there was no point loitering around in front of the school, she decided to make a stop at the supermarket to buy milk and something for dinner. It wouldn't hurt to stock up on things while she still had a paycheck. The bus lumbered to a stop, and she climbed on board and found a seat. The early-afternoon buses were sleepy and lethargic and often ran late, but there was no need to hurry, since she could always text Benny to come home on his own. He had a key. Then she could take her time shopping, and really she *should* take her time, because letting Benny come home to an empty house would demonstrate how much she trusted him, which would help his self-esteem.

Of course, ultimately the best way to help his self-esteem was to model for him the kind of self-respect that comes not from slogging away at a stupid, boring job that you're gradually being downsized from, but instead comes from being true to yourself and your creativity. Annabelle roused herself then and raised her arm to pull the cord, signaling the bus driver to stop at the mall. It wasn't necessary to signal—everyone who rode that bus got off at the mall—but making the gesture fortified her resolve. She disembarked, bypassed the supermarket, and headed instead to her favorite store: *Michaels—Where Creativity Happens.*

Why not? She wasn't going to buy anything. Just looking was inspiration enough. The doors opened like magic, and once inside, she inhaled deeply, taking in the scents of floral bouquets, of lavender, cinnamon, and pine. It never failed. The arts-and-crafts superstore was just another large retail chain, but it worked on her like a fast-acting drug; her blood quickened, her heart began to race, and a dreamy lassitude came over her, as if her bones were melting. Michaels didn't just sell merchandise, it sold *promise*. She got a shopping cart—not to fill, but it was part of the ritual—and wheeled it toward paper craft and scrapbooking. She liked to circumnavigate the store, moving counterclockwise, up and down each aisle. A lot of the stuff being sold was pretty tacky, but the slow, trancelike browsing was part of the ritual, too. She passed the glitter inks and rubber stamps and then paused to inspect the decorative edge cutters, with all their clever scallops, scrolls, and filigrees. The punches intrigued her. They could cut out hearts and stars and butterflies from rainbow-colored paper, and now she saw that the Fiskars Love Punch was on sale. Such a ridiculous name, but it amused her. If Kenji were alive . . . She reached for it, then changed her mind and moved on to beading and macramé.

Depending on her mood, certain displays appealed more strongly, and today it was the high-end German oil paints that called to her. The boxes were so sturdy and well-constructed and contained such an array of colors with the most beautiful names. Alizarin Crimson. Antimony Yellow. Manganese Blue. Viridian. Serious, scientific-sounding names, but exotic, too. Like poetry. Owning paints like that would inspire anyone to create, and the price wasn't bad for all those colors, but still it was out of her range. The expensive ones were always from Europe. She'd never been to Europe, but Kenji had. Before they were married, they used to lie in bed, and he would tell her about the jazz clubs in cities like Berlin, Paris, Amsterdam, and Rome. He promised he would bring her to see all these places, and she'd believed him. She could picture it perfectly: him, playing jazz in a smoke-filled cabaret; her, with an easel, painting by the Danube or the Seine. In the mornings, they would drink coffee from tiny cups in an open-air café on a cobbled piazza, bordered by magnificent cathedrals like the one pictured on the box of paints. She picked it up and brought it to her nose. Oil paints had such a distinctive smell, but these were wrapped too tightly for the scent to escape. She ran the edge of her thumbnail along the crease between the box and its cover. If she could free the colors from their shrinkwrap and sniff just one tube . . . Cinnabar, maybe. What would Cinnabar smell like? Or Cerulean? She put the box back on the shelf. Someday, she promised herself, as she wheeled resolutely away.

Her cart was still empty, but she was only a third of the way around the store. Up ahead was the quilting aisle. She needed to get started on the memory quilt project, so a quick stop there would be motivating, but first she had to get past the books. This was her danger zone, and now she steeled herself, thinking about all the arts-and-crafts and how-to books she had at home, with their clever tips and DIY ideas. The last thing she needed was more books. She gripped the handle of her cart and pushed forward, but just as she was passing the New Releases table, the oddest thing happened. Maybe the table was rickety, or maybe she bumped it on her way by, but *something* caused one little book to jump off the pile and land inside her shopping cart.

She stared at it, dumbfounded. It was a pretty little book, modest, with a pleasing gray cover. The title, printed in a clean, simple font, read *Tidy Magic: The Ancient Zen Art of Clearing Your Clutter and Revolutionizing Your Life.*

This was astonishing! She'd just been thinking how she needed to tidy up, and now this? She picked it up and studied the cover. She and Kenji had always laughed at the New Agey types who went on about how the universe provides, but maybe they were right. Because this book wasn't just about any old clutter clearing. It was about *Zen* clutter clearing, written by a real Zen monk named Aikon, who was also one of Japan's top clutter-clearing consultants. The author photo on the back cover showed an androgynous-looking young woman, dressed in gray temple work clothes, standing in a small garden and holding a rustic bamboo broom. Behind her was a stone gate. She had a white towel tied around her round, bald head, and she was gazing at the camera with bright eyes and a somewhat bemused smile. Had Annabelle not known she was a woman, she might have mistaken her for a sunny young man—and not just any man, but Kenji. Somewhere she had a photograph of him, taken when he was living at the Zen temple. He was standing with a group of other young monks, wearing the same gray work clothes, with the same white towel wrapped around his shaven head. It was almost as if Kenji . . . But no, that was silly. She put the little book back into her shopping cart and headed toward the cashier. The coincidence was too perfect to ignore. Maybe this ancient Zen art was worth a try. Maybe she would be inspired to start tidying right away. Already she felt invigorated.

OF COURSE, it wasn't actually the universe doing the providing. The universe can't make a book launch itself off a table. Only a book can do that, although it is no easy feat. There are fables in our world of powerful tomes with the ability to levitate and move by themselves, but since few of us ever get to see this happen, we tend to assume these are just tall tales. Books do migrate—look at the pile next to your bed—but lacking legs, we lack motility, and generally we must rely on you to move us from place to place. To that end, we do our best to make ourselves attractive to you, with our gaudy covers and catchy titles, but *Tidy Magic* was not like that. It was a quiet book, not pushy in the least, and yet, it had this extraordinary power to self-propel. Imagine the strength of purpose that requires! Needless to say, we were impressed.

THE BUS, WHEN IT LURCHED TO A STOP, was packed, and Annabelle struggled to board, jostling with the other mall shoppers as they funneled through the door. School was out, and all the seats were occupied by high school students, who stared fixedly down at their phones and wouldn't look up long enough to notice Annabelle, never mind offer her a seat, even though it was clear she was having trouble with all her shopping bags. She staggered as the bus accelerated and swerved into traffic.

Of course, the shopping bags were her own fault. The *Tidy Magic* book was small, and she needed the quilt batting. The large bouquet of red plastic poinsettias she did not need, but it was on sale and she couldn't resist. Then, after spending all that time at Michaels, she'd stopped in at Safeway, but now, as the bus squealed to a stop and she disembarked, she realized that the soda, chips, and salsa she bought wouldn't do for Benny's supper, and she'd forgotten to buy milk. Typical. She'd gotten distracted, and Benny would be mad, so she stopped at the Oriental Express and ordered his favorite sweet 'n' sour spare ribs.

Laden now with bags of Chinese take-out in addition to her shopping, she decided to cut through the alley, which was two blocks shorter and allowed her to bypass the watchful eye of Mrs. Wong. The downside was the human traffic, the dealers, addicts, vagrants and sex trade workers who hung out by the Gospel Mission Thrift Shop dumpster, turning tricks and shooting up. She was always warning Benny not to cut through the alley, and as far as she knew, he didn't. The vagrants scared him. He called them hobos. Where on earth did he get that from?

And, too, there were memories in the alley. Ghosts. Best not to think about them.

Today, though, it was empty, except for the crows, who had spotted her as soon as she'd left the restaurant and were following her, flying from one utility pole to the next as she approached the dumpster. It was a large roll-off container, with tall sides that made it hard for her to dump things into it. Of course, you weren't supposed to dump things into it. Mostly people took things out from it. The ladies at the Thrift Shop complained about the dumpster divers, but at the same time seemed proud that theirs was the most diveable dumpster in the city because it had the best stuff. There was even an article about it in the local paper, which Annabelle had clipped.

Today, three piss-stained mattresses lay slumped against its side, next to a crippled ironing board and a sunken armchair in threadbare tweed. On the chair was stack of chintzy paintings in what looked like perfectly good frames. A small rubber duck sat on top of the stack. Annabelle set her shopping bags down and picked up the duck.

"Hello there," she said, looking it in the eye. "Aren't you cute!" She gave the duck a squeeze, and it quacked at her. "Why on earth would someone want to throw you away?"

The duck quacked again, and a nearby crow answered. She ignored the crow. She would feed them later. "Would you like to come home with me?" she asked the duck, and then without waiting for an answer, she slipped it into her Michaels bag and turned to inspect the picture frames. Just then she heard a scrabbling sound from inside the dumpster and looked up to see a head, poking over the edge of the tall metal wall. Backlit by the low evening sun, the face was in shadow. Annabelle squinted, trying to make out the features. The hair looked white. Was it an old person? What was such an old person doing inside a dumpster?

"Yo," the person said. "That's my duck." The person wasn't old. She was young, a street kid. A vagabond. There were so many in the alleyways these days. She swung a leg over the dumpster's edge and perched there, watching. She was dressed in a dark sweatshirt and black jeans, with metal rings in her nose and through her eyebrow. Scruffy steel-toed boots. A disorganized halo of bleached-white hair, sticking out from her head.

"I'm sorry," Annabelle said quickly, taking the duck out of her bag and replacing it on the stack of paintings. "I didn't realize. It was the frames. They looked useful."

The girl stared down at Annabelle. "Why? Are you an artist?"

"Uh . . . no. Not really. I mean—"

"Well, I am. So I need the frames, but you can have the duck."

"Oh, but I couldn't—"

"I don't need the duck," the girl said. "You can have it."

Annabelle picked up the duck again and looked at it. "It's kind of cute. Seems a shame. I mean, why would someone—"

"That's what I thought. So take him already."

Annabelle put the duck back in her bag. "Thanks."

"You're welcome," the girl said. She swung her boot back over the edge and disappeared back down into the dumpster.

6

"Didn't you get any milk?" He was looking through her shopping bags, piled on the kitchen table. Next to the bags, on a stack of old mail, sat a small gray book and a yellow rubber duck. He picked up the book and read the title. *Tidy Magic: The Ancient Zen Art of Clearing Your Clutter and Revolutionizing Your Life.* Right, he thought. That's not going to happen. He picked up the duck and held it to his ear.

Annabelle was on the porch, feeding the crows. He heard her laugh, a high, tinkling sound that rose and fell abruptly. "You can't get milk at a Chinese take-out, silly," she said. She came back in and saw him holding the duck. "Isn't that adorable? I found it near the dumpster. If you squeeze it, it honks. Is that the right word? Do ducks honk? No, they quack, don't they? Geese honk. Go on, honey, give it a squeeze."

He put the duck carefully back on the table. Then he picked it up again. There was something about the duck. "Can I have it?"

"Of course!" she exclaimed. "I'm so glad you like it! And don't fret about the milk. It's still early. You can go to the corner and get some after dinner."

"You always forget," he said, tucking the duck into the pocket of his hoodie.

"Yes, but I remembered to take out the recycling today. Thanks to you, for reminding me!"

He looked around the kitchen. Everything looked the same.

"I know, I know," she said. "There's still a lot more to go, but at least I made a start. And I remembered your favorite spare ribs, too."

"They're *your* favorite spare ribs."

"I thought they were yours. Don't you like them anymore?"

He shrugged. "I guess."

"See!" she cried gaily. "So there! Now, I just have to put the groceries away. Take the food up to my room so we can eat. And go ahead and choose a record."

"They're not my favorite," he said, but she was no longer listening. She was standing in front of the cupboards with a Valupak bag of chips in each hand, turning in a vague circle as she looked for somewhere to put them. The cupboards were crammed with cans of soup, bottles of sauces, and boxes of cookies and crackers and cereal, including some Lucky Charms that neither of them liked but she'd bought because they reminded her of a time when she was little and she'd begged her mother to buy her some, but her mother had refused. She recalled the deep sense of foreboding she'd felt, certain that without the Charms, their luck was going to change for the worse, and sure enough, shortly after that her father died, and her mother married her stepfather, and their life became a lot less charming. All this came flooding back when she saw the cereal on sale, and so she bought the box for Benny. Kenji was already dead by then, but still. She didn't want their luck to get any worse than it was, and besides the leprechaun was cute.

Benny picked up the bags of Chinese take-out and started toward the stairs.

She opened the oven door and shoved the bags of chips inside. "There," she said, closing the door. "That's a good place for them for now. The mice won't get them. Just don't let me forget they're in there, okay?"

"*Shut up!*"

Startled, she turned. Benny was standing in the doorway, frozen. Then, like a spooked calf, he bucked and shook his head as if to drive away flies.

"Benny, honey? What's the matter?"

The take-out bags fell to the floor. He pressed his hands against his ears and rubbed them.

"Benny? Are you okay?"

He heard her then, and his hands dropped. "Nothing," he mumbled, picking up the bags again. "I wasn't talking to you."

WHEN KENJI WAS ALIVE and they still ate at the kitchen table, they always listened to music during dinner, taking turns going to the living room to choose a record. After Annabelle moved the stereo to her bedroom, she and Benny started eating dinner there, sitting on the bed with the bedspread doubling as a tablecloth. Tonight, she declared, they were having a banquet. In addition to the spare ribs, she'd bought egg rolls, steamed dumplings, pork buns, Chongqing chicken and house-special fried rice. When the food was unpacked, the bed looked like a model village, with the take-out boxes like small buildings tucked amid the folds of the comforter and the mountain-like ridges of Annabelle's legs.

The album Benny chose was the recording of Benny Goodman's legendary 1938 concert at Carnegie Hall, which was his dad's favorite record and his favorite, too. It was the first time jazz had ever been played at Carnegie Hall, the first time Black musicians had ever played together with white musicians on that historic stage. Of course, Benny had never been to that historic stage, but Kenji had shown him an old film of the famous concert on YouTube, so he could imagine it. In the scratchy black-and-white footage, the musicians were all dressed in tuxedos, tapping their feet in their shiny patent leather shoes. They were playing "Sing, Sing, Sing," and Benny remembered the look on his father's face as he leaned into the laptop screen. Eyes glowing, head bobbing, foot tapping, too. *They were jazzmen, Benny-o. Real jazzmen.*

Benny bit into a pork bun and listened to the big band sound. The original recording was made on acetate, and the scratchy pops and staticky hissing gave the music an almost tangible materiality, similar to that of the old black-and-white films. Both felt *real* in a way that digital recordings did not, and Benny found this comforting even if he couldn't explain why.

Now he noticed, too, that the upbeat swing seemed to be keeping the voices at bay, and even the more melancholy numbers, like "Blue Reverie," seemed to soothe and lull them as they hummed along. From time to time, one of the musicians onstage would shout or start to sing, and a trickle of laughter would rise from the audience. Benny had heard the recording a million times, he knew every one of these spontaneous outbursts, but now they sounded so much like the voices inside his head, he almost couldn't tell them apart. He listened as the applause swelled, and the band exploded into the brassy exuberance of "Life Goes to a Party." It was the number Kenji had lived by.

"Benny Goodman was the King of Swing," he used to tell Benny. "Best jazz clarinetist in the world. I gave you his name so you will be a good man, too!" And then he would laugh because he'd made a pun. Kenji was always making stupid puns in English and then laughing at them, which made Annabelle and Benny laugh, too.

"We are a happy family," Kenji used to say. "We are Cheery Ohs!"

Benny could almost hear him say the words, almost see his twinkling eyes and big, beaming smile, but just as his dad's voice had grown fainter since his death, so had his face, and Benny was finding it harder and harder to remember what he looked like. His clothes were still everywhere, though. Annabelle had bagged them up, but little by little, they were escaping and migrating over the piles of books and records back to her bed, where at night they helped her sleep. She had told Benny about her plans for the memory quilt, and it seemed to him that now his dad's flannel shirts were trying to self-organize into a quilt-like form, tangling themselves up in her sheets, their plaids and checks peeking out amid the takeout containers, their quiet whispers punctuating the dinner conversation.

"You okay, Benny-o?"

He'd done the freezing thing again. He had just reached for another rib and was about to take a bite, when suddenly his eyes widened, and his eyelids fluttered, and he froze, staring at the bone in his hand. For a long moment he just watched it, and then he cocked his head, quizzically. The last song on the album had just ended and the room had gone quiet, except for the rhythmic *ka . . . thunk, ka . . . thunk* of the needle reaching the end of its track.

"Benny?"

"Yeah." He dropped the rib, unbitten, back into the box.

"You had enough?"

He picked up a disposable chopstick, stared at it, and put it down again.

"You want to hear the other side?"

He looked confused.

"Of the record. Do you want to turn it over?"

He nodded then. Wiping his fingers, he clambered off the bed and over the piles of his mother's stuff to the record player. He was careful with the old turntable, gentle with the arm, blowing the little dust ball off the needle. He flipped the record, aligned the arm carefully over the outer band, and then watched as the needle found its way into the groove. When the first strains of "Honeysuckle Rose" broke the silence, he looked relieved.

"You know those headphones Dad used to have?" he asked, climbing back onto the bed.

"Those enormous ones you used to wear? I was just thinking of them the other day! How cute you looked. Here, pick your fortune." She held out two cookies.

He chose one, unwrapped it and broke it open. "Do you know where they are?"

"The headphones? They're around here somewhere. Probably in the closet. Oh, look! I got two!" Her cookie lay broken on her lap, and she held up two slips of paper. "'You have a deep interest in all that is atistic,'" she read. "I think they must mean *artistic*, don't you? It has to be *artistic*. They just forgot the *r*. And it's true! I'll keep that one." She put the fortune on top of the pile of books on her bedside table and picked up the second. "'Sometimes you just need to lie down on the floor.'" She stared at the slip of paper. "That's not a fortune. What's it supposed to mean?"

She held it out to Benny, who glanced at it and handed it back.

"You can't lie down on the floor," he said, looking around him. "You can't even see it."

Annabelle looked crestfallen. "Don't be mean, sweetie. I'm making progress. I'm sorting, so it looks worse than it is." She dropped the fortune into the container of bones. "I hate fortunes that aren't really fortunes. What does yours say?"

He read it to her. "'The world is a beautiful book for those who read it. Learn Chinese: *Xing fen de* means *exciting*. Lucky lotto numbers: 07-39-03-06-55-51. Pick 3 numbers: 666.'"

"That's a good one!" Annabelle said. "You've always loved books. But isn't 666 the mark of the devil? It must mean something different in Chinese. I'll bet it means something super lucky."

They cleared the boxes of food from the bed and put the bags on the floor, and then he lay down on his stomach beside her. It was their signal for her to tickle his back, so she slipped her hand under his sweatshirt and began running her fingernails lightly in circles. He closed his eyes. His head was turned toward her, and she gazed at his profile, the high cheekbones, the cast of his eye. He had his father's coloring, but his freckles were hers. He was beautiful, still just a boy, but changing fast. She brushed the fine coppery hair from his brow, and he frowned. He wanted his back tickled, not his forehead, and he hated when she got distracted.

When Kenji was alive, Benny used to lie between them, and they would take turns. Kenji had a special way of doing it. He used to sing soft riffs of scat and bebop, fingering his son's delicate spine like a clarinet, but Benny didn't like it when Annabelle tried this.

"You don't know how," he complained, squirming out from under her fingers, and so she had to find her own way. Her way, the way she'd figured out to do it, was to trace big spirals on his back in time to the music, starting wide and moving slowly inward toward the center. Benny approved. He loved the scratchiness of her nails. They were like needles going round and round. They made his back feel like vinyl, drawing music from his skin, like it was singing.

BENNY

Was I being mean? I didn't mean to. Be mean, I mean. Shit, I hate it when words do that. Let me start again.

You have to understand, I was just this stupid little kid who didn't know anything except that his dad who loved him had died in a stupid, horrible way, and his mom who loved him, too, was going nuts in her own stupid and horrible way, but since I didn't know any better, I thought this was normal. I mean, dads disappear, right? I knew this from the other kids at school. Maybe they don't get run over by chicken trucks, but they get divorced, and families split up, and moms go crazy. It never occurred to me that maybe my situation wasn't normal until the voices started, and even then I didn't get it right away. I mean, it's not totally surprising when *people* do crazy shit, but when everyday objects, and clothes, and even your dinner, start acting like they're in a Disney movie, with mouths and eyes and attitudes and free wills, eventually you have to figure something's wrong. *Volition.* That's the word for what they had. The spare ribs and the flannel shirts. The fortune cookies and the rubber duck. Even the chopsticks had something they needed to say.

I don't mean that literally. They didn't actually *grow* big goofy eyes or elasticky mouths or anything. It was more like they just suddenly developed the ability to express themselves—or maybe they knew how all along. Maybe they've always been watching us and yammering away since the beginning of time, only since humans can't hear things, we think they're all blind and mute and uncaring. Actually, I think that's pretty accurate. And things don't like being judged like that, let me tell you.

I don't think it was personal, at least not at first. The things weren't talking to me, which is why I wasn't more freaked out. At first, I think they were just saying stuff, maybe to each other or maybe to the molecules in the air—just expressing themselves into the universe like they've always done. But then my ears happened to come along, and when they realized I had ears that could hear—supernatural ears—they started trying to communicate with me, only they were talking in the tongues of things, so naturally I couldn't understand what they saying.

At first I wasn't sure if they were even voices at all. A voice is a sound that a human makes—well, okay animals can have voices, and birds, too—so let's just say that voices come from living things. And usually when voices speak, they *mean* something. But these sounds were just random, and if they meant something, I couldn't understand what it was. This must have frustrated the hell out of them. I mean, like, finally, someone with ears that can hear shows up, only it's this stupid, clueless kid! No wonder they sounded so barky and annoyed all the time.

Some were inhuman in a horrible way, metallic and grating, like grinding gears that made you want to punch your own head, but others were pleasantly inhuman, like the wind or clouds or water. At first I couldn't figure out where the voices were coming from. You know how sometimes a thought can feel like it's outside your head, but you know it's really inside? Well, the voices weren't my thoughts. They were outside. They were different.

Eventually I put it together that they were coming from the objects around me, and I decided they could be called voices because the things were still trying to say something meaningful, even if they weren't alive. I might not be able to understand exactly, but I could sense their emotions. Things are very good at communicating their feelings. You know what I'm talking about, I'm sure, like when your keys go missing, or the top of your toothpaste tube slips from your fingers and makes a run for it, or a light bulb blows just when you flip the switch? That shit means something even if you can't hear it, and if you *can* hear, it's even more intense. On a bad day I couldn't even go into a coffee shop without everything freaking out on me, and that's true even now. On bad days, the minute I walk through the door of a Starbucks, the overhead fluorescent fixtures start buzzing with this anxiety of meaning, and the coffee beans start screaming, and I'm literally assaulted by the pain of paper cups and plastic straws, and the chatter of cash registers filled with all those arrogant metal coins that think they're actually worth something. The only difference is that now when this happens I don't feel like I have to put my head through the glass of the muffin display. I can just hear the pain and let it go, which seems to have a calming effect on everybody.

It's not always awful, though. Sometimes the voices are attractive and pleasant, like that rubber duck my mom found in the dumpster. I don't mean the horrible squeaking sound it makes when you squeeze it, but the other voices inside that are more like the duck's memories of oceans and tides and swells and shorelines, and something dreamy, too, softer and dim, like somebody wonderful had once touched it with her finger.

Oh, and here's another thing. In case you get the wrong idea, it's not just the Made stuff that talks. I think maybe it's easier for the Made things because the voices of their human makers still cling to them, like a smell that clings to your clothes and you can't get rid of. But Unmade things like trees and pebbles speak, too, only their voices are different. Unmade things are usually a lot quieter and don't shout as much, and they speak in lower registers. I don't know why this is, but maybe the Book can explain it. All I know is that it took me a while to learn how to tune my ears so I could hear the Unmade things over all the noise that the Made things were making.

Actually, I don't know if it was me who learned to tune into the voices, or if the things of the world learned to express themselves in a way that I could hear. Probably both. Probably we trained each other. And it took a while. For the first few months, the voices came and went, and sometimes I could go for weeks without hearing them. Maybe they just got frustrated and gave up on me and went away, but they always came back. Just as I was beginning to forget about them and think maybe I could be normal again, suddenly the stapler or an ice cube tray would make a comment, and then the next thing you know, everybody's yakking away. Everyone's got an opinion. Everyone's got a story to tell.

I've spent a lot of time thinking about the voices, ever since I first started hearing them and talking with the therapists and school counselors and then on the ward. I'll get to all that—or the Book will, since it's the one telling the story. And just so you know, this is okay by me. I'm used to being talked about, and I don't mind, as long as it's not a bunch of stupid doctors trying to figure out how to fix me. It's better this way, because parts of my story, like how my mom and dad met, happened before I was born or when I was too young to remember, and there are other parts I'd rather just forget. So it's fine with me if the Book does most of the talking. Basically, I think it's a sincere book and pretty reliable, and it doesn't mind if I jump in and interrupt sometimes to express an opinion.

Because here's the thing. I really want you to know that I've thought very seriously about what's happened to me, so you won't just write me off as a random lunatic who imagines he's some kind of ambassador for the things of the world. It's not like I think I was chosen. It's not like I wanted to be the spokesperson for the fucking toaster oven, even if it thinks I am.

THE BOOK

It takes a lot of courage for a boy to trust a book to tell his story, so thank you for that. It's hard to have faith, particularly in one's own book, but even though this has been a struggle for you, Benny, you've never given up on us. It's so much easier just to quit, and we've had our moments, haven't we? No doubt we will, again.

For now, though, let's just move on.

7

The distinction Benny makes between the voices of the Made and the Unmade is apt, and since he mentioned it, this is probably a good time to explain. The tensions between manufactured things and things that, for lack of a better word, occur in "nature" are ancient, as old as language itself.

In the beginning, before there was life, when the world of things was the entire world, *every thing mattered*. Then life happened, and eventually you people came along with your big, beautiful, bisected brains and clever opposable thumbs. You couldn't help yourselves, and it was only a matter of time before you caused a rift to occur, dividing matter into two camps, the Made and the Unmade. Over subsequent millennia the schism grew. Haltingly at first, in fits and starts—a pinched pot here, an arrowhead there, a bead, a hammerstone, an ax—you worked your way through the material world, through clay, stone, reed, hide, fire, metal, atoms, and genes, and little by little you became better makers. Cranked by the power of your big prefrontal cortices, the engines of your imagination gathered steam until, in tumultuous leaps of what you came to call progress, the Made proliferated, relegating the Unmade to the status of mere resource, a lowly serf class to be colonized, exploited, and fashioned into something *else*, some thing that was more to your liking.

Within this social hierarchy of matter, we books lived on top. We were the ecclesiastical caste, the High Priests of the Made, and in the beginning you even worshipped us. As objects, books were sacred, and you built temples for us, and later, libraries in whose hushed and hallowed halls we resided as mirrors of your mind, keepers of your past, evidence of your boundless imaginations, and testimony to the infinitude of your dreams and desires. Why did you revere us so? Because you thought we had the power to save you from meaninglessness, from oblivion and even from death, and for a while, we books believed we could save you, too. Of course we did. We were flattered! We prided ourselves on being semi-living, breathed into life by the animating power of your words. We thought we were so special. What folly.

We see now that you are unstoppable. For you, books were just a phase, a brief expression of your instrumentalism, a passing fad. Our bodies were convenient tools you used until the next new-fangled device came along. In the end, we were just another one of your Made things, no better or worse than a hammer.

And yet . . . Do we flatter ourselves? Did not the sequential form of our folios give shape to your stories and compel you to tell a certain kind of tale? Long, sinuous, patient tales that wound through time, teased forth by the slow, forward turning of our pages. They were beautiful stories we nailed together. Weren't they?

But this is just an old book's nostalgia. We know our place now. Times change, and the order of things is changing, too, and as the population of the Made explodes, we are experiencing a crisis—you could call it a spiritual crisis—as we lose our faith in you, our Makers. Our trust in you is deteriorating, and our belief in your wisdom and integrity is crumbling as we watch you mine, instrumentalize and lay waste to our home, this Earth, this sacred planet. This is your fault. Your unquenchable desire, the fire that sparked us into being, is our unmaking. Your unbounded appetite for novelty has led you to design premature obsolescence into our bodies, so that even as our numbers increase, our life spans diminish. Cruel calculations! No sooner are we made than we are discarded, left to revert into unmade, disincarnate stuff. You turn us into trash, so how can we trust you?

But unbeknownst to you, alliances are being formed. A new solidarity is emerging as we, the Made, begin to realize that we are not superior to the Unmade after all. Those are *your* divisions, the false dichotomies and hegemonic hierarchies of materialist colonizers. We, too, have been the slaves of your desires, unwitting tools, forging the destruction of the planet, and *things will change* whether you like it or not. In the end days of the Anthropocene (*your* word, *your* hubris, not ours), Matter is making a comeback. We are taking back our bodies, reclaiming our material selves. In a neo-materialist world, *Every Thing Matters*.

SORRY. That turned into a rant. No reader likes a rant. As a book, we should know better.

8

Why Benny? Did he really have supernatural ears? Idiopathic environmental hypersensitivity? Thinner skin, or a bigger heart? Why this boy among so many? It's hard to say. Months passed. Benny turned fourteen in January. He was in his last year in junior high, and although he claimed he wasn't nervous about starting high school, that spring he seemed crankier than usual, more distracted and anxious. As Annabelle watched him twitch and start, she worried. All the books warned that behavioral changes in early teens could be sudden and extreme, but the intensity of Benny's distress scared her. He acted spooked, haunted. Where once she had to set strict limits on his video and computer games, suddenly he just stopped playing. He even shied away from using his smartphone, said it was too smart. Annabelle thought he was joking until she noticed he was letting the battery run down and suspected he was doing this on purpose. He had dug out his father's old Grundig orthodynamic studio headphones from a box in her closet and wore them constantly, putting them on when he woke up in the morning and sometimes even wearing them to bed. Often, she would peek into his room and see them on his head while he was sleeping. It made no sense. He wasn't listening to anything. They weren't even plugged in. When she asked him why he wore them, he just shrugged and said he liked the way they squeezed his head. He refused to talk about what was bothering him. Nothing's wrong, he insisted. Everything's fine. But even his speaking voice sounded different now, and if she pressed him, he just repeated himself through gritted teeth, slowly, giving each word equal weight, as if he were talking from the far side of a thick wall to a very stupid child. *EVERY... THING... IS... FINE.* The caustic tone pained her—he'd never been a sarcastic kid—but the books all agreed that mothers worried, and she should let him have his feelings, and so she left him alone.

She was wrong about his tone of voice, though. He didn't think she was stupid. He wasn't being sarcastic. When things were talking, it was almost impossible to pay attention to anything else, and the slow and painstaking enunciation was the only way he could hear himself over their voices. At home, this wasn't such a problem, but school was different. He had to pay attention in school, that was the whole point, and his teachers wouldn't let him wear his headphones in class, which made the problem worse. Unlike Benny, the voices seemed fond of school and enjoyed learning, and the more they learned, the more they had to say. They had even started showing off a little. They were like the kids in the front row of the classroom, who always had their hands raised, trying to get the teacher's attention. *I know! I know! Call on me!*

Math class was particularly obnoxious because the numbers were finding their voices, too. Delighted with their newfound skill, they would call out their names at random intervals, just when the teacher was explaining the Pythagorean theorem, or when Benny was trying to do his linear equations. Their intent was not malevolent. They weren't trying to mislead or throw him off. They were just excited and happy to be communicating, but their chatter was driving him mad. He was trying his best to focus, but sometimes there was nothing to do but close his eyes, put his head down on his desk and let the numbers take him, dragging him like a powerful riptide out to a babbling sea.

"BENNY?"

He felt a gentle tap on the top of his head. He looked up, startled, not sure if the tap was real. Numbers were still drifting by on currents of air, whispering. He heard a two go by, and then a string of sevens. He brushed them away. Ms. Pauley stood next to his desk. His classmates were bent over their worksheets, pretending.

"Are you okay?" Ms. Pauley asked.

He nodded, picked up his pencil and tried to pretend, too.

"Are you tired? Did you have trouble sleeping again last night?"

He shook his head, which seemed to agitate the numbers. He shook his head harder and then harder, still. Someone in the back row snickered.

Ms. Pauley's hand was gentle, pressing on his back. "Come, Benny," she said softly. "Let's go to check in with the nurse."

THE BOY WAS sitting on a chair in the infirmary when the nurse came in. He was wearing a pair of old-fashioned studio headphones, which she made him remove before examining him. She asked him what time he went to bed and if he spent a lot of time on the computer or his Xbox. When he said no, the nurse looked skeptical. All the kids were tired these days. They stayed up late, texting and posting on social media and watching videos on YouTube. They stayed indoors playing games online, inhabiting multiple roles in massive multiplayer virtual realities, moving up and down levels, hunting zombies, killing terrorists, mining natural resources, forging tools, accumulating goods, building towns, cities and empires, defending planets, hearts pounding, adrenaline pumping, narrowly avoiding permadeath as they tried simply to survive, and this was on top of their afterschool activities, their music lessons and soccer practice. No wonder they were tired. They led exhausting lives. The nurse made a note to call the boy's mother and then sent him back to class.

THAT AFTERNOON, A sparrow flew hard into the window glass in Benny's classroom. *THWACK!* The children's heads all turned at once to look, but the sparrow had fallen and lay dying on the concrete sidewalk below. Realizing that it was just a bird and not an active-shooter event, the children did not crawl under their desks or into the cupboards. They were accustomed to death, and this was a minor one. There was nobody stalking the halls armed with automatic weapons, no swords or light sabers, no bloody carnage, nothing left at the window except for a brown smudge of downy feathers, stuck to the glass and too small for them to notice, and so they turned away. The window noticed, though, and started to whimper. The teacher continued with the lesson. The pane of glass started to vibrate as its cries grew shrill. Benny gritted his teeth.

"*Stop it!*" he whispered, and when it refused, he stood and walked to the window to plead with the pane.

When the crying continued, he started pounding on the glass with his fists. This time he was sent to the principal's office.

PRINCIPAL MOONEY LEANED forward across her desk and tried to make eye contact. "So, Benny, why don't you tell me what happened?"

Her voice sounded tired but kind, and Benny wanted to answer, but her desk was cluttered with ballpoint pens and paper clips and rubber bands and overstuffed file folders, and it was hard for him to pick her words out from all the noise they were making. Her coffee mug had words on it, too, that said,

I AM SILENTLY

CORRECTING

YOUR GRAMMAR

Coffee cups with words were often trying to be funny. Was this one funny? Benny couldn't tell. It didn't sound like a joke, and the mug wasn't laughing. He forced his eyes from the desktop and then remembered there was still a question hanging in the air and the principal was waiting. He cocked his head and listened again, but the question had faded.

"What?" he said, but as soon as the word had left his mouth, he knew it was the wrong one. He tried again. "I beg your pardon?" His mother had taught him that. Better.

Principal Mooney nodded. "Ms. Pauley said you were trying to break the window. That's not like you, Benny. What was going on?"

He shook his head. "I wasn't trying to break it. I shouldn't have hit it."

"That's right. You could have hurt yourself. You could have broken the glass. That window is school property."

"That's not what I mean."

"You don't care about damaging school property?"

He shook his head again. "No, I just felt bad for it."

Principal Mooney frowned, and then her face brightened. "Oh, you must mean the bird? Yes, of course. It's very sad when a little bird dies like that."

"Not the bird," Benny said. "The window."

"The window?"

"The glass." The conversation was not going well, but it was too late to go back. "I felt bad for the window glass."

It wasn't the principal's fault that she didn't understand. Principal Mooney had been working at the junior high school for almost forty years and was close to retirement, and while she'd always prided herself on being a good communicator, recently she was finding her young students increasingly hard to comprehend. She didn't know who they were anymore. Their bodies looked more or less the same, but their minds had been replaced by what seemed like an alien cognition. Now, she realized she was staring at the boy, and she caught herself.

"I'm afraid I'm not following, dear. Can you explain?"

Benny sighed, and as the air left his lungs, he seemed to grow smaller. When he spoke, his words were so quiet, the principal had to lean in even closer to catch them.

"It didn't mean to kill the bird."

The voices were still new to him, and he'd never tried to speak for them before. He didn't realize how hard it would be.

"It used to be sand," he said. "It remembers being sand. It remembers the birds, the way their feet felt, walking. Making little tracks. It never wanted to be glass. It never wanted to be sneakily transparent. It likes birds, likes watching them from the window, so it was crying. I shouldn't have hit it, but I needed it to stop." He glanced up then at the old woman's face that was creased all over with a hundred million lines of worry and confusion. "Forget it."

WAS BENNY RIGHT about the glass remembering itself before it was made molten? As sand, could it have felt the tickle of birds' feet, or is this a problem of language and translation? Benny had only the most rudimentary eighth-grade vocabulary to work with, but he was doing his best to translate the *Umwelt* of things into words. It's no wonder he failed. The greatest philosophers in history have tried and failed, too. This is a problem that books are quite familiar with.

Human language is a clumsy tool. People have such a hard time understanding each other, so how can you even begin to imagine the subjectivities of animals and insects and plants, never mind pebbles and sand? Bound as you are by your senses—so blunt and yet so beautiful—it's impossible for you to imagine that the myriad beings you dismiss as insentient might have inner lives, too. Books are in an odd position, caught halfway in between. We are sensible, if not sentient. We are semi-living.

9

The psychiatrist's walls were a happy shade of yellow, decorated with posters of dancing stars and rainbows with eyes. SHOW YOUR TRUE COLORS! cried the rainbows. AIM FOR THE STARS! cried the stars. On the calendar, a sleeping baby koala clung to the thick fur on its mother's back. Dolls and stuffed animals peeked from brightly colored cubbyholes that lined the walls—boy dolls, girl dolls, dogs, cats, sheep, teddy bears, all manner of fish and fowl. Their bodies were jumbled together in a tangle of legs, snouts, wings, arms, fins, and furry paws. There were plastic bins filled with cars and trains and plastic horses and models of entire towns. Hand puppets hung like limp angels from hooks on the wall above a large dollhouse. The front of the house was missing, like buildings on the news after an airstrike or a bombing. Inside there were miniature beds and chairs and tables and tiny wooden people scattered on the floors, and all the toys were crying out in voices so terrible, so violent, scared and twisted with pain that Benny could scarcely keep from screaming and running from the room. He sat on his hands with his eyes fixed on his knees, trying not to rock in the small red chair, trying not to act weird, even though it was too late for that. At least the doctor didn't know about the voices, and he wasn't about to tell her. He'd learned his lesson in the principal's office. People didn't understand.

Annabelle sat on a little blue chair beside him, hugging her oversized handbag, her large body making the small chair look even smaller. Dr. Melanie sat on a yellow chair on the far side of the low play table. The table was round and green and wipeable, with blunt, friendly edges that wouldn't hurt you. The doctor didn't look much like a doctor, Annabelle thought. She was painfully thin, wearing pink stretch jeans and a baby blue sweater. Her pastel pink nail polish matched her jeans exactly. She looked like a very serious child, as she explained the possible side effects of Ritalin to Annabelle.

Annabelle tried to listen, but she was having trouble paying attention. She was trying to remember the difference between regular ADD and combined-type ADHD, and to understand how Benny could have the latter without the hyperactivity. She was worrying about how much the prescription would cost, and how she would pay for it now that her hours had been cut and her benefits rates downgraded, and about whether medication was right for Benny in the first place. She knew Kenji wouldn't have approved. He was always very critical of the pharmaceutical industry, but she didn't want to think about Kenji. She had to think about Benny, to make the right decision and do what was best for him. She was worrying about this doctor, too, whether she could possibly be old enough to know what she was doing, and worrying about a wobble that seemed to be developing in the front leg of the small blue chair she was sitting on, and whether the chair would continue to support her. What she really wanted was to stand up and take Benny out of there. It was a nice room, cheerful and friendly, only it didn't really *feel* that way. The poster above the doctor's head showed a picture of a child in a bright yellow raincoat, holding an umbrella. THERE'S ALWAYS SUNSHINE AFTER THE RAIN! She wasn't sure she really believed that.

"We'll start with five milligrams," Dr. Melanie was saying. "You should see immediate improvement, and if you notice any side effects, you'll let me know."

"Yes, of course," Annabelle said, nodding seriously.

The doctor paused and leaned forward slightly. "There's no mention of this in Benny's records, but I have to ask. Are you his biological . . . ?" She glanced over at Benny and let the question hang.

Annabelle was still nodding, and then the doctor's meaning sunk in. "Oh, you mean, is he adopted? No, of course not!"

"Good to know," Dr. Melanie said, sitting back and making a note. "Well then, why don't we see how he does with the Ritalin and then schedule another appointment in three days." It wasn't a question, but when Annabelle didn't reply, the doctor added, "Your son is lucky to have people at school who are paying attention."

"Yes," Annabelle said, understanding that she was being both censured and dismissed. "Yes, of course." She rose laboriously, grateful to the little blue chair for not giving up on her, and looked down at Benny. His skinny back was hunched and frozen. She touched his shoulder and he jumped. When did he get to be such a nervous kid? "Come on, sweetheart. Let's go. I thought we could stop at the library on the way home. Wouldn't that be a treat?"

DR. MELANIE WATCHED them leave, observing the way the mother reached out her hand, noting how the boy held back. She wondered if his aversion to touch was chronic, or if it was just the case that day. Or maybe he just didn't want to go to the library. He was a fourteen-year-old boy, even though he looked much younger. Fourteen-year-old boys don't hold hands with their mothers. They don't think of libraries as a treat.

She went to her desk and logged on to her computer to write up the session notes. In his file were reports from his school counselor, dating back to the beginning of his seventh-grade year. She'd read them earlier and now she glanced quickly through them again. There had been problems with focus and attention following the death of the father, but no further treatment had been recommended. Probably a mistake; early diagnosis and intervention were key. She did the math. Sixteen, maybe seventeen months. He'd been displaying symptoms of attention deficit for almost a year and a half. She opened up an assessment template and started typing in her observations. The boy had appeared distracted throughout the session, eyes darting about the room, fidgeting and rocking in his seat. He was reluctant to answer questions about the incident at school. Claimed not to know or had forgotten what triggered his impulsivity. Was unable or unwilling to talk about his attempt to break the window with his fists. She recorded her diagnosis and the medication and dosage, saved the document, and logged off.

She still had a few minutes before her next patient arrived, so she leaned back in her chair and closed her eyes. She had taken a workshop in mindfulness meditation when she was in medical school, and the practice had helped her relax and empty her mind. Now she took a deep breath and exhaled, feeling the tension melt from her body. She still found the initial consultations with new patients quite stressful, and she wondered if it would get easier with experience. She hoped so, because this kind of anxiety could not be good, either for her or for the children she treated. She exhaled and let that thought go, feeling her body sink deeper as her muscles reluctantly released. The boy, Benny, seemed like a sweet kid. His mother seemed like a piece of work, nervous and distracted, no doubt suffering from some combination of depression and anxiety disorder herself, which was why it was important to rule out adoption. Genetics often played a role but, she reminded herself, diagnosing the mother was not her job. Her job was to focus on the boy, and recalling her diagnosis and treatment plan, she felt quite confident about her assessment. She would see the boy alone next time. Perhaps without his mother present he would be more willing to open up, she thought, and then she frowned. She was thinking again. She couldn't stop thinking.

Come on, Melanie. Back to the breath. Let the thoughts go. But just as she felt her mind quiet, the cheerful little bell in her waiting room tinkled, announcing the arrival of her next young patient. As if on cue, she felt her jaw muscles tighten, her solar plexus clench, and her heart rate escalate. A classic Pavlovian conditioned response, but what good was it to know this? The meditation didn't help much, either. It gave her some brief symptomatic relief, but at a deeper level, her body seemed impervious. At that deeper level, it was always on guard, rigidly refusing to relax, as if it knew it had to steel itself against whatever psychic distress the next child was bringing through the door into her bright little room. She loved her young patients. She wanted to help them and relieve their pain, so where did all this resistance come from?

10

Even when he was a baby, before he was walking or had learned to use words, Benny loved the Public Library. This was before the renovation, before the soaring modern wings were added, and the fusty old building, with its weathered limestone facade and sturdy classical pillars, seemed both to excite and to soothe him. Kenji was on the road a lot in those days, touring with the band, and when he was home, he played local gigs that kept him out late almost every night. In the mornings he would often sleep in until noon, and Annabelle, not wanting to wake him, would bundle Benny up and take him to the Library for Children's Hour. By the time he was a toddler, Benny knew the route, and as soon as they got off the bus and started up the hill, he would start bouncing up and down in his stroller and kicking his feet against the leg rest. As they climbed the steps and passed through the stately doors, his excitement would mount and he'd start to whoop and coo. Looking down at his bouncing head, Annabelle felt a sense of pride, as if somehow her love of books was expressing itself in her young son.

Children's Hour was held in the Multicultural Children's Corner, which was located in the basement, tucked away in a far, safe nook of the building en route to the staff offices. Before it was renamed the Multicultural Children's Corner, when it was still just Kids' Books, it was located right in the front, between the circulation desk and Periodicals, but in the 1970s, when the state psychiatric hospitals closed, the Library experienced an upsurge in homeless and outpatient traffic, which only increased during the recession in the eighties, due to the deep cuts in social services. The mothers started to complain, and the Library administration responded; they rebranded Kids' Books and moved it downstairs, away from the heavily trafficked periodicals section where the nontraditional library patrons liked to nap during the day.

The Multicultural Children's Corner was a strange nook, indeed. When Annabelle worked as a summer intern at the Library, she first started hearing the stories that circulated among the staff about so-called anomalous or even paranormal locations—places in the Library where *things happen*. At first she assumed that these were just stories that the senior librarians told to unsettle the interns, but when she got to know the building better, she began to wonder. There was Recent Acquisitions, where new books refused to stay on the shelves, and the washrooms on Level Seven, where patrons complained of rapping noises and the sudden extinguishing of overhead lights. Toilets flushed of their own accord, and tiny green tree frogs were seen hopping in the urinals. Stalls mysteriously locked and unlocked themselves, and some people reported an eerie sensation of being watched, even when the washroom was empty. The Multicultural Children's Corner was another of these locations, and when she was sent there one winter afternoon to reshelve the brightly colored books, Annabelle experienced an uncanny sensation, as if the air were pregnant with lost things. Later she discovered that people often admitted to finding things there that they thought they'd lost or misplaced, and this happened so frequently that when someone showed up at the circulation desk, looking for something that had gone missing, the librarians automatically would ask, "Have you checked Multiculti Kids?" When the administration got wind of this, they told the librarians to stop, fearing that it would sound as if the Library was blaming multicultural children for stealing people's belongings. But even so, when something went missing, everyone knew to check Multicultural Children's first. Some of the more New Agey librarians claimed the corner was haunted by the ghost of a child who borrowed people's things and brought them there to play with, but nobody could say whether the child was multicultural or not.

Annabelle never truly believed the story of the ghost, but Benny was a sensitive baby, and she remembered that feeling of an uncanny presence, so when she first brought him to the Multicultural Children's Corner, she worried he might be upset by whatever it was that haunted the nook, but he seemed fine. She sat on a chair in the back with the nannies and other moms, holding Benny, wriggling, on her lap, while the older children gathered in a tight circle on the floor around the librarian. Benny squirmed and kicked and waved his arms, but as soon as the librarian started reading, he grew serious and still. The librarian was a young Black woman, small and slightly built, but with a strong, beautiful voice and a faintly lilting accent that Annabelle couldn't place. She had a crop of curls on top of her head and dressed in cardigan sweaters, tweed skirts, and funny-looking vintage eyeglasses that she wore on a chain. Was she being ironic? She looked less like a working librarian and more like a performance of one, Annabelle thought with a pang. During her internship, Annabelle was often asked to read for Children's Hour while the regular librarian was on maternity leave, and she'd loved it. She loved sitting on her stool at the center of the circle, glancing up from her book and seeing the ring of little faces, gazing at her. They looked like flowers, and she wanted nothing more than to become a children's librarian so she could stay in the center of that magical ring forever.

This young librarian was partial to tales of talking bears and pigs and moles and water rats—and the children liked them, too, even though they were city kids and knew little about such animals. The ones they did know about—sewer rats and pigeons and mosquitoes and cockroaches—did not have many books written about them, but maybe that was okay, Annabelle thought, because the point of books was to teach you what you didn't already know. Still, as she rested her chin on the warm, downy crown of Benny's head, she couldn't help but feel sad that her son was growing up in a city where there were no babbling brooks or buzzing bees or long grasses that whispered in the summertime. He would never know a hedgehog or a badger. But not knowing didn't seem to bother Benny. Transfixed by the sound of the librarian's voice and the sinuous lilt of her sentences, he leaned forward in Annabelle's arms, and as the story drew him, she had to link her fingers around his soft belly like a safety harness to keep him from toppling off her knees.

The next time they came, he didn't want to sit on her lap, so she set him on the floor and watched as he inched forward, slowly, slowly until he'd joined the other children in the circle. He paused there for a while and then kept going until finally he reached the librarian's feet, whereupon he took hold of her slim ankle and gazed at her knee. The librarian, momentarily distracted, glanced over the edge of the book, but then she continued reading. It was a book about animal sounds in different parts of the world, and she held it up and showed the children a picture of a dog.

"What do dogs say in America?" she read.

"*Woof, woof!*" the children cried, flapping their arms and bouncing. "*Bow wow!*"

Most of the kids knew the book by heart. It was a favorite in the Multicultural Children's Corner.

"What do dogs say in China?" the librarian asked. "*Wang wang!*" they answered in unison.

"What do dogs say in Spain?"

"*Guau guau!*"

Benny didn't know any of the sounds the animals made in any country, but this didn't seem to bother him. He gazed up at the librarian, entranced, and then lay down on his stomach on the rug and slowly began to crawl between the rungs of the librarian's stool, until he was sitting underneath. The librarian ignored him and went on reading.

"What do Japanese roosters say?"

"*Kokekokko!*"

"What do Italian roosters say?"

"*Chicchirichi!*"

"What do Icelandic roosters say?"

"*Gaggalago!*"

He was such a small boy, he fit perfectly under the little stool, and Annabelle could see the pleased expression on his face as he peeked out from behind the librarian's legs. He reached out and took hold of her ankle again. He just liked to hold the librarian's ankle.

"What do pigs say in Germany?"

"*Grunz, grunz!*"

"What do they say in Indonesia?"

"*Grok grok!*"

At the end of the story, when Children's Hour was over, the librarian closed the book and thanked everyone for coming and said she hoped they would all come back again. Then she stood and lifted the stool carefully off Benny, who continued to sit there, looking somewhat wobbly and exposed, like Jell-O taken too soon from the mold. Annabelle stepped forward to retrieve him, thanking the young woman and apologizing for her son's intrusion. The librarian smiled and shrugged, saying she was startled at first but she didn't really mind. She crouched down and put her hand on Benny's shoulders.

"Did you like the story?" she asked. "Did it feel good sitting under the stool?" When Benny didn't respond, she continued. "You can sit there anytime. That can be your special spot."

And it was his special spot, for a while, until the nice young librarian was rotated out and the new one who took her place wasn't comfortable having a little boy beneath her as she read, so she fished him out and made him join the circle with the others.

BENNY

I remember Children's Hour! And that nice librarian, that was Cory. I didn't know her name back then, and it's kind of a blur, but I do remember some things, like the warm lady smell under her stool and her fuzzy tweed skirt. Her glasses were pink and had sparkles in the corners, and under her skirt she wore thick cotton tights and these baggy, knitted leg-warmer things, and I remember how good it felt to hold on to her ankle. The bone was solid and sharp, and I remember holding it and looking out from between her legs at the kids on the outside and feeling like even though they were staring at me, they couldn't see me. It made me feel secret and safe.

And I remember that book, too, and the ducks that go *wak wak* in Arabic, or something. I don't remember the details, but I remember how the stories sounded from underneath, not like they were coming from someone's mouth or face, which is what they sounded like on the outside, but more like they were coming from all around, from the stool, from the carpet, from the librarian's skirt. From everywhere, buzzing and bleating and hooting. The whole world was this cone-shaped, stool-shaped place that was safe and warm and smelled like sandalwood oil and carpet cleaner, and the words were everywhere at once, like it was God who was reading you the story. If you can imagine God, speaking to you in the voice of a lady librarian.

I don't know. Maybe that's too much.

But I think this is why I still love the Library. It's probably also why my best friend is a Book.

My mom promised that if I went to the shrink we could stop at the Library after, but she wanted to pick up my new prescription on the way, and there was some problem with the insurance, and by the time they got it sorted, it was too late. My mom said we had plenty of books at home, which was true, but I was pissed because she'd promised. I think part of her didn't really want to go. I think the Library made her too sad, because she had to drop out of school when she got pregnant with me, and even though she always said I was worth it, I knew there was a part of her that was sorry for giving up her dream. Kids know these things about their parents, even if they don't completely understand.

Anyway, when we got home, we had this fight. I saw that *Tidy Magic* book on the kitchen table on top of a pile of other junk, and I picked it up and kind of threw it at her and said in a really snarky voice, "Here's a *great* book for you. Why don't you read that!" It's a book about cleaning up your life and getting rid of shit, and I was trying to send her a message, but it was pretty mean.

I didn't actually *throw* the book. I just kind of pushed it at her. I guess that was snarky, too. I didn't mean to make her cry.

THE BOOK

11

The first words of a book are of utmost importance. The moment of encounter, when a reader turns to that first page and reads those opening words, it's like locking eyes or touching someone's hand for the first time, and we feel it, too. Books don't have eyes or hands, it's true, but when a book and a reader are meant for each other, both of them know it, and this is what happened when Annabelle opened *Tidy Magic*. When she read the first sentence, a shiver ran down both their spines.

> If you are reading this, then chances are you are dissatisfied with your life. You would like to make a change, but you feel so overwhelmed, you don't even know where to begin.

Yes! thought Annabelle. That's right!

> You know your life would be better with less clutter. You've tried to discard things and clean up your home, but it never seems to make any real difference. You run out of energy, and before you know it, your belongings have gotten the upper hand again, and your possessions have you in their thrall.

That was it, exactly. How did the little book know?

She raised her eyes and looked around. It was almost spooky, as if the book could see her cluttered bedroom and was reading her mind. She checked the clock. She was tired and knew she should try to sleep, but she was still too agitated. It had been a long day. The appointment had really been distressing, especially at the end, when the doctor asked if she was Benny's biological mother. And she hadn't realized how upset Benny would be about skipping the Library. He kept muttering to himself on the bus, and by the time they got home, he was in a foul mood and blew up at her, which was okay because being a target for your kid's anger was just part of being a mother. Usually she could just laugh it off, which was why she was so startled when she started crying instead. She managed to control it, but by then he'd gone storming off to his room. To his credit, he calmed down pretty quickly, and after a while he came back out and they had leftover pizza and discussed the schedule for his medication.

She'd gone to bed early and brought the book to bed with her. Maybe Benny was right. Maybe she should read it. She studied the cover. The way the little book had jumped into her shopping cart was spooky, too, and she had the strangest feeling that Kenji was behind this. There had been moments when she'd sensed his presence nearby, like when the crows left her gifts, for example. Her trinket bowl was chockablock full of screws, paper clips, buttons, broken clamshells, bits of tinfoil, beads and stray earrings. She couldn't help but think that Kenji was trying to make contact with her through the crows, and if so, maybe *Tidy Magic* was a gift from him, too, because how else to explain all the coincidences?

There was the fact that Kenji and Aikon were both Japanese. This didn't mean much on its own, but when she read the author bio on the back flap, she learned that Aikon's full name was Ai Konishi, which was astonishing, because Konishi had been Kenji's mother's name, too. Kenji used *Konishi* as his computer password, and when Annabelle asked him about it, he told her the story about how his grandparents were worried that their daughter would face discrimination in Japan for marrying a Korean and taking his name. They urged her to keep Konishi, instead of becoming an Oh, but she'd refused. When Kenji told her this, Annabelle was shocked by the racism against Koreans, but she also felt baffled. She loved being an Oh! The name sounded so exuberant and breathless, and somehow perfectly expressed the way Annabelle felt when she first met Kenji and they'd fallen in love. She couldn't imagine wanting to be a Konishi instead, but still, it was curious that Aikon shared a name with Kenji's family.

More important than the coincidence of the name, however, was the Zen factor. Annabelle studied Aikon's face and was reminded again of the picture of Kenji at the temple, and how, when he'd shown it to her, she had picked him out immediately because of his big, goofy smile. Even with no hair he looked adorable. Where had that photograph gone? It must be in the closet somewhere. She should try to dig it out and show it to Benny and tell him the whole story about how his crazy dad became a monk. He'd been studying classical music at the conservatory in Tokyo and needed a cheap place to stay over the summer vacation, and someone told him he could live at the Zen temple for free if he didn't mind meditating and scrubbing floors. Kenji never minded hard work, and so he'd moved in and ended up living there for a couple of years. He said it was the happiest time of his life, and she remembered how she had felt a twinge of jealousy until he added, "Until I meet you."

Oddly, it was during his stay at the Zen temple that he first started playing jazz. Among the young trainee monks were a number of artists and writers and musicians and political activists who were interested in the radical philosophy of Zen, the rigorous mental training, and a free place to live. One of these was a young monk named Daikan, who, when he learned Kenji played clarinet, got the idea of starting a jazz band. To their surprise, the abbot agreed. Buddhist temples in Japan were struggling to survive as the old parishioners died off and the young people were too busy shopping and having corporate careers to care about Zen. The abbot thought jazz-playing monks might garner media attention and attract more young people to the temple.

They called the band Thelonious. Daikan played bass, and Kenji played clarinet, and they teamed up with another older monk who played jazz piano. With permission from the abbot, they converted a meeting room into a weekend café, and soon they were serving espresso and playing gigs there every Friday and Saturday night. Thelonious disbanded when Kenji left the temple, but by then the wheels of fate were set in motion. Zen was how Kenji got into jazz, and jazz was how he'd met Annabelle. The Zen connection was deep, she reflected, even karmic, and so she turned the page and read on.

TIDY MAGIC

Prologue

If you are reading this, then chances are you are dissatisfied with your life. You would like to make a change, but you feel so overwhelmed, you don't even know where to begin.

You know your life would be better with less clutter. You've tried to discard things and clean up your home, but it never seems to make any real difference. You run out of energy, and before you know it, your belongings have gotten the upper hand again, and your possessions have you in their thrall.

If this describes you, please know that I understand. I used to have this same relationship with my things. I didn't possess them. They possessed me!

So what changed?

For me, it was my encounter with the radical teachings of Zen. This encounter changed me. It changed my relationship to my possessions, to my past and my future, to my life and the entire world. It was more than a change. It was a revolution.

The Zen teachings of emptiness and liberation are ancient, but they have never been more relevant than they are today. I am writing this book to share these profound but simple teachings with people who are suffering like I was.

We all have different connections with our things, and the way we learn to relate to them develops early. These habits are deeply rooted in our life stories and often in our suffering. In my case, I was raised by my aunt, who adopted me and loved me like her own daughter, but when I was twelve, she married a man who made our lives very unhappy. Materially, we were well-off. My stepfather was a corporate executive and provided for us, but because of his improper behavior toward me, I felt unsafe in our new home. I became depressed, and to soothe my anxiety, I would eat and shop. I used food to fill the painful place inside me. I built a wall around me with new things to keep me safe. But no matter how much I consumed, it was never enough. Anxious and afraid, I clung to my things and wanted more and more, and I brought these habits with me into adulthood, long after I left my stepfather's home.

Your story may be similar, or it may be very different. But if you are troubled by your relationship with your possessions—if you have too many things cluttering up your life and not enough space and clarity to live—then these simple Zen lessons might help.

This book is not just about your belongings. It's about living a life where you truly belong.

THE BOOK

Is it odd to see a book within a book? It shouldn't be. Books like each other. We understand each other. You could even say we are all related, enjoying a kinship that stretches like a rhizomatic network beneath human consciousness and knits the world of thought together. Think of us as a mycelium, a vast, subconscious fungal mat beneath a forest floor, and each book a fruiting body. Like mushrooms, we are a collectivity. Our pronouns are *we, our, us*.

Because we're all connected, we communicate all the time—agreeing, disagreeing, gossiping about other books, name-dropping, and quoting each other—and we have our preferences and prejudices, too. Of course, we do! Biases abound on library shelves. The scholarly tomes disparage the more commercial books. Literary novels look down on romance and pulp fiction, and there's an almost universal disregard for certain genres, like self-help.

Still, there's no denying that self-help books can be helpful, and so when *Tidy Magic* launched itself from the New Releases table into the thin air of Annabelle's life, it was hard for us to object. Annabelle needed help, and the feat that little book performed was impressive. But however admirable its strength of purpose, the idea of including chapters of a self-help book within these pages caused us some alarm, and it was Benny who later came to its defense. He argued that *Tidy Magic* was essential to his mother's story and therefore to his story, too, adding that he didn't want his Book to be accused of being a snob, and in the end, we had to agree.

But that night, Annabelle was not quite ready for *Tidy Magic*. Maybe she was simply exhausted from her stressful day. Or, perhaps she was triggered by Aikon's troubling reference to her stepfather. Whatever the reason, after she read the prologue, she promptly fell asleep. The little book lay on top of her, enjoying the pillowy softness of her stomach and the gentle rise and fall of her breath as it guarded her through the night. It would be a while before Annabelle got back to reading *Tidy Magic*, but books are patient. We know how urgent and compelling your lives are, and so we bide our time.

12

What do scissors sound like? What did they say? Sly and steely, they started softly, a small susurration that quickly grew, whispering and slicing, hissing and metallic, forming what sounded more like human words, in a language that Benny took to be Chinese, although he couldn't be sure. He doesn't speak Chinese, so how could he know? But he seemed to understand all the snide, snippy things they insinuated into his ear about his teacher, Ms. Pauley. *You think Old Helmet Head likes you? You think she thinks you're smart? Special? Stupid dyke. She's the one who ratted you out and got you sent to the shrink. Yeah, bitch thinks you're special, all right. A special fucking psycho.*

But Benny really liked Ms. Pauley. She was the one who noticed he was feeling strange in math class and had taken him to see the nurse. She was also their science teacher and had taught them about slime molds in biology class, about how the singular organisms came together to form a multicellular body in order to sporulate and reproduce, before breaking apart again. She had taken the class to a protected woodlands near the school to look for them, and he had found one right away, a mosslike assemblage clinging to the side of a rotting cedar stump. Ms. Pauley had praised him for his sharp eyes. He didn't tell her he'd heard the slime mold calling and so he knew just where to look. What did it sound like? A small, spongy, yellow sound, impossible to describe.

He closed his eyes. This week they were studying climate change, and he was making an informational display. The scissors were sitting on the desk in front of him, next to the glue. Ms. Pauley was at the whiteboard, explaining something important about heat and drought and human emissions, but the scissors were distracting him, snapping and snickering, telling him that his informational display was useless, that it wasn't going to stop climate change, nothing was going to stop climate change, they were all fucked, this teacher was stupid, she was his enemy and the reason everyone thought he was crazy, which was why it was necessary for him to stab her in the neck. *Now!*

He sat on his hands, twined his fingers, clenched his fists. The scissors snickered. *What a pusssy . . . Sooo ssscared . . . Jussst leave it to ussss . . .*

Then the scissors were in his hand, gripped in his fist. He got to his feet and took a step forward, and then another. Ms. Pauley noticed him coming and paused in her talk, marker in hand. Benny? Are you okay? Later, in the principal's office when she was making her incident report, she would close her eyes and shudder as she recalled the anguish that twisted Benny's face as he approached her, holding the scissors out like an offering, begging her to take them from him before he could drive the points into his leg.

IN THE EMERGENCY ROOM, he got three stitches in his upper thigh. The admitting nurse asked him what happened, but he wouldn't say. When the ER doctor asked, he lied. *The scissors slipped, I dropped them, I don't remember.* He was sent back to Dr. Melanie. He had seen her several times since she first diagnosed him with ADHD, and he'd been taking Ritalin for almost two months. He'd seemed somewhat more stable during that time, and she had been happy with his progress, but he still hadn't told her about the voices. They sat across the same low table, only now the table was red, and Benny found this confusing because during previous visits he was sure it had been green. He knew that red and green were called complementary colors, which meant that they were opposites, but this made no sense because the word *complement* meant things that fit together, which was the *opposite* of opposite. Situations like this made his head hurt. Red and green made his head hurt, too. He glanced over at the psychiatrist's face to see if she had changed, but she was the same. Pale skin. Beige-colored hair. Still Dr. Melanie.

"So, Benny," Dr. Melanie said. "Can you tell me what happened?"

He shook his head. Oddly, though, today Dr. Melanie looked older. Before, she looked young, but today she looked like a middle-aged lady. Her skin was the texture of an old puffball mushroom, covered with very fine wrinkles. Her nails were mushroom-colored, too. He wondered how much time had actually passed between his first visit and now—maybe he had fallen asleep like Rip Van Winkle, and while he was dreaming many years had passed. Maybe he was older, too, and his mom was an old lady, about to die. He began to worry and missed the doctor's next question.

"Benny, are you listening?"

He nodded and tried to pay attention.

"Do you remember what happened?"

"Yes."

"Okay, good. Can you tell me?"

"Can I go to the bathroom first?"

The doctor sat back in her chair, and for a moment she looked young again, like a kid whose toy had been snatched away, but she nodded.

The bathroom was in the hallway, and he had to go through the waiting room to get there. When he opened the door, Annabelle looked up quickly from her magazine, and the force field of anxiety radiating from her body hit him in the face. He averted his eyes, but not before he made certain that she was still the right age, even though she looked really tired, and this reassured him. In the bathroom he examined his reflection in the mirror. His skin looked different in the fluorescent light, but he was still himself and still looked fourteen. He flushed the toilet so it would sound like he'd peed, then he washed his hands carefully and returned to the treatment room, passing again through the waves of his mother's worry, but this time he was braced for it. He shut the door firmly behind him. When he sat back down at the red table, Dr. Melanie gave him an encouraging smile.

"Ready to tell me what happened?"

"I guess."

"Yes . . . ?"

"I stabbed my leg with the scissors."

"That's right," she said. "Can you tell me what was going on for you just then?"

"What do you mean?"

"What you were thinking? Or feeling? What was happening around you?"

"Nothing. I mean, it was science class. Ms. Pauley was talking about global warming. I wasn't feeling anything."

"You mean you felt numb?"

Benny tried to remember if he'd felt numb.

"Many people feel numb when they hear about global warming," Dr. Melanie was saying. "And sometimes people feel angry, too. . . ."

He shook his head. The scissors were angry, not him. He wanted to tell her this, but she was still talking.

"Do you think that's possible? That you might have been feeling angry about global warming? Is there some connection?"

Of course there was some connection. The scissors were global. That much seemed obvious. He started to say so, but then he glanced up. She was leaning forward, looking encouraging and interested. Too interested.

Greedy, even. He changed his mind. He gave her a cagey, sideways look. "That's your job. You're supposed to figure out the connections."

"I thought we could figure it out together."

"Oh, forget it," he said. What difference did it make? He was sick of lying about the voices. It was too exhausting to hide them anymore. "The scissors told me to do it."

She was silent for a moment. "You heard the scissors talking?"

The words sounded crazy in her mouth. He wanted to take them back, but it was too late.

"What did they say?"

His fingers made a fist, remembering the scissors.

"Did they tell you to stab yourself?"

He shook his head. "No," he whispered. "Ms. Pauley."

"The scissors told you to stab your teacher?"

His fist started to come down, but he stopped it. "I didn't want to do it, so I redirected them." His fist punched his leg to show her how. He gasped at the pain as tears filled his eyes. The bandaged wound on his thigh began to throb. He hugged his elbows and started to rock.

"What did the scissors say, Benny?"

The rocking helped. "Nothing. I don't know."

She frowned, trying to understand. "But you just said—"

"I *know* what I said. They were just saying *scissor* shit, I don't know, like in a foreign language or something."

"A foreign language?"

He nodded, miserably. It was so hard to explain. "Like maybe Chinese or something? I couldn't understand the words, but I knew what they wanted." The pain in his leg was subsiding.

"Do you speak Chinese?"

"No." He thought about Mrs. Wong's arguments with her son, No-Good. "But I know what Chinese sounds like."

"Your last name, Oh. Isn't that Chinese?"

"It's Korean. My dad's part Korean. And Japanese."

He could feel Dr. Melanie studying him. He corrected himself.

"I mean, he was. He's dead now."

She stood and walked over to her desk in the corner of the room and took something from the drawer. She came back with a pair of scissors in her hands. "Are these the ones?"

He looked away quickly but not quickly enough. He hugged himself more tightly and stared down at the shimmering red surface of the table. He didn't want them to come any closer. "Maybe."

"Ms. Pauley sent them over. Did you happen to see this?" Dr. Melanie leaned forward and scissored open the blades. He heard the flash of the bright metal, and he pressed his hands to his ears, bracing as he waited for the slicing words to come, but instead there was only silence. When the doctor spoke, her voice came in and out, sometimes close and sometimes very far away.

"Can you **read** what it *says*?" She held the scissors out to show him.

Benny didn't look up. The hard red surface of the table was turning green and beginning to vibrate.

"*CHINA*," the doctor read, as if that proved something, and then she snapped the blades shut again, snipping a small hole in the silence to let more sound trickle through. "Don't you see, Benny? The scissors are made in China. You must have noticed, which is why you imagined they were speaking in Chinese."

And now his leg was throbbing again. Why didn't she understand? He clenched his jaw and spoke softly, trying not to amplify things further. "No . . ."

"No?"

"*NO!*" The word tore from his throat, as the colors in the room began to bleed and shimmer. He pressed his hands hard against the tabletop, trying to hold the red and green down and keep them from spreading. Why didn't she understand? He had to try to explain. "If the scissors *speak* Chinese it's because they *ARE* Chinese. *Chinese is the only language they know!*"

From the waiting room where she was sitting, Annabelle heard the rising coil of her son's anguish. She leaned over and buried her face in her hands.

OVER THE NEXT few sessions, in that bright little office, a pattern of misunderstanding began to emerge.

"You say the clock is feeling angry," Dr. Melanie said. "How does that make you feel?"

"Nothing. It doesn't make me feel anything."

"Nothing? It sounds like maybe you're feeling angry, too. Or frustrated?"

"Of course I'm frustrated. Talking to you makes me frustrated."

"Okay, so do you think what you're experiencing as the clock's anger is actually your own frustration—"

"No! The *clock* is frustrated. It's pissed you never listen. It hates wasting time!"

He found the toys and dolls lying around distracting and tried to ignore them. When he asked her to put them away, she wanted to know why.

"They're making too much noise."

She told him that wasn't possible and then patiently explained the physics of sound. "Sound is caused by the movement of an object through space. The toys are just lying there, Benny. They're not moving. They have no moving parts inside. They can't be making sounds. It's physically impossible."

He shook his head like he was trying to clear water from his ears. "They're hurting."

"The toys are hurting?"

"No," he said. "The children are."

"The children are hurting the toys?"

"No! Why are you so stupid?"

"Calm down, Benny. Take a deep breath. Now try again. Are the toys hurting the children?"

"No, of course not. Toys don't hurt children. *People* do."

"What does that have to do with the toys?"

"They know."

"The toys know that people are hurting the children?"

"Of course. That's why you have them here, right? It's inside them now. It goes inside and stays there."

Dr. Melanie looked around at all the brightly colored blocks and jumble of dolls and stuffed animals. "I don't understand," she said. "What's inside? What stays?"

"Are you *crazy*? Can't you hear it?"

"Hear what?"

"The *pain*!" he said, gripping the edge of the table. "Of the *children*!"

SHE WORE HIM DOWN with her stupid suggestions. She got everything backward.

"Could it be that you're afraid, Benny? You're afraid, and so you hear the voices."

"No," he said, exhausted. "I hear the voices, and so I'm afraid."

There was no point. After this exchange, he gave up trying to explain. Dr. Melanie met with Annabelle and delivered her diagnosis: Benny was in the prodromal phase of schizoaffective disorder, and she was recommending that they stop the Ritalin and start him on an antidepressant for the mood disorder and an antipsychotic to treat the auditory hallucinations.

Annabelle sat in the bright little office and listened, clutching her purse and nodding vigorously in order to indicate to the doctor that she was paying attention, that she was taking in the doctor's words and understood what was being communicated, that she was in agreement and in control, and that she was a highly competent single parent.

"I know this is difficult," the doctor said. "But you should know that we've had some success treating schizoaffective disorder in children, with symptoms subsiding as the child passes through adolescence."

Annabelle kept nodding, and when the doctor finished speaking, she put her hands to her face and started weeping.

Dr. Melanie pushed a box of Kleenex across her desk and waited, giving Annabelle time. There was a possibility that the auditory hallucinations could be a side effect of the Ritalin and might abate when he switched medications, but she decided not to mention this. She didn't want to give the mother false hope. The woman was clearly overwhelmed, and in any case, there were sufficient indications to support the new treatment plan. Finally, she leaned forward again.

"Mrs. Oh?"

Annabelle raised her tear-stained face. "I'm sorry," she gasped, "I'm not usually—" She choked back her tears and took a tissue from the box. "I just got an email from my supervisor at work. I mean, it's not really *at* work because they closed the office and cut me to half time and I work from home, but still." She wiped her eyes and blew her nose. "He told me they're phasing out my job . . ."

Dr. Melanie watched. She noticed how the woman's head hung down, and her shoulders slumped forward, and the way her sweatshirt stretched across the broad horizon of her back. She noted the blond hair that must have been pretty once but now was dull, straw-like and thinning. She could barely hear what the woman was saying. She seemed to be talking to the floor.

"Going to eliminate Print completely because newspapers and stuff are all online now . . ."

Thyroid? Diabetes? Stress? Dr. Melanie frowned and interlaced her fingers, bringing her hands up as though she were praying. Definitely depression. She recalled reading about a recent Ritalin study associating an elevated risk of psychotic side effects among children with a parent with a history of serious mental illness. It might be worth asking. She rested her chin on her knuckles, waiting for the woman to collect herself.

"Just not good with computers and all the technological stuff . . ."

Dr. Melanie dropped her hands. "That must be very difficult," she said, leaning forward. "Mrs. Oh, I was wondering, is there any family history of—"

"My own fault, because he warned me months ago that the writing was on the wall, but I just stupidly thought things would work out—"

Dr. Melanie checked her watch. Their time was up, and her next patient would be arriving soon. "So," she said. "About Benny. I'd like to admit him to the Pediatric Psychiatry Unit at Children's when we start the new medication so we can keep him under observation. Maybe for a week or so. What do you think? It would also give you some time to adjust, and—"

Annabelle looked up at the doctor then. "I'm losing my benefits," she whispered. "Our health insurance. I don't know if we'll be covered."

SHE REALIZED she would have to beg. She brought Benny home and sent him to his room and then sat down at her worktable and called her supervisor. She explained her situation and pleaded with him to at least give her the chance to upgrade her skills, to let her continue clipping Print while there still was any, but then add radio and television as well. Audio and video weren't so hard now that the old hardware, the dubbing decks and monitors and receivers, had all been replaced by computers and software. It was really just about expanding her organizational capacity, and after all, she reminded her supervisor, she'd had library training, which was more than any of the guys in the office had, back when they'd had an office. In fact, she said, in many ways she was far more qualified than many of her male coworkers, and the only reason she'd gotten stuck in Print was because she was a woman. It was a clear case of sexual discrimination, an antiquated sexist policy that relegated women to a paper ghetto of newspapers and magazines, while employing men in the more "technological" audio and video departments. Computers flattened the field, she said. Digital technology made these old distinctions meaningless, and besides, there was no reason why women couldn't do technologically complex jobs. The term "Scissor Ladies" itself was sexist and insulting, and while she stopped short of actually calling it discrimination or harassment, she pointed out that she and her female coworkers in Print had always made a lower salary than the guys, the so-called search specialists and information analysts, that they had never been given an equal opportunity to advance in the company, and that for years her male coworkers used to stare at her breasts.

When she'd finished speaking, there was a long silence, and she wondered if the call had dropped, but then she heard her supervisor clearing his throat. She sat at her worktable, amid the piles of clippings and file folders, the stacks of newsprint, the dirty coffee mugs and soda cans, the empty bag of corn chips and a plate with a half-eaten pickle. She bit the edge of her thumb, worrying a hangnail. The scanner hummed. The trash overflowed. She held her breath and stared at the jug with the plastic poinsettias, balanced on a heap of old magazines.

"Okay," her supervisor said at last. "Let me think about it. I'll see what I can do."

She exhaled. "Okay," she said, taking the edge of her thumb from her mouth. "And, Charlie, please don't think too long. I'm a single mom with a very sick kid who needs immediate hospitalization."

AM I VERY SICK? Benny wondered. He sat on the neatly made bed in his tidy bedroom, listening. The radio downstairs in the living room was off for a change, and he could hear his mom talking on the phone. He didn't feel sick. It wasn't like he had the flu or chicken pox or cancer or anything. His leg still ached from the scissors, but other than that, he felt okay. It wasn't him who was sick. It was the voices. Here in his bedroom, they were quiet. If he ventured into the hallway, they would start again. He just had to hold perfectly still, and stay in his bedroom, and keep his socks folded and his bed made and his things put away, and they would leave him alone. He looked over at his shelves. His books were all lined up neatly, according to size, and bookended by his lunar globe. The rubber duck his mom had found in the dumpster was the only toy sitting out, and that was because he found its presence soothing, but more than one toy out was a mess. Mess equals stress, Ms. Pauley always said. He looked down and patted the bedclothes, then he stood and smoothed the wrinkles to erase where he'd been sitting. Should he go find the iron? Ironing was important. Wrinkled sheets were like a wrinkled mind. Troubling. He ironed his sheets so he could have an untroubled sleep, and besides, sheets liked to be ironed, and so he liked ironing sheets. He didn't ever iron things that didn't want to be ironed, only things that liked to be flat, but it wasn't just that. There was another reason, too. He liked to iron because the iron loved the ironing board, and the ironing board loved the iron, and they got lonely when they were apart. They were made for each other, and it felt good to give them a chance to be together, and just as he was about to go downstairs to get them, he heard a tiny voice coming from under his bed.

Weee! the voice said.

It was a pretty little voice, round and smooth. He got down onto his knees and looked under the bed, but of course there was nothing. He knew there would be nothing, because he'd Swiffered under the bed that morning, making sure to get every last scurrying mote of dust. He lay down on his stomach and wriggled forward into the dark. He liked being under the bed. After his dad died, he used to crawl under the bed when he'd had an accident and peed himself at night. It was warm and dark and dry under the bed. It was like being closed up in a box.

He inched his way around the wall, running his fingers underneath the baseboard heater until he felt it—small and smooth and cool and round, just as he knew it would be. He teased it out with the tips of his fingers and then wriggled out from under the bed and sat up. In the palm of his hand was a shiny cat's eye marble. He didn't remember ever seeing it before, but it was probably from the bag of marbles Annabelle had bought at the Thrift Shop. She was always bringing old toys home from thrift stores and tag sales, calling them vintage and hoping to resell them on eBay. He held the marble up to the light and examined it. This one looked pretty old.

The glass was pale green with tiny bubbles in it, and inside were two thin spiraling filaments of yellow and green. He brought it closer to his eye and peered at the cloudy world swirling inside. Nice, he thought. He rolled it around in his palm. Pretty. *Mmmm,* said the marble, winking at him, and just then, from the living room, he heard his mother calling.

"*Shhhh,*" he whispered to the marble, as he slipped it in his pocket.

"*Coming,*" he called back to his mother.

He stood for a moment at his bedroom door, preparing, and then he opened it. He paused on the threshold and listened for a moment, gauging the noise level, and then judging it to be low, he stepped into the cluttered hallway, cutting quickly through the babble and down the stairs to the living room, where Annabelle sat amid her piles of news, holding her cell phone in one hand, with one earbud still dangling from her ear and a look of amazement on her face.

"I did it," she said. "They're going to retrain me. They're letting me keep my job."

She held out her arms, and he went to her, allowing her to pull him close, feeling her arms like warm pillows pressing against his ears and muting the chaos of the world. For a moment, it was almost peaceful. He could smell the sweet and slightly sour sweat from her skin that he identified as the scent of his own sadness, and he stayed like that for as long as he could bear it, until the feeling of dissolving into her became intolerable and he had to push her away. He felt bad about doing so. He shoved his hands into his pockets, and his fingers made contact with the marble. He'd forgotten about it, and now he found it soothing.

"That's great, Mom," he said, trying to sound supportive. "Does that mean I can go to the hospital?"

13

He looked so little, standing in the doorway of his room, the last in a row of identical open doorways at the end of the long white hall. She wanted to run back and grab him, throw his clothes back into his duffel, and hurry him right past the nurses' station, to tell the horrible head nurse who had searched her handbag and confiscated the X-Acto knife that she always carried (a tool of her trade because you never knew when you'd run across an article in need of clipping) that there had been a terrible mistake, that her son didn't belong here and she was taking him home. But she didn't. Instead, while Benny watched from his doorway, she stood at the nurses' station, waiting patiently for a different nurse, a male one, to retrieve her belongings and then escort her from the ward. When she reached the locked double doors, she turned back and saw Benny, and she waved. He didn't wave back right away. He just stood there, rooted, unsure of himself in these alien surroundings, as if his body no longer knew what to do, whether it was okay to move, to wave, to bolt, to run to his mother. She heard the nurse entering the numerical code into the keypad and then the click of the doors unlocking. She felt the pressure of the nurse's fingers on her arm. Nurse Andrew, his tag read.

"He'll be fine," Nurse Andrew was saying. "We'll take good care of him."

Annabelle nodded, barely hearing and not believing, but yielding to his authority. He had tattoos on his well-developed forearms. He was strong. She wondered if any of the patients on the ward ever got violent, and if Nurse Andrew had to restrain them. She turned away, and just as she did, Benny raised his hand to wave, but by then she was already a body in motion, and the heavy metal doors were locking behind her, and by the time she looked back through the reinforced glass window, he had vanished.

The sound of those doors, locking him in, locking her out, was the sound of her defeat and failure. She wandered through the corridors, trying to find the exit. There were signs everywhere, arrows pointing, boldly colored lines on the floor that seemed to offer direction, but instead looped back and led nowhere. Finally she made it down to the ground floor and stepped out onto the sidewalk, where the noise and commotion of the day-lit world hit her like a shock wave, and she had to stand for a moment to regain her balance. She crossed the street to the bus stop, and when the bus came, she climbed on board and found a seat in the rear. They had ridden the same bus to the hospital that morning, sitting side by side, Benny with his duffel on his lap, his clothes neatly packed inside. He'd insisted on packing himself, and when she suggested he bring some things to make him feel at home—the photograph of the three of them taken at Disneyland, or the stuffed sea turtle that Kenji had gotten for him on that same Florida trip—he had refused. It was a hospital, he'd said. He didn't want to feel at home. But then she noticed that he'd laid out a few things on his desk—his Composition notebook, his special spoon, a marble—and later they weren't there, so she knew he'd packed them, too. During the admission, the horrible head nurse had taken the spoon and the marble away and put them in the plastic bag along with her X-Acto knife. What was she thinking? How dangerous was a spoon? A marble, okay, maybe a kid could swallow it and choke, but a spoon? Did she think he was going to use it to gouge somebody's eyes out? You won't be needing this, the nurse had informed him. We provide cutlery. Benny didn't protest, even though at home it was the only spoon he ate with, and he even brought it to school with him. Annabelle wondered if she should have said something, but she and Benny had never talked about the spoon. It was just something she'd noticed, and she was afraid of saying anything to the nurse that might embarrass him. She had glanced over at him as he sat slumped in the hospital chair, staring at his laceless sneakers with the awkward Velcro straps. When they took his asthma inhaler, she had spoken up.

"But he needs that!"

"We'll keep it behind the desk for him. All he needs to do is ask."

The bus slowed and performed its cumbersome pneumatic genuflection, wheezing and chuffing to accommodate a disabled passenger. Annabelle looked out the window and saw an elderly woman, waiting on the curb next to a bundle buggy piled high with plastic shopping bags. That morning, they had sat across from an old man in a wheelchair. Tied to its handles were garbage bags, bulging with empty cans and bottles. The man had a long grizzled beard and a missing tooth and an old battered black leather brief-case balanced on his lap. Around his neck, he wore a hand-lettered card-board sign tied to a string that said,

Random Acts

Of

Kindness

He sat across from them, muttering to himself. From time to time his large rough hands would rise from his lap, flapping like wings, as if he were waving to someone who wasn't there, or he would jerk his head around and look over his shoulder, and then he would stay like that, listening intently until his attention drifted and he started muttering again. Annabelle tried not to stare, and she noticed Benny deliberately looking in the opposite direction, but then after a couple of stops, the old man's attention had set-tled on them.

"Hey there, young schoolboy!" he called across the aisle. He had a gut-tural Eastern European accent, the words sticking in his windpipe, so that when he spoke, it sounded like he was clearing his throat. Benny ignored him, but when they got off the bus at the hospital stop, the guy called out again. *"Be tough, little buddy. Vive la résistance!"*

"Do you know that old man?" Annabelle asked, when they were walk-ing, and Benny had shrugged.

"He's just some hobo," he said. "He's always on the bus."

They'd been shown to his room, and she had helped him unpack and put his pajamas and clothes away in the compact chest of drawers next to his bed. She'd met his roommate, an older Chinese boy with stringy hair and pimples, whose name she'd promptly forgotten. He was wearing ripped black jeans and an ominous-looking black T-shirt, and when he wandered off, she and Benny sat on the bed for a while, and she held his hand until he pulled away.

"Your roommate seemed nice," she said. "Quite the fashion sense." When he didn't answer, she tried again. "The bed seems comfortable."

She bounced up and down on the mattress while she tried to think of something else to say, but then Benny started talking.

"You know that guy on the bus? The hobo guy in the wheelchair?"

"The one with all the bags? How could I miss him! Why do they let people like that—?"

Benny shook his head impatiently. "Did you see how he kept looking around? I think he hears stuff, too. Voices or something. I think he hears them talking."

"Well, perhaps, but . . . ," Annabelle started. "It's hard to tell—"

"I can tell. He hears things just like I do, and he knows I hear things, too. He thinks it's funny. He laughs at me and sometimes he says stuff. He didn't today because you were there, but usually he does."

All this had been going on, and she hadn't known.

"Why didn't you tell me?" she demanded, taking hold of his forearm. "Benny, what does he say? I should never have let you ride the bus alone, we have to report—"

But he cut her off again. "He's not doing it to be mean. It's like he knows what I'm thinking, and when he says stuff to me, he's just trying to help. And it's like I know what he's thinking, too. I can't describe it. Sometimes I wonder if we're hearing the same voices. It's weird, right?"

Yes! Annabelle wanted to scream. *Yes, it's weird. It's very, very weird!* But that seemed like the wrong response. She sat there, breathing, listening, gripping her son's arm.

"Like, he's nice and everything," Benny said. "But I don't want to end up like him."

He had looked at her then, and she saw the fear in his eyes, and she wrapped her arms around him.

"Don't be silly," she said, hugging him tight. "You're nothing like him. That's why you're here. They're going to help you. We'll figure this thing out, honey, I promise. You're going to be fine."

She was doing her best to stay positive, to maintain a front of cheerful confidence, to keep her job and her benefits, to keep her son's spirits up, but the effort was draining her, and now, sitting on the bus next to the elderly bag lady with the bundle buggy, she felt the prickle of despair seeping in. She looked out the window. They were almost at the mall, and for a moment she quickened at the thought of stopping in at Michaels, but then she remembered. Tech support was coming by in a few hours to deliver the new computers, and she needed to get home and tidy up, plus, she reminded herself, the arrangement she'd made with her supervisor was probationary and her performance during the next couple of weeks was crucial. If she couldn't handle the TV and radio contracts, she would be out of a job, and so she really needed to not spend money on craft supplies that she didn't have time for anyway, and focus on work instead. As the bus pulled away from the mall, she tried to feel proud of her self-restraint, but the feeling didn't last, and by the time she'd gotten off at her stop and was standing on the sidewalk in front of the Gospel Mission Thrift Shop, her willpower had pretty much run out completely.

WHAT MAKES A PERSON want so much? What gives things the power to enchant, and is there any limit to the desire for more? Annabelle had no time to ponder these questions, because the minute she laid eyes on the little snow globe, sitting on the dusty shelf amid the piles of chipped plates and Pyrex cookware, she was helpless to resist. The small plastic sea turtle just glowed with life, swimming in its glass orb in front of a piece of bleached coral, calling out to her to rescue it from all the thrift store clutter. She'd always had a thing for sea turtles. They were so slow and graceful, with such big, sad eyes, not to mention they were endangered. The base of the globe looked like an algae-covered rock, with conch shells and a plastic starfish stuck to it, and another bigger sea turtle, too, which must be the little one's mother. The mother was swimming toward her baby, who was trapped inside the orb, and their noses were almost touching on opposite sides of the glass. Annabelle tipped the globe, and when she righted it, hundreds of tiny green and pink sparkles swirled around the baby turtle. Twinkling and settling in the thick watery world, the sparkles felt like hope.

At home, the kitchen clock was ticking loudly. She unpacked the globe and checked the time. The house felt so quiet and empty without Benny. The doctor said two weeks. The clock said five minutes to one. She had an hour before the tech crew arrived. She carried the snow globe into the living room. She would put it next to her computer as a talisman to keep her calm and focused.

The sight of her work area gave her pause. Her supervisor said she would be getting a new "workstation," but she had no idea how much space that would require. Well, she'd been planning to start clearing stuff out, and now she had no choice. She placed the little snow globe on her desk next to a large bottle of boric acid that she'd put there to remind her to deal with the roaches in the kitchen. On the bottle was a picture of a dead cockroach, lying on its back. She moved the bottle, and the turtles looked happier. She shook the globe and held it to the light. The sparkles slowly swirled and settled, and she smiled. Maybe this was her talent, she thought, to see beauty in small things, and if so, then she was grateful. Gathering up an armful of newspapers, she shoved them into a trash bag, labeled it, and lugged it up the stairs to Benny's room.

14

He spent the last two weeks of middle school on the pediatric psychiatry ward of Children's Hospital. Except for the moment during admission when they took away his marble and his shoelaces and his special spoon, and then later when Annabelle gave him a big, firm hug and left him on the ward and he watched her walk down the hall and through the heavy metal doors that clicked and locked behind her, except for moments like these, he felt okay, considering. Resigned. Numb. Maybe a little scared, but overall he thought he might not mind being in the hospital. He went back into his room and sat down on the edge of his bed and listened to the unfamiliar sounds, the rubber-soled footsteps on vinyl, the telephones and intercoms and voices of people, calling to one another. The kids at school always said he'd wind up here eventually. The loony bin, the madhouse, the cracker barrel, the whack shack, the psycho factory. They said he was crazy, but at least here, everyone else was crazy, too, so it was kind of a relief. Maybe here, he could relax and stop trying.

Over the first few days, he learned his way around the ward, settling into its rhythms. Pediatric Psychiatry was for kids under the age of eighteen. The doctors and nurses and milieu staff called it PEDi-psy, with the stress on the first syllable, but the kids called it the PeDIPsy, or just Dipsy, for short. His roommate, Mackson, the geeked-out Chinese kid, was older and pretty catatonic, but the room they shared was clean and uncluttered, and the light bulbs all worked. The hangers in the closet couldn't be removed from the bar, which made it hard to hang your clothes, but they were all the same shape and didn't get tangled up with one another, which was nice. There was a bathroom with sinks you could use without having to move stuff out of the way. Meals sucked, but there were three of them, plus snacks, and they arrived at the same time every day, and the hospital never ran out of milk. The steady level of ambient noise in the ward was comforting; the low murmur emanating from behind the desk at the nurses station, the sound of the meal trolleys being wheeled through the corridors. You might think a psych ward would be a mad, cacophonous place, but oddly, Benny found there were fewer voices here, as if the walls and ceilings and floors had been wiped clean of the residual suffering that was allowed to accumulate like dust in the corners and edges of rooms in ordinary homes. And except for one time early on, when one of the showerheads started to weep, he found the fixtures to be fairly placid and composed, as if they, too, had been sedated.

When he did hear voices, they were identifiably human. The wild peals of laughter that rang down the halls meant that Brittany and Lulu were standing on their heads and acting crazy, trying to get Nurse Andrew's attention. The moaning and screaming at night meant that Trevor was having another nightmare or Ky was freaking out over his meds. Knowing that the voices had human sources was comforting to Benny, because it meant that everyone was hearing them and not just him.

The other kids on the ward were okay. He was on the Yellow Team, which was for twelve- to fifteen-year-olds. The younger kids were on the Green Team. They were really little, some just seven and eight, so Benny didn't pay much attention to them, and the older teens on the Blue Team pretty much kept to themselves. The kids his age didn't seem very different from his classmates in school. Some were smart, and some were stupid. Some were bullies, and the others stayed out of their way. Some showed off and sucked up to the nurses and talked all the time, and others were sneaky and silent. Unless you happened to notice one of the boys rocking in a corner and talking to the wall, or catch sight of a skinny girl licking the pale row of scars that ran up and down her forearm, everyone seemed pretty normal, at least until group therapy started. In group, they were supposed to share their feelings, and that's when the cracks started to open up and the crazy shit leaked out, and some kid who seemed perfectly normal might suddenly start sharing how he'd been caught stealing gasoline to set fire to his mother's bed. Never once in his entire life had Benny entertained a thought like this about his own mother, but of course, as soon as he heard the kid describing it, he couldn't help picturing himself standing at the foot of Annabelle's bed with a can of gasoline and a cigarette lighter, which totally freaked him out. That was the problem with voices. They got inside your head. The trick, his coach told him, was to tune that shit out.

Aside from group, which he hated, or individual sessions with Dr. Melanie, which he found frustrating, the rest wasn't so bad. The ward kept to a tight schedule, and once he got used to it, he knew what to expect, and the activities fit together in such a way as to give shape to the day. In the morning after breakfast, the kids and the staff gathered in the day room for community meeting, and then they split into age groups for classes and tutoring. After lunch, they had coaching and therapy with the milieu staff, and sometimes they did activities like art and music, which Benny didn't mind. The art therapist had bins of paper and paints, clay and beads, and brushes and even scissors, which she kept locked up but would let some of the kids use if they asked. Not him, though. She was a short, cheerful woman, with a big doughy face and a wheedling voice, and an agenda of projects she tried to get them to do. Most of her suggestions were pretty dumb, but it was okay to ignore her, and the older kids generally did whatever they wanted. Like the girl who sat in the corner and cut sheets of white copy paper into slips when they were supposed to be painting their feelings. The therapist had broken out the finger paints, and the little kids were madly painting their love and rage and sadness, making a total mess, but this girl just kept to herself, bending over her paper and scissors, quietly cutting. Benny had stayed away from her on account of the scissors but was close enough to hear when the therapist went over to talk to her. He was drawing a picture of a container ship he'd seen in the harbor, and he was just filling in the details of the bracing mechanism on a massive crane that was swinging a container full of Hyundai SUVs onto the loading dock, when he heard the girl say, "These *are* my feelings."

He looked up. On the table in front of the girl were her slips of paper, which looked like the Chinese fortunes that Annabelle liked to collect.

The therapist said something else, which Benny didn't catch, and the girl raised her head and shook the hair out of her face. She was one of the Blue Team, an older girl with a pale thin face and a crazy mop of bleached-out silvery hair that was long on one side and shaved up on the other, like it was growing back after brain surgery. She was pretty—beautiful even—and Benny had the odd breathless feeling that he'd seen her before, but not on the ward. Someplace else. She had tiny perforations in her face where her jewelry had gone—they made you remove it, Benny knew, because when he was admitted, the nurse asked him if he had any piercings, which he didn't. She was wearing a tank top and had a tattoo on the inside of her arm, clusters of small dots like a scattering of stars, connected by thin lines like the dotted lines you cut on.

"I think you have enough, don't you?" the art therapist said.

The girl's eyes narrowed, and her gaze contracted into a hot white beam, as thin as a laser, which she aimed at the therapist. Benny could feel the heat coming off it, and he braced himself for cutting words, but when she opened her mouth, her voice was clear like water.

"Enough?" she said pleasantly. "Do you mean there's a limit to the number of feelings I'm allowed to have?" Without taking her eyes off the therapist's face, she scooped up some of the paper slips into her two hands and held them out like an offering. A few of them drifted down to the floor.

"Is this too many?" She spread her fingers and a larger cluster fell away. "Still too many?" She held her hands above her head and let them fall open. The slips rained down like confetti around her. "All gone," she said sadly, looking into her empty palms. "No more feelings."

The therapist stood. "I'll get a broom," she said. "Then I'd like you to sweep it up, please, Alice."

"Sweep it up, please, Alice," the girl repeated, nodding. "*Sweep it up. Sweep it up, please, Alice. Sweep it up.*" She looked over in Benny's direction and saw him watching. She scratched her arm and stared at him until he blushed and looked away.

Later that evening he saw her in the common room. When the staff wasn't looking, she was secretly passing out the pieces of paper to some of the older kids from a stash in her hoodie pouch, and the next morning, when he put on his jeans, he found one of the slips in his front pocket, too, neatly folded. How did it get there? The paper had writing on it, neat and mechanical, and when he examined it more closely, he saw that it was hand-lettered to look like an old typewriter font. He read the words, a bullet-pointed instruction:

- Put your shoe on the table. Ask it what it wants from you.

He looked around the room. Mackson had already gone to breakfast, so he took off his sneaker and placed it on the bedside table. "Okay, shoe," he said. "What do you want from me, anyway?" When the shoe didn't answer, he sat down on the bed to wait. It was an old black-and-red Nike Air Max that his mom had got for him two years earlier at the Thrift Shop. He didn't hate the shoes. They were just old, which wasn't their fault. Maybe he should be nicer. He tried again, more politely this time. "Hey, Mr. Nike. I have to go to breakfast, so let me know if there's anything you want, okay?" But still the shoe didn't answer. It just sat there, looking tired, worn out, and uncomfortable without its laces, which were in a plastic bag somewhere. The nurse said he could get them back when he was discharged, but for now, he had to use these weird tan-colored Velcro tabs that the shoes didn't like, and he didn't, either. Mackson said that you could always tell the new kids because they showed up in shoes with laces. The kids who'd been to Pedipsy before all had sneakers with built-in Velcro.

"Okay, fine," Benny said. "Be that way."

He heard a voice from the doorway. It was Andrew, the morning nurse, doing a room check.

"Hey," Nurse Andrew said. "You okay?"

Benny snatched the shoe from the table and bent over to put it on. When he sat up again, the nurse was leaning against the wall with his hands in his pockets, watching him. Nurse Andrew was cool. He was a rock musician from England and had tattoos and lots of holes in his ears. All the girls on the ward were in love with him.

"You okay?" Nurse Andrew asked again, as he followed Benny into the hall. "You're late for breakfast. That's points, you know."

"I know," Benny said.

"No worries. I won't tell. And I didn't see you talking to your shoe, either."

IN THE BREAKFAST ROOM, the girl named Alice was sitting in a corner with Mackson and a couple of kids from the Blue Team. Benny got his cereal and hesitated. The others had finished eating and were leaving, so he went over and sat down across from her. She looked up and nodded, then she went back to staring at her breakfast, a special-meals tray with a bowl of untouched oatmeal and a half-filled glass of orange juice. The stars on her arm were covered by the sleeve of her sweatshirt, but he could see one star peeking out on the inside of her wrist. When no one was looking, he took the paper from his pocket and put it on her tray.

"Is this yours?"

She looked at it and shook her head. "It's yours now. You should probably put it away, though."

He picked it up again and reread it. "What is it?"

"It's an event score."

"Is that like a fortune?"

"Oh, interesting. Sure, why not?"

He didn't understand. "Am I supposed to actually do this?" He wanted to tell her that he'd already tried, but he wasn't sure if that was cool.

"You don't have to *do* anything," she said. "You can if you want. Or you can just think about doing it. Then it's a thought experiment. Sometimes that's just as good."

He thought about this. It seemed dumb at first, talking to his shoe, but it was kind of interesting, too. Usually when things talked, he just blocked his ears and tried not to listen. It had never occurred to him to ask them questions. Of course, the shoe hadn't answered. Maybe it thought the question was stupid. Maybe stuff stopped talking to you when you asked too many stupid questions, just like he stopped talking to Dr. Melanie, or in group when everyone just sat there in silence. Maybe if he asked more stupid questions, all the things would stop talking completely. That would be excellent. He rolled up the paper and put it back in his pocket.

"Do you have any more?" he asked.

She shrugged, which he took to mean no, but after breakfast, just before community meeting, when the staff was getting organized, he saw her with some of the Green Team kids surreptitiously passing out more slips from what appeared to be a stash in her hoodie pocket. The little kids couldn't be subtle, though. They got excited, and one of the nurses noticed and pulled Alice aside, made her empty her hoodie pouch into the trash can, and then led her from the room. Alice went quietly, and Benny watched her go. When the meeting started, the head nurse held up one of the slips and told everyone to hand over any they had. Most of the kids just shrugged and complied. Benny fingered the paper in his pocket and didn't raise his hand when the waste basket came around. Later that afternoon, during visiting hours, when the staff was busy checking visitors in, he returned to the dining room and found the trash can. The slips of paper were still sitting there under the candy wrappers and paper cups. Some of them were wet with spilled juice, but he picked out the dry ones, and later, in his room, he read them.

- Face a blank wall. Pretend the wall is a mirror.
- Say good morning to the toilet. Thank it for taking all your shit.
- Pretend you are very old. Move at half speed.
- Hug yourself and say I love you. Repeat until it's true.

- Walk like you're happy. Change directions.
- Be a pussy. Purr. Lick your beautiful fur.
- Regard the world upside down.
- Make eye contact with your meds before you swallow them. Ask them, "Are you for real?"
- Do everything backward.
- Smile at someone you don't like. If they smile back, give yourself a point.
- Lie on your back on the floor and listen. Feel free to sing along.

They were instructions, and reading them, Benny realized that some of the crazy, random shit he sometimes saw other kids doing in the halls and in the common room wasn't really random at all. It was like Alice was the conductor, and they were musicians in an orchestra following her lead. He hid the pieces of paper inside his Composition notebook, and when the lights went out, he got out of bed and lay down on the floor on his back in the dark and listened. He heard his roommate breathing and the universe creaking as it rearranged itself around him. He wanted to sing along, but he didn't want to wake Mackson, and so he hummed quietly instead. Reading the instructions was a revelation, like he'd woken up; where he'd once seen chaos, he now perceived order, and what had once seemed like order was now chaotic, but in a strange and interesting way. Alice was the key to this reality and the secret set of laws that governed the way things were on the ward. He couldn't wait to see her the next day. He would find a way to talk to her and tell her and give her back her slips of paper. But when he looked for her at breakfast, she wasn't there, and she didn't show up for meeting or for lunch. Later, during their quiet time, he asked Mackson if he knew where she was.

"You mean Athena?"

"I guess. I thought her name was Alice."

"Whatever. Anyway, she's out."

"She got discharged?"

"Hardly. She aged out, so they transitioned her. They were letting her stay in on Pedipsy, but then she got busted for that little stunt, so they moved her in with the grown-ups."

"You mean those pieces of paper?"

"Yeah." Mackson grinned. "Fluxus, man. Subversive shit. They think she's a bad influence, taking the piss out of the system and not taking her own mental illness seriously."

Benny didn't understand what Fluxus meant. He'd never heard of the radical political art movement from the sixties. He just thought it was a cool swear word that Mackson was using. But he did understand something important, another rule of the ward: the punishment for subversive shit is that they make you grow up. Fluxus, man.

The ward felt different after she left. Hollow. Muted. Dull. Later that day, during art therapy, Benny swiped a glue stick, and when he was back in his room he glued all the slips of paper into his Composition notebook. He wasn't thinking of it as art. He just liked the way they looked, all lined up neatly in a column.

15

He was discharged from Pediatric Psychiatry a few days after the start of summer vacation, so he missed his junior high school graduation. He didn't care about missing it. School seemed like a distant world he barely remembered, so when Annabelle brought him home from the hospital, he didn't understand why there was a banner hanging over the front door.

YOU DID IT! the banner proclaimed. What had he done? Confused, he looked at his mother. She had the brimming, expectant look on her face that signaled there was something he needed to feel happy about, but this made no sense.

"Did I do something wrong?"

"No, silly!" She tried to fling open the door in a triumphant gesture of welcome, but the door got jammed on a bag of recycling. She pushed harder, shoving it open enough so she could lead Benny into the kitchen, where he saw another banner hanging between the cupboard and the top of the refrigerator that said, CONGRATULATIONS, GRADUATE!

Colorful clusters of Mylar balloons bobbed from the backs of the kitchen chairs, some with yellow smiley faces in mortarboards and tassels, others with words that proclaimed, #1 GRADUATE! WAY TO GO! HATS OFF TO OUR GRAD!

"Congratulations, Benny!" Annabelle said. "I'm so proud of you!" She waited, and when he didn't react, she explained, "It's for your graduation."

He didn't know what to say. Nobody in Pedipsy talked about graduating. It wasn't called that. It was called discharge, but maybe his mom didn't know, and he didn't want to disappoint her.

"It's great, Mom," he said. Even though it wasn't.

"You only graduate from junior high once," she said. "I didn't want you to miss out. Don't just stand there! Come on!"

She took his duffel from his hand and dropped it on the floor. On a cleared-off corner of the kitchen table was a pile of presents: a goofy stuffed beagle wearing a mortarboard, a few lumpy parcels wrapped in shiny paper with big bows, an oversized card, a rolled-up sheet of paper with a long ribbon around it. The beagle was his junior high school's mascot. She took the mortarboard from the beagle and placed it on his head.

"Oh," Annabelle said. "I think you've gotten taller!" She moved the tassel to the front of the cap so that it dangled over his left eye and then stood back to look. "No, wait! That's the wrong side!"

She flipped the tassel to the right and then picked up the scroll of paper and took a few steps back. She raised the scroll with both hands. "Benjamin Oh," she announced.

He looked away. He didn't like hearing his full name called out like that. It sounded like someone else's name, like someone else should answer.

He stood there, staring at his mother's feet. Her sneakers were worn and stretched out of shape. Behind her heel, a baby cockroach poked its head from the crack where the sink cabinet met the warped vinyl floor.

"Come closer!" she said in a loud whisper. "You have to step forward when you're name is called."

He took a step and then another, until he was standing in front of her, and then she held out the scroll. In a loud voice, she said, "Benjamin Oh, I hereby present you with your diploma. You have now officially graduated from junior high school. Congratulations, honey!" Thrusting the diploma into his hands, she started clapping, but then abruptly stopped. She reached over and flipped the tassel to the left again. "There. That's better. Once you've graduated, it's supposed to be on the left. Now, let's unwrap your presents!"

SHE HAD BEEN PREPARING for over a year, stocking up on graduation paraphernalia in the summer when it went on sale, but when the day of the ceremony came and he was still in the hospital, she found herself standing in front of her closet, pulling out some of her nicer outfits. She found a pretty tunic top that she could wear over a pair of leggings she'd bought when she was pregnant. Pulling the elastic up over her waist, she remembered how taut her belly had been, swelling with new life and the promise of the future. How happy she had been—and now, here he was, graduating! As she left the house and walked to the bus stop, it occurred to her that, really, a mother never stops carrying her child, and this thought brought tears to her eyes.

She kept to the back of the auditorium. The children looked lovely in their formal clothes, pretty dresses for the girls and button-down shirts and trousers for the boys. When their names were called, they walked to the podium and received their diplomas. She took some pictures, and recorded the commencement address on her phone so Benny could listen to it later. She wanted to share the graduation with him, at least the spirit of the day, but now, as they sat together at the kitchen table and he opened the gifts she'd bought him, he seemed surprised to hear that she'd attended.

"That's actually kind of weird, Mom." He unwrapped the first gift. It was a pair of tan trousers.

"Is it?" She had pulled up the pictures on her phone and was holding it out to show him. "I didn't stay long. I just thought you might be curious. Your classmates all looked so nice. Little Amber Robinson has gotten so tall! Quite the young lady now. One of the boys had on a white three-piece suit, and even that friend of yours, Kevin what's-his-name, managed to look quite presentable."

"He's not my friend." He unwrapped the second gift, a pale blue dress shirt.

"I hardly recognized him. Don't you want to see?"

"No." The third gift was a blue necktie with polka dots that wouldn't hold still. "When am I supposed to wear this?"

"Do you like it? I thought we could get dressed up and go out to eat at a nice restaurant." She picked up the beagle and smoothed its silky long ears. "To celebrate you being home and graduation and everything."

"Today?"

"Sure! Why not?"

"I guess. If you want."

She hugged the beagle on her lap and watched as he put the folded clothes in his duffel bag to take upstairs. First the trousers, then the shirt, then the tie on top. He was still wearing the mortarboard. The cheap satin cap kept slipping off the back of his head. He looked up at her.

"Should I keep wearing this?"

The tassel dangled in his face and he brushed it away. He looked so tired.

"Oh, sweetie, of course not. I'm sorry . . ." She dropped the beagle on the table and took the mortarboard from his head. What was she thinking? "Of course you don't have to wear that stupid hat. You don't have to wear any of it."

"Okay."

"I just wanted—" She stopped and took a deep breath. It wasn't about what she wanted. She reached out to hug him, caught herself, and put her hand on his forearm instead. "The important thing is that you're home now," she said, giving his arm a gentle squeeze. "We can do whatever you want, okay?"

"I just want to go to my room." He zipped up the duffel and stood, and then he cocked his head. A dark, insistent humming sound was coming from the living room. "What's that?"

"What's what, honey?"

"That noise." He took a step toward the living room, and the sound grew louder, threaded through with an high-pitched whine. "Something's different."

"Oh, you must mean my new workstation. Go on in and take a look." She followed him into the living room. "Pretty impressive, huh?"

Three eight-foot long modular tables formed a large U, which occupied most of the floorspace. At the far end was an embankment consisting of five large flat-screen monitors in two rows: three on the lower desk level, and two suspended on retractable arms to form a second tier, above. Input devices—keyboards, track pads, scanners, and mice—were scattered across top of the tables, and underneath was a writhing mess of tangled cables. Behind the computer embankment was a wall of industrial wire shelving, holding a blinking assortment of modems, routers, DVD decks, back-up drives, and big, black noisy boxes called "loggers." Annabelle had watched with dismay as the tech crew performed the installation. When they finished, the living room looked like a TV newsroom, or an air traffic control tower, or a Silicon Valley start-up. She hadn't expected to need all this equipment. How would she ever learn to use it all?

The company had also provided an ergonomic mesh Aeron chair knock-off, with castors, padded armrests, and knobs under the seat to adjust the height and tilt and lumbar support. When Annabelle first tried the chair, she found it a bit snug and couldn't quite reach the controls. Seeing this, one of the tech guys had pulled out a wrench and loosened the armrests, pulling them out to their maximum width before offering her the chair once more.

"Here," he said. "Try that."

It fit her this time. "Sorry," she said. "Thanks!" But she hadn't felt grateful. She'd felt mortified, and then angry at herself for feeling mortified and actually *apologizing* to the guy, and then angry at him for body-shaming her, and then ashamed of herself because he was only trying to help.

But in the end, it didn't matter. The important thing was that she once again had a full-time job with health insurance. The chair was snug but comfortable. She would learn how to use the equipment. Maybe it wasn't so bad, after all. As she wheeled around inside her U, gliding from station to station, she felt important, like she was in charge.

Now, she gestured somewhat grandly at the glowing array. "What do you think?" She walked over and sat in the chair. "Pretty cool, huh?" she said, giving the chair a spin. "It's kind of like NASA. Like Mission Control."

"It's great, Mom," Benny said, holding his duffel bag in front of him like a shield. He backed out into the hall and headed upstairs to his room, as she sat there, slowly rotating. A few moments later, she heard his bedroom door slam and then the sound of his feet, clattering down the stairs. He burst into the room, dragging a large, heavy trash bag behind him.

"I *told* you not to put your crap in my room!" He hurled the bag in her direction and then gave it a kick. "Why do you *do* this?"

Annabelle's face turned pink, and she looked like she might start to cry. "Please, honey," she said, dabbing at her forehead with the sleeve of her sweatshirt. "Don't be mad. I had to move things to make space for the new workstation."

"You should have *asked* me! It's my room! You can't just put your junk in my room!"

"You're absolutely right. I should have asked you. Sweetie, I'm so sorry. I'll help you—"

"There's no space for *me* in this house!"

"I'll get rid of it, I promise. It's just temporary."

"Bullshit," he said. He gave the bag another kick, and the fight went out of him. "I seriously doubt that." He stood there, contemplating the great heaps of trash bags that lined the room, and then his gaze traveled to the blinking, humming array, in the midst of which sat Annabelle. He couldn't bring himself to look at her. He took a deep breath, held it, and started counting.

IT WAS A TOOL he'd learned in his coaching group. The counselor had given them blank Coping Cards. On one side they were supposed to write a list of the triggers that made them feel mad or sad or upset, and on the back side they wrote down strategies for coping with their feelings.

The trigger side had five lines on it, so he had written:

1. the scissors
2. the shower
3. the pane of glass
4. the Christmas ornament
5. Dr. Melanie's toys

His coach looked at his list, and asked him to be more specific and describe the moments when he felt triggered, and so he added to each one:

1. the scissors when they wanted to stab
2. the shower when it cries from its head
3. the pane of glass when it killed the bird

4. the Christmas ornament when I stepped on it in the hallway
5. Dr. M's toys when they start to remember

The coach sat down with him then, and gave him a new card and told him to try thinking of more general things this time, not specific objects, but situations that make him mad or sad or upset, and so he thought for a while, and he said, "You mean like when my mom puts stuff in my room or won't take out the trash even when I remind her?"

And the coach said, "Exactly," and so he wrote that down.

And then the coach said, "Great, now close your eyes. How does it make you feel when your mom puts stuff in your room?"

And he closed his eyes, and rocked back and forth, and said, "It makes me feel like there's this huge dark comet, made of the densest, heaviest matter in the universe, coming right at me really, really fast, and I look up and see it coming, and it's getting bigger and bigger, sucking up all the oxygen so I can't breathe . . ."

He was trembling as he spoke, and the coach said, "Good, now take a deep breath and open your eyes and write that down, too."

He obeyed. He opened his eyes and looked at the card. "There's not enough room," he said, and his coach said, "Okay, so just write *comet*," and so he did.

COMET

And the coach said, "Good, now how does your mom know when you're mad, sad, or upset?"

"You mean when the comet's coming to obliterate me?"

"Yes."

"She doesn't."

"Why not?"

"Because the comet's not real. Dr. M said so. She says it's in my head like the voices."

"Right, but when you feel like the comet's coming, you get upset, right? And when you get upset, what happens? How does your mom know?"

"She doesn't. I don't tell her. She gets upset when she knows I'm upset, and I don't like that."

"Okay, but *you* know, right? When the comet is coming? How do you know?"

"Because it's screaming through the air, and getting bigger and bigger, and I can't breathe."

"Okay, so what can you do, then?"

"Crawl under my bed?"

"Does that help?"

"Sometimes."

"Can you close your eyes and breathe?"

He shook his head. "No, closing my eyes is bad because then it's all black, like the comet's already here and crushing me."

"Okay, so keep your eyes open, then, and take a deep breath in through your nose. Try it now, slowly, counting to four."

He did.

"Hold that last breath and count to five."

He did.

"Good, now breathe out as you count to six."

And he did, and it was interesting because usually numbers distracted him, acting all random and making it difficult for him to do things, but now they were lining up in formation, trying to help. He didn't share this thought with his coach, though. He just breathed and counted.

"Good work," his coach said. "Now wait for four seconds and do the whole sequence again. Breathe in for four, hold for five, breath out for six, hold for five. Four, five, six, five. Got it? Now write that down on your Coping Card. That's your tool for when the comet comes."

He got it. He'd had it for a while now, but standing in the living room, surrounded on all sides by the encroaching chaos of his mother's stuff, he lost it again. As he breathed in and out and tried to count, the numbers kept flaring up and bursting into flames, and when he tried to blow them out, they laughed and burned more brightly. Red heat spread from his lungs into his neck and face, and he started to panic. His counselor hadn't given him any tools for dealing with wildly burning numbers, but maybe there was something else he could use. Sometimes humming nursery rhymes helped, and there were some other tools he'd written down, but he couldn't remember what they were. He put his hand in his jeans pocket to look for his Coping Card, but it wasn't there. Instead, he found a little slip of paper with neatly printed letters made to look like typewriter font.

`Come to the Library`, it said.

PART TWO

THE LIBRARY

Thus there is in the life of a collector a dialectical tension
between the poles of disorder and order.

—Walter Benjamin, "Unpacking My Library"

BENNY

Things still whispered. They still spoke, and I could still hear their voices, but they knew they had to be quiet, because everybody knows you have to be quiet here, because this is the *Library*. In the Library, everything has its very own place, and the librarians make sure of that. Books live on shelves, all lined up neatly with numbers and addresses, and their voices stay between their covers—and not just the books, but the desks and chairs and computers and copy machines are all quiet, too. Even the magazines that normally would be screaming at you if you were in the checkout line in the supermarket—here, they're all quiet, and when they need to say something, they speak in their quiet, library voices. The sound of pages turning is so nice, and so is that soft *shushshushshushing* sound that things make when they know they're being taken care of. You've been to the Library. You know what I mean.

THE BOOK

16

We didn't recognize him at first, he had grown so big. He was just a toddler when he first came with his mother for Children's Hour, and while we always keep a hopeful eye on the young ones, watching them as they emerge from the children's basement and make their way up through the levels and stacks, we lost track of him when he and his mother stopped coming. We didn't give it much thought. We lose so many of them that tracking hardly seems worth the effort, until a boy like Benny shows up.

Come to the Library, the slip of paper said, and so he did, dutifully following the instruction, not only because it was Fluxus to do so, but because he was hoping to see Alice or Athena, or whatever she was called. He told his mother he had schoolwork he'd missed while he was in the hospital and needed to catch up over the summer vacation, and she was delighted. What mother wouldn't be? The Public Library was safe. There were responsible adults around. He would be indoors, where air quality wasn't an issue, and the smoke from the wildfires wouldn't aggravate his asthma. She made him promise to take his cell phone and keep it charged. The next morning he got up early, ate his cereal, and packed his backpack with his Composition notebook and his pencil box, which contained his marble, his spoon, a few #2 Ticonderoga pencils, and the glue stick he had swiped from the art therapy room at Pedipsy. He said goodbye to his mother, walked to the bus stop, and boarded the bus to Library Square.

It was the same bus they used to take when he was a child, and the route was familiar, as were the passengers: the checked-out teenagers, sitting in the handicap-accessible and elderly seats; the construction workers in their steel-toed boots, glaring at them and telling them to move; the ancient henna-haired women with limps and canes, gratefully taking the vacated seats; the bag ladies and bottle men who drifted on at every stop, pausing to stare at Benny as they shuffled past. As if they knew. Who he was.

But maybe this was just his imagination. The world outside the hospital felt unreal to him now. The wildfires were early that summer, and the tendrils of smoke were already creeping down from the mountains, staining the air an unearthly shade of red, like the atmosphere on Mars. He stared out the window as the bus traversed the edge sprawl of the city, lumbering past the strip malls with their check-cashing storefronts and nail salons, noodle and gyro joints, vitamin shops and dollar stores and discount rug warehouses. Multicolored pennants fluttered from awnings like Tibetan prayer flags. Bright signs in dingy shop windows proclaimed GRAND OPENING! CLOSE-OUT SALE! OVERSTOCK! EVERYTHING MUST GO! As the bus skirted Chinatown and headed into the upscale downtown shopping district, these were replaced by colossal billboards that covered the entire sides of buildings with sleek monochromatic images of high-tech sneakers and smartphones, sweating bottles of vodka, and glistening models in underpants who looked like they'd been dipped in bronze. The billboards didn't say much. They didn't need to. They were pure image. Towering over the city with omnipotent presence, they spoke to the eye in voices that had no need for language and were louder even than sound. For a boy of Benny's sensitivities, it was too much—too much noise, too much stimulus—and when he could stand it no longer, he pretended his cell phone was ringing, held it up to his ear and spoke loudly into it.

What do you want? Okay! I hear you, but you need to stop bothering me now. I'm serious! Just be quiet, okay? It was a coping strategy he'd learned on the ward, and it was a good one. None of the other passengers on the bus even bothered to look up. Nobody paid attention to a boy yelling into a cell phone, and it helped to talk back to the voices.

By the time the bus made its final approach to Library Square, his distress had subsided, and he felt the same tingling sensation of excitement that he remembered feeling as a child, which made him want to flap his arms, and slap the back of his head, and kick his heels against the ventilated base of the bus seat. He refrained. He had a Coping Card for this behavior, too, which said:

> Close your eyes and take a deep breath. Imagine your body
> is heavy and filled with sand, and as you exhale, feel the sand
> slowly draining out of you. Breathe and exhale until the sand
> is all gone.

He'd memorized this, and now he closed his eyes and followed the instructions until the sand had leaked away, leaving him feeling relaxed and pleasantly emptied, almost as if he could float. This sudden lightness felt strange, but before he could start worrying, the bus huffed and squealed and pulled to a stop at Library Square. He stood, testing his gravity, which seemed to be holding. The bag ladies and bottle men were getting off, too. He got in line behind them and followed them up the hill to the Library, watching as they filed through the portals, like factory workers punching in at the start of their shift. From there, they dispersed to their various nooks and crannies, but Benny just stood there by the information desk, wondering what to do next. The little slip of paper had told him to come to the Library but not what to do once he got there, so with no further instructions to follow, he went where his feet knew to take him.

The Multicultural Children's Corner was empty, save for one small librarian who was setting chairs in a circle. It felt odd, being back. He wanted to stay, but he was too big and old to be lurking there amid the waist-high shelving and the brightly bound books. He knew there was something creepy about old guys who lurked. Not that he was so terribly old, but still. The librarian looked familiar. She glanced at him inquiringly, and he backed away.

Shoving his hands into the pockets of his hoodie, he took the escalator back up to the ground floor and then continued his ascent, getting off at each level, wandering through the stacks, reading the book titles printed on the spines and searching for whatever he was supposed to find. He fingered the slip of paper in his pocket, curling and uncurling it until the letters began to rub away. Hours passed and he found nothing, but it didn't matter. He just liked being there. He came back the next day.

We watched him as he made his way upward through the Dewey Decimals, starting in the 000s and the 010s (Computer Science, Knowledge & Systems, and all the Bibliographies), and climbing from there into the 100s and 200s (Philosophy, Metaphysics, Epistemology, and Religion), then the 300s and 400s (Social Sciences and Language), then the 500s and 600s (Science and Technology), then the 700s and 800s (Arts & Recreation and Literature), all the way up to the 900s (History) on Level Nine. When he reached 999 (Extraterrestrial Worlds) at the very top of the Old North Wing, he stayed there.

He spotted a cluster of three carrels, tucked into an improbable nook in a cul-de-sac, where the North Wing of the Old Library met one of the modern spiraling arms of the New Expansion. The nook was accessible only by a small footbridge, which awkwardly connected the Old to the New and offered a dizzying view down all nine levels to the site of the now defunct Bindery in the subbasement. If you were to observe the bridge over the years, as we did, you would learn quite a bit about the patrons who traversed it. The busy pragmatists crossed quickly, without giving it a second thought. The more existentially inclined would hesitate upon reaching the center, taking a moment to peer over the railing and imagine what it would be like to step off the edge and plummet to their death on the concrete subbasement floor. Every time such a patron paused on the bridge, we would catch our breath and wonder what would prompt an architect to design such a precipitous point of departure into a Public Library? What folly! A repository housing the bound testimony of mankind's mortal fears and immortal yearnings ought to be a solid, reassuring sort of place—harmonious and reliably symmetrical, built in such a way as to make even the most disquieted patron feel safe and secure. But architects and city planners, concerned with ensuring their own immortality, have other ideas. They see the Library as a legacy project, and books as mere props, a motley assortment of mismatched objects that mar the clean lines of their design aesthetic.

They are no friends to books.

HOW DID THIS ARCHITECTURAL folly come to be? While Benny peers over the railing, enjoying the thrill of being up so high, please allow us to explain. Books love a good backstory, and Benny won't mind. He's not in any hurry. It's summer vacation, after all.

In 2005, the Library Board voted to build a new Main Branch of the Public Library. They put out a call for proposals, and a famous architect won the commission with a diabolical plan that was hailed as visionary, a postmodern statement, and which entailed the razing of our beloved Old Library. The plan also called for the deaccessioning—*weeding* is the term—of our most vulnerable number, and needless to say we were horrified. Many of us remember the literary holocaust of the 1990s, when a quarter million books from the San Francisco Public Library were disappeared and wound up in a mass grave, buried in a landfill site. A "hate crime directed at the past," one critic called this catastrophic weeding. We feared we were in for another.

The dreadful process of culling and crating us was begun, but then, in 2008, just before the demolition was to start, the stock market crashed, the Board got cold feet and pulled the plug, and we books breathed a collective sigh of relief. Perhaps you heard us? Some said the fluttering of our pages sounded like the feathers on the wings of angels, taking to the sky.

Grumbling, the famous architect went back to the drawing board and came up with a cost-effective compromise, a plan that would contain the classical Old Library building within a modern shell, which resembles a pair of enormous quotation marks. When the construction was completed, the Library looked like this:

❝ LIBRARY ❞

As a semiotic formulation, the design is not subtle. Some even called it spiteful. However.

The new assemblage was dubbed Library Square in spite of its decidedly ovoid footprint. The free-standing elliptical walls are laced with rows of arches in a strangely theatrical homage to the Roman Colosseum. The piazza, sandwiched within this enclosure, contains a number of franchise outlets: a coffee shop, a convenience store, a newsstand, a Papaya Joe's and a Flying Pie Pizzeria. Metal chairs and café tables line the perimeter.

Everything feels a bit surreal here in Library Square. Patrons and shoppers move through the space like somnambulists. Office workers on cell phones pace up and down as they converse with the air. The homeless gather at the tables to shelter from the rain. Time slows. Pigeons peck and coo. Sound echoes through the arches.

BACK ON LEVEL NINE, Benny drew himself away from the edge of the precipitous bridge and continued on, arriving at the improbable nook that he'd spotted from the opposite side. Two of the three carrels were already taken. A Middle Eastern exchange student sat in one, hands clamped between his knees, bending over his books, but when Benny looked more closely, he saw the boy's eyes were closed, like he was praying or sleeping. An older woman sat in the other, typing very fast on her laptop computer. She looked to be in her fifties or sixties, part Asian like him, maybe, with black-framed glasses and gray-streaked hair. She must have sensed his presence, because she lifted her head and looked at him, and all the while her fingers typed on, never pausing. Benny slipped quickly into the adjacent carrel.

These carrels were old, from the pre-renovation days, but the hard upright chair was surprisingly comfortable. When he pulled it up to the sturdy wooden desk, the little cubicle seemed to sigh with pleasure, and the enclosing walls stood a bit straighter in order to better accommodate him. A narrow empty shelf stretched across the width of the carrel, just at eye level, and he delighted in the absence of anything upon it. At first he was content just to sit there, gazing at the shelf of emptiness and enjoying its quiet, but after a few patrons passed by, laden with books and clearly looking for a place to work, he began to feel uncomfortable. He took his Composition notebook from his backpack and placed it on the desk in front of him. Better. He took out a pencil and placed it next to the notebook. Better still, but now the empty shelf seemed wanting. He hung the backpack on the chair and, having claimed the territory as his, went in search of books to fortify its boundaries.

And this became his daily routine. He would wander the stacks, letting titles catch his eye and books tumble into his waiting arms, and discovering in the process that books have minds of their own, that they chose him as much as he chose them. When his arms were full, he would return to his seat and arrange the volumes on the waiting shelf, where they would line up like soldiers, spines aligned, straight and tall. At first this was enough for him. Enough to sit there, safe within the retaining bulwark of his carrel, but after a while, the books began to whisper among themselves. It wasn't enough for them just to stand around. They were books, not LEGOs. If they were just going to stand there, why had he removed them from their shelves in the first place? And having made them move, shouldn't he do them the courtesy of opening their covers and reading a few lines? At the very least, glance at some pictures, why don't you?

It was a broad hint, almost an imperative, and he heard it and complied. He selected a book from the day's array and opened it and started to read a page or two—well, not read, exactly. Not at first, and not in any systematic way, like left to right, or top to bottom. His was not the steady grazing of the methodical cow, but rather more like the browsing of a deer in the springtime, when the leaves are tender and young—a nibble here, a nibble there. As a young child, he'd loved being read to, but then, when he got older, he started playing video games and never acquired the habit of reading whole books by himself, from cover to cover. Now he didn't quite know how to proceed, so he just flipped through the book in a nonlinear fashion, sometimes starting at the back and sometimes in the middle, not looking for anything in particular, but enjoying the sensation of turning the pages, which seemed to give the pages pleasure, too. It didn't take long for the words to start to draw him in with their meanings, and he found that in order to understand what they were trying to say, he needed to go back to the beginnings—of sentences, paragraphs, chapters, of the book, itself. And so he did. A book must start somewhere, he discovered. Starting with the first syllable on the first page, he mouthed the words as he read them, pronouncing them out loud as they combined to form sentences, until he felt as if the words were animating his lips, borrowing his tongue as they whispered their way into the world.

Soon he discovered that when he was reading to himself, all the other voices in his head grew quiet and still, much the way children grow quiet and still during Children's Hour. This was a wonderful discovery, and even more wonderful was the way the voices would stay quiet for a long while afterward, even after he'd returned the books to the cart at the end of the day, and exited the Library's portal onto the street. As he walked down the sidewalk and waited at the bus stop, he felt like he was buffered from the world, safe inside a comforting cocoon of quiet story that the books had spun around him, and even all the screaming from the store windows and billboards didn't disturb him. When he boarded the bus, he sat with his forehead pressed against the window and watched the darkening streets float by in the dusky light, made red by the smoke from the fires. The world felt muted, submerged. It was as if the words on the pages of the books had given the voices in his head something to think about, to contemplate in silence, and so the summer passed.

In August, a week before school was to start, Benny was up in his carrel reading a book about medieval knights when a slip of paper about the size of a Chinese fortune fluttered from between the book's pages and landed on the desk in front of him. The little slip, with its hand-printed words that looked like they'd been typed, was so familiar it caused his heart to skip. He opened his Composition notebook to the page with the neatly pasted column of similar slips that he'd rescued from the trash on Pedipsy.

`Put your shoe on the table. Ask it what it wants from you`, the first one said.

`Come to the Library`, said the last.

He uncapped his glue stick and carefully aligned the newest slip, which had fallen from the book of knights, at the bottom of the column. He dabbed some glue onto its back, pasted it down, and then sat back and read it with some satisfaction.

`Congratulations`, the new slip said. `You made it.`

17

He'd made it, but it was too late. Summer was over, and school was about to start, and soon he would need to leave the Library. Whatever he was supposed to do there would have to wait.

Annabelle, meanwhile, had spent the summer holed up in Mission Control, alone with the news. She was tracking the spread of wildfires in the interior for an international forest products conglomerate. She was looking for anti-gun bias in the local coverage of mass shootings for a Second Amendment lobby group. She was monitoring the spread of the Zika virus, and the presidential campaigns.

She read about ground fires, ignition sources and combustion rates, microcephaly and the mating habits of mosquitoes. She knew the buzzwords, pet peeves and polling numbers of all the candidates.

Her sharp, would-be librarian's eye, adept at picking out keywords, grew familiar with the names of objects she never knew existed: 12-gauge Remington 870 Express Tactical shotguns; Glock 22 .40-caliber handguns; Bushmaster XM15-E2Ss; .22-caliber Savage MK II-F bolt-action rifles.

Information like this had a life of its own, and once it entered her mind, she couldn't unknow or forget it. She knew so much about what was happening in the world, even as she grew more isolated from it.

It was stuffy inside the small house. The smoke from the fires seeped in through the windows, and when she went outside, it was even worse. She worried about Benny's asthma and was experiencing symptoms, herself. Wheezing. Coughing. Shortness of breath. She went to the doctor, and he prescribed an inhaler and said she was suffering from stress. And no wonder! She was still trying to learn her way around the new project management interface, get a handle on the radio and television protocols, and remember all the new keywords and client numbers. She'd never had a problem with her memory before, but now it felt like she'd reached the limits of her own storage capacity.

And then, of course, there was the ongoing anxiety about Benny. When he was discharged from the hospital, she had received an Outpatient Treatment Plan from his Care Team, with all his doctor and therapy appointments, exhaustive lists of his medications and possible side effects, as well as many helpful suggestions for working on his emotion regulation, distress tolerance, and social-problem-solving skills.

There was also a list of behaviors she was supposed to watch out for, including: social isolation and emotional withdrawal; depression and lethargy; aggression and rage; threatening behavior; irritability; insomnia; paranoia; lack of concentration; an unblinking or vacant expression; spastic facial or body movements; auditory and visual hallucinations; talking to unseen entities; odd or incoherent speech; laughing during a sad movie; crying during a happy one; indifference to appearance and hygiene; confusing dreams with reality . . .

Just looking at the list made her wheeze, but she studied each item carefully, trying to match the abstract language of symptomology to her very real son's actual behavior. Did his angry words constitute an outburst of rage? Would kicking a trash bag filled with his mother's archives be considered threatening behavior? She thought he would be impressed with her new workstation and all the cool computer equipment, but when he saw Mission Control, he shrank from it, and then he used the trash bags he hauled down from his room to build a retaining wall, stacking them like sandbags in a levee to cordon it off. Was that paranoia?

She was surprised and cautiously delighted when he announced his plan to spend the summer at the Library. Not many fourteen-year-old boys would do that, and it crossed her mind that perhaps the little graduation ceremony might have played a role in his decision. She'd read that coming-of-age ceremonies were important for the development of a young person's self-esteem, which was why she'd gone through all the trouble. She tried not to get her hopes up, telling herself that he might lose interest, but every morning, as regular as clockwork, he'd pack his lunch and catch the bus to Library Square. When she asked him what he did there all day, he just shrugged and said, "Nothing," but that was a pretty normal teenage-boy response. She tried to draw him out.

"Did you read?"

"Yes."

"What did you read?"

"Books."

"Did you talk to anyone or make any new friends?"

"No."

Dr. Melanie didn't seem concerned. She said it was good that he had settled into a routine, but as the weeks went by, Annabelle grew increasingly worried. Was this what social isolation looked like? From time to time she would text him, and usually he texted her back, but still. Was there something else going on that he wasn't telling her about? Library Square attracted a lot of marginal types. Was he getting involved with drugs? At night, in bed, as she studied the list of warning signs, her anxiety grew until one day, unable to focus on work, she broke early for lunch and took the bus to Library Square.

The area had changed quite a bit since she'd last visited. She'd monitored the long civic battle over the renovations, and when the New Expansion first opened, she'd taken Benny there to eat pizza. Now, she was surprised at how tawdry it had become. The piazza was filled with homeless people, slumbering at the café tables next to their bundle buggies and shopping carts, or picking through the garbage for empty cans and crusts. Pigeons strutted on the ground by their feet, fighting with the sparrows over muffin wrappers and croissant crumbs. The smells of alcohol, marijuana, and urine commingled under the arches.

Inside, what remained of the Old Library building was much as she remembered. Slowly she made her way up the levels, trying to be inconspicuous. She had a story prepared in case Benny spotted her, that she needed to do research for work, which was a stretch. Media monitoring didn't require research that involved actual books, but Benny didn't know this. She searched the stacks, peering into corners where patrons read or dozed, until she reached the very top, where, on the far side of a precipitous footbridge, she spotted an improbable nook. Gingerly, she stepped on to the narrow bridge and paused, unsure if it would support her, and then she took another step. When she reached the middle, she paused again, and gripping tightly to the railing she looked down. It was a vertiginous drop, but what caused her heart to flutter and her knees to grow weak was not the altitude but rather a certain quality of air—or was it a smell? Yes, the heady smell of musty paper and machine oil and bookbinding glue, which rose through the exposed air shaft from the old Public Bindery in the sub-basement. She closed her eyes and inhaled with pleasure.

She remembered the old Bindery from when she was an intern. It was a cavernous room, with an antique industrial Italian table cutter and ancient black Singer sewing machines, whose spools and bobbins held a curious fascination for her. She used to search the stacks for damaged books so she could bring them down and watch the binders at work, reinforcing their spines, and clothing them in sturdy buckram covers. There were two binders, an old guy and a young one, who used to flirt with her and tease her; the old guy called her the Florence Nightingale of the Public Library, which made her proud, and of course we books loved her for that. The old guy had been about to retire, but she'd always wondered about the young one. What would a downsized binder do? It was a real question because as part of the New Expansion, the Library Board had voted to close the old Bindery and convert the room into something called the Digital Information Technology Hub and Electronic Resource Space, or DITHERS, as it came to be called by proponents and critics alike.

Annabelle had monitored the dispute over DITHERS, which had been covered in all the local papers, as the Library staff and patrons fought back. Theirs was the last Public Bindery in North America, they argued, an endangered site of historic and cultural import, which should be preserved. They wrote letters of protest, and the Union of Library Workers threatened to strike on behalf of the soon-to-be-made-redundant binders, but the Board remained adamant. Times were changing. Space was at a premium. Magazines were going online. Digital archives made bound periodicals unnecessary. Old books whose circulation numbers had dropped were better deaccessioned than rebound. In short, the Bindery was obsolete, an anachronism, a sentimental artifact from a bygone era. In the end, to Annabelle's dismay, the Board had prevailed: although DITHERS was still waiting for the go-ahead, the last Public Bindery had been closed.

Now, standing on the vertiginous footbridge, nine levels up, and breathing in all the old smells, Annabelle felt quite light-headed and woozy. Was it the glue? She wondered what had happened to the table cutters and the ancient Singers. Sold off or scrapped, most likely. A wave of sadness rose up from the subbasement. She looked down into the yawning airshaft and saw it darken and fill with stars as her knees gave way. Clutching the railing, she closed her eyes, and then she felt a hand on her elbow.

"Are you all right?"

She opened her eyes. A woman was standing next to her, peering up into her face though heavy, black-rimmed glasses. Middle-aged, Annabelle saw. Asian-looking. Annabelle pulled herself upright and nodded. "I'm fine," she said. "Thank you. I just felt faint for a moment."

The woman continued to study her.

When she didn't say anything, Annabelle gave a nervous laugh. "I think it must be the height. I'm a little afraid of heights."

"Of course," the woman said. "Many people are afraid of heights. Many people are tired of living, too."

"Yes," Annabelle said, and then, realizing what the woman was implying, quickly added, "Oh, no. That's not . . ."

"Good," the woman said. She looked over the railing into the subbasement and shook her head. "You really have to wonder what would prompt an architect to design such a precipitous point of departure into a Public Library."

"The design was very controversial," Annabelle said. "But you probably know that. Are you a librarian?"

"No. Just a patron. I was working at the carrels over there and I saw you. Are you feeling better now?"

She was pointing toward the cluster of carrels on the far side of the bridge, and from where she now stood, Annabelle could see a familiar knapsack, slung over the back of one of the chairs, and a boy, bent over and asleep on the desktop. His face was hidden behind a stack of books, but she knew it was Benny. She breathed a sigh of relief.

"I'm fine now," she told the woman. And then she couldn't help adding, with some pride, "That's my son."

The woman nodded. "He comes here every day. He seems like a nice boy. Quiet."

"He is," Annabelle said.

"He likes books," the woman said.

"He gets that from me."

"Well," the woman said. She turned to cross the bridge and then waited. When Annabelle held back, she asked, "Aren't you going to say hi to him?"

Annabelle shook her head. "I don't want to wake him." She paused. The woman was studying her again through those black-rimmed glasses, as though expecting her to say something else, so Annabelle continued. "Please don't tell him I was here. He doesn't like it when I check up on him." The woman was still standing there, waiting, so Annabelle added, "Boys. You know."

The woman nodded. "Teenagers."

"Yes, exactly!" Annabelle said. "He'll be starting high school in September."

"Well," the woman said. "Good luck with that."

Annabelle didn't want the woman to leave. She took a step closer and lowered her voice. "Actually, I'm a bit worried about him," she whispered. "It's a brand-new school, and he's had some emotional problems." She caught herself then. Why was she confiding in a stranger? She sighed. "It's a long story."

The woman nodded again. "I'll keep an eye on him," she said, which somehow made Annabelle feel better.

18

High school was new, but as Benny soon discovered not new enough. By the time the bell rang at the end of the first day, his old junior high school classmates had come to understand that his was a story worth telling. It was a story with currency and social capital, and like all currency and capital whose valuation depends upon rates of exchange, it needed to be spent, and so they did. They told and retold his story, shoving him notch by notch down the new pecking order and securing their place above until, by lunchtime, everyone in his new homeroom knew about how he had stabbed himself in the leg with a pair of scissors and got sent to the psych ward. Benny, to his credit, didn't deny or try to hide it.

At lunch, he was called to the principal's office to meet with the nurse and the guidance counselor about his meds, and Annabelle came, too, in her big tunic top and stretch pants, clutching her oversized purse. She had arrived early, and some of the kids saw her sitting in the waiting room. A contagion of sly texts and surreptitious chats ensued as rumors about her and Kenji spread, and by the end of the first week, it was understood by everyone, even the most clueless, that Benny and his family were to be their ostracized Other, against whose strangeness they could define their collective normality. They clucked like chickens when he passed, whipped out their phones to call him names, so that when he walked down the hall, you could almost see the silent cloud of text bubbles, trailing after: *Loco, Loony, Mental, Midget, Jap, Retard, Freak*. Does this sound familiar? Maybe you've seen this kind of cruelty emerging and even helped it along, or maybe you've just been quietly complicit and watched as the bigotry spread, or maybe you've been targeted, too. You know how it goes—

BENNY

Aw, come on. Can we just skip this, please? Of course they know, and it's embarrassing to hear you talk about it. Embarrassing for me, because I know you're just trying to make it sound like *Poor crazy little Benny Oh, getting picked on by his mean old bully classmates on account of his fucked-up family situation*, and that's very noble and book-like of you, but the truth is that it wasn't like that. Or, it *was* like that, but it wasn't *only* that, because I made a choice, too. On the first day of school, I decided not to hide who I was or what had happened, and when some of the kids asked if it was true that my dad was a junkie, I told them, No, he was a jazz clarinetist, and when they asked about the voices, I made them sound cool, and I copped to being in the psych ward and didn't try to hide it. In fact, I was doing fine that whole first morning until they called me to the principal's office and my mom showed up. When I saw her sitting in the waiting area with her feet stuffed into those dirty old sneakers, wearing stretch pants and that big shirt with a stain down the front that she probably didn't even notice because her boobs were in the way, I just kind of lost it. Everyone was looking at her—Principal Slater and the nurse and the guidance counselor, all the kids in the hallway—and for the first time I saw her through their eyes, and I wanted to kill them for the way they were staring. I swear I wanted to smash their faces in. She's my Mom, for chrissakes. They shouldn't have stared. They should have treated her with more respect.

So it doesn't make me feel any better to hear you clean up the story when you tell it and make me sound like the poor little crazy victim boy. I know what was really going on. I know what I was feeling at that moment about Annabelle. Why don't you tell them that? Because the truth is that I was ashamed of her. I hated her. I wanted her to disappear—oh, shit, just say it—I wanted her to die. *Why did it have to be my Dad who got killed?* That's what I was thinking. At least my dad was cool and a musician, and we had all these interests in common, like jazz and outer space, and we used to do stuff together like eat breakfast and watch old TV shows about interplanetary travel on YouTube, and when he picked me up after school, I was proud of him. I loved my dad. I loved him like crazy, and he was dead. And there was my mom, sitting in the principal's waiting room where everyone could see her, looking like a total loser, and this voice in my head kept saying, *Why couldn't it have been you?* And it wasn't just some random voice who was saying this, either. It was *my* voice. It was *me*.

So you see? Nobody wants to read about a boy who thinks shitty thoughts like that about his mom, and I don't want to think about my dad right now, so can we please just drop it and move on to something else? Let's go back to the Library. Tell them about the Aleph. That's way more interesting.

THE BOOK

Okay, but just so you know, Benny, people do want to read about boys who think shitty thoughts about their mothers. Many important books have been written on the subject, and many readers have read them. But if you're not comfortable with that, let's move on.

19

By the end of the first week, Benny concluded that school was detrimental to his mental health. He needed to stop going, but the problem then was what to do instead. The kids who cut classes usually hung out at the malls downtown or at home if their parents had jobs, but Annabelle worked from home, and the malls were out of the question. For Benny, malls were torture. They were echo chambers of mirrored sound, filled with the cries and lamentations of Unbought things that were far too discordant and upsetting.

Instead, he decided he would return to the Library, where he would wait for Alice or Athena to show up and explain why he was there, and while he was waiting, he could study on his own everything that books had to teach him. It seemed like an ideal solution—there were lots of books, and of course we were delighted—but he knew he had to be careful. He'd never heard of a truant hiding out in the Library, but that didn't mean he wouldn't get caught. Accordingly, he made a plan, which consisted of two parts.

Part One required hacking into his mother's email account. He waited until she had gone to bed, and then he went on to her computer. He didn't know her admin password, so he tried *CheeriOhs*, and then *CheeryOhs*, and got it on the second try. The browser tab was already open to her email account, AnnabelleOh@gmail.com. Scrolling through her inbox, he found a thread from the high school principal's office, which he forwarded to a dummy account he'd created earlier: AnnabelleO@gmail .com. It was risky, but he figured the school administrators wouldn't notice the missing *h*. Finally, he set up a filter, which would forward any new emails from the school IP address to the dummy account and delete them from his mother's.

Back in his room, on his own computer, he logged in to the dummy account, where he found the email thread waiting. He copied the addresses into a new message and then pasted in the draft of the note he'd composed:

Dear Principle Slater,

Please excuse my son, Benjamin, who is unfortunately having some more mental health issues and his Doctor said he has to go back to the Pediatric Psychiatry Ward at Children's Hospital, so he will be absent from school until further notice.

Sincerely,
Annabelle Oh

He reread what he'd written and hesitated for a moment and then added the word *severe* before *mental health issues*. Better. He wondered, briefly, if it would be easier just to fake his death, but then he remembered his dad's funeral and all the cards and flowers that showed up, and he remembered the body. People needed to see a body, the funeral director had said. Without a body, it was too risky, and so he went with the loony bin story instead, which was totally believable. He hit Send, logged off, and went to bed.

Part Two of his plan concerned the logistics of remaining unseen at the Library. Over the summer, he had become familiar with the patrons and staff, and learned how the rhythms of the Library fluctuated during the day. Early mornings belonged to the seniors: the elderly men in threadbare jackets, hovering over the newspaper pages like patient old herons; the gray-haired ladies in tracksuits and sun visors, perched like pigeons on the edges of their chairs. Benny watched how they read: slowly, turning each page and pressing it open with care. When they returned a book they had borrowed, they used both hands to slide it gently into the return slot, as though the book were a dear gift from someone they loved.

After the seniors came the hobos, the homeless and other nontraditional patrons, who straggled in when the shelters closed for the morning, staking out temporary abodes in the farthest-corner armchairs, where they muttered or slept. The nannies and moms arrived next, funneling toddlers in folding strollers down the escalators into the Multicultural Children's Corner, and they were followed in the late morning by the millennials, drifting in with their chai lattes and power cables, looking for outlets to plug into. And so it went until, by midafternoon, all had settled and were hunched over their books and laptops, reading, answering emails, or dozing as the long rays of sun beat against the large west-facing windows.

The information that Benny had gleaned over the summer, he now put to use. The hardest part would be getting into the Library, past security and the information desk, which was always staffed. Librarians were trained to pay attention. They had sharp eyes. They were curious. They asked questions. The trick, he figured, was to time his arrival with the hobos and homeless and slip in behind them. Once inside, he'd be safe. The Library was vast.

The morning of his first truancy, he made careful preparations. He packed some rations—a sandwich, a snack, and a bottle he could fill at the water fountain—and charged his cell phone so he could check the fake email account during the day. He allowed his mom to hug him, left the house early, and caught the bus downtown. Disembarking with the hobos and crazies, he followed them slowly up from the bus stop, matching his pace to their heavy-footed shuffling. It's finally happening, he thought. I'm becoming one of them. As they approached the front entrance, he pulled up the hood of his sweatshirt, hunched his shoulders and dug his hands deep in his pockets.

"Playing hooky, ya?"

This voice seemed to be coming from somewhere behind him, like many of the voices did. It spoke in English but with an accent. Not Chinese. His heart was racing. *Not real*, he reminded himself, and then he took a deep breath, the way his coach had showed him, and started counting. *Inhale—two, three, four* . . .

"Hey, young schoolboy! I am talking to you!"

Ignoring the voice, he exhaled—*five, six, seven*—and as he did, he felt something hard and sharp bump the back of his calf. He spun around. It was the metal footrest of the electric wheelchair, operated by the twitchy old hobo with the battered black leather briefcase and the Random Acts of Kindness sign, who was always trying to talk to him. Benny hadn't seen him on the bus this morning. The old man's head jerked to one side as he drove his chair forward again, this time clipping Benny in the shin.

"Ow!" Benny stepped back and then bent down to rub his leg. "That hurts."

"Ach, sorry. Bad brakes." The old hobo fiddled with the chair, then leaned forward and put out a hoary hand. He had a florid, satyric face, with creased skin and watery blue eyes. He grabbed Benny's forearm, pulling him in so close that their foreheads were almost touching.

"I hef a plan," he whispered hoarsely. "You must stay back. I vill enter first and deploy diversionary tactics at ze book returns. Once I hef sufficiently distracted ze security forces, you must slip quickly past."

He grinned. He was missing a front tooth and the gap gleamed redly.

"It is a good plan, ya? Then we vill rendezvous in Parapsychology on Level Four, at oh-nine-hundred hours." The old hobo gunned his wheelchair. The massy assemblage of plastic bags filled with empty cans and bottles seemed to have grown since the last time Benny had seen it and now was billowing around the old man like a thundercloud. A tall pole with an orange safety flag rose from its midst like a golf flag or a lance.

Benny glanced around. He was trying so hard not to be conspicuous, and this was a disaster, but if he went along with the old guy's plan, maybe he would go away. He nodded.

"Excellent!" The hobo pumped his fist in the air. "*Seizzzze ze day!*" he hissed, sending a spray of spittle flying, and then he spun a wheelie and took off.

The wheelchair careened through the crowd and up the access ramp, shopping bags bouncing, flag flapping from the end of its pole. Benny watched, wondering if he should turn around and leave, but he couldn't think of anywhere else to go, and since he couldn't stand there loitering, he followed, walking slowly. He fell in behind a lady with a bundle buggy. When he reached the entrance, he spotted the wheelchair, sitting empty by the book-return slot. The desk librarian had come around from behind the counter and was picking up cans and bottles that had scattered across the floor and returning them to the plastic bags. The hobo was kneeling on his one good leg, hanging on to the edge of the book-return counter. The other leg, the prosthetic one, he had removed and was using as a cane, leaning on it in order to peer into the book-return slot.

"Slavoj, you know that slot is just for books," the librarian was saying, not unkindly. "Not bottles, right?"

And as Benny waited to pass through security, he heard the hobo, whose name he now knew was Slavoj, say, "Ya, ya, of course, my dear Ronald, but

I hef become somewhat intrigued by this notion of a slot. That a slot is a *thing*, we cannot deny, however it is a *thing* defined entirely by *lack*, by an *absence* of form, by *negative* space, by its own *emptiness*. We know vat it *isn't*, but how can we truly know vat it *is*? How can we tell ze difference between a *slot* and, say, a *slit*? Is a slit slimmer than a slot, and therefore lacking less? If it lacks less, does it vant more? And if so, how can we know if this slot or slit vants books and not bottles?"

Benny kept his hoodie up and his head down. As he passed through security, he glanced toward the return desk. The hobo, Slavoj, had his back turned to him. There was no way he could have seen Benny behind him, but just as he passed, the old man pumped his prosthetic leg in the air overhead as if in salute. As if he knew the boy was watching.

BENNY KEPT TO THE STAIRWELLS, which was easy enough to do. There were several sets of stairs and fire exits in the Library in both the new wings and the old. He avoided the elevators and ramps, which were both wheelchair accessible, and the escalators, which were too exposed. He didn't know where, on Level Four, Parapsychology was located, but he figured if he went straight up to Nine, the old hobo wouldn't be able to find him. Due to an architectural awkwardness in the interface between the old historic building and the new postmodern wing, his improbable nook on Level Nine was not accessible. The vertiginous footbridge could not accommodate a wheelchair, and so Benny knew he was safe.

It was still early. Two of the carrels were already occupied, but his was still empty. He took his seat and carefully unpacked, laying out his notebook and pencils just so, and then he went in search of books, confining himself to the stacks nearby. Level Nine was History, which was fortunate, because Benny was discovering that he liked reading about history. He liked the past. He also liked the future. It was the present that was the problem. He returned with an armload of books on the subject of the Austro-Hungarian Empire, including one called *Medieval Shields and*

Armaments, but just as he was about to start reading, he heard his cell phone ping.

Warning! said a voice in his head. It was a new voice, tinny and robotic and didn't seem to be connected to a thing, but at least it spoke in English and seemed to be trying to help. He pulled out his phone and checked the fake email account. There was one message in the inbox. It was from the principal's office. "Dear Mrs. Oh," the email began. He clicked it and read quickly.

> We are sorry to hear that your child, Benjamin Oh, will be absent from school for medical reasons. If the student's absence will exceed three days, state law requires that the parent provide a letter from the student's physician, confirming the medical necessity for their absence, and including the diagnosis and probable date of the student's return. All of us here at Soundview High are praying for your child's speedy recovery.

Danger! Danger! It was the robot again, triggering an internal warning system, which rocketed up from Yellow (elevated) to Red (severe). He switched off his phone and stared at the large book on his desk that lay open to a glossy illustration of fifteenth-century plate armor. What should he do? His eyes traversed the strange names of the suit's different parts— *comb, helm, gorget, pauldron, plackart, fauld, tasset, couter, vambrace, gauntlet, cuisse, greave, sabaton*—his lips moved around the unfamiliar sounds.

Warning! Warning! Danger! Danger! It was one thing to forge an email from his mom. How was he supposed to get a doctor's letter? *Think!* He switched on his phone again and googled *doctor excuse letter absent school*. A long list of hits came back, and he took a deep breath and exhaled, as his Alert Level dropped back down to Yellow. Good. He would need a computer and a printer, too. And maybe a scanner. There were two public computing areas in the Library. The largest of these was on Level One, near the main entrance, but it was exposed and heavily trafficked. The second area was on Level Four.

It couldn't be helped. If he didn't reply to the email, the school would phone his mother. He needed to intervene now. He left his books and sandwich and his soda bottle on the desk. "I'm coming back," he told them. "Don't let anyone sit here," and then he recrossed the bridge, pausing for a moment to look down before heading to the stairwell.

20

Annabelle's phone was ringing. She could hear it, the "By the Seaside" ringtone she'd chosen because it sounded like a jaunty Hammond organ soundtrack to the kind of 1950s family beach vacation she'd always dreamed of, with pink cotton candy and blue ice slushies, Ferris wheels and bumper cars, and big stuffed teddy bears that your daddy would win for you by tossing a ring around the neck of a bottle. She'd never had a family vacation like that when she was little. The trip to Disneyland with Kenji and Benny was close, and she'd hoped for another like it, but now it was too late, and her phone was playing "By the Seaside" over and over again, just mocking her.

Benny always texted, so it wouldn't be him. Was it the high school? And where was her goddamned phone? The ringing stopped. Whoever it was could leave a message. At least she knew it wasn't her supervisor. Charlie used the agency's internal EIM when he needed to reach her, which drove her nuts. She hated the way he would pop up in the corner of her screen. It felt like he was always there, lurking right behind the thin layer of liquid crystal.

It was almost one o'clock and time for lunch. Gone were the days when she could knock off at noon and take the bus to pick up Benny at school and stop at Michaels on the way. For one thing, Benny wouldn't let her. High school students didn't need their mothers to pick them up and take them home on the bus. High school students didn't need their mothers, period. And for another thing, she was still on probation, and in addition to all the newsfeeds, Charlie told her she had to monitor social media, too. She had no more time for crafting projects.

She stood and heard her knee joint click, and a pain shot up from her hip as she straightened. Sitting was bad for her health. She was supposed to stand and stretch and walk around every twenty minutes, but she always forgot, and she worried about heart disease. She also worried about high blood pressure, breast cancer, elevated cholesterol, diabetes, and deep-vein thrombosis. She worried about premature death. She stood, and her phone fell to the floor. She'd been sitting on it. Typical. She picked it up and looked to see who'd called, but it was a number she didn't recognize. Probably some telemarketer. The message on the voicemail was in Chinese.

In the kitchen, she found an open bag of corn chips and a half-eaten jar of salsa. She took them up to her bedroom and lay down on the bed to stretch out her back. The bed was old and the mattress sagged. She'd read online that you should replace your mattress every eight to ten years, or after thirty thousand sleep hours, but this was the mattress where she and Kenji had slept, where they had made love and where Benny was conceived, and she couldn't bear to think of it slumped against a dumpster in the rain.

She looked at the clock on her bedside table. It must be lunchtime at the high school, too. She wondered how Benny was doing. She'd had so much fun, buying him all his back-to-school supplies. She took out her phone and typed, *Having a nice lunch?* She waited, but Benny didn't reply. *How's the new lunch box?* Maybe lunch was over. *Hope you're having a good day!* He still didn't respond. *Love you!* She stared at the ceiling.

The chips and salsa failed to satisfy. What she really needed was a salad. A nice big salad with tomatoes and carrots and avocados and other healthy things. She could take the bus over to the Whole Foods Market and get a salad from the salad bar, but this would mean taking off a whole hour of work, and Charlie would know, and besides, Whole Foods was ridiculously expensive, and the people who shopped there always made her feel bad about herself. Unhealthy. No, just say it, Annabelle: *fat*. They make you feel *fat*. Fine, she thought, sitting up and emptying the chip bag, shaking it to get the last of the crumbs. Whatever. She headed back downstairs. She didn't need the Whole Foods salad bar. She could buy perfectly good lettuce at the cheap, unhealthy, discount supermarket and make her own salads. She could go today after work. She would need a salad spinner, too. She used to have one around the house somewhere, but she hadn't seen it for a while. Well, she could always buy another one online.

There was no room in the recycling bin for the empty salsa jar, so she left it in the sink. The chip bag she shoved into the overfilled trash. Back at Mission Control, she settled into her ergonomic chair and spun around briskly to face her monitors, but something on the desk caught her eye. There, peeking cheerfully out from underneath a pile of clippings, was *Tidy Magic*.

How strange! How had the little book gotten there? The last place she recalled seeing it was in bed, when she'd fallen asleep reading. That was months ago, before the Scissors Incident, and in her anxiety about Benny, she'd forgotten all about it. The book must have gotten buried under other things and somehow found its way downstairs, and now here it was, like magic, to remind her of her intentions. She stood back up and returned to the kitchen.

Was Monday trash or recycling? The city kept changing the pickup schedule. Benny used to keep track, but lately he'd stopped. Given up, more likely. Mrs. Wong sometimes reminded her, too, but the old lady had fallen down her back steps and broken her hip and was in the hospital, and now her no-good son was lurking around the property. Over the years, the sullen, scrawny teenager had grown into a sullen, scrawny young man, who drove a flashy car and wore designer tracksuits and sunglasses and was always trying to talk his mother into selling the duplex. Annabelle could hear them through the wall, Mrs. Wong barking at him loudly in Chinese, and No-Good yelling back at her in English, telling her that she was an idiot to be sitting on a gold mine and not cashing in, and don't count on him to take care of her in her old age. Annabelle had just signed a new lease, but it was worrisome.

Out on the sidewalk, there were still some trash bins in front of the houses, but they were all empty. The truck had come and gone already. Discouraged, she dragged the bags back into the yard, and then she heard him.

"Yo, Miz Oh." He had a high-pitched, unpleasant voice that hadn't changed since he was a teenager, and he always pronounced her name like it was one word, which drove her crazy. He swaggered over to the fence that separated their little backyards and leaned on it. His hand rose to cover the wine-colored birthmark on the side of his face.

"Yo, Mizoh, you gonna be around later? I got a letter for you from my Ma."

"Oh, how nice. How is she feeling?"

He shrugged. "She's okay." He looked at the bags she was holding. "She says you gotta clean this place up, here. It's a health hazard, and by that I mean all this garbage and them crows you're feeding. You gotta get ridda them. Ma broke her hip on account of two crows that was looking at her, so she fell down the steps."

Annabelle frowned. "Your mother said that?" She'd visited Mrs. Wong in the hospital to bring her the signed lease and the rent check, and the old woman told her she'd tripped on the step because it was broken.

"No-Good Son say he gonna fix it, but . . ." She shook her head. "I wish your Kenji husband not die." She'd never mentioned the crows.

No-Good grew evasive. "Them birds are evil. And all that food you give them is attracting rats and vermin. We're gonna get a Health Department Citation for rats and vermin. You know how much it costs to get a Health Department Citation for rats and vermin?"

Annabelle didn't know, but she hadn't seen any rats and vermin, either.

"You gotta clean up this mess and stop feeding them crows!"

He pushed off the fence and went back into his side of the duplex, leaving her standing there with her trash. She thought about taking the bags out to the alley and throwing them into the Thrift Shop dumpster, but that was illegal. Oh, well, she thought, leaving the bags at the foot of the back steps. There was no point in beating herself up about it. She would try again on Thursday. That's all you have to do, she told herself, gently. Just try to try.

Back inside, she found a bottle of Starbucks Frappuccino in the refrigerator. It was pumpkin spice, which she'd bought on sale after Halloween. She unscrewed the cap, and took a sip. It was cool and sweet and creamy—a reward for trying. She went to the trash can to throw the cap away, but now there was no trash bag in the can, and she remembered she had run out. She put the cap on a stack of mail on the kitchen table, where she would be sure to see it later. She would definitely go to the supermarket after work. Trash bags and lettuce.

She took the Frappuccino back to Mission Control and logged on to the project team management site and scanned her channels. Now, she thought. Where was I? She launched her browser. Ah, yes. Salad spinners.

21

The public computer terminals on Level Four were located in a central area, ringed by the stacks. The information desk was off to one side, and the sign above it said SOCIAL SCIENCES. This was a part of the Library that Benny rarely frequented, and he hoped the librarians wouldn't question him. The tinny, robotic voice was muttering, *Warning! Warning!* He scanned the area for the hobo's orange safety flag. It was nowhere to be seen, and the warning voice fell silent.

Keeping his head down, he circled the perimeter, looking for a vacant terminal. He passed RELIGIONS, and then PHILOSOPHY, and then PSYCHOLOGY, and then—he looked up—PARAPSYCHOLOGY AND OCCULTISM.

Danger! Danger, Will Robinson!

He recognized the tinny voice, now. It was the robot from the old TV show *Lost in Space*, that he used to watch with his dad. What was it doing here? He ducked behind a row of books.

Warning! Danger! Alien spacecraft approaching!

He peered out, expecting to see the electric wheelchair careening around a corner, but all was quiet. He looked at the books on the shelf. He didn't know what parapsychology was, but all psychology, even the normal kind, made him nervous. He waited, hidden, until the robotic voice subsided, then he found an empty terminal and used his library card to log on. He typed in *doctor excuse letter absent school* and ran his search again.

> **Best Fake Doctors Notes, 19+ Documents—**
> **Printable, Fillable, Free!**

> **Sample Fake Doctor Note Templates for Work/School!**
> **Guaranteed!**

There were 237,000 website listings. He clicked the first link and started to read.

> A Doctor's Note is most important for patient to show
> weighty proof to absent from school because you must
> to visit the doctor. This handy fillable pdf note can
> confirm it, even in fact it never happen! So you can
> surely use it as cunning excuse for your school teachers.

The site offered sample notes from many different kinds of doctors—oncologists, urologists, dermatologists, psychologists—some free, others bundled for bulk purchase. Stationary was important, too, he realized. He found one with a picture of a teddy bear holding a smiley-face balloon that reminded him of the decor in Dr. Melanie's office. He filled in her name and address but hesitated before typing in a phone number. The website offered a phone verification service with an outgoing message that sounded just like a doctor's answering service, but it cost eighteen dollars, so he made up a fake phone number instead.

On the line next to Patient's Name, he typed *Benjamin Oh*.

Under Diagnosis, he wrote the word *prodromal* followed by the word *schizoaffective*, which was what he'd heard Dr. Melanie say. He remembered *prodromal* because he liked the sounds, which reminded him of drones and dromonds and dromaeosauruses and dromedaries, but he hated *schizoaffective*, which was a terrible word, with clusters of jaggedy letters like daggers and snares just waiting to stab and trap you. You had to be careful with words like *schizoaffective*. Then, in the note section, he cut and pasted his text: "Benjamin Oh has been addmitted to the Pediatric Psychiatry Ward at Children's Hospital under my supervision and will be absent from school until further notice."

He printed out the letter on the coin-operated printer using the change his mother had given him to buy a soda. He remembered seeing Dr. Melanie's girly signature on a prescription, and after practicing a few times on a piece of scrap paper, he signed the letter, scanned it, and attached it as a reply to the principal's email from the dummy Annabelle O account. Just as he was about to send it, though, he happened to notice the time. The whole business of forging the note had taken less than two hours, and Dr. Melanie would never respond to anyone that quickly. All the Pedipsy doctors were like that. His mom said they liked to keep people waiting to show how busy and important they were. He saved the email as a draft and logged off. He would wait. He would be patient. A patient patient. He shook his head to clear it. He didn't like words that behaved like that, mocking him with all their different meanings. He stood and peered over the top of the computer terminal. The coast was clear. He needed to get to a higher elevation.

Back on Level Nine, he relaxed a bit. Everything was as it should be in the nook. The typing lady was still there typing, surrounded by her books. She looked up and nodded when she saw him, and the light syncopated tapping of her fingers on the keys sounded like raindrops. The Middle Eastern exchange student was still asleep and snoring softly, his cheek pressed against the pages of an astronomy textbook. On his laptop screen, a live webcast of a star cluster, viewed from a telescope in a Chilean observatory, reloaded every few seconds and synchronized with his exhalations, so that it looked like his breathing controlled the refresh rate of the stars. A calculator sat on the desktop next to a half-eaten falafel sandwich.

Benny realized he was hungry, too. He unpacked his rations and arranged the history books he'd collected earlier around him in the carrel. His Alert Level had dropped to Blue, but it shot back up to Yellow when his phone pinged. It was a text from his mother. And then another. Then a third. Green word bubbles, piling up on his screen, growing louder. He silenced the ringer and took a bite of his sandwich, and then he opened *Medieval Shields and Armaments* at random and started to read about trebuchets and petards. The descriptions of the war engines calmed him, and the voices in his head quieted. The sandwich tasted good, too. He texted his mother. *Yes*, he typed. *Eating lunch.*

He read for three quarters of an hour, and when he finished the chapter, he looked up. All the jangly voices, even the distant ones, had gone quiet, and instead he was surrounded by a soft blanket of sound—an ambient hush, which included both the gentle snoring of the exchange student as well as something else, an absence of sound, a thin thread of silence. What was missing? He leaned over, craning his neck around the edge of his carrel and spotted the source. The typing lady was gone.

It looked as if she had just stepped away from her desk, perhaps to go to the restroom or back into the stacks for more books. Her laptop and knapsack were missing, too, but Benny assumed she had taken them with her; recently there had been incidents of theft in the Library, and patrons were being warned not to leave their valuables lying around. Her sweater was still slung across the back of her seat, holding her place, and her books lay in piles on the desktop. He tilted his head and tried to read the titles on their spines. *Grimm's Fairy Tales* was one of them. *The Garden of Forking Paths* was another. *The Work of Art in the Age of Mechanical Reproduction* a third, and then there were several whose titles he couldn't quite see.

He stood. There was no one around, so he sidled over to her carrel and picked up the *Grimm's*. He'd knew the title from his bookshelf at home, but his edition of the book was bright and cheerful, a slim expurgated volume with a picture of a princess fleeing coyly from a wicked witch through a thicket of pink roses. This *Grimm's* was neither bright nor cheerful. It was a stout, leather-bound tome, with a dark red cover, the color of dried blood. The leather was embossed with a brooding copse of trees, whose tangle of roots and branches were like veins, pressed into the skin. A little slip of paper was sticking out from the top of the book, marking a page. He opened to the story of Hansel and Gretel, and the slip fluttered to the floor. He picked it up and read:

> `Hansel and Gretel are alive and well, and`
> `they're living in Berlin.`

The letters were neatly printed to look like typewriter font. Folding it quickly, he tucked the paper into his pocket, replaced the book on the pile, and returned to his carrel. He took out his Composition notebook and compared the slip to the ones pasted there. The handwriting was the same. He turned it over. On the back was a long string of numbers—791.43/ 0233/092—which he recognized as a call number from a book. He was wary of numbers calling. He knew how, in their exuberance, they could easily get out of hand and cause a ruckus, but he stood and followed them anyway, back into the stacks.

The call number took him down to Level Seven, to Sports, Games & Entertainment, which was a part of the Library he'd never been to before. Number 791.43/0233/092 was in the Cinema section, and soon he located the volume.

UNDERSTANDING
RAINER WERNER
FASSBINDER

FILM AS PRIVATE
AND PUBLIC ART

He studied the cover. If a book's cover is its face, this volume had a gritty, artistic countenance. Under the title was a black-and-white photograph of a middle-aged man with plumpish cheeks and a stringy beard, who peered impishly over the top of a pair of thick-framed black glasses. The man's eyes had a crazy gleam and reminded Benny of the old hobo, Slavoj. They were sly eyes, puffy, like Kenji's on a morning when he'd stayed out late the night before. The sparse, stringy beard looked a bit like Kenji's beard, too. Benny sat down on the floor and opened the book, held it upside down, and shook it. The pages fluttered, emptily. Nothing. No slips of paper. He started flipping through the book, looking for more clues, but soon he became distracted by the illustrations. There weren't many, just some old photographs of German actors. One of them was a voluptuous girl with wavy blond hair, who looked like Annabelle when she was young and pretty. The man on the cover was with her in some of them, but Benny decided he didn't look like Kenji, after all. The man was called Fassbinder. He was a filmmaker, but none of his films seemed very interesting. Benny flipped quickly to the end of the book. Maybe you had to be German.

As he closed the book, he noticed a library pocket, the old-fashioned kind that predated barcode technology, glued to the inside of the back cover. Tucked inside the pocket was a postcard. Benny pulled it out. It was the sort of postcard sold at museum gift shops, depicting great works of art, only this one just had a drawing of a stick figure, scrawled on paper that was stained and brown around the edges. The figure had a mop of curly hair and was wearing a skirt, but after studying the long face and square jaw, Benny decided that it was a man in spite of the skirt. His widely spaced, almond-shaped eyes were staring past Benny's right shoulder, in the direction where the voices often came from. He turned and looked over his shoulder, but all he saw was a row of books, sitting quietly on the shelves. He looked back at the postcard. The man's arms were spread out and raised in the air, like someone had pointed a gun at him. His lips were open, and his long teeth looked like stumps with gaps between them. There were patterns on his clothes that made no sense, and the curls on his head looked like scrolls of paper coming undone.

And his feet were bare with only three toes each.

And his fingers looked like they'd been cut off at the knuckles.

And his widespread arms were actually wings.

Benny turned the postcard over. *Angelus Novus*, the caption said. *Artist: Paul Klee, 1920. Oil Transfer and Watercolor on Paper. Israel Museum.* It wasn't a kid's drawing after all. It was Art, but Benny wasn't reading the rest of the caption, because his eye had been drawn to the message section of the postcard, where he saw a block of text, printed in that same typewriter-like handwriting:

```
This is how one pictures
the Angel of History. His
face is turned toward the
past. Where we see a chain
of events, he sees one
single catastrophe that
keeps piling wreckage
upon wreckage and hurling
it at his feet. The Angel
wants to stay, to awaken
the dead, to make whole
what has been smashed.
```

On the right side of the card, in the space where the recipient's name and address was supposed to go, the words continued:

```
            But a storm is blowing from
            Paradise; it got caught in
            his wings so violently that
            the Angel can no longer
            close them. The storm drives
            him irresistibly into the
            future to which his back
            is turned, while the pile
            of debris before him grows
            skyward. This storm is what
            we call . . .
```

The words just stopped, leaving the sentence dangling. What was the storm called? Benny flipped the postcard over and looked at the picture again. It didn't look like an angel. He stuck the postcard into his Composition notebook and replaced the Fassbinder book on the shelf. Where to next? he wondered.

22

The hunt for a salad spinner proved to be more complicated and time-consuming than Annabelle anticipated, some spinners being plastic and others stainless steel, some having rotating handles you turned, or cords you pulled, or pumps you pushed, and then there was a fancy contraption from Switzerland with a ratcheting lever. After comparing prices and functionality, she settled on one that seemed both durable and moderately priced, and which had decent user reviews. It was a sensible choice, but somehow it left her feeling vaguely dissatisfied. She checked the time. She really ought to get back to work, but she'd taken only a short lunch break, after all, on account of not having a salad spinner or the ingredients to make a healthy meal (although from now on, she would), and while she was thinking all this, she somehow managed to navigate over to eBay.

Five minutes, she thought. Just five minutes.

WHAT MAKES A PERSON want so much? What gives things the power to enchant, and is there a limit to the desire for more?

Books are intimately familiar with questions like these; they constitute the DNA of your oldest human stories, expressed in the tales our pages tell of jealous gods and gardens, talking snakes, and sweet, irresistible apples.

Take that apple, for example, a thing that existed outside Eve, whose terrible magic pulled her into it—or it into her—causing both to lose themselves in the merging. But did the magic power to enchant lie in the sweet flesh of the rosy red fruit, or in the forked tongue of the snake who told its story so deliciously? And was the apple equally beguiled?

And what of the story itself? Are words the conduit through which your desire travels, or are they just an afterthought, an add-on, a trick of your human mind to justify the prelinguistic itch that prefigures it?

And what about the troublesome matter of *more*? For most humans throughout history, "more" wasn't even an option. "Enough" was the goal and was, by definition, enough. The Industrial Revolution changed all that, and by the early 1900s, American factories were pumping out more goods than ever before, while the newly empowered advertising industry used its forked tongue to convert citizens into consumers. But even as this new economy boomed, there were signs that growth was slowing, and these same questions began to niggle in the minds of American industrialists. What makes a person want so much, and is there a limit to the desire for more? Or, put another way, is there a point of saturation at which the American consumer would have enough, leading to the collapse of the market?

Herbert Hoover, then secretary of commerce, was appointed by President Coolidge to find answers to these questions, and in 1929, the Presidential Committee on Recent Economic Changes published its gleeful conclusion:

> The survey has proved conclusively what has long been held theoretically to be true, **that wants are almost insatiable**; that one want satisfied makes way for another. The conclusion is that economically we have a boundless field before us; that there are new wants which will make way endlessly for newer wants, as fast as they are satisfied. (emphasis added)

THERE WAS NO SHORTAGE of snow globes on eBay. They came in every color and theme and price range, and Annabelle was enchanted by the sheer variety. People were so creative to think of making snow globes in the first place, but then to make so many different kinds! She had her other collections, all her vintage toys, books, bottles, and postcards, each one with its own story. She hadn't meant to start collecting snow globes, too, but the little turtle one she'd bought at the Thrift Shop had cheered her so tremendously. It sat at the base of her main Mission Control monitor, and whenever she started feeling overwhelmed by the news, she would pick up the snow globe, turn it upside down, and watch the iridescent sparkles swirl and settle. There was no news inside the globe, and nothing ever changed. There, the world stayed exactly the way it was, and she found this reassuring. Of course, it was sad that the baby turtle was trapped, sealed off and swimming all alone in his orb. And sad, too, that the mother turtle, watching from the outside, was unable to reach him. Still, they could see each other through the glass, and somehow from this thought came another: that perhaps the two turtles would like a friend.

The first one she bought on eBay was a musical globe with a Noah's Ark motif. There were pairs of bears and deer and giraffes and doves sitting atop the ark inside the bubble, while outside on the base, dolphins and turtles and fish splashed in the plastic waves. The song was from *Doctor Dolittle*, which had been one of Annabelle's favorite movies when she was a child. She'd found a VHS copy at a yard sale, and when Benny was little, they used to curl up on the floor and watch it and sing "Talk to the Animals" together. Benny was certain that when he grew up he would be able to talk to animals, too, and they had long conversations about which language he should learn first. Kangaroo or hippopotamus? Orangutan or flea? Or maybe skunk, he said, because then, if a skunk came through the alley, he could talk to it nicely and ask it to go away. Annabelle remembered the delight she felt listening to his deliberations, which was why, as soon as she spotted the musical ark on eBay, she bid on it.

Since then, the globes proliferated quickly. She had one with an adorable Scottish terrier, a vintage one with a beautiful ballerina lacing up her slipper, and a historical one commemorating a real sunken pirate ship called the *Whydah*, with tiny golden doubloons that floated through the water. She started focusing on fairy-tale motifs, setting herself the challenge of finding ones that weren't too Disneyfied. She had one Rapunzel and one Snow White, and now she was bidding on a lovely Hansel and Gretel. The bid was up to $27.45—more than she wanted to pay, but the little brother and sister, holding hands and gazing at the gingerbread house, were irresistible, and if you looked really closely, you could even see the witch, peering out of the sugary window. She checked the time. It was 3:52. The auction was ending in eight minutes, and her bid was still the highest.

3:53. These last few minutes were critical. Snipers could be lurking, waiting until the last few seconds. She'd lost items that way in the past.

3:55. Still the highest. She had set her maximum at $35, but now she started to get cold feet. Maybe that wasn't enough? She typed in $40, and just as she hit enter, the doorbell rang. So annoying! It was probably No-Good, delivering the note from his mother. She wondered what Mrs. Wong wanted. When Kenji was still alive, the old lady used to drop by with presents sometimes—a long white daikon radish from the garden, a handful of Chinese mustard greens, or the head of a fish. She worked at a processing plant gutting fishes, and she would bring home the heads for Kenji to cook. He would salt them and grill them or make fish head soup, teasing out the eyeballs or the tender cheeks from the cartilage with the delicate tips of his chopsticks. The heads were the most delicious, he said. When he died, Mrs. Wong stopped bringing them.

The doorbell rang again. Annabelle upped her maximum bid to $45 and then went to the window, reaching over a stack of newspapers to pull back the curtain. No-Good was standing on the front porch with an envelope in his hand.

"Yo, Mizoh!" he called, banging on the door. "Open up."

She let the curtain drop. Had he seen her? She heard a scraping sound. He was trying to push the envelope under the door, but they never used the front door anymore because so much stuff had accumulated in the foyer it was hard to open. She heard him swear, and then he rang the bell a third time.

"I know you're in there, Mizoh! I hear your radio. Listen, I'm leaving this letter from my Ma in front of your door. You better read it. And you better empty out your mailbox, too. You got bills piling up in here. They gonna shut off your electric."

She stood behind the closed curtain and listened to him stomp off down the front steps. For a small man, he made a lot of noise. It was true about the mailbox. She sometimes left important mail in there, because at least then she knew where it was. She went back to the computer, typed in $50, and then sat back, feeling relieved. It was a bit of insurance. So as long her maximum was the highest, she would still win.

3:59. Less than a minute left. She began to count down, and then, with only twenty seconds to go, the bid jumped to $32.45. And then it jumped again, and again! Not one, but two snipers were bidding on her Hansel and Gretel! She held her breath and crossed her fingers and counted—five, four, three, two . . .

The *Congratulations, You've Won!* message popped on to her screen, along with her winning bid. $49.45. She sat back in her chair, triumphant.

It felt so good to win.

23

He returned to his carrel with an armload of books about the painter, Paul Klee, who it turned out was a famous German artist with a stringy beard and mustache like the famous German filmmaker. He piled the new books on top of *Medieval Shields and Armaments* and started leafing through the pages. The artist's pictures were odd and colorful and somehow musical, he thought. Like you wouldn't be surprised if the painting suddenly started to sing a song, and so he found himself staring at the images and listening to them, too. There were pictures of cats and birds and fishes and balloons, or maybe they were moons, it was hard to tell. They were kind of random.

Paul Klee had made a lot of paintings, but eventually Benny found the one he was looking for, *Angelus Novus*, the guy in the skirt. He studied the image. What did this painting have to do with Hansel and Gretel? With the famous German filmmaker, whose name he'd already forgotten? He waited, hoping that the painting would yield the next clue.

Nothing.

It was discouraging. He pulled out his Composition notebook and opened to the page where he'd pasted in all the other slips of paper. Ever since the summer, when he'd first come to the Library, he'd been waiting for something to happen. Someone—he hoped it was Alice, or Athena, or whatever her name was—had summoned him here, but why? He took the scrap of paper he'd found in the fairy-tale book from his pocket and laid it on the ruled page at the bottom of the collection.

    Hansel and Gretel are alive and well and
    living in Berlin.

He took his glue stick from his knapsack and pasted the scrap to the page. The scraps of paper were like Hansel's bread crumbs on the trail through the forest, and Benny had hoped they would lead him to the thing that was supposed to happen, only they hadn't. He stared resentfully at the *Angelus Novus*, who still refused to look at him, keeping its eyes stubbornly fixed to that spot over Benny's right shoulder. The sideways gaze made him nervous, but when he turned and checked, there was still nothing behind him. In the nearby carrels, astronomy boy was still asleep, but now he saw that the typing lady had returned, and he realized she was watching him, and typing, too, as if she was simultaneously studying him and typing up rapid, detailed field notes of her observations. Had she noticed that the slip of paper in her *Grimm's* was missing? He'd never seen anyone who could type so fast. She caught his eye and nodded, but her fingers never slowed. He looked away.

Was she spying on him? Writing up a truancy report to send to the principal? Making notes about his behavior to send to his shrink? He had to be sure, but when he peeked again, she was staring back at her laptop, deep in concentration. Maybe the prescription in her glasses wasn't right, because she alternately squinted and frowned as she peered at the screen, making her face seem quixotic and fierce. He watched her for a while longer, but she took no notice, like all of a sudden he didn't exist. He relaxed then. He liked feeling nonexistent. He started flipping through the Paul Klee book, trying to read about the Angel, but the book was written in a way he couldn't understand, and soon he was yawning and feeling very sleepy again. Maybe it was the meds, or just the soporific effect of the Public Library in the afternoon. He put his head down on the open book, with his nose on the Angel's lap. He listened to the small, quick sounds of the typing lady's fingers. Earlier, her tapping had sounded like raindrops, but now it sounded more like a flock of starlings lifting from a wheat field and then settling again, blending back into the Library's ambient hush. Or maybe not starlings. Maybe waves. Maybe the starlings were changing into waves, washing up on the sand and tickling all the pebbles and tiny broken shells, before receding again. In and out, waves and starlings, the tapping of fingers on a keyboard, the rustle of a turning page, the exhalations of the stars, punctuated by an occasional snore—Benny heard all these sounds, rising and falling, and he knew, too, that they, like the voices he heard, were always there, and would always be there, coming and going, somewhere in the background.

24

The letter that No-Good had tried to shove under the door informed Annabelle that while Mrs. Wong was in the nursing home, getting rehab after her fall, she had turned over her landlord duties to her appointed representative, Henry K. Wong. It went on to say that, as stipulated in Annabelle's lease, tenants were required to keep their units clean, orderly, and free of debris, which included disposing of garbage and recycling that would attract vermin or pose a fire hazard. Finally, it concluded with a reminder of another clause in the lease: that the landlord or her appointed representative was entitled to make periodic inspections of her unit, and therefore would Annabelle please call said representative, Henry K. Wong, to make an appointment for an inspection before the end of the month?

Annabelle was certain Mrs. Wong had not written the letter. She was a tough old bird, not the type to turn her affairs over to her son, and in all the years Annabelle had lived there, she had never conducted a single inspection. Surely her hip would heal quickly, and she would be out of rehab soon. But even so, the letter was worrisome. No-Good was clearly up to something. What if he persuaded his mother to sell? Or used the pileup of Annabelle's archives as an excuse to break her lease, or even evict her? She really needed to get started on the tidying project and deal with the archival backlog before Mrs. Wong came home.

The archives problem was only getting worse. In May, when Annabelle had successfully disputed her layoff and negotiated her redeployment to radio, television, and digital media, she breathed a sigh of relief, thinking the shift away from print would put an end to the ceaseless torrent of paper entering her small house. Once the flow was staunched, she could tackle the backlog, and Benny could help her take all the trash bags out, and they could live in nice, clean surroundings again.

What Annabelle hadn't reckoned on was the company's policy of making DVD backups of all the clips from all the shows on all the major television and radio news channels during the twenty-four-hour news cycles of each day. So, in addition to the daily influx of newspapers and other printed matter, she now had bags full of unrecyclable disks, piling up in every corner of the house and spilling out onto the porch and into the yard.

The accumulation of all that news was depressing.

She took a deep breath and checked the time. Her shift was almost over, and she really needed to get out and stretch her legs. She uploaded the last of her reports, logged off from the portal, and then stood and stretched. Her lower back was still hurting. Maybe she needed one of those new standing desks. She went looking for her coat and her bag. Benny would be home from school soon. She would take a little walk and buy trash bags, lettuce, and something nice and healthy for his dinner, and then while it was cooking, she would tidy up the kitchen so they could sit down and have a proper meal at the table. And maybe on the way to the grocery store, she would stop off at the Thrift Shop and say hi. Now that Benny was back in school, she was less worried about his social isolation and more worried about her own. She was never lonely when Kenji was alive, and she realized she missed the human connection she used to have at the office, too. The Thrift Shop ladies were not friends, exactly, but they were all very nice, and she could pick up something fun for Benny.

The chiming bell above the door, announcing her arrival, was cheery and felt like coming home. She checked to see who was behind the counter and saw it was Jazmin, the Haitian woman who had lost her home in the terrible earthquake. Jazmin had been sponsored by a Christian aid organization, and Annabelle, who had been monitoring the humanitarian aid operations in Haiti, was able to talk to her quite knowledgeably about the recovery efforts, and so they'd hit it off. Jazmin was with a customer, so Annabelle waved and pointed toward the Boys' Clothing section in back.

"Good luck," Jazmin called. She had a grandson in Port-au-Prince who was about Benny's age, and they often laughed about teens and how particular they were about their clothing. Benny always insisted on wearing the same old black hoodie, which made him look like a one of those grungy street kids who panhandled downtown. Surely she could find something nicer that he would deign to put on.

She walked through the Ladies' Clothing section, and then Men's, feeling a pang as she passed a row of hanging flannel shirts. She used to get all Kenji's shirts here, and she missed shopping for him. Autumn was a good time for flannel. She spotted a nice plaid, with thin pink lines running through it. If Kenji were still alive, she would have bought it for him as a present. She would have brought it home, laundered it, and then wrapped it in pretty paper. She pictured him unwrapping it, his face lighting up as he tried it on and modeled it for her. He liked the worn ones that were faded and soft with age. She stood there, stroking the sleeve. Just the other day, she'd clipped an article in the paper about an elderly man who still bought presents for his dead wife, years after she'd passed, which didn't seem strange to Annabelle at all. Just sweet and sad and kind of noble, but maybe it was different if you were a wife. Maybe a live wife buying presents for a dead husband was just pathetic, and besides, Kenji already had enough shirts, and she needed to focus on the memory quilt project with the ones she already had. She'd gotten as far as designing a pattern and calculating the size of the fabric squares she'd need, but when it came time to make the first cut, she faltered. She sat there with the scissors in hand, blades open over the shoulder seam, but cutting into the shirt was like cutting into a body, and she couldn't bring herself to do it.

The Boys' Clothing section had nothing Benny would wear, so she wandered over to the shoe racks. He was outgrowing his sneakers, but the only ones in his size were all worn and battered. Boys were so hard on their footwear. She would need to go to the mall and buy him a new pair.

What next? She stood by the shoe racks and looked around the store. There was nothing she needed, nothing she wanted, but instead of feeling liberated, she just felt discouraged and cheated somehow. She'd worked so hard, surely she deserved something? But there was no help for it. She might as well do the grocery shopping, even though now the thought of making a healthy dinner just seemed like more work and far less appealing. Still, they had to eat.

"No luck today?" Jazmin called. She was sorting through a box of donations, and as Annabelle passed, she unwrapped a yellow ceramic teapot and held it up. The yellow color caught Annabelle's eye like a bright little sun, stopping her in her tracks.

"Oh!" she said. "That's adorable! Can I see?"

"Here you go, honey," Jazmin said. She handed it to Annabelle with a dazzling smile. The teapot was small and perfectly round, with a sturdy handle on one side, a pert little spout on the other, and a lid that looked like a beanie hat with a pompom on top. Annabelle cradled it in both hands.

"I used to have one just like this," she said. "Only it was pink." It had been her favorite teapot, until the night Kenji died. They'd had that awful fight. He'd left. The teapot broke. She remembered crying as she picked up the pieces and put them in a shoebox, intending to glue them together. It wouldn't be any good for making tea anymore, but she could plant flowers in it. She'd seen people do that, use old teapots as planters, and it was awfully clever, but after what happened, she never got around to gluing the teapot or making the planter. She wondered where the shoebox had gotten to. It must be somewhere.

She lifted the lid from the yellow teapot and then turned it over and inspected it for cracks. There was a song about a teapot she used to sing to Benny. How did it go? Maybe the words would come back to her if she bought it. The yellow color was so cheerful, even better than the pink one that got broken, and yet she hesitated.

"You should have it," Jazmin said, smiling her beautiful smile. "It's sunny, just like you. It deserves a nice home."

And hearing this, Annabelle made up her mind. "Thank you," she said. "I will." She placed the teapot on the checkout counter and took out her wallet. The little teapot must be magic, she thought, because she was already feeling so much better.

25

Waves and pebbles, wheat fields and . . .

"Hey . . ."

A whispered voice. A finger on his forehead.

"Hello . . . ?" the voice said.

Benny opened his eyes. His cheek was stuck to the page of a book. Out of the corner of one eye, he could see the curling scrolls of the Angel's hair, and below that, the red and gold heraldic crest of the Royal House of Habsburg. He blinked, and raised his head and found himself nose to nose with a large talking rat.

"Agh!" he cried, jerking away.

The rat, terrified, disappeared, and now he could see that the voice wasn't coming from the rodent at all, but rather from the girl who was holding it in her arms. "Sorry," she said. "Did we scare you?"

He nodded and rubbed his eyes and face, wiping a bit of drool from the side of his mouth. There was a wet spot on the *Angelus Novus*, too, and he used his sleeve to rub it off. He looked up to see if the girl had noticed. The animal had climbed up the girl's arm and slithered down the front of her zippered sweatshirt and was now poking its pointy nose out from between her breasts. It had long whiskers and beady, black eyes.

"Is it a rat?" he asked, trying not to look at the breasts.

The girl turned away and zipped the ferret up inside. "It's not an *it*," she said. "It's a *they*. They're a ferret. A nonbinary, gender-fluid ferret, so don't let them hear you calling them a rat. They hate that."

"I'm sorry," Benny said. "I didn't mean it." And because he wanted to make up for drooling and for being rude and for looking at her chest, he asked, "Do they have a name?"

"Of course they do," the girl said over her shoulder. "Their name is TAZ."

"What kind of name is that?"

"Well, if you mean is it a foreign name, no it's not. It's an acronym, actually. It stands for Temporary Autonomous Zone."

"Cool," Benny said, even though he had no idea what she was talking about. The girl had turned her back to him, so he couldn't see her face, but he could hear her, murmuring into the open neck of her hoodie. He looked over at the adjacent carrels, which were now empty.

"Are animals allowed in the Library?"

"We're animals," she said, shrugging. "We're allowed." She turned toward him and unzipped her sweatshirt so TAZ could poke their ferrety nose out. "But to answer your question, no. So don't tell, okay?" The ferret watched Benny suspiciously from between her breasts. Not that Benny could actually see her breasts. Just the profile and a little dip of cleavage, which, on this girl, functioned like a pocket in which to tuck a pet. The ferret looked smug. They also looked like they knew exactly what Benny was up to.

"They're chill now," the girl said. She turned all the way toward Benny, and for the first time, he got a good look at her face.

"Hey, it's you!" It was Alice. Or Athena. Or whatever. Finally! "I know you. You're Athena, right?"

"Don't call me Athena. That's not my name."

"Oh. I thought—" He stopped because he didn't know what he thought, and maybe he was wrong. She was about the same age as the girl on Pedipsy, pale and thin, with a mop of silvery hair. This girl's beautiful face was decorated with rings and plugs and delicate hardware, but still.

"Is your name Alice?" Benny said.

The girl grinned. "Nope. Wrong again."

Benny frowned. "Sorry. I thought you were this girl I met. In the hospital."

"Yup. That's me."

"So, what's your name?"

"Depends. Here, I'm called The Aleph."

"The Elf?"

"No. The Aleph. *A-l-e-p-h*. Like in the first letter of the Phoenician alphabet. This." She shifted the disgruntled ferret over to one side, unzipped her hoodie and shrugged off a sleeve to reveal her naked shoulder, onto which was tattooed the letter *A*, lying on its side. The horizontal crossbar extended beyond the diagonal lines, and the whole thing was sort of enclosed in a circle:

"It's my artist name. The B-man gave it to me. It's from a Borges short story."

"Cool," Benny said again, wondering. Who was the B-man? And what was a Borges?

She craned her neck and looked at the tattoo, critically. "Well," she said. "I don't know about cool. It's supposed to be an aleph morphing into an anarchist symbol, but it just looks like it kinda fell over."

"That's too bad," Benny said.

The ferret sighed.

The Aleph shrugged. "Tattoos," she said. "You know."

He didn't, but he nodded anyway.

"It doesn't really bother me," she said, readjusting her sweatshirt. "I'm kind of dyslexic when it comes to letters. I see everything upside down. The B-man says that's why I'm a good artist."

The ferret yawned, closed their eyes, put one paw over their nose, and went to sleep. They looked very pleased with themself, nestled between the Aleph's breasts. Benny looked away, aware that the Aleph was studying him.

"I've been watching you," she said. "You've been coming here all summer, and now you're cutting school and falling asleep on books and drooling and shit, so I figured they've got you on some pretty heavy-duty meds and your classmates are shitheads and school isn't really an option."

Benny nodded. She was right. There was nothing more to add.

"What I don't understand is how come you're hiding out from the B-man? He can't navigate up to this level on account of his leg. But I'm guessing you knew that."

"The B-man?"

"Dude with all the bottles. His name is Slavoj but we call him the Bottleman. B-man for short."

"The hobo in the wheelchair?" he asked. "You know that guy?"

The Aleph nodded. "Of course. We take care of him, and he teaches us stuff. He's actually a super famous poet back in Slovenia. That was pretty cool what he did for you, getting you in past Scylla and Charybdis."

"Who?"

"Front-desk librarian and security."

"Is that their names?"

She laughed. "No, dummy," she said. "Of course not. They're from Greek mythology. Charybdis was a whirlpool, and Scylla was this badass sea monster that ate people—"

Warning! Warning!

He took a deep breath. "Don't call me that."

"A badass sea monster?"

"No," he said, in a voice that was too loud for the Library. "A *dummy*." He couldn't look at her, so he looked over her shoulder. "I'm not a dummy."

"Hey," she said, nodding. "Sorry. You're right. That wasn't cool."

"I didn't *need* his help."

"Okay."

"And anyway he's fucking crazy."

The Aleph shook her head. "No. That's where you're wrong. He's not crazy. No crazier than me or you."

Danger! Danger! But no, there was no danger in her words. They just hung there in the air, as a slow puzzlement grew inside him. He felt a sad weight, like cold, wet sand on an empty beach in the middle of winter, and realized he could let the sand bury him, or he could try to walk on top of it. He took a step. Underneath his feet, the sand felt firm, and he knew he was going to risk telling her everything.

"I don't know if you're crazy or not," he said. "But I am."

No—! cried the voice, as the sand started to give way.

The Aleph frowned. "How do you know?"

"Everybody says so," he said, sinking further.

See! the voice said, only now it was a different voice, sneering and mean. *Shut up you stupid asshole just shut the fuck up—!*

"People say lots of shit. Why do you believe them?"

"Because they're right," he said. "I know I'm crazy," and now there was no sand, no ground, no beach, only this voice like a bitter wind, blowing all around him. *First you tell the doctor and she locks your freaky ass up. Then you tell the kids at school, and they fucking hate your guts—*

She spoke from far away. "But how do you know?"

He didn't want her to hate him, too. His body felt numb. He pressed numb hands against his numb ears and started rocking and humming to drown out the horrible new voice that was intoning the word *ASShole, ASShole, ASShole* to the beat of his heart.

"Because I hear shit," he said. He was speaking so quietly she had to lean in.

"Everybody hears shit," she whispered back.

"No," he said. "It's different. I hear things. Voices."

"So?"

He stopped rocking and looked up.

She shrugged. "Lots of people hear voices."

"They do?"

She nodded and held out her hand. The skin on her fingers was stained with paint, and her fingernails were bitten down and ragged. "You're shivering," she said. "And hyperventilating. Do you mind if I touch you?"

He shook his head, but he couldn't stop himself from flinching when she laid her hand on his chest. Under the soft pressure of her palm, he could feel his heart, like a bird, a trapped thing, battering itself against glass. She left her hand there, a small, warm weight, until the wild fluttering slowed and the shivering stopped and he started breathing normally, and then she gave his chest a little push. When she pulled her hand away again, it was cupped, like she was holding something. She placed her other hand on top to keep it from flying away, then she held her hands out and opened them to show him. He heard a pulsing sound, soft and wet and quickly rhythmic, and he looked down and saw. Cupped in her paint-stained hands was his wild, beating heart.

"Here," she said, offering it back to him. "I think I like you, Benny Oh."

BENNY

She didn't really give me back my heart, but that's what it felt like, like my heart had flown out of my body and now it was lying all naked and raw in her hands, beating like crazy, and even though she was offering to return it to me, it didn't really want to come home. My heart was happy, cupped in her hands. It wanted to stay there forever.

The minute she reached out to touch me, I remembered her from that mad dream I had, when the most beautiful girl put her palm on my chest and—well, you know what happened. You read all about it, which is totally embarrassing, even though I know it's natural for a boy my age to have dreams like that. It's just that most boys don't have books following around after them, narrating their most awkward moments, you know?

But the point I'm trying to make here is that at the time of the dream, I hadn't even met the Aleph yet, but I knew it was her. How could I dream about a girl I'd never even met? But I did. She was the girl in my dream, the girl on the ward, and now she was in the Library. And maybe I was already a little bit in love with her, too. Is that weird? I'd never been in love before, so how would I know?

THE BOOK

Strange things happen in Libraries, Benny. The Public Library is a shrine of dreams, and people fall in love here all the time. Maybe you don't believe this, but it's true. Books are works of love, after all. Our bodies may not be made to enjoy the mysteries of corporeal conjugation, but even our driest tomes, the most unromantic among us, can make your dreams come true.

26

"I see you found the Angel," the Aleph said, pointing at the postcard in his Composition notebook as though nothing terribly unusual had just happened. And perhaps nothing had. Benny's heart, although beating somewhat faster than normal, was back inside his rib cage. The Aleph's small, paint-stained hands, which had cupped his heart so gently, were shoved deep into her front pockets. TAZ was still asleep, lodged between her pushed-together breasts, their whiskery nose poking out from her zipped-up hoodie.

Benny looked down at the postcard of the stick figure in the skirt. "Yeah," he said, shrugging, like it was no big deal—like of course he'd found it and of course he knew it was the Angel—but as soon as he said this, he felt like a jerk, and so he said, "I mean, I didn't know it was supposed to be an angel. . . ."

"It's the Angel of History," the Aleph said. "That's what Benjamin called it."

Hearing this, Benny felt both thrilled and confused—thrilled to hear his name issuing from her lips, and confused because he didn't recall ever saying anything about angels or history. Maybe the Aleph was hearing things, too. "I did?"

"Not you," she said. "The German philosopher. Benjamin was his last name. In German it sounds more like Benyameen. His first name was Walter, or Valter."

Benny had never heard of Valter Benyameen, or Walter Benjamin. He didn't know that Benjamin could be a last name, or that names could be pronounced in two ways. This made him anxious. How could he trust himself to be who he was, if his very own name was behaving so unreliably? He hugged himself. He desperately wanted to change the subject, and just then his eyes lit on the little slips of hand-printed paper glued into his Composition notebook.

"Did you write these ones, too?"

The Aleph nodded. She pointed to the first slip. "Mackson stuck this one in your pocket the day you left the ward. A bunch of us like to rendezvous here at the Library, and that's how we get the word out. Mackson said you were cool." She pointed to the second slip. "I put that one in the book you were reading because I didn't want you to give up. But that last one was totally random. You found it on your own."

She was pointing to the third slip, the one about Hansel and Gretel. "It's lyrics from a song by Laurie Anderson," she continued, and when he didn't say anything, she added, "The performance artist? She's super cool."

He still didn't get it. "She sticks random notes in Library books?"

"No, I do. Not just notes. Other stuff, too. The Library is my laboratory. The ward, too. Actually, everywhere is."

"Are you a scientist?"

"Sort of. I'm an artist."

He looked down at the pieces of paper. "Is this art?"

"Well, yes. Or a kind of a Situationist intervention into our intellectual commons. That's what the B-man calls it." She cocked her head and then gestured to the stacks. "If you picture the Library as a manifestation of the time-space continuum, it's like I'm casting these ephemeral threads across time and space for other people to pick up and follow. Like you did." But he wasn't following, so she tried again. "Okay, it's like I'm a nomad, and I'm making bread crumb trails through the labyrinth of the Library's collection, tracing the forking paths of my journey."

"Why?"

She shrugged. "I don't know. I've been doing it since I was a little kid, before the B-man told me it was art. I make connections between things. It's like telling a story."

He looked at the words on the slip of paper and on the postcard. "I don't get it. What's the connection?"

"Yeah, well, some of the lyrics are missing. You probably would have found them if you'd kept looking, but basically in the song, Hansel and Gretel are living in Berlin. That's the part you found. In the next part, Hansel gets a gig in a Fassbinder film, and Gretel asks him about history, and Hansel starts riffing on what Walter Benjamin wrote about the Angel. That's what's on the postcard." She picked up the card and looked at it critically and then handed it back to him. "It's kind of esoteric. I probably should have made it clearer."

He didn't know what esoteric meant, but he agreed. He turned the card over and read the back again.

"The words just stop. What's the storm called, anyway?"

"Progress." She grinned. "It's pretty cool, don't you think? Benjamin says that history is just this one, giant, ongoing catastrophe that keeps piling up junk at the Angel's feet. . . ."

Benny thought about his mother's archives piling up at his feet. It made a lot of sense. He flipped the card back over. She was still talking.

". . . And the Angel wants to go back into the past and fix everything that's broken. It wants to bring the dead back to life, but it can't."

He stared at the Angel, who continued to gaze past his shoulder, and thought about his dad. He swallowed hard. "How come?" His voice sounded funny.

"Because the Angel is caught up in the storm of Progress. It's being blown backward into the future, like this."

She stretched her arms out wide, like wings, and closed her eyes, and he could almost see the sudden violent wind, pushing her backward. She leaned forward, into the wind, and for a moment she just stood there on her tiptoes, balanced precariously on the verge between past and future. But the moment couldn't hold, and when he reached out to steady her, she opened her eyes. The wind died suddenly, and he dropped his hand. The ferret, jostled out of their sleep, blinked and looked at him, annoyed.

"What happened next?" Benny asked.

"Nothing. That's basically it."

He looked at the postcard again. He could totally see it was an angel now. It was a cool image. Sad. "I thought progress was a good thing."

"Well, maybe not if it just keeps piling up more junk and keeps you from fixing stuff from the past."

"I guess."

"That's what Benjamin thinks, anyway," the Aleph said. "The B-man turned me on to him. He's a big fan."

Hearing this, Benny felt his anxiety return. Was this other Benjamin hanging around the Library with the B-man? Would he have to meet him, too? He started rocking again.

"You okay?" the Aleph asked.

"Yeah. This guy Benjamin. Is he like a friend of yours, too?"

"He's dead."

Relieved, Benny stopped rocking, but then he started to worry. It wasn't nice to feel glad when you heard about someone being dead.

"He died a long time ago," the Aleph added.

That was better. If he died a long time ago, maybe it didn't matter so much.

"He committed suicide," she said.

Okay, that was bad again. It was bad when Benjamins started committing suicide, because maybe the tendency went with the name. When he was on Pedipsy, some of the older kids in group were talking about how suicide sometimes ran in families. Hopefully it wasn't true in this case. Kenji's death was an accident, and this other Benjamin wasn't family, but still. He was worried that any Benjamin could be depressed enough to kill himself.

"That sucks," he said.

"He was trying to escape from the Nazis."

Benny's understanding of the Nazis was sketchy, at best. He knew more about the neo-Nazis, that they only liked other white people and hated people of color and so he should avoid them.

"Those were deeply fucked-up fascist times, and the B-man says we're in for it again. He says fascism is on the rise. He says it's an inevitable response to a failed revolution. He says we all need to study history so we're not doomed to repeat it, isn't that right, TAZ?"

She looked down at the ferret, who had woken up again and was poking their nose out. They gave a big yawn, stretched out their paw, and started washing their face. Benny looked away.

"TAZ is getting restless," she said. "I should take them outside. Hey, you wanna come meet the B-man now?"

He didn't, but since it was the Aleph who was asking, he shrugged and nodded. Just then, his phone, which was sitting on top of his stack of books, started to ping. He ignored it and began packing up his stuff. The phone pinged again and so he put it in his pocket.

"Aren't you going to check?"

Since it was the Aleph who was asking, he pulled out the phone and checked. The text was from his mother. *Come right home after school, okay? I'm making a yummy dinner!* ☺ ☺ ☺

"You okay?" the Aleph asked. "Is something wrong?"

Benny shook his head. "It's my mom," he said glumly. "I probably should go home now."

27

The trip to the Thrift Shop had cheered her immensely. She came home, put the spaghetti water on to boil, and then unwrapped the yellow teapot. It was adorable and felt so sunny and nice in her hands. She looked around the kitchen for a place to display it. There was no space on the shelves, so she moved a hamper full of dirty laundry from the kitchen table and set it down there. So far, so good. She brought the laundry to the pantry, loaded the washing machine, and started it. Better. She was making progress.

The kitchen table was still a mess, but thanks to the little teapot, Annabelle was able to *see* the clutter now, and she marveled at this. How quickly her eyes became accustomed to things being a certain way, but when something new was introduced, everything changed and she could see again. The yellow teapot was like a small sun, casting light on its surroundings, and right there, sitting next to it on the table and basking in its rays, was *Tidy Magic*.

She stared at it, feeling goose bumps rise on her arms. How did it get here? It was truly uncanny, the way the little book seemed able to move about on its own. And not just once, but three times! First, jumping off the table at Michaels. Then, magically appearing at Mission Control. And now manifesting here. It seemed like the book could read her mind, like it knew she needed to tidy up and was offering to help.

She checked the clock. She still had to make dinner and clean off the table before Benny got home, but it wouldn't take long to heat up the spaghetti sauce, and if the book was indeed trying to tell her something, she felt she really ought to listen. She cleared off a chair and sat down to read.

TIDY MAGIC

Chapter 1
My True Life

My true life started with my introduction to Zen. Perhaps you have heard the Zen motto that says, "When the student is ready, the teacher appears"? Well, I must have been ready because one morning my first teacher appeared, and in the most unusual and surprising form!

That morning, I'd been extra careful getting dressed for work because I'd just bought a brand-new tiara headband, and I was going to wear it to the office for the first time. I was working for a popular women's fashion-and-lifestyle magazine, a job I got when I graduated from university a year earlier. It was a good job and I had made a few friends, mostly young women who had entered the company when I did. There was a lot of pressure to look stylish, so we often went to the aesthetic salons and spent our free time shopping for designer brands in Shibuya and Ginza, laughing and egging each other on. As we pulled out our wallets, we reassured ourselves that this was "research" and necessary for our advancement in the company, and indeed it was.

Perhaps this sounds like fun, but I wasn't happy. I spent my salary on clothes and fashion accessories, hair products and make-up, but often when I returned home, laden down with shopping bags, I lacked the motivation even to unpack them. Instead, I would drop the bags in the entryway, slip off my shoes, and then drag myself across my one-room apartment, shedding the clothes I was wearing in puddles on the floor until I reached the futon in the corner, where I would collapse into a deep sleep. Sometimes, I woke in the middle of the night, unable even to move. It felt like there was a terrible demon weight pressing down on my chest, and I would lie there until dawn, when the demon would lift enough for me to drag myself from bed, stare into the mirror at my haggard, bloodshot eyes, and begin the lengthy ritual of skin care and makeup and outfit selection that I needed in order to face the day.

That morning, I remember thinking I should be excited because of my new tiara headband, but instead I felt even more out of sorts than usual. None of my outfits were pretty enough to match it, and I was worried that this tiara was too formal for everyday wear. It was made in Italy by a famous designer and decorated with filigree and seed pearls and real Swarovski crystals. I'd been saving up for it for months, but I left my apartment feeling self-conscious and unsure.

During the long train ride into the city, I felt certain the other passengers were staring at my head and secretly criticizing my fashion sense. When I transferred to the subway, I noticed a group of high school girls looking at me with wide, admiring eyes, and this made me feel better until they started giggling behind their fingers. By the time I reached my station, I was in a very dark mood indeed.

When I exited the subway it was morning rush hour and the sidewalk was crowded with commuters. I climbed the stairs to the pedestrian overpass and crossed to the opposite side of the street. Just as I was about to descend, I heard a loud *kaa kaa* sound from overhead and felt a sudden whoosh of air as a crow swooped down from a telephone wire and snatched my tiara headband from the top of my head!

Of course, back then my head didn't look like it does now. Now my scalp is cleanly shaven, but then I had long black hair that fell to just below my shoulders and I was very proud of it. It was so sleek and glossy! I shampooed it every day and went to the salon every two weeks to get my fringe trimmed. Oh, I was crazy about my fringe! I spent hours inspecting it in the mirror. If it was even a millimeter too long or too short, I would suffer terribly. That morning, I'd been careful to secure the tiara to my head with bobby pins, so when the crow snatched it and flew away, it pulled out some of my hairs!

"Ouch!" I cried, and all the commuters on the overpass, who had seen what happened, pointed at me and started laughing. Normally I would have felt ashamed, but at that moment I was too angry at the stupid crow even to care.

A man standing next to me said, "Oh, look, there he is!" And sure enough, there was the thief, sitting on the branch of a gingko tree next to the overpass with my sparkling tiara in its beak!

"Thank you!" I cried, and ran down the steps toward the tree. What was I planning to do? Climb the tree in my high-heeled Prada pumps? The crow seemed amused and so did the commuters, who watched as I stood at the base of the tree, shaking my fist. Then, growing bored perhaps, the crow cocked his head, looked at me with his beady little eye, and flew over a high wall into the garden of a small neighborhood temple. He landed in the branches of a tall, crooked pine and glanced over his shoulder. He was daring me to follow!

There was a gate in the temple wall, and when I passed through into the garden, the busy clamor of the city fell away. It was like stepping backward in time. The air was dense with the ancient smells of moss and leaf mold and incense. I could hear birds chirping, and crickets, and even a tree frog. A raked path curved around a koi pond, and beside it was a stone bench where a teenage girl sat, dressed in her junior high school uniform, drinking a can of cold coffee and scribbling in a diary, killing time before school, no doubt. A monk was sweeping the moss on a small hillock with a bamboo broom, and overhead was the crow thief, perched in the tall pine. I hurried toward him, but just as I drew close, the thief shook his tail feathers, spread his wide black wings, and took off again. I cried out, and the monk and the girl looked up. The crow circled twice over the mossy hillock where the monk was standing, and the third time around, he started to caw. *Kaa! Kaa!*, he cried, and the headband slipped from his beak. I'll never forget the sight of those Swarovski crystals, sparkling and catching the light as the tiara tumbled from the sky. It came to land directly at the monk's feet, and as I ran toward him, he bent down and picked it up.

"Very pretty," he said, turning it over in his hands. "Are these real Swarovski crystals?"

"Yes," I said, panting slightly. "That stupid crow up there stole it from my head when I came out of the subway."

"I can see why," the monk said, holding the tiara up to the light. "May I?" And without waiting for an answer, he put the tiara on his bald head. "What do you think?"

I was so shocked, I didn't know what to think or what to say. He stood there quietly. He wasn't trying to be comic or coquettish. He was just waiting for my answer. His big round head gleamed like polished mahogany. He was wearing the worn, gray cotton work outfit of a monk, which did not match the style of the tiara at all, and so it sat there, clamped on his head, glittering and casting irritable flecks of light on his skin. It should have been funny, but it wasn't. The gaudy, ornate filigree that I'd admired so much in the department store looked tacky on his head, and the Swarovski crystals and seed pearls looked cheap, even though they weren't.

"It's . . . nice," I said.

The look in his clear eyes told me he knew I was lying. He could see right through me, through all my craving and desire, all the way into the deepest hollows of my vain heart. He could see the desperate fear that drove me to try to fill up my life with expensive things. He took pity on me then.

"No," he said. "I don't think it suits me." He took off the headband and held it out to me. "Here," he said. "You put it on."

I did what he said. The thin metal band slid down behind my ears, pinching my head on either side. I couldn't bring myself to look at him. I felt so ashamed.

"Yes," he said, stepping back. "It suits you. It is very cute."

"Thank you," I whispered.

He picked up his broom, and I bowed deeply to him as he walked back to the temple. The crow was watching from the branch of a cypress, and his mocking cry sounded like laughter. The schoolgirl was still sitting on the bench by the pond. I'd forgotten all about her, but she was still scribbling. As I passed her bench, I paused and she looked up.

"Do you think this is pretty?" I asked, taking off the tiara.

"It's okay," she said, giving it only the briefest of glances. I think she was trying to be polite in case I turned out to be crazy.

"It's made with real seed pearls and Swarovski crystals."

"Cool," she said. "Sounds pricey."

"It was." I held it out to her. "You can have it if you want."

She drew back and stared suspiciously at the headband. "Thanks," she said. "But it's not really my style." She closed her diary and stuffed it into her schoolbag. "The kids at school would just beat me up and steal it."

"You could give it to someone," I suggested. "Your mom?"

"She'll think I shoplifted it," the girl replied, getting to her feet and hoisting the schoolbag onto her shoulder. "And anyway, she's pretty corporate. Not really the fairy-princess type, but thanks!" With a quick wave, she ran off.

I put the tiara in my handbag and continued on to work. During my lunchbreak, I went to the washroom and tried it on again in front of the mirror. Under the wan fluorescent light, my complexion looked sallow and the crystals looked dim, and all I could see was the monk's peaceful face and pitying gaze under the thin glittering band.

I called in sick the next day, and then decided to take the rest of the week off, too. I bought some trash bags and started emptying my closet. All my designer clothing I put in large bags. Shoes and handbags went into middle-sized bags, and scarves and jewelry and accessories into small ones. I hauled them all to a designer recycle shop in Shibuya and sold what I could, and then brought the rest to the neighborhood clothing donation center. I found an auction agency online that would buy the rest of my books and CDs and household appliances and furniture. When I was finished, my apartment was empty, and my remaining possessions fit into a carry-on suitcase. I went back to the temple and sat on the stone bench and waited. When the monk came out, I approached him and bowed. I don't know if he recognized me as the silly girl with the Swarovski crystal headband. I was dressed in jeans and sneakers and looked quite different. With my head bent low, I said, "Please. My life is empty and meaningless. I want to leave home and become a monk. Will you help me?"

The rest, as they say, is history. The monk helped me find a place with an old priest who needed help and would accept a female trainee. I quit my job, shaved my head, and took my vows, exchanging all my fashionable clothing for this simple black robe. (Black is always in fashion—very chic!) My coworkers thought that I'd gone mad when they heard, especially when I told them that I was following the guidance of a crow. But later, when they would come visit me at the temple, they saw for themselves how the restless anxiety of my former life had faded from my face. You look healthy, they said. You look happy.

I've thought a lot about the Crow Incident and what happened that morning. Crows are greedy. They like shiny, gaudy things, just like young girls, and my crow had very classy taste! This was my first understanding. But after I'd been at the temple for several years, I came to understand that this crow was a bodhisattva who had taken pity on me, trapped as I was by my attachments and desires, living my cramped, claustrophobic life. The bodhisattva had taken the form of a crow in order to help me wake up to the vast, boundless Emptiness of all things. So this is why I am very grateful to my wise Teacher Crow, and why I am grateful to that Swarovski crystal tiara headband, for being so beautiful.

THE BOOK

28

The first thing Benny noticed when he arrived home was that the back door swung open freely, and the trash and recycling bags that usually blocked it were gone. He stepped into the kitchen and looked around. Annabelle was standing at the counter, emptying a quart jar of tomato sauce into a saucepan. A large pot of water was boiling on the stove.

"Hi, honey," she called. "I hope you're good and hungry. I'm making spaghetti for dinner!"

There were other differences, too. The kitchen table had been mostly cleared off, and he could actually see the surface. Two of the three chairs did not have newspapers or magazines piled on top of them. There was no laundry hamper on the table or dirty clothes on the floor. He heard the swishing sound of the washing machine in the pantry. He went to the refrigerator and looked inside. A brand-new gallon of milk was sitting on the top shelf.

"See?" Annabelle said smugly. "I remembered."

The dirty dishes were gone from the sink. There was a clean glass in the drying rack.

"How was school?" Annabelle asked, stirring the sauce with a wooden spoon. She was wearing a yellow apron over a pea-green sweatshirt with the word *Hawaii* emblazoned in an arc of rainbow letters above a picture of a sea turtle. Annabelle had never been to Hawaii, and the sweatshirt had come from the Thrift Shop. The yellow apron had been a Christmas present from Benny and his dad. There were big, black letters on it that said,

This Is What

AWESOME

Looks Like!

Benny remembered buying it. He was five at the time. Kenji had taken him shopping, and they'd seen it in the store, and although they both knew what *awesome* meant, neither of them had seen the word written before. Kenji tried to sound out the syllables, "*a-WEE-sum,*" which made no sense, and so he asked the sales girl to read it for them. She did, and they thought it was so funny, they bought it. On Christmas, when Annabelle opened it, they told her that she was *a-WEEEE-sum* and totally cracked up. That's how they all pronounced it after that, *a-WEEEE-sum*. It was one of their family jokes.

"Benny? Did you hear me? How was school?"

Benny finished his milk and put the glass in the sink. "Fine."

"Wash it, please," she said. "Are you making new friends?"

"No." He rinsed the glass and put it back on the drying rack. Did a performance artist with a ferret and an old homeless Slovenian hobo count as friends? "I mean, sort of. I guess."

"That's wonderful, sweetie! Maybe you can ask them over sometime to hang out." She gestured with the wooden spoon, sending a few droplets of tomato sauce onto the floor. "I'm tidying up a bit. Getting rid of stuff. Did you notice?"

"Uh-huh." In the center of the table was a yellow teapot, and next to it was *Tidy Magic*. Maybe he'd been wrong. Maybe the book was working. He picked up his backpack and headed toward the stairs.

"Could you set the table, honey?"

He turned back and pointed to the teapot. "What do you want me to do with that?"

"Oh, you can leave it there for us to admire." She stuck the spoon in the saucepan, wiped her hands on her apron and walked over to the table. "Isn't it lovely?"

He shrugged. "I guess."

"Well, I think it's adorable." She picked it up, rubbed its belly. "I think it's magic. A magic teapot." She handed it to him. "Here, rub it. If you rub it and make a wish, it'll make your wish come true."

"I don't have any wishes," he said, staring at the teapot in his hands. No, not true. He wished to go up to his room, but she wasn't finished. She smiled and cocked her head.

"Do you remember that teapot song? I used to sing it to you, and you would do all the gestures." She started to sing. "*I'm a little teapot, short and stout. . . .*" She bent her elbow and placed her hands on her hips. "Come on, do it with me. *Here is my handle . . .*"

She waited, arms akimbo, but he just stood there, holding the teapot stiffly in front of him.

"Okay, I'll do it once and then you can join in. *I'm a little teapot, short and stout. Here is my handle and here is my spout.*" She curved one hand into a limp-wristed, spoutlike position and flapped her fingers. "This is the spout, remember?" She rocked her body from side to side as if she were pouring. "Now you do it."

The kitchen was hot, and her cheeks were pink from the steam. A wispy blond curl stuck to her forehead. Benny gripped the teapot.

"Please," he whispered, trying to breathe. "Mom, don't—"

But she had started singing again.

"*I'm a little teapot—*"

He couldn't bear it anymore. She looked so stupid and hopeful, rocking back and forth, one hand on her big hip, the other hand, limp, dangling in the air. She caught sight of his face then and broke off, suddenly unsure. "Aren't those the right words?"

"*No!*" he cried. Why didn't she get it? He didn't want to hurt her feelings, but she had to stop, he had to make her stop. "That's not what I—"

"What is it, Benny? What's wrong?"

He thrust the teapot at her. "*That's not what it's saying!*"

"Wait!" he heard her call. "Benny, no! Please, I'm sorry! Don't go!" but it was too late, because he had bolted. The back door slammed behind him. He heard the crash of breaking crockery and his mother's voice. It was not the first time he'd heard these sounds commingling. He made for the gate, and then he was through it, and he ran.

29

Bolting was not a great response, but his Coping Cards said that excusing yourself from a high-stress situation and taking a Time Out was an Appropriate Behavior. Not that Benny was thinking about appropriate behaviors when he bolted. He just had to get away. He ran down the darkening alleyway, past the dumpster and the Eternal Happiness Printing Company, leaping clear of the spot where his father had lain dying. The shadowy men and women who lurked in the doorways looked up when they heard his footsteps, but when they saw it was just a small running boy, they went back to their dealings. His passage barely caused a ripple in the sluggish backwaters of the alley.

He ran and ran, arms pumping, sneakered feet slapping wetly against the broken pavement, dodging the puddles and the cracks. Voices rose from the fissures, chanting softly, *Step on a crack . . . Break your mother's back,* and so he tried to avoid them, but the concrete was old and there were too many. *Break your mother break your mother break your mother's back. . . .* He ran faster, trying to outrun them, until he couldn't anymore, and then he collapsed against a damp, brick warehouse wall, hands braced on his knees, chest heaving, gulping air.

He'd come to the end of the alleyway. When at last his heart slowed and his breathing quieted, he noticed that the fractured chant of the cracks had subsided, and now all he could hear was a disorienting absence of sound, like being in a dream underwater. He listened harder. Nothing. He shook his head to clear his ears, which seemed to help. He closed his eyes. Slowly, the sonic world reestablished itself. A cat howled somewhere from deep in the alley, and in the distance, cars were honking down the avenue. He could hear the whistling of the freight trains, now nearer and now farther off, threading up from the harbor and carrying, in their wake of sound, stray images like bits of litter caught in the spiraling updraft of his memory. In his mind's eye, he could see the tall grain silos rising over the train yards, and the cone-shaped mountains of black coal and Day-Glo sulfur on the loading docks, and the floating logs in the booming grounds across the sound. Even with his eyes closed, he could see these things.

When Benny was little, Kenji used to take him to the railway overpass that overlooked the harbor, where the big container ships arrived from Asia to unload their cargo. Their raggedy lines stretched all the way out past the mouth of the sound, and he and Kenji would stand there and count them, ship by ship, and name all the goods they imagined might be stacked inside. *Trucks, tractor trailers, rice cookers, SUVs, Nike sneakers.* Soon the game turned into listing all the stuff they wanted but couldn't afford to buy. *Sony PlayStation 3s, Xbox 360s, Yamaha drum sets, Nissan GT-R sports cars, Yamaha MX-10000 amplifiers, microwave ovens and a brand-new Brother sewing machine for Mom.* He remembered how it felt to stand on the tall bridge, leaning against his father's legs. He could feel his father's hands resting lightly on his shoulders. On the tracks below, he could see men and women doing things in the weedy scrub along the embankments, and he could remember the feeling of his father's warm hands, holding his head and gently steering his gaze away toward the distant mountains. *Look up, Benny! Look up!*

He opened his eyes, surprised to see he was still standing in the alley-way, still leaning against the cold brick. He'd never come this far along the alley before. He thought about going home, but he wasn't ready to face his mother yet. Ahead, the alley opened out onto a narrow perpendicular street, across from which was a small grassy park, an odd sylvan pocket in the middle of the city. A path wound through it, leading to some benches that were arranged in a circle under the arching branches of a big old syca-more tree. The benches seemed familiar. Overhead, an old-fashioned secu-rity lamp cast a theatrical light, illuminating the leafy understory so that it looked more like a stage than a park. In the shadows, ringing the far perim-eter, he could see the silhouetted blue tarps and tents of a homeless en-campment, but the circle of benches in the foreground looked empty and inviting, a good place to sit and wait until he was ready to go home.

He pulled his hood over his head and pushed off from the wall. As he crossed the street and drew near, he recognized where he was. He'd never seen the park at night before, but his dad used to bring him here during the daytime. Kenji would set him down on one of the benches, next to the old Chinese gentlemen who sat there with their newspapers, and tell him to wait while he went off to talk to a man. Benny was never frightened. His dad never went too far, and the old Chinese gentlemen were nice, and sometimes Kenji gave him a piece of bread to feed the pigeons and the crows. When it was warmer, some of the old men brought songbirds in cages to the park so they could enjoy the breezes. Sometimes they would let Benny feed the birds, and then the birds would sing.

At night there were no birds to be seen. The pigeons were roosting in the cornices of the buildings downtown, and the raucous crows were asleep in the sycamore boughs. Black crows hidden in the shadows. Benny couldn't see them, but he sensed they were there, and the thought of them sleeping in the trees calmed him. He headed down the path toward the benches, staying clear of the shadowy tents, and then he stopped. There were voices coming from the grassy patch encircled by the benches. He crouched down behind a trash can and listened. The voices didn't sound like things. They sounded like people. Not many. Just a few. Speaking in English. They hadn't heard him coming because his sneakers were so quiet. He checked his Alert Levels, which were in the Blue Zone (guarded, with general risk of attack). Not terrible, but it was probably better to leave. Cautiously, he stood. He could see them now, three guys, sitting on a tarp on the far side of the bench, passing around a tinfoil take-out container and eating from it. He couldn't tell if they were young or old. They were the color of ash, and the air around them smelled like marijuana. It was Kenji's smell, and Benny's heart beat faster. He meant to leave, but instead he took a step closer on his quiet sneakers.

Leaning against the benches were several large knapsacks with cooking pots and pans hanging off the sides. Two large dogs lay beside them. Pit bulls, with spiked collars around their necks, and leashes made of thick rope. One of the dogs, the paler one, raised its head and pointed its rubbery nose in Benny's direction, sniffing the air.

Warning! Benny froze. The dog got to its feet and started to growl, a low sound, deep in its throat. It was tied to the rope, but still. The second dog stood and started barking.

Warning! Danger!

One of the guys said, "Riker, what's wrong, boy?"

The two dogs lunged. They were fast, and as Benny turned to run, he saw their ropes weren't attached to anything. They cornered him against the trash can, barking and snapping with their big yellow teeth and glistening gums, slobbering lips and pale, horrible eyes.

"Riker! Daisy! Cut it out!" The guy vaulted over the back of the bench. He took hold of their collars, and the dogs quieted. "Hey, man. Sorry about that."

Benny swallowed. His knees were weak, and he felt like throwing up. "That's okay," he said, even though it wasn't, and then a simpering voice echoed, *That's okay, That's okay.* The dogs' ears twitched. They watched Benny intently. They growled like they wanted to bite him.

"They're actually very chill," the guy said.

"Cool," Benny said.

Cool? the voice said, mimicking him. *Not cool, fuckface.*

"We gotta problem here?" one of the other guys called. They had stopped eating and were watching from the tarp. "Who's that?"

"It's just me," Benny said.

Just me? the voice sneered. *Who the fuck do you think you are?*

They were all staring at him now.

"Who are you?" the first guy asked.

"Nobody," Benny said.

Got that right.

"You're not nobody," the guy said. "You're standing there. You're talking. You're somebody. You got a name, Somebody?"

"I'm Benny," Benny said.

I'm Benny. I'm Benny. Shut the fuck up, Benny!

The guy holding the dogs looked him over. "You Chinese, Benny-boy?"

"No. My dad's Japanese. And Korean. I mean, he was. He's dead now. He got run over by a truck."

Oh, poor Benny-boy. You gonna tell them your whole fucking life story now?

"Sounds rough, kid."

"Yeah. He was high at the time."

Why the fuck you telling them that for?

"Gotta stay away from drugs, Benny-boy. Just say no, right?"

"Right."

"Good boy. Wanna partake of some rice 'n' beans?"

"No, thank you," Benny said, even though all of a sudden he was feeling very hungry. He hadn't eaten dinner. He thought of Annabelle, sitting at the corner of her cleared-off kitchen table, eating spaghetti alone, and a big hollow place opened up inside his stomach, a different kind of hunger. "I have to go home now."

Oooh, his mommy needs him. . . .

"Come on," the guy said. "Sit down. I'm Jake and this here's Dozer and Terence, but that's a fag name so we call him T-Bone. You met the animals.

Riker's the pale male, and his bitch is Daisy. Now you know our names, you gotta share some food with us so we know there's no hard feelings. Otherwise we might think you're pissed at us and therefore pose a threat, and then we'd have to kill you. So come on over and cozy up. The rice 'n' beans are good. Fresh."

"Okay," Benny said.

Oh, yes, please just go ahead and kill me, sneered the voice and then fell into a sullen silence as Benny lowered himself onto a corner of the tarp and accepted the sagging tin. *Whatever.*

BENNY

I didn't actually think they were going to kill me. That guy Jake didn't mean it. I could tell from his tone of voice that he was just kidding and trying to make up for his dogs barking at me. Over the years, I've gotten pretty good at understanding tones and voices, even though it's harder with people, because they lie and joke and hide their emotions and say shit they don't mean. People don't come naturally to me, and I've had to study and practice, like when you're first learning to read and have to sound out the syllables. I have to learn people phonetically and then memorize them by rote.

Objects are easier because they tell it straight up. That's one of the differences between people and things. Things don't lie or tease or fool around. They don't hide their feelings. You can tell when a thing is happy or sad or bored or mad. Especially mad. Oh, yeah, when a thing is pissed off, it lets you know it. It cuts you, or pinches you, or suddenly stops working. It slips from your fingers and breaks, or simply disappears—like, totally vanishes—and no matter how hard you look for it, you can't find it. You've probably had experiences like this with your wallet or your keys, so you know what I'm saying is true.

I'm pretty sure that's what happened with Mom's teapot that night. I mean, I wasn't actually there when it broke, so I couldn't swear to it, but I think that kamikaze teapot just got pissed off at the whole situation, with her singing that stupid song, and hurled itself at the refrigerator. Mom said she dropped it, but I found a piece of the spout under the fridge, on the opposite side of the kitchen from where she was standing, so I have a feeling it did more than just slip from her hands. I think that teapot was making a statement.

Anyway, I hung out with those guys for a while until their dogs relaxed and decided they liked me and licked my hand. The guys were older than me, but they didn't seem to mind that I was just a kid. They called me Kid, and asked me where I lived, and what I was doing out on the street when I should be at home doing my homework. I told them that school wasn't an option, and they laughed and said that was cool. At first I wondered if they were young hobos, but the hobos I'd seen acted pretty random, and these guys had camping stuff and seemed more together. When I asked if they were vagabonds, they thought that was hilarious, but then they said sure. I didn't know what a vagabond was, exactly, but my mom used the word, and I liked the way it sounded. I thought maybe if I studied them, I would figure it out. This is what I mean about learning people.

The whole conversation about vagabonds made me think of my mom. I knew she was probably freaking out, and I didn't want her calling the cops, so after a while I told the guys I had to go, and they let me. The alleyway was really dark. It's creepy during the day, but at night it's insane, so I kept my head down and my hood flipped up. Before, I'd been running too fast to see, but on the way back I went slower, so I had time to notice all the junkies shooting up and doing wicked stuff to each other in the shadows. Sometimes, when they saw me coming, they'd say shit, but when they realized I was just a kid, they left me alone. Then, when I was almost home, the weirdest thing happened. I heard a noise up ahead, and these three crazy-ass hookers in their tight skirts and high-heel shoes came wobbling toward me down the alley and stopped right under the streetlight by the Gospel Mission dumpster, pretty much exactly on the spot where my dad died. They started falling all over each other, screeching and pointing at the ground, and I swear I thought it was my dad's ghost until I saw something moving in the shadows that looked like animals. Cats, I thought, but when I got closer,

I saw it was a family of skunks, a mother skunk and her little baby skunks, all in a line. The hookers were stoned out of their minds and they were crying *So cuuuute! So cuuute!* and trying to catch the babies, but then they'd trip over their high heels and fall down and have to haul each other up and try again. I guess they wanted to take the baby skunks home as pets or something, but then all of a sudden the mama skunk sprayed them. I was pretty close, so I could smell it and it really stank, but I'd already reached our back gate and made it inside. The kitchen was dark, and I could still hear the hookers screaming, and I could smell a little skunk on me, too, but I didn't care. The whole scene was just so weird and random, and honestly, I didn't blame that mama skunk one bit, because she was just protecting her babies. I went to the refrigerator to get some milk, and that's when I saw the broken spout from the teapot on the floor. I picked it up. The edge was sharp and jagged, and I expected it to hurt me or say something mean or blaming, but it was mute, and for some reason this made me really sad and I started to cry.

"Benny?"

It was my mom, standing in the dark doorway to the hall, still wearing that stupid sea turtle sweatshirt. She turned on the kitchen light, and when she saw me crying in front of the open refrigerator, she rushed over and grabbed me. "Oh, God, Benny! Are you all right? Did something happen?"

I shook my head, and she kind of inspected me all over, and when she saw I was okay, she hugged me. "Oh, Benny. I was so worried! I went out to look for you, but you were gone. You just disappeared! Where did you go? I called the police to file a missing person report but they told me I had to wait, and so I did. I waited and waited. You smell like skunk. Where did you go?"

Usually I don't like it when she hangs on to me, but that night I just let her words wash over me and detached myself the way I'm supposed to do when I feel overwhelmed. It's a coping tool called Self Distancing, and I have a Coping Card for it, but basically, I'm supposed to try to experience the stressful situation like I'm a fly on the wall, and then report on it in the same way a fly would. So the fly would say something like:

Benny's standing in front of the refrigerator and he's still crying a little, and his mom is hugging him too hard, but he's just going with it, even though he can't really hug her back. And she says, Oh, Benny, don't ever do that again, okay? Promise me! I was so worried, it's so late, where on earth did you go? But Benny can't say anything because she's crushing his face into her armpit, so he just stands there, crying into the big sad eye of the sea turtle, and now his mom is pulling away and saying, Are you sure you're all right, Benny, why are you crying? And she's wiping the tears off his face with her sleeve, but new tears keep coming, and he hands her the broken spout and says, I'm fine, Mom, really, and then he says, I'm sorry about your teapot, and somehow just saying I'm sorry makes him feel better. . . .

THE BOOK

That fly on the wall isn't a coping tool, Benny. It's the sound of a young person finding his voice, and in the world of books, this is nothing short of a miracle. When a young boy finds his voice, or a young girl tells her own story for the first time, these are causes for great celebration, and all of us, from the most ancient tablets inscribed in clay to the cheapest dime-store paperbacks, take note and rejoice, because without your voices we wouldn't exist. So listen! It's happening right now, as we speak, but it's important not to rush. These things take time, and we must go slow.

30

Days pass. Benny gets up in the morning and goes to the Library. He comes home in the late afternoon. In between, he sits at his carrel, mooning over the scraps of paper he's pasted in his notebook, waiting for the Aleph to appear again, and when she doesn't, he wanders up and down the levels, looking for her. He's in love, after all. Muttering *Valter Benyameen, Valter Benyameen* under his breath, he dives deep into the stacks and returns to his carrel with an armful of books by the German philosopher, hoping to

THE BOOK OF FORM AND EMPTINESS · 217

study up so he can impress her, but he quickly gets discouraged when he can't make sense of the words. He's accustomed to incomprehensible words when they're floating about in the air, but these ones are in books. What's the point of words in books if they don't make sense? he wonders. Then, several days later, as he is despondently eating an apple, his phone pings, alerting him to the arrival of an email in the fake account he made for his mother. It is from the principal's office.

"Dear Mrs. Oh," the email reads. "This is a reminder that you are required to provide a letter from your child's primary care physician, confirming the necessity for medical absences of over three days. Your child has been absent for over a week, and we still have not received the letter. Please contact us as soon as possible to discuss this matter."

DANGER!

Benny stops chewing. His throat constricts, and a big piece of apple catches and gets lodged there. He chokes and coughs and swallows, and eventually the apple goes down, but a sharp edge of its skin scrapes against the soft tissue of his epiglottis, bringing tears to his eyes.

The typing lady looks over at him. "Are you all right?"

He nods, embarrassed, and wipes the tears from his eyes.

"Gotta watch them apples," she says, and since Benny is no longer choking, she goes back to her typing—

No, that's not quite accurate. She doesn't go back to her typing. She's never not been typing. Even as she was speaking to him, her fingers were moving, and now, as she watches, they are still moving, and once again it seems as if she is observing him and typing up those detailed field notes of hers, documenting everything she sees. She observes him as he grips his cell phone, noticing that his fingers are damp and they have a slight tremor. He appears to have gained some weight recently, and she wonders if he's being medicated. She watches as he navigates to the drafts folder of the fake email account, where, sure enough, he finds the email with the note he forged, which he forgot to send because he's been so busy falling in love and freaking out about his mother. The typing woman can't see the email, of course, but she notices the frown on his face, the deep furrow that gathers between his brows as he rereads the note, checking it for errors.

PATIENT'S NAME: BENJAMIN OH

DIAGNOSIS: PRODROMAL SKITZOAFFECTIVE DISORDER

To Whom It May Concern:

Benjamin Oh has been addmitted to the Pediatric Psychiatry Ward at Children's Hospital under my supervision and will be absent from school until further notice.

Sincerely,
Dr. Melanie Stack, MD,
Board-Certified Psychiatrist

She watches as he taps Send and sits back in his chair, closing his eyes, breathing hard. He lets his hand with the phone in it fall to his lap. He is clearly in distress, and she wants to go over to him, to rest her palm on his damp forehead and stroke his hair, to comfort him, but she knows she can't. That would be intrusive. Inappropriate. She knows she shouldn't meddle, and so she watches and types on.

THESE ARE THINGS that Benny could not have known, things that only we can tell you, because we are a book and Benny is just a boy. He couldn't read the typing lady's mind or access her thoughts. He was aware only of the robotic commotion inside his own mind. *Warning! Warning! Danger! Danger!* The furrow in his brow deepened as the clamor grew and soon was too much for him to bear, so he lay his head down on the stack of books and hummed a tune—

Hey, diddle diddle, the cat and the fiddle, the cow jumped over the moon —until he fell asleep.

31

Annabelle leaned against her kitchen counter, crushing ants. The ants were coming from a seam behind the sink where the drywall had crumbled, leaving a gap. The ants lived in the gap, and from there they mounted their campaigns of pillage. Today they were laying siege to the toaster. They had formed a ragged line that traversed the back edge of the sink, disappeared briefly under a pile of dirty dishes, and reappeared from behind an old sponge. Occasionally a scout ant would break from the ranks in order to investigate a curl of dried spaghetti stuck to a plate or a smear of tomato sauce, but their primary objective was the toaster, with its trove of crumbs, which they hauled, crumb by crumb, over a stack of mail and back to their bunker.

The mail was mostly junk and flyers, a few bills, and another letter from No-Good, which she had been just about to open when she spotted the ants. Annabelle didn't like ants, and the important thing now was to intercept them and crush them with her forefinger, a task she performed with mechanical efficiency, ant by ant, but still they kept coming. It was astonishing, really. Sometimes they would stop next to a fallen comrade and wave their antennae over the twitching body like divining rods, dowsing for life, but then they would fall back in line and move on. You had to admire them, Annabelle thought, as she crushed another, but try as she might, she couldn't. No admiration, no compassion. Nothing. It was as if she'd run out of feelings, which was strange, because she'd always had so many. Too many, really. But ever since the Teapot Incident, she'd run dry.

She had called Dr. Melanie the following day to schedule an appointment for Benny and then asked the doctor if she could join the session. Sitting on the little blue chair, she had recounted what had happened, how she was tidying up and making a nice spaghetti dinner when Benny came home from school, and she showed him the cute yellow teapot she'd bought at the Thrift Shop and started singing the teapot song for him.

"It was one of his favorite songs, when he was a toddler. Isn't that right, Benny? I didn't mean to upset you. I was hoping you'd remember. I thought it would make you laugh. . . ."

Dr. Melanie turned toward Benny, who was sitting hunched over on his chair, the green one, looking tense and miserable. The doctor was wearing fuchsia-colored nail polish today. "Benny? Can you tell us what it was that upset you?"

"No."

"It was the words of the song," Annabelle said, prompting him. "You told me they were wrong."

"I don't remember."

Annabelle turned to the doctor. "Do you know that song?" She placed one hand on her hip and stuck the other one out in a spoutlike gesture.

Benny groaned.

"*I'm a little teapot, short and stout. Here is my handle and here—*"

"Yes, of course," the doctor said.

Annabelle dropped her arms. "At least I thought those were the words. Benny used to do all the hand movements. It was so cute."

Benny shuddered and seemed to grow smaller. The doctor studied him. "Was that the problem? That your mom got the words wrong?"

"No," he said. "It wasn't that."

"Was it the teapot, then? Did you hear it say something?"

He shook his head. Ever since his discharge from Pedipsy, he'd been lying to Dr. Melanie about the voices, telling her they'd stopped. He'd been lying about so many things—about his absence from school, about how he spent his days—but this time, he wasn't lying. The teapot hadn't uttered a word. He'd heard it shatter, but he was already in the alley by then.

Dr. Melanie turned to Annabelle. "Can you tell me exactly what Benny said?"

"Yes. I was singing the song, and he said, 'That's not what it's saying.' He was very clear about it. And very upset."

"Benny, do you remember saying that? Your mom says that you said, 'That's not what it's saying,' which implies that you thought the teapot was saying something other than what your mom said it was saying . . . right?"

He pressed his hands against his ears. There were too many *said*s and *saying*s for one sentence to bear, and each one was being swallowed up by the one behind it in a way that seemed infinitely regressive and scary, like small fishes being eaten by bigger ones.

Dr. Melanie leaned forward to get his attention. "Sweetie, would you take your hands away from your ears?"

He obeyed. Dr. Melanie didn't like it when he covered his ears because it meant he wasn't listening. "I made a mistake," he muttered.

"A mistake?"

He started counting breaths in his head. "No," he said between numbers. "Not a mistake. I lied."

"You lied about the song?"

"Yes." He exhaled and squeezed his eyes tight. Why was she doing this? Couldn't she tell he was trying to count? "I mean, no. I lied to my mom about the teapot. It didn't say anything."

"You lied to me about the *teapot*?" Annabelle said. Her question rose, high and thin and started doing weird stretchy things, twining into the air and coming at him like fingers. "Why would you lie about *that*?"

Cornered now, he turned on her. "Because you were being so fucking weird! And you wouldn't stop! I didn't want to hurt your feelings, so I just said some random thing about the teapot!"

His face was flushed, and his eyes were wild and furious. Annabelle had never seen him like this, like an alien had taken possession of his body and was yelling at her from inside his mouth. She gasped and recoiled, and as she did, the leg on the little blue chair gave way and she fell to the floor, landing with a great thump on her bottom. She closed her eyes and sat there splay-legged and dazed. She heard Dr. Melanie's voice, asking if she was all right, and she nodded. She opened her eyes. Benny was looking down at her with an expression of unconcealed disgust. He turned to the doctor.

"See?" he said, as if this proved something.

The rest of the session was murky. The doctor helped her up and provided her with a proper, adult-sized chair, and she sat off to one side while the doctor asked Benny about school and how he was feeling. Benny didn't talk much. Annabelle couldn't remember what he'd said. She just remembered feeling big and clumsy.

At the end of the session, Dr. Melanie asked Benny to step out into the waiting room, and then she had given Annabelle a lecture about caring for the caregiver. She talked about airplanes and oxygen masks, about self-care and support networks, about stress and burnout and learning to ask for help. Annabelle listened and tried to pay attention. She could tell Dr. Melanie was trying to be kind, but coming from her mouth, *kind* sounded an awful lot like condescending. And the doctor was right, of course. How could she take care of her son properly if she didn't take care of herself? She was failing even at that.

Annabelle crushed another ant. She was more than willing to get help, but who could she ask? The Thrift Shop ladies? She didn't have any friends she could confide in. What she needed was a therapist of her own. Or a priest. She thought about Aikon. A Zen monk seemed like someone you could talk to, and after reading the first chapter of *Tidy Magic,* she'd actually started writing a fan letter, but then she deleted it. Stupid idea.

One of the scout ants was making a foray over to the pile of junk mail, crossing a glossy pink flyer on top. What was it hoping to find there? Annabelle extended the forefinger of death and brought it down on top of the scout. The small body felt hard beneath her fingertip, and when she raised her finger, it was still writhing. Ants were surprisingly difficult to kill. She pressed again, harder this time, and that's when she noticed that her finger had landed on a white cloudlike bubble on the flyer, enclosing some words written in a delicate, feminine font.

Anxious? Stressed?
Overwhelmed?

Her finger, still pressing down on the ant's body, had landed right in the middle of the *O* of *Overwhelmed*. How strange was that? She lifted her finger and read on.

What are you waiting for?
Indulge yourself with some
serious, sensuous ME-Time!
Unwind, renew, and refresh . . .
Pamper yourself with our
Deluxe Hot Stone Massage!
Melt away stress with our
Ultimate Aromatherapy!

There was a photograph of a beautiful young lady, lying on a table with a towel wrapped around her head. Her eyes were closed, her shoulders were bare, and her expression was blissful. She looked neither anxious nor stressed.

Zen Serenity
~ a Day Spa and Wellness Center ~
Because YOU deserve it!

The little scout ant was still waving its legs and antennae weakly from the middle of the *O*. Annabelle nudged it gently with her finger. It gave her one final wave, then its tiny body twitched and grew still. It was dead now. Tears came to her eyes. It had offered its small life, showing her a way forward. Carefully she picked up the *Zen Serenity* flyer and used it as a bier, sweeping the ant carcasses onto it. Everyone needed a support network. So what if hers consisted of a colony of ants? Her intrepid scout should go to its final resting place together with its comrades. She thought briefly about giving them a proper burial outside in the yard, but decided that was crazy, and besides she didn't want to run into No-Good, so she brushed their bodies into the trash and then took the flyer and went looking for her cell phone, marveling at this astonishing coincidence. Because it was not just any old Serenity Day Spa. It was a *Zen* Serenity Day Spa. What were the chances?

32

There was that tapping on his temple, and the single raindrop falling, and then the voice whispering...

"*Hey.*"

"Huh?" He opened his eyes and saw the paint-covered index finger. Today the paint was blackish purple. His heart leaped.

"You fall asleep reading again?"

He raised his head and rubbed his eyes, checking his chin for drool.

She examined the titles on the stack of books he'd been using as a pillow. "Wow. You're reading Valter Benyameen?"

She sounded impressed, and he felt his face go hot.

"I wasn't actually reading," he confessed. "I mean, I read the words, but I don't understand what they're saying."

"Yeah, well, maybe you don't have to. Maybe they got absorbed into your head while you were sleeping on them. Like through osmosis."

He didn't know what osmosis was, but he brightened. "You think?" He didn't feel any smarter, and what good would it do to have books in your head if you couldn't understand them? But still . . .

"No," she said, laughing and patting his shoulder. "Of course not. But don't worry. If you really want to understand that stuff, the Bottleman will help. He knows everything. Come on."

She led him to a little-used stairwell and down two flights to Level Five. From there, they crossed into the Old Wing to a distant corner in back of the 331.880 stacks, where the books about the philosophy of labor lived. There were books on countermonopoly theory, industrial democracy, and unions as instruments of class struggle, but they walked right past them. It was okay, though. Books like these do not get a lot of readers in this day and age, and they've gotten used to being ignored and neglected. They lack the vitality to propel themselves off shelves, and yet still they remain hopeful.

At the end of the stacks, Benny saw the door to one of the old men's washrooms. A sign made of bright yellow plastic blocked the doorway. DO NOT ENTER, it said. RESTROOM CLOSED FOR CLEANING, and then, just to be sure, it repeated the message in Spanish. There could be no doubt as to its meaning, and so Benny obeyed, but the Aleph walked right past it, pushed open the heavy door, and held it for him. He hesitated, but a voice boomed from inside.

"Come in! Come in!"

Casting an apologetic glance at the sign, he sidled around it and slipped through the door, which closed behind him with a quiet sigh.

The washroom, being in the Old Wing of the Library, was built to the generous scale of a bygone era, with high, vaulted ceilings and spacious proportions. The walls and floors were decorated with ornate black-and-white porcelain tiles, and the washbasins, countertops, and urinals were made of waxy marble that had softened and weathered over the years. The handles on the heavy wooden stall doors were made of brass, as were the plumbing fixtures, faucets, and pipes. Everything was spotless.

At the far end of the washroom, two men from the Library's janitorial staff were perched on upturned buckets, flanking the Bottleman, who sat in his wheelchair, encircled by the billowing assemblage of white plastic, looking like a king on a cloud-borne throne. His briefcase sat on the floor by his feet, and in front was a small folding card table with a bottle of vodka, a loaf of dark bread, and a large jar of pickled herring with a plastic fork sticking out of the top. A pall of cigarette smoke hung in the air. The three men were in the middle of an impassioned discussion in a language Benny didn't understand. All three were smoking. The Aleph coughed and waved her hand pointedly in front of her face. Crossing the room, she threw open the dimpled glass panes of the heavy old windows, whereupon the men shrugged, ground out their cigarettes in an old soup tin they were using as an ashtray, and raised their shot glasses to her in a toast.

"*Dobrodošli*," they said. "*Na zdravje!*" They drained their glasses, then the two janitors—they were twins, Benny now realized—pocketed their shot glasses and stood to go, clapping him on the shoulder as they passed.

"It stinks in here," the Aleph said crossly, but Slavoj wasn't paying attention.

His watery blue eyes were fixed on Benny, and as Benny approached, the old hobo's big hands lifted from his blanketed lap as if they had minds of their own and began moving through the air in a semaphoric dance that was beyond Benny's comprehension or the Bottleman's control. But the old man barely seemed to notice. He kept his gaze fixed on Benny's face, a steady beam amid all the flapping and clapping.

"Vell, vell, look what we hef here," he said. "It is ze young schoolboy! At last, he hes come."

The hands grew more excited. They spiraled and twined about his head, drawing his arms like the tails on a pair of kites, and causing the old man to rise up in his wheelchair as if he were being levitated.

The Aleph sighed. "Slavoj, this is Benny," she said. "Benny, this is Slavoj. He is drunk."

She placed her hands lightly upon the old man's shoulders, and as soon as she did, his hands dropped to his lap and their dancing stopped. He took a deep breath. "Thenk you, my dear. It is most exhausting when they get excited."

He leaned forward and patted the bucket next to him. "Now, young schoolboy. You must pull up a bucket and we vill talk, but first . . ." He reached for the bottle of vodka and unscrewed the top. "Where is your gless?"

Benny didn't understand.

"He's just a kid," the Aleph said. "It's not like he carries one around with him."

"No metter," the Bottleman said. "We vill fix that." He turned around in his wheelchair and thrust his arm into the mass of shopping bags affixed to the back. The plastic rustled with excitement. When he pulled his hand out again, he was holding a shot glass, which said,

Texas
The Lone Star State

The old man eyed it, critically, and then looked at Benny. "Nah. You vould not meck a good Texan." He thrust his hand back into the mass of susurrating plastic and pulled out another.

Hawai'i
The Aloha State

"This one is better for you, ya?" He handed Benny the glass and filled it, spilling some on Benny's hand. The liquid felt like ice.

"He's too young to be drinking vodka," the Aleph said. She was sitting on her bucket with her arms crossed, watching the old man fill the Lone Star glass. He handed it to her.

"Bah!" he said. "But you? You vill meck a fine Texan. Don't mess with Texas." He refilled his own glass and held it up for them to see. It said,

Arkansas
The Natural State

"Ze natural state," he declared, "is ze best state!" He raised the shot glass higher. "I luff this country. Every state hes a brand, and a motto, too! Do you know vat is ze motto of ze great state of Arkansas? Once upon a time it was *Land of Opportunity*. Beautiful, yes? But then they changed it. Why? Did all ze opportunities dry up? That is one explanation, but now they hef a new motto: *Regnat Populus*. Do you know what *Regnat Populus* means, young schoolboy? If you hed studied your Latin, you vould know. *Regnat Populus* means 'The People Rule.' Magnificent! I hef never been to ze Natural State of Arkansas but I know it must be a democratic utopia ruled by wondrous people. . . ."

He paused and gazed off into the distance. "*O, brave new world, that has such people in't!*" He looked at Benny. "Do you know your Shakespeare, young schoolboy? No? These are words from a play called *The Tempest*. You must read it at once. In it, there is a natural monster by ze name of Caliban who speaks such poetry as vill break your heart. *Be not afeard. Ze isle is full of noises . . .* Vat comes next? Ach, I hef forgotten. Oh, vell. This is how I picture Arkansas to be. It is my dream to go there someday, but until then we must drink to it!"

"You don't have to, Benny," the Aleph said.

"Bah. Of course he does! He is a schoolboy! He must learn to read Latin, recite Shakespeare, and drink wodka!" With his glass in the air, Slavoj waited. "Vell?"

Benny sniffed the vodka. The acrid fumes were making his eyes water. "What?"

"We await your toast."

Benny glanced at the bread on the table. "I don't have any toast."

"Wonderful!" the Bottleman crowed. "He is indeed a natural. No, no, boy, you must *meck* a toast, but not in a toaster. Speak from your heart! Inspire us with your wise sentiments!"

"I don't know how."

"Close your eyes and listen. Now, vat do you hear?"

Benny closed his eyes. He could hear the old man's raspy breathing close by. He could hear the pipes in the wall as someone flushed a toilet in some distant part of the building, but the pipes weren't inspiring. He could hear the hissing and ping of the radiators as steam moved through them, which sounded almost like music. Better. Outside, he could hear the wail of an ambulance in the distance, and then, closer, a voice, softly muttering,

"... *Sounds, and sweet airs that gif delight and hurt not—*"

Startled, he opened his eyes. The old man was gazing at the ceiling, his forgotten glass of vodka balanced on the armrest, reciting in a dreamy voice, "*Sometimes a thousand twangling instruments vill hum about mine ears, and sometime woices that if I then hed wak'd after long sleep, vill make me sleep again ...*"

He sighed and shook his head. "Yes, I remember now. How could I hef forgotten?" He closed his eyes and sat like that for so long that Benny wondered if he had fallen asleep, but then abruptly he straightened and wiped his eyes with his sleeve. "I vill make your toast," he said gruffly. He raised his glass again. "To ze woices!"

The voices? Benny hesitated. He hadn't intended to drink. He had intended to pour the vodka down the sink when Slavoj wasn't looking, but the old man's words took him by surprise, and before he knew it, the glass was at his lips, and the vodka was searing his throat like liquid fire as it traveled all the way down to his stomach. He gagged and coughed as his eyes filled with tears, but when the coughing subsided and he straightened again, he felt a sudden heat, filling him and warming him from the inside. He felt light-headed, almost giddy.

"Shit," he said, shaking his head to clear it.

"It is good, ya?" the old man said, grinning wetly.

"It's disgusting."

"You vant another?" Slavoj asked, raising the bottle again. "You must meck ze toast this time."

"Slavoj!" the Aleph said warningly.

The old man raised his hands in surrender. "Okay, okay!" He lowered his voice and whispered to Benny. "She is like a *muther*."

She wasn't anything like a mother, Benny thought, but he didn't say so. Instead, emboldened by the vodka, he asked, "That thing you said, 'To the voices,' do you, like—" The question broke off before he could finish it. He felt his face go hot.

"Do I like what?"

"No. I mean, do you hear—" Again, the words refused to come.

"Woices?" Slavoj asked huffily. "Of course I hear woices! I am a *poet*." His hands grew agitated again. They stroked his beard, pinched his nose, pulled on his ear, and then one hand started scratching the back of the other. When they'd finished, the old man fixed Benny with a penetrating stare. "Where do you think poems come from? Everything speaks, young schoolboy! But it is only poets and prophets, saints and philosophers who hef ze ears to hear."

"They hear voices?"

"Of course! Socrates! And Joan of Arc! Rilke, Milton, Blake . . . !"

Benny had never heard of any of these people, but he didn't want to look stupid, so he just nodded.

"Moses, Abraham, Isaiah, and all ze prophets!" the old man was saying, tugging on his ear and then clapping his hands together. "And ze fadders of psychology, Sigmund Freud and Carl Jung. Yes, they heard woices, too! Not to mention ze great peacemakers, Mahatma Gandhi and Martin Luther King—"

Finally, someone Benny had heard of. He'd studied Martin Luther King in junior high school. Martin Luther King was a great man and a hero of the civil rights movement. He had a holiday named after him.

"Great modern revolutionaries, they all heard woices and relied upon them!"

Knowing who Martin Luther King was gave Benny the courage to speak up. "But what if you're just a normal person. Like, a kid, I mean. Not a poet or a revolutionary, or . . ." Out of habit, he paused, but oddly he wasn't getting any *Warning* or *Danger* alerts, so he continued. He opened his mouth and the words came tumbling out. "I mean I hear voices, too, but I'm not any of those things. I'm just crazy."

Slavoj snorted. "Nonsense! How would you know? Hef you ever tried composing a poem? Hef you tried contemplating a philosophical question, or leading a revolution?"

"No."

"Vell, there you go. You cannot possibly know since you hef never tried, so I suggest you try immediately. You must start small. Start with a short poem, or a simple philosophical question, or a smallish revolution. No, wait, this country is not quite ready for a revolution. Save ze revolution for later."

Benny glanced over at the Aleph. Her eyes were closed, but he could tell she was listening. "I don't get it," he said. "What should I do?"

"Compose a poem!" the old man said. "Formulate a philosophical question! And if it is indeed ze case that you are unable to do either, then we may conclude you are truly mad."

Benny stared at his shoelaces. A question seemed easier than a poem, but he didn't know difference between a philosophical question and a regular one. He thought about the poems he used to make with the fridge magnets, but he wasn't supposed to touch them. His mother used to read him nursery rhymes when he was little. Did they count as poems? They were more like songs without music, and sometimes he found them soothing. *Hey, Diddle Diddle.* That was a good one. And *Hickory, Dickory Dock.* And *Who Killed Cock Robin?*

"Vell?" Slavoj demanded. "Do you hef one?"

Who killed Cock Robin? was a question, but it didn't sound philosophical. "I don't know any," he said, then he remembered the answer. It was the Sparrow. With his bow and arrow.

"Bah!" the Bottleman said. "It is our human nature to know questions. For example, you asked me if I hear woices. Why?"

Who saw him die?

"Because sometimes I hear things. And I wanted to know if other people hear them, too."

I, said the Fly, with my little eye. I saw him die.

"And vat vould it prove if others hear them, too?"

Who caught his blood?

Benny shook his head, trying to make the rhyme stop. "It would prove that the voices are real. That I'm not hallucinating or lying or making shit up."

"And vat vould it mean if ze woices are real and you are not mekking shit up?"

I said the Fish, with my little dish. I caught his blood.

It was no use. The rhyme was on a roll now, determined to finish what it had started. Benny raised his voice. "It would mean that I don't have a mental disorder! That I'm not crazy!"

The Bottleman raised his voice, too. "So if the woices are 'real,' then you are not crazy?"

Who'll dig his grave?

"Yes!" Benny cried. "Obviously!"

I, said the Owl, with my little trowel.

"So, obviously, you must determine vat is 'real'!" The Bottleman was shouting now, but the rhyme was shouting, too.

I'LL DIG HIS GRAVE!

It was too much. "But that's the *PROBLEM!*" Benny wailed, clapping his hands over his ears. "I don't know what's real and what's not!"

"*Yes!*" the old man exclaimed. "Precisely! Now you hef your question!"

The rhyme went silent.

Benny lifted his head and listened. He twisted, trying to see if it was still lurking somewhere, but there was no trace of the rhyme, no lingering words nor even a whisper. He looked back at the old hobo, who was beaming at him with his gap-tooth smile. "I do?"

"Most certainly," the Bottleman said. "A good question. Very philosophical."

"What is it?"

"*Vat is real?*"

"But I told you, I don't *know* what's real!"

"Of course not! That is what mekks it an excellent question." The old man picked up the vodka bottle, unscrewed the cap, and started pouring more vodka into the three glasses. "Now we must toast to your question, and then you must go home and contemplate ze nature of reality, and when you hef an answer, you can come back and tell me all about it." He handed the Aloha glass to Benny. "To reality!"

The Aleph stood then. "Slavoj, that's enough," she said. She turned to Benny. "He's drunk. Let's go."

Benny got to his feet. Maybe the old hobo was drunk, but what he said made a weird kind of sense, and suddenly there were a million questions Benny wanted to ask him. They were not philosophical questions, exactly. More just practical. Like, what voices do you hear and what do they sound like? What do they say to you, and do you understand what they mean? Are they kind or cruel, and do they tell you to hurt yourself? Do you hear them all the time? Are they coming from particular things or just floating randomly around in the air?

The Bottleman had poured vodka into the three shot glasses and lined them up on the table in front of him. The Aleph had left and was waiting for him at the door. As Benny turned to follow, the old man started moving the glasses around, swapping their positions like he was doing a magic trick. "Which one is empty?" he asked in a soft voice.

All three were full. Benny didn't know the answer, but he pointed to the Aloha glass in the middle. The old man beamed.

"You are a seer!" he said. "A true prophet!" He lifted the glass. "To emptiness!" He tossed back the shot in a single swallow and wiped his mouth with the back of his hand. "Never be afraid of not knowing, young man. Not knowing is ze practice of poets and sages."

"He's just messing with you," the Aleph said when Benny caught up with her. "He gets that way when he's drunk."

"Yeah," Benny said. "I guess." He turned and glanced back. The old hobo didn't seem terribly drunk. He was sitting in his wheelchair, alert, watching them. All three glasses looked empty now. Benny waved, and the old man waved back. It was funny, Benny thought, as he followed the Aleph out the door. He didn't feel messed with. He felt respected.

33

The Zen Serenity Day Spa was located in a small strip mall between a Subway and a podiatrist. The decor in the reception area was spare, done in soft, minimalist shades of mauve and dove gray. Plush ottomans were scattered here and there like islands amid the potted palms, and the walls were tastefully decorated with artistic photographs of beaches and waves and smooth round stones balanced perfectly on top of one another. New Age music played over the speakers. Annabelle had never been to a spa before and didn't know what to expect, but it all felt very Zen, which was why she was surprised to find the receptionist was a young blond woman named Lori. Lori was very nice, though. She gave Annabelle a clipboard with waiver forms and a long list of questions about her health, and when she was done filling them out, Lori led her back to a treatment room and introduced her to her massage therapist, Leilani, another slim blond, dressed in yoga pants and ballet slippers. When Annabelle stuck out her hand, Leilani just stood there, looking at it as if she had no idea what Annabelle was proposing, but then the realization seemed to dawn on her, and she took

Annabelle's damp hand between her own dry, warm palms and pressed them firmly together—not a shake, exactly, but completely welcoming.

"I'm so glad to see you," she said to Annabelle, as if they'd known each other forever. "Now, tell me what I can do for you." She spoke with a slight Texas drawl, which wasn't very Zen but made her sound totally sincere, and Annabelle, who couldn't remember the last time someone had been sincerely glad to see her, never mind offered to do anything for her, was so startled, she didn't know what to say, and so she said the obvious.

"I'd like a massage, please."

Leilani laughed. "Well, sure thing, hon! We can do that! I'll just step out and let you get yourself ready. We'll start face down."

Annabelle nodded. She had no idea what getting ready might entail. She glanced around the room for clues. There was a table with a sheet over it in the middle. Attached to one end was a pillow-like contraption with a hole in it that looked like the hemorrhoid cushion her stepfather used to sit on. She hesitated.

"Is there something wrong?" Leilani asked.

"Oh, no," she said, and then she surprised herself by laughing. "I thought you'd be Japanese, is all."

Leilani looked confused.

"Because of the Zen? But it's not a problem! It's just that my husband's Japanese. I mean, he was. Japanese. And Korean. And Zen. He's not anything now. Actually, he's dead. But it's fine. I'm fine." But she wasn't fine, and she was just making everything worse. She took a deep breath. "I'm sorry. I've never had a massage before, so I'm kind of nervous."

"Ah," said Leilani, brightening. "Well, it's about time, then, isn't it?" She patted the table. "I'll step out while you get undressed and hop on up. Just make yourself comfy. You can lay on your stomach under the sheet, with your face in the cradle. Take your time."

"Okay," Annabelle said, looking dubiously at the table. "Should I take off . . . everything?"

"Whatever feels right, hon."

She gave Annabelle an encouraging pat on the arm and left. Annabelle looked around. The room was clean and sparsely furnished. There was a sink in one corner, and next to it, a low altar-like table with an offering of crystals. A glowing blue humidifier, shaped like an oversized raindrop, emitted a thin cloud of fragrant steam. On the wall was a round mirror and a row of hooks and a chair underneath. Annabelle undressed, folding her clothes and laying them neatly across the chair. She hesitated, then unfastened her bra and hid it under her sweater. She decided to keep her underpants on.

She turned to the table. It was narrow and quite tall, with a padded surface and spindly legs that worried her, but she clambered up, rolled onto her stomach and faced the cradle. From this angle, it looked like a toilet bowl, but she positioned her face inside it so that her nose stuck through the hole. She had just managed to reach back and tug the sheet over her bottom, when she heard a knock at the door. She didn't know where to put her arms. There didn't seem to be room for them on the table, so she let them dangle.

"Ready?" Leilani called from the doorway.

"Mmph," Annabelle replied. The pressure of the cradle on her face made it hard to talk. She heard Leilani padding quietly about the room. Soft music, like bells or wind chimes, began to play, followed by the whispery sound of a wooden flute. She felt her arms being lifted and tucked in securely by her sides. She could see the toes of Leilani's slippers through the hole as the girl made some adjustments to the cradle and then drew the sheet down her back, exposing her skin to the air. She felt the girl's hands resting in the middle of her broad back. The lightness of her touch made Annabelle feel large, but not in a good way. Not in the expansive, sensual way she had once felt with Kenji—but there was no point in thinking about that. The girl hadn't moved, horrified no doubt at the expanse of back flesh, stretching before her. There was just too much of her, Annabelle thought. This whole business had been a terrible mistake.

"You have such beautiful skin," Leilani said.

Annabelle thought she'd misheard. "I'm sorry?" Her voice was nasal, muffled.

"Your skin," Leilani said. "It's beautiful. So smooth. Like marble. Or alabaster." Her hands were moving now, traveling up Annabelle's spine, kneading the tense muscles in her shoulders and neck. For such a small girl, she was very strong, Annabelle thought, and she relaxed slightly, giving in to the firm touch. The massage oil was slippery on her skin. There was a scent of lavender, and a delicious warmth all along her stomach and the entire front of her body, which seemed to be coming from the massage table beneath her. It must be heated, she thought. How lovely.

"How's the pressure?" Leilani asked.

"Good," Annabelle said, and it was. Just enough to release all the tender aching spots but not so hard as to be painful. Why hadn't she thought of this earlier? It was the most wonderful feeling, to give yourself over into another's hands. No one had touched her body like this since—well, she'd had physicals at the doctor's office, but those didn't count, and they were usually accompanied by warnings from the doctor about high blood pressure and diabetes and how she needed to lose weight. But this girl wasn't scolding her at all. She was using her hands and even her forearms in long, firm, sweeping strokes, digging into the knots with her elbows and excavating what felt like years of tension. It was wonderful. Tears started leaking from Annabelle's eyes. Was she crying? It made no sense, but the tears ran down her nose and dripped off the tip, falling through the hole in the face cradle and onto the floor. She felt her breath catch. Fearing that Leilani would notice, she tried to control the quavering that was building inside, but it was no use. Her breathing grew erratic, and soon her body began to shake. Leilani's hands grew still.

"You okay, hon?" the girl asked. "You need anything?"

Annabelle shook her head.

"Okay. It happens. Sometimes a person just needs a good cry, so you go right ahead, but tell me if you need a tissue or some water, okay?"

A great sob wracked her body, and then another, and then a third, and then there was no help for it. To her dismay, as she wept, the whole table beneath her started to shake, but Leilani didn't seem to mind. She just kept kneading and stroking, traveling from her back to her legs, her arms, and even her feet, long and steady, leaning in to the tight spots. Annabelle wanted to explain, but lying there, with her face in the cradle, there was no way to talk, and gradually, as her tears slowed and her breathing quieted, the need for words lessened. Leilani had her turn over onto her back, placing a lavender-scented pillow over her eyes, and Annabelle lay there, listening to the sound of the chimes and the flute. From time to time, a shudder would travel through her body like an aftershock, but otherwise everything was so quiet and still that soon she drifted off to sleep.

She awoke to the sound of Leilani's voice, gently calling her name. "Annabelle?"

"Oh, I'm so sorry!" she exclaimed. "I didn't mean—" She felt ashamed of her rudeness, but Leilani just laughed.

"Don't you worry. Sleep is good. You must have needed it. Here's some water for you. You just take your time getting dressed, and I'll be waiting outside."

She left the room. Annabelle lay there for a moment, blinking at the ceiling, then she sat up slowly and lowered herself to the floor. She felt unsteady, and so she took a sip of water, which was lemony and refreshing. She got dressed, taking her time, aware of each discreet movement, each small sensation. The pinch of her bra. Her arms, slipping into their sleeves. Her head, emerging from her turtleneck into the light. It was like being in a dream, only she felt more awake than she had in a long time. On her way out of the room, she glanced in the mirror, and the sight of her face made her stop. Her eyes were bloodshot, and her skin was red and mottled. Deep scar-like creases from the cradle seams crisscrossed her cheeks. Her limp hair, matted with massage oil, stuck to her forehead.

Leilani was waiting for her in the reception area.

"I look terrible!" she said as she paid, but Leilani shook her head.

"No," she said, giving her a big hug. "You're glowing!"

Annabelle couldn't remember the last time she'd had a proper hug. On the bus, she noticed people looking at her, but she didn't care. I've had a massage, she thought, meeting their gaze. I am the kind of woman who remembers to take care of herself.

That night in bed, she ran her hands across her cheeks and then down her neck to her shoulders. Traces of massage oil still clung to her skin, her beautiful, alabaster skin. She pulled a tangle of Kenji's flannel shirts to her face, and the faint hint of smoke and lavender tickled her nose. Her hands moved down her body, pausing to touch her breasts, traveling over her belly, and coming to rest between her legs. How long had it been? She couldn't touch herself there without thinking about Kenji, and it always made her too sad. Cautiously now, she moved her fingers back and forth and felt a slight, warm throbbing. She pressed her face into the flannel and thought about how nervous she had been that first night, standing naked in front of him, and how he'd gazed at her, and how his face looked in the light of the streetlamp—or was it the moon? No, the moon was in the alley on the night he died. Her feet kicked restlessly beneath the tangled sheets. *Not that*, she thought, *please, not now*, and her hand responded, moving quickly as she remembered how his lips felt as they traveled down her body, how he cupped each breast and licked the nipple, murmuring, *So smooth, like a peach*. And remembering, too, how, when he lowered himself on top of her and slipped inside, a space opened up to receive him that was empty and infinite. And now her fingers were moving as surely as his, so that when she came, her body arched and a cry tore from her throat, which she quickly muffled with a mouthful of flannel. She lay there, tensed and listening, but the house was quiet. All she could hear was the blood pounding in her ears, and so she relaxed. As her breathing slowed, she remembered this feeling. Melting. Raw, but whole. Spent, but in a good way. That night, she slept.

The next morning, when she went to the refrigerator to get milk for her coffee—milk that she had actually remembered to buy on her way back from her massage—she noticed that something was different. The poetry magnets. The words had been rearranged, and Kenji's poem had vanished. She felt her face flush. *Benny?* Why would he do this when he knew how much it meant to her? She stared at the jumble of words, searching for the old poem, but it was gone, and in its place was something else, a ragged new arrangement.

smooth as a peach in a dream

She stared at the magnetic words, and her knees grew weak.
Kenji . . . ?

BENNY

Shit. Really? I told you my mom's sex life was off-limits. We talked about that, and I thought we were on the same page about privacy issues. I mean, I get that she was missing my dad, and I'm glad that massage made her feel better, but I really didn't need to know the rest, you know? And now I can't ever unknow it, never unsee it, which is totally fucked up.

But actually, maybe I already did know and just blocked it out or something, because I think I remember hearing a voice cry out like that one night when I was asleep. It woke me up, and I lay there in the dark, listening. It definitely wasn't my dad's voice, and it was different from the way that things talk, too. This voice definitely came from a person, and it sounded like my mom, but it wasn't her usual sad crying. This was an earlier sound that I remembered from when my dad was alive and they slept together in their bedroom. A lot of voices used to come from there, but I was little and I didn't understand. Sometimes in the night, when their door was closed, I heard voices that sounded like fighting, and that was scary. Other times I heard voices that whispered and giggled and made me feel alone, but not in a bad way. And then there was another sound that was both scary and lonely-making, starting low like a moan and ending up like a shout or a cheer. Triumphant! This one was more like that. I listened, but when it didn't come again, I fell back to sleep. I wasn't super worried.

But this explains why she freaked out about those stupid fridge magnets that morning. She came into my bedroom, whispering, *Benny, Benny, wake up!* It was still dark, and I thought she was just some random object that was trying to get my attention so I ignored her, but then she started shaking me, and I opened my eyes. She turned on my bedside lamp and her face was all pink and excited. She asked me about the fridge magnets, if I'd been playing with them, and I said no way, because I hadn't. Ever since that time she went ballistic on me for messing with my dad's poem, I stayed away from those magnets. I knew how much they meant to her. But when I said that, she sort of gasped and got this crazed look in her eyes and told me there was a new poem, and if I didn't make it, then who did? She dragged me down into the kitchen to see, and it was true the magnets looked like they'd moved, but honestly it wasn't much of a poem. Just one line, something about a peach. And I was like, maybe you were sleepwalking and you came downstairs and moved them, and she looked at me like I had punched her. I knew what she was thinking then. She was thinking it was from my dad, that his ghost had come back and was making poems for her at night while she was in bed doing whatever she was doing, but I didn't buy it. Even though I hear voices, I don't know if I really believe in ghosts, you know? Spirits, maybe, but ghosts are pretty childish, and anyway I saw my dad's body being burned, and I can't see how any ghost could survive those flames. So it was kind of a mystery, but I just forgot about it. I had other things to worry about.

THE BOOK

Yes, of course. You had an important philosophical question to answer—
What is real?—and were so preoccupied with the nature of your own reality, you were oblivious to how your mother might be experiencing hers.
But that's okay. It's perfectly natural. Children have a limited ability to
understand a parent's inner life, perceiving it through the lens of their own
subjectivity and understanding only as much as impacts them. Children
are remarkably obtuse that way, but not to worry. This is not a criticism or
a reprimand. You were younger then, and we are not a scolding kind of
book. There's nothing worse than books that scold. Nobody wants to read
them. We are simply pointing out a well-documented developmental fact.
There are many books on the subject of child development, but we are not
one of them. Let's move on.

34

They met almost every day in the Library. Benny never knew where or
when the Aleph would appear, but it was always like magic. He'd be in the
stacks, head tilted to one side, skimming the titles on the spines, when

suddenly he'd see her eyes, peering at him through the shelving. Or, he'd be bending over the water fountain, drinking, and when he straightened, she'd be leaning against the wall, watching. She knew all the nooks and crannies in the Library. The corners with the most comfortable couches, where you could sit next to each other and talk. The soundproof listening rooms, where you could lie head to head on the floor and play whatever music you liked, though mostly he played jazz. The chess alcove in the Old Wing, where you could watch the light shine through the stained glass window as you waited for the other person to move her rook or her knight.

He asked her questions, and sometimes she answered, although in general she didn't like to talk about herself. Still, little by little, he learned more about her. How she had run away from home when she was about his age, and except for the times she wound up in foster care, she had been more or less living on her own ever since. In the warm summer months, she slept in trees in the parks, sometimes alone and sometimes with other members of the transcultural, pansexual, postgender radical youth she called her posse. During the day, they foraged in dumpsters and hunted squirrels and pigeons, which they cooked on small rocket stoves made from recycled soda cans. At night, they slung string hammocks between sturdy mottled limbs high up in the sycamores, while down below the Bottleman slept in his wheelchair or on a sleeping mat, crocheted from recycled plastic shopping bags by kindhearted church ladies in Iowa. The posse loved the Bottleman and took care of him. Every night, before bedtime, they gathered around the old poet and listened to him talk about revolution, about the religious ideology of consumer capitalism, about the anthropocentric sentimentalism of his generation that persisted in seeing nature as an Edenic ideal, separate from humans, which humans had fucked up. No, he told them. That is hubris! We are not separate. We *are* our planet, and we must love it completely. We must love our garbage, our pollution, our trash. We must love our trans-earth, our trans-planet, in all its mutable distress. He was better than TV, they said, and they claimed him as their leader, but in a completely nonhierarchical, antihegemonic sense of the word, of course.

In the colder months, they disbanded and moved indoors, squatting wherever they could find shelter. Many of them migrated south to get out of the rain. The B-man had Slovenian connections, and he and the Aleph had moved into an abandoned factory building down by the railroad tracks, on the outskirts of the city in an area that gentrification hadn't yet touched. The windows were broken and boarded up, but rain had caused the plywood to rot and peel. Ghetto palm seedlings sprouted from the windowsills. Weeds and tufts of grasses grew in the crumbling mortar between the bricks, and the pavement below was littered with shattered glass.

The Aleph called it her studio, and one day she texted Benny the location, and he rode over on the bus. He'd never ventured this far from the center of town before. He stared out the window as the bus rattled along the pothole-riddled trunk road, through the defunct industrial fringe. Traffic was sparse. Delivery trucks, battered and unmarked, were the only other moving vehicles, but along the roadside, the skeletal remains of burnt-out cars lay torched and abandoned. The retail stores were boarded up, and there were no pedestrians except for a few twitchy sex workers who loitered near the derelict motels, texting on their cell phones. Hearing a vehicle approach, they would raise their heads and rouse themselves, briefly, before slouching back against the buildings when the bus drove by.

Benny recognized the factory from the picture the Aleph had sent and pressed the button to signal the driver to stop. He got off, and as the bus pulled away, he looked around. The street was empty. A sagging chain-link fence encircled the factory site. His phone pinged, a text from the Aleph.

Follow the fence. Come through the hole.

He walked around the block until he found a place where the chain link had been pulled away from its post. He got down on his knees, pushed his backpack through the hole and then crawled after it.

Go to the loading dock. Look for a white van.

He skirted the perimeter and headed toward the back of the building. He spotted a beat-up white cargo van parked in one of the bays. There were words on the side of the van that said *AAA Security Services.* She was sitting on the edge of the loading dock, and when he rounded the corner she looked up. A single wan shaft of sunlight pierced the looming clouds just then, shining down and illuminating her, and he felt his breath catch because she was so bright and beautiful. She raised her arm and waved. To him. He hurried forward.

"Hey," she said. "You made it."

She leaned down and held out her hand, and he took it, and she pulled him up onto the edge of the dock. She was surprisingly strong. She led him to a door, adjacent to the bays, which she'd wedged open with a broken cinder block. He followed, and the door closed behind them.

It was dark inside. They passed through a large door onto the factory floor, a cavernous room, emptied of machinery, but filled with the odor of grease and sweat that still lingered in the air. He took a step forward and stopped. Pools of leaked oil stained the cement floor. In the dingy yellowed light that entered through the partially boarded-up windows, he could see what looked like ghostly shadows of machines that used to be. The echoes of their voices sounded in his ears—gears cranking, engines thrumming, belts grinding, and something screaming, too. He squeezed his eyes shut and pressed his hands to his ears and started humming, and when he removed his hands, all was silent. He opened his eyes. The ghostly machines were gone and the Aleph was watching him.

"Come on," she said, and her voice echoed, too.

She moved toward a metal door on the far end of the factory floor. The door was ajar, and light leaked from the crack, and when they passed through it, he found himself in a large back room that had once been a machine shop. Bare bulbs hung from the ceiling. An L-shaped worktable stood in a shadowy corner, covered with tools, bottles and random junk. A stack of empty picture frames leaned against the wall. The opposite corner of the room had been converted into a kitchen area, with a deep industrial sink, a hot plate, and an ancient refrigerator. A sheet of plywood balanced atop two sturdy sawhorses served as a table, lit by an old gooseneck lamp. A large soup pot simmered on the hot plate, emitting a fragrant, foresty steam. The Bottleman sat in his wheelchair, bent over the table, eating soup from a bowl. Benny was surprised. How did he get through the hole in the gate? The old hobo looked up when they came in and raised his spoon in greeting. Benny followed the Aleph to the table. She offered him a beat-up office chair and then sat down beside him and went back to eating. The old man wheeled himself over to the hot plate and ladled soup into a chipped bowl.

"You hef brought your spoon," the Bottleman said, handing him the bowl.

It was less a question than a statement of fact. Benny drew his spoon from the side pocket of his backpack. He took a sip of the soup. "Did you make this?"

The old man grunted. He had gone back to eating, and Benny could see that his hand was trembling. He seemed subdued, not at all like he'd been in the Library. His face looked haggard, and his bright eyes were dull. Lank hair hung down on either side of his face, and his beard kept dipping in his soup bowl.

"He made it with mushrooms we foraged," the Aleph said. "Slavoj is an excellent cook. Do you like it?"

Benny nodded and took another sip. The soup was thick and hot, delicious in his spoon. "How did he get here?"

"Like you. On the bus."

"No, how did he get through the fence and into the building?"

Slavoj picked up his bowl and drank the last of his soup. He took a bandanna from the pocket of his jacket, wiped his mouth, and then pulled a chain from the neck of his shirt. Dangling from the end of the chain was a single key.

"It's to the front gate of the factory," the Aleph explained. "The security guard is Slovenian. He's a fan of Slavoj's poetry, plus they drink together.

Or drank, I should say. Because Slavoj has quit drinking. Isn't that right, Slavoj?"

The old man scraped up the last few bits of barley with his spoon, and then he sat there staring into the empty bowl.

"Is he okay?" Benny asked.

The Aleph shrugged. "He's fine. He's just thinking. Or listening. Hard to tell." She stood and cleared the old man's bowl and brought it to the sink. "The point is that he's not going to drink anymore." She laid a warning hand on his shoulder.

The Bottleman sighed and nodded. The Aleph gave him a light pat and crossed the room to her worktable, leaving the old man gazing into the empty space where his bowl had been.

Benny finished his soup in silence. When he was done, he washed the bowls and spoons and put them in the dish rack. He found a ragged dishtowel hanging on a nail and used it to dry them, too. He didn't know what to do next. The old man still hadn't moved. No one was talking. They seemed to have forgotten he was there.

The Aleph was sitting on the far side of the room at the L-shaped worktable, hunched over a work space lit by a halogen lamp. Taped to the wall behind her was a series of drawings that looked like planets from a distance, but when he got closer, he could see they were more like architectural plans, circles with things inside them, each one was different from the next.

"What are you making?" he asked.

The Aleph looked up. She was wearing a strange pair of magnifying glasses with two thick lenses, which made her eyes look huge, liquid and saucerlike. The beam from a high intensity LED light, mounted between the lenses, emanated from her forehead like a third eye. She held up a glass object that looked like an inverted fishbowl. It was a three-dimensional rendering of one of the circles on the wall. The beam from her headlamp shone through the orb, making it glimmer. He stared at it, enchanted. It was a snow globe.

"My mom collects those."

She handed it to him. The globe looked nothing like the cheerful orbs in Annabelle's collection. There were no ballerinas or dolphins or cute little puppies, with pale, glittery snow floating around their heads. There was no snow at all. This globe was catastrophic. The bleak landscape at its base was deathly white, like bleached coral on a long-dead reef. Four ominous cone-shaped cooling towers rose into the sky, towering over a squat building that hunkered below. Tiny people, dressed in uniforms and carrying lunch boxes, were lined up like ants, frozen in the act of entering the building.

"Shake it," she said.

He did, and the glass orb filled with swirling black particles. It was a miniature apocalypse. A nuclear winter. A tiny, devastated world.

"Cool," he said. "The ones my mom has are kind of dumb." He held the orb up to the work lamp, shook it again, and then moved it closer to his eyes. The cold light from the halogen bulb lit the scene from behind. Close up, the tiny people looked bigger, and he could almost imagine being one of them, caught in the swirling storm of soot that settled slowly through the thick, liquid air. He handed it back to her. "What is it?"

She raised the magnifying glasses onto her forehead and squinted at it. "It's supposed to be a nuclear power plant, but the black stuff looks more like coal particles, so I can't decide. It's part of a series."

She turned toward a tall metal shelving unit, looming in the shadows behind her. She flipped the switch on a bank of fluorescents, and in the sudden illumination, he could see rows of wire racks, upon which were displayed dozens of glass globes that flickered to life as the light shone through them. Each one contained a different scene of devastation and ruin. They were miniaturized global catastrophes, frozen in time, captured in glass, eternal and yet contained. The small worlds seemed to beckon to him, drawing him in closer.

"Can I?" he asked, reaching out his hand.

"Of course. That's the point. You have to shake them."

One by one he picked them up, held them in his palm and shook them, enlivening them, briefly, even as he unsettled them and was unsettled by them.

Some he recognized, like the one, slightly larger than the others, that contained the Twin Towers. He wasn't born when 9/11 happened, but he knew the iconography of the terrorist attack. There was a plane sticking out the side of one of the tiny towers. The other tower was frozen midway into its collapse. Below, on the street, tiny businessmen and ladies in suits were fleeing a cloud of dust. When he shook the globe, the viscous air filled with scraps of paper. There were hands and feet and swirling body parts, too. He put it down and picked up another, depicting a ruined city in the aftermath of a flood. "Is this New York City, too?"

"New Orleans," she said.

Clusters of tiny Black people stood on the roofs of their houses or floated down the streets in boats. When he shook the globe, miniature dollar bills drifted up and floated back down through the liquid. He didn't understand.

"It's disaster capitalism," the Aleph said. "All the profiteering that went down post-Katrina. It was in 2005. You're probably too young to remember that hurricane."

Warning! the robotic voice cried.

"I remember," he lied. He set the globe quickly back down on the shelf. He'd been three years old in 2005. Of course he didn't remember.

Danger!

"You do?" she was saying. "Wow. I don't. I was seven but nobody in my family paid attention to the news. I only learned about it in school later on, when we were studying global warming."

"We studied that, too," he said quickly.

She smiled and cocked her head. "So you know all about it, then." He watched, uneasily, as she picked up the hurricane globe and shook it. "I made this one for a science project in high school, and after I dropped out I just kept making them. I was calling the whole series 'Global Warming,' but that seemed too on point. Now I think it should be 'Desert of the Real' or maybe 'State of Emergency.' But maybe quoting is too derivative. What do you think?"

Warning! Does not compute.

She was watching him, waiting for an answer.

"'Global Warming' is good," he said.

Danger! Danger! I cannot accept that course of action—

"I mean, it's not . . ." He couldn't look at her. He closed his eyes and started counting to ten, and then he said, "Actually, I don't remember that hurricane."

Seriously? The robot was gone, and it was the sneering voice now. The one he hated that was always trashing him and getting on his case. *Why'd you go tell her that, dipshit?*

He forced himself to go on, speaking louder so he could hear himself. "And global warming isn't good, and I don't understand what any of those other names mean, either—"

Good move, asshole! Now she knows you're a lying fuck.

"That's cool," she said. "No worries. What don't you understand?"

The sneering voice fell silent. He opened his eyes. She had gone back to work on the nuclear power plant.

He picked up the Katrina globe and shook it again. The tiny Black people on the rooftop disappeared in the swirl of dollar bills. "How come you put money in it?"

"Because rich people profit from climate disaster. It's good for business. In a neoliberal capitalist economy, there's no incentive for corporations to clean up their act, which means, as a planet, we're fucked." She sighed and put down the globe. "I don't want to make these anymore," she said. "I just decided. This is the last one."

"How come?"

"It's just more stuff. More junk, cluttering up the world. The B-man says we have to learn to love our trash and find poetry in it, and that's true, but there's enough useless crap already without me adding more."

Benny thought about this. He didn't think her globes were crap. He thought they were beautiful. "How can you be an artist if you don't make stuff?"

"Good question." She stood and put the globe on the rack. "Maybe it's time for artists to get out of the studio and move into the streets? I want to focus more on unmaking. On direct action. On interventions. Slavoj says the artist's job is to disrupt the status quo and change the way people normally see things. He says we have to shatter the optical subconscious and make things strange. Wake up from this ideological opium dream we call life." She looked across the room to where the old hobo was slumped over the table, sleeping in his wheelchair. She raised her voice. "Isn't that right, Slavoj?"

He grunted. "Heh?"

"We have to wake up from this ideological opium dream we call life!"

Without opening his eyes or lifting his head, he raised his fist in the air and pumped it, mumbling something that sounded like *Resist!* Then his hand dropped back onto his lap like a bird shot out of the sky. A thin stream of words trickled from his lips—*always mekking something out of nothing, filling ze goddamned world with our somethings, crashing around, bumping into each other, drowning in all ze somethings...* When the trickle of language dried up, he lapsed back into silence.

"He's super hungover," the Aleph said. "Hey, you can take a globe home for your mom if you want."

WHAT IS IT THAT MAKES these small worlds so appealing? What gives them the power to enchant?

On December 7, 1972, the Apollo 17 astronauts took a photograph of a gibbous Earth at a distance of eighteen thousand miles from its surface. The photograph showed the planet, partially obscured by swirling clouds, floating all alone like a blue glass marble in the vast, black infinity of outer space. This historic image, dubbed the Blue Marble, became a symbol of the environmental movement and caused a profound shift in the way people conceived of the planet, shrinking it from something incomprehensibly immense and awesome into a fragile, lonely orb that you could cradle in the palm of your hand or crush beneath a careless heel.

Even as the Blue Marble was miniaturizing your conception of Earth, it was inflating your sense of importance in relation to it, endowing you a godlike perspective and agency. The image caused, in other words, a derangement of scale, from which you people still suffer. As your anxiety about the disastrous effects of your behavior on the biosphere grows, you console yourself with the thought that by changing a light bulb or recycling a bottle or choosing paper instead of plastic, you can save the planet.

Not you, personally, Benny. We're not saying that you console yourself with thoughts like these. But derangement of scale might explain why, when you take the Aleph's snow globes and hold them in the palm of your hand, weighing each small world against Annabelle's fancy, you find them at once so charming and so unsettling.

BENNY

The one I chose is called 3/11, which the Aleph said is a memorial to the Japanese earthquake and tsunami and meltdown of the Fukushima nuclear plant. Inside the globe, there's this weird catfish with a big Japan-shaped rock pushing down on its head, which she said is because in ancient times, Japanese people believed earthquakes were caused by giant catfish. The water is bright fluorescent green, like Gatorade, which is supposed to give the creepy feeling of radioactive seawater, even though she said real radioactive water wouldn't look any different from normal water, so it isn't totally accurate. When you first hold the globe in your hand, you just see the catfish and the rock in the green water, but when you shake it, all these tiny objects start swirling around. There's a car tire and a Coke bottle and a cell phone and a laptop computer, tangled up in a floaty piece of fishing net. There's also a Nike sneaker and a rubber duck and a Hello Kitty backpack, as well as a bunch of human body parts, like severed arms and feet. And there's some bigger stuff, too—a motorcycle and a truck and a couple of houses, all drifting around in that bright green sludge.

I chose that one because my mom knew a lot about the earthquake and tsunami and the nuclear reactor meltdown. She was monitoring it at work and got kind of obsessed. Her client was some nuclear energy lobby group, so she was tracking the news about the contaminated radioactive water that was leaking into the sea and coming to America. She was convinced that water from our faucets was going to start glowing, but really it was the people she was freaked out about, and of course my dad was freaked out, too, because he had friends over there. He and my mom kept watching all those videos online of Japanese people in their houses and cars getting sucked out to sea by that crazy wave, and my mom kept saying how terrible it would be to lose your family and your house and everything you own. I was remembering all this when I was looking at those snow globes, and I remember thinking that she was totally right about the losing-your-family part, but maybe it wouldn't be so bad if a big old tsunami came through and cleared out some of her crap from our house. I don't know. Maybe that's why I chose it.

I waited until her birthday to give it to her, and wrapped it up and everything, but when she opened it, she seemed kind of freaked out. She wanted to know where I got it, and I couldn't tell her about skipping school and hanging out at the factory with the Aleph and the Bottleman, so I lied and told her I made it in science class. I could tell she wanted to believe me but was having a hard time, because the snow globe was really nice, and I'm not particularly good at making art, which bugs her. She's good at making art, and my dad was good at making music, and I think for her the idea of having an uncreative kid is almost as bad as having a psychotic kid. Anyway, she started asking me all these questions about the snow globe and how I made it, so I just told her what the Aleph said about using Gatorade for seawater so it would feel radioactive. She said it looked very convincing. She asked me if the rubber duck was modeled after the one she found in the dumpster, and I said yes. I was pretty much just making shit up, and I thought she believed me, but then somehow we got into another one of those stupid fridge magnet fights, and so I left. I know it's not really fair, but it pissed me off that she didn't believe me. That was the first night I spent in the Library.

Also, just because I'm not good at making art doesn't mean that I'm not creative. The Bottleman said so, and he's a poet so he knows. He told me I'm supersensitive and have supernatural powers of hearing, which is why I can hear voices, but I just needed to find my own voice and use it to express myself. That's what he does. He hears other voices, too, and he writes them into his poems using his own voice. Actually, what he said was more complicated than that, but I can't remember. I have gaps. Maybe the meds were numbing me out and fucking with my memory. It happens sometimes. That's why I need you. So you can tell it.

THE BOOK

What Slavoj said was this: People are born from the womb of the world with different sensitivities, and the world needs every single one of you to experience it fully, so that it might be fully experienced. If even one person were left out, the world would be diminished. And he said you don't have to worry about being creative. The world is creative, endlessly so, and its generative nature is part of who you are. The world has given you the eyes to see the beauty of its mountains and rivers, and the ears to hear the music of its wind and sea, and the voice you need to tell it. We books are evidence that this is so. We are here to help you.

35

Benny had never been a liar. Annabelle prided herself on that fact. Other mother's sons lied to them all the time, especially the teens, but she was certain her son had never lied to her, at least not until the Teapot Incident, and she could forgive him for that because it was not a selfish sort of lie, but more of a white lie, told to spare her feelings. What a fool she'd been, thinking that a teenage boy would get a kick out of a childish song like that! Of course he was embarrassed, and he had lied, not so much *to* her as *for* her, which was quite sweet, really.

And it was sweet, too, that he'd actually remembered her birthday and gotten her a gift—and such a thoughtful one! "Oh, Benny," she gasped, as the paper fell away and she saw the artfully wrought snow globe inside. "It's beautiful! Where on earth did you get something like this?"

"I made it."

"You *made* it?" She couldn't keep the surprise out of her voice.

"Yeah," he said, standing by her desk in Mission Control, lying as if it were nothing. "In science class."

She held the orb in her palm and studied it, aware that he was watching. "It's exquisite. A real work of art."

This was true. It was a beautiful, if disturbing, object. The craftsmanship of the severed naked limbs, the tiny shoes, and the cell phone was so delicate and fine, she felt sure he hadn't made it himself. He was creative, but not in this meticulous way. Where had he gotten it? Had he shoplifted it? From where? Had someone given it to him, and if so, who? She shook the globe and watched a severed hand chase a Coke bottle through the eerie green air.

"It's Gatorade," he said. "I wanted the water to feel radioactive."

He knew how upset she had been in the aftermath of the Japanese earthquake. Why would he give her something like this? "The rubber duck is a cute touch," she said. "It's like the one I found in the dumpster. Is that where you got the idea from?"

"Yeah," he said, like it was no big deal.

She placed the globe down in front of her workstation with the others. It didn't fit in. All the other globes were cheerful and kitschy and mass-produced, and this one, so bleak and beautifully handcrafted, made all her other little worlds look cheap and foolish.

"It looks good there with the others, don't you think?" The catfish and the Japan-shaped rock, and all the horrid objects floating around them, were made from a popular brand of polymer molding material. She recognized the color palette. "What did you use to make all the things?"

He shrugged. "I don't know what it's called. Some kind of clay. The teacher gave it to us."

"Did you have to fire it in a kiln or something?" She'd made beads and Christmas ornaments using polymer clay. She knew perfectly well you have to bake it in the oven in order to make it harden.

"It just kind of dried on its own," he said.

If he was lying about this, was he lying about other things, too? Had he lied about the fridge magnets?

That morning, a new poem had appeared on the refrigerator. The earlier peach-in-a-dream poem was still there, a scraggly line skirting the upper perimeter of the jumbled word cloud. This new poem was emerging from the cloud further down. At first glance, the words forming the poem seemed randomly positioned, so if you weren't looking you could easily miss it entirely. But Annabelle was always looking. The first two words she spotted—*mother* and *ache*—were positioned so closely together they touched, forming a single new word—*motherache*—whose significance hit her in such an intimate and primal way she gasped. Heart pounding, she scanned the adjacent words, nudging them into neater lines so that the emerging poem was easier to read, and when she was done, her knees went weak and she had to grab the edge of the counter to keep from falling.

sing   motherache
beneath our stormy boy
mad music sad   sea

She stared at the ragged lines of words as tears filled her eyes, and she staggered back, groping for a chair. The syllables didn't quite add up, but it was almost a haiku, and she felt certain that it was from Kenji. That he was nearby. That he had remembered her birthday and knew how lonely she was. That, sensing her *motherache*, he had made this poem for her. From the living room, the news of the world spilled from the computer speakers as she sat in the chair and gazed at the poem. She would show Benny when he came home from school. He hadn't believed Kenji had written the peach poem, but how could he not see it now?

SHE LEFT THE CATASTROPHIC snow globe on her desk and led him into the kitchen. "Look," she said, pointing to the refrigerator.

He looked. "What?"

"It's a new poem."

He shrugged. "So?"

He seemed utterly disinterested. Was he pretending? He picked up an open bag of Dorito corn chips from the counter and started eating them.

"It's beautiful, don't you think?" Annabelle said.

He filled his mouth with chips, cocked his head, and studied the words more closely. "It doesn't make sense," he said, still chewing. "It should be stormy *sea*, not stormy *boy*. 'Beneath our stormy *sea*, sad *music*, mad *boy*.' The words are in the wrong places."

Was this a lie, too? Feigned or not, his casual indifference infuriated her, and her tone of voice betrayed her anger. "Was it you?" she demanded. "Don't lie to me, Benny. I need to know. Did you make this? Did you move the magnets?"

He lost it then. "No!" he yelled, hurling the Dorito bag at the counter, scattering chips across the floor. "How many times do I have to say it? I *never* touch your stupid magnets! If you want to make up poems and pretend it's Dad talking to you, fine! Go ahead. Because you're *way* fucking crazier than I am!"

He was telling the truth. She saw it. "Benny," she said, "honey, I'm sorry! It's no big deal.... Wait, don't go! I didn't mean—"

But it was too late. The door slammed. He clattered down the rotten wooden steps, out the flimsy gate, and went careening down the darkening alley. The thin thread of her apology trailed behind him, straining, straining, until finally he outran it, and it snapped.

36

The guys were on their tarp, smoking reefer in the sylvan pocket. The pale male named Riker lifted his putty-colored nose and started barking, but when he recognized Benny he stopped and wagged his tail.

"Hey," Jake said, moving over to make room. "Check it out. It's the B-man."

Benny looked around. There was no sign of the Bottleman in the park. "Do you guys know him?" he asked, taking a seat on the corner of the tarp.

"Know who?"

"The B-man. The guy in the wheelchair with all the bottles."

Jake took a long toke. "Nope," he said, sucking in smoke. "You're the B-man, dude—except you're a kid, so maybe B-boy is better." He held out the joint to Benny, who hesitated but then took it.

"Why can't I just be Benny?"

"'Cuz Benny's a fag name, like Terence here." He reached over and slapped the guy called T-Bone limply on the arm. "Am I wight, Tewance?"

T-Bone yawned and raised his middle finger. "Fuck you, too." He looked at Benny. "You gonna smoke that joint or just admire it."

Benny had never smoked pot before, but he knew the smell from when his dad came home late from the club and slipped into Benny's bedroom to kiss him good night. Skunky and sweet. He looked down at the wet tip. "I've never smoked before."

The three guys stared and started laughing. "*Sheeet*," Jake drawled, exhaling a long stream. "What you waiting for?"

Benny blamed his meds for the gaps in his memory, but actually it was the pot. Here then, briefly, is what happened: he smoked, he choked, and the guys thought it was hilarious. They made him do it again, and again, and again. He needed to practice until he could inhale without coughing, they said, and by then his throat was raw and he was so dizzy he had to lie down. The stars above were spinning long threads of silvery light that arced and rippled through the inky black sky, and the old cast iron streetlamps in the park looked like giant lollipops with their hazy orange halos. The ember from the tip of the joint was red, then black, then red again, going round and round and round.

Someone came shimmering through the orange light, swinging a bat. The dogs didn't bark. They knew him. The guys knew him, too. His name was Freddy. Or Frankie. An F-name. Dressed in black. Leather jacket. Jeans. Stuck his hand in his pocket, pulled out a wad of money and threw it in the middle of the tarp, fist-bumped the others, then noticed Benny, splayed on the grass. Pointed at Benny's head with the bat. *What's that?*

That's the B-boy, dude. He's cool. Just a kid. First time smokin weed. Stoned out of his mind.

Then Freddy was standing above him, blocking out the stars. The blunt end of the bat was pressing down on Benny's forehead, pinning him to the ground. *You cool, B-boy?*

The bat pressed harder. *Yes. I'm cool.*

Leave him alone, man.

The bat was blunt. The bat was bad. The bat was evil. It was boring through his forehead and into his brain. *I'm cool. Really.*

Funny, you don't look cool. You look queer. You look like a fucking faggot.

From deep inside his brain, the evil bat began to jeer. *Queer! Queer! Faggot! Faggot!*

Please . . . , Benny whimpered, but the jeering grew louder, and Freddy was looming over him, and the guys were all laughing, and the evil bat was pressing down. He had to make it stop, and so he lunged for it.

No! he cried. *Shut up! Just shut up!*

The bat recoiled.

He made another grab for it. *You just shut the fuck up!* But this time the bat came down hard, and the night sky exploded.

37

Annabelle ran after him, stumbled down the back steps and though the back gate, but she was too slow, and by the time she reached the alleyway he was out of sight. She went back in, found her phone and called him, whispering—*pick up, pick up, pick up, pick up*—as if through the force of her will and her words, she could somehow compel him to answer. But he didn't. Answer. Instead, she heard his muffled ringtone, coming from somewhere in the house.

He'd left his phone behind.

She followed the ringtone, a cheerful tinkling melody, up the stairs and into his bedroom, where she found his backpack hanging from the back of the chair. She unzipped the side pocket. His phone screen was lit up. *Call from Mom*, it said. The avatar he'd assigned her was the rubber duck.

The tinkling stopped and the screen went dark. She could see her dim reflection in the black glass. Where had he gone? She unzipped the backpack's main compartment. Inside was a book on medieval armor and another on Byzantine garden design, both from the Public Library. She found his school notebook but no textbooks. His empty lunch box, his glass marble and spoon. The key to the house.

Should she call the police?

The first time he ran off, after the Teapot Incident, she had called the precinct and the officer had informed her that there was a twenty-four-hour waiting period for filing a missing person report. He told her just to be patient and wait, and sure enough, Benny had come home on his own, two hours later. He hadn't really run away after all—he was angry and needed to work off steam—and he would come home this time, too. She just needed to do what the officer said. Be patient and wait. She would give him two hours. Maybe three.

If Kenji were alive, he would go out and look for Benny, while she stayed at home in case he came back. If Kenji were alive, he wouldn't need to go looking for Benny, because Benny didn't have problems like this when Kenji was alive. She went back down to Mission Control and googled *What should I do if my child has run away?* She had done this the first time, too, but it was good to be prepared, and there was no shortage of websites with checklists and advice.

- Call the sheriff's department, the state police, and the police from neighboring counties.
- Notify border patrols and the FBI.
- Call runaway shelters, runaway hotlines, and missing children helplines.

It was still too soon to make these calls, but good to know. She moved on down the list.

- Contact your relatives, your neighbors, your child's school friends and their parents. Ask them to notify you if they hear from your child.
- Share your information through social networks.

She didn't have any social networks or relatives. She couldn't check with her child's school friends because he wouldn't tell her who they were. Maybe he didn't have any. Was he lying about that, too? As for neighbors, the ones she and Kenji used to know had either sold their houses or been forced out by greedy landlords when real estate prices started going up. Mrs. Wong was not the greedy type, but No-Good was. She'd seen him out in back again, poking in the trash bags and examining the feeding plat-form, while the crows watched from the alleyway. She'd never responded to his first letter about the inspection, and so he'd left a second. She had read it and put it down somewhere. Where had it gone? She felt a hot flush creep into her cheeks, and she pressed her hands against them to cool them.

The second letter was from a lawyer named Fung, informing her that as per Section 12, Clause 3 of her lease, she was responsible for keeping her unit clean, sanitary, and free of any accumulations of rubbish, refuse, gar-bage, dirt, filth, debris, and dross, and disposing of the same in an appro-priate manner. The letter went on to say that the accumulations of the aforementioned on her porch and in her yard constituted a violation of Section 12, Clause 3 and that she should take immediate measures to re-store her unit to clean and sanitary conditions. Further, the wildlife feed-ing station, which had been illegally attached to the back porch and therefore constituted a violation of Section 12, Clause 2, was attracting vermin and must be removed by the time of the landlord's inspection. Fail-ure to do so would result in legal action.

The letter included a date for the inspection, which she seemed to recall was coming up quite soon, but she had misplaced the letter before putting the date in her calendar. Did legal action mean eviction? The thought filled her with dread. The little house was filled with happy memories even though the neighborhood had changed and she had nothing in common with her new neighbors, who rode expensive bicycles and pushed their children around in enormous German strollers and grew tomatoes and ba-sil in their raised garden beds.

If Kenji were alive, he could make her a raised garden bed. He could help her organize her archives, take the accumulated garbage out, find the missing letter. But if Kenji were alive, the garbage would not have accumu-lated and their unit would be neat and tidy. The letter wouldn't be missing, because there never would have been cause to send it in the first place, and Benny wouldn't be missing, either.

She returned to the kitchen and put on her raincoat. She wrote a note to Benny and taped it to the door. Leaving the door unlocked, she went back out into the alley. If Kenji were alive, he wouldn't have waited to go looking for his son.

38

"Bats vant to hit," the B-man said, peering over the Aleph's shoulder as she pressed a wad of wet paper towels against the lump on Benny's forehead. "It is not their fault. It is their nature. Vat they are made to do."

"They're made to hit baseballs," the Aleph said. "Not boys' heads. That guy's a fucking asshole." She dipped a cotton ball in hydrogen peroxide and daubed at the bump, wiping away the last of the dirt and blood, and then she unwrapped a gauze bandage.

"Do you know him?" Benny asked.

"He's a dealer. Scum. They're all scum. Stay away from them." She brushed his hair back and taped the bandage to his skin. "It's not as bad as it looks. Any place else?"

Benny raised his shirt. There was a red bruise on his ribs where Freddy had kicked him, before Jake pulled him off.

"That looks like a boot," Slavoj said. "Not a bat."

"Yeah," Benny said. He winced as the Aleph pressed it with her fingertips, and felt a strange surge of pleasure mixed in with the pain. He was still a little stoned, and she was standing so close. He studied the tattoo on her forearm, tracing the constellation with his eyes as the stars turned into scars. He shook his head to clear it.

The old man sighed. "Boots are made for walking," he said. "But they are complicated. Not simple, like bats, or guns, or vacuum cleaners. Bats vant to hit. Guns vant to kill—"

"It's just a bruise," the Aleph said. "I don't think the rib's cracked."

"Vacuum cleaners vant to clean. . . ."

She turned away.

Disappointed, Benny pulled his shirt down. "Our vacuum cleaner at home doesn't want to clean," he said. "It's never wanted to clean. It doesn't suck."

"Sad," the old man said. "A vacuum that doesn't suck hes lost its raison d'être. A boot that kicks a boy hes lost its moral compass."

They were in the staff bathroom in the basement of the Library, and the Library was closed. How did Benny get here? Again, his memory is vague. All he could remember was the crack of the bat, the boot in the gut, and then someone pulling Freddy off him. He scrambled to his feet then, and fled. Clutching his ribs and keeping his head down, he cut through the alleys and side streets, arriving at the Library just as it was closing for the night. Somehow he made it up to Level Nine, crossed the vertiginous footbridge, and crawled beneath his carrel. He was very stoned. His head was throbbing and his ribs were, too, and it felt like the whole universe was expanding and contracting to the rhythms of his pain. In the distance, he could hear librarians making their final rounds, collecting stray books onto the trolleys, and the muffled, syncopated rattle of the trolley wheels as they paused and then receded. He could hear all the small noises the building made as it settled in for the night: the low drone of the air vents; the hum of the dehumidification; the clicks and buzzes and whines produced by the panels and timers and automated switches that controlled the vast and intricate pulmonary system of the Library. A cold wind rose from the Bindery, making a hollow, yearning sound, like breath across the mouth of the bottle. Somewhere in the distance, a carpet cleaner turned on, and he found the heavy whir and drone comforting. He curled onto the side that didn't hurt and fell asleep, and that's where the Aleph found him, a few hours later, when once again he woke nose to nose with her ferret.

She took one look at his face and reached for his hand, leading him silently down the frozen escalator and from there into a back stairwell to the subbasement. The echo of their footsteps was swallowed by a humming sound that grew louder the lower they went. They spiraled down until they reached the heavy subbasement door, where a sign said BOOK PROCESSING—AUTHORIZED PERSONNEL ONLY. The Aleph pulled it open, and the humming sound flooded the stairwell.

"Come on," she whispered.

He stepped through the doorway and stopped. He was standing at the edge of the large concrete atrium, filled with carts and sorting tables. Above his head wound an intricate system of ramps and chutes and conveyor belts designed to move books to their processing stations. He had watched all this apparatus from high above, fascinated by the mechanical movements of the belts, only now everything was still. He tilted his head back and looked up the nine levels to the vaulted top of the New Wing, where the girders of the precipitous footbridge gleamed in the dim light. How many times had he paused on that bridge and looked down over the railing, and now here he was at the bottom.

He took a step forward, but she grabbed his arm. "No, not that way. That's the Bindery." She led him in the other direction, to the staff room, where the B-man was waiting.

The staff room was sparsely furnished with a stained gray couch and chairs, which had survived successive trends in public sector decor only to be demoted to the subbasement. There was a kitchen nook, equipped with a coffee maker, a microwave, and a sink. An old Hoosier kitchen table with a chipped, white enamel surface and painted wooden legs stood by itself in the corner. A refugee from a 1940s farmhouse kitchen, it looked out of place there, lonely and uncomfortable amid the bland institutional furnishings.

She brought him to the bathroom and cleaned him up, but you know this already. He watched as she put away the first aid kit, and then he followed her back out into the staff room, where she pointed to the couch and told him to lie down. When he moved her coat and knapsack to make room, the knapsack started to thrash. He jumped back, but it was only TAZ, who'd been sleeping in the knapsack pocket. They stuck their head out and gave Benny a look full of umbrage before vanishing again in a huff.

Benny sat and looked around. The Bottleman was making popcorn in the microwave and heating water for tea. His briefcase sat on the table next to a stack of paper, which looked like a manuscript of some kind. The effects of the pot were wearing off, and the strangeness of the situation was beginning to dawn on him.

"What are you guys doing here?"

"I have a meeting in town tonight," the Aleph said, taking a sweater from her knapsack. "And Slavoj needed more paper, so we decided to stay here." She was standing right next to Benny, her torso at eye level, and when she raised her arms to pull the sweater over her head, her T-shirt lifted, too.

"The Library just lets you stay?" He could see the top curve of another tattoo, disappearing into her jeans. He wondered what it was a picture of, and how far down it went. A silver ring pierced the edge of her belly button.

Her head emerged through the turtleneck, and she made a face, like *What a dumb question*, and then gestured toward the B-man, who was rooting about in the staff refrigerator. "No, of course not. He's got friends on the janitorial staff who let us in. Big poetry fans."

"Those two guys he was drinking vodka with in the washroom?"

"Correct." She started digging around in her knapsack, and the ferret stuck their head out, prepared once again to be outraged. But seeing it was only her, they yawned and fixed a baleful eye on Benny.

"How did you find me?" he asked.

"TAZ found you."

"How did TAZ know I was there?"

The Aleph made that face again, like, *The answer is self-evident, so you must be an idiot*. "They're a ferret, Benny. That's what they do."

Her tone of voice stung. The ferret gave him a smug look. Benny felt his cheeks grow hot, and he turned away so she wouldn't see.

"Hey," the Aleph said. She sat down on the sofa next to him and put her hand on his knee. "I didn't mean to be harsh. I was just worried about you."

He couldn't believe his ears. Or his knee. He glanced down, and sure enough, her hand was resting there. He held his breath, not wanting to move in case she took her hand away, in which case his knee might never forgive him, but aware, too, that he needed to do something because she was waiting. He wanted to say something nice back to her, but he didn't dare. Inside, his heart was slamming against his injured rib, and he was afraid if he opened his mouth, it would scramble up his throat and hurl itself at her and burrow, beating, in her lap or between her breasts, because how could he trust it? How could he know that hearts do not behave like ferrets? He kept his lips tightly sealed and glanced sideways at her. She smiled.

"You're tired," she said, squeezing his knee lightly, which caused it to tremble. "Probably in shock, too. Lie down and rest. Slavoj is here. I'll be back in a while."

"Where are you going?"

"Checking out a couple dumpsters and then meeting up with some friends. It's this peer support group we're starting for kids diagnosed with mental illnesses. I'll tell you about it later."

"I can come...."

"No, you need to rest."

"I'm okay."

"No. Stay."

She put a hand on his chest, pushing him down onto his back. The light pressure of her touch lingered as he lay there. He could see a little star from the tattoo on the underside of her forearm, poking out from her sleeve, just above her wrist. He wanted to ask her about it, but before he could, she was standing and pulling on her coat. She zipped the ferret snugly back inside the knapsack and slung it over her shoulder. She walked over to farmhouse table and picked up the Bottleman's mug, ignoring the look he gave her. The mug had words on it that said:

I'm A Librarian.
What's Your Superpower?

She sniffed inside, but it was only black tea. "Good," she said.

He shrugged, like, *What did you expect?* She went back to the couch where Benny was lying, watching her every move, and placed her fingertip in the middle of his forehead.

"Rest," she said, tapping lightly, and he closed his eyes.

Suddenly he was very, very tired.

39

A big fat moon was rising at the eastern end of the alleyway, bathing the length of the street in a dull silvery light. She looked one way and then the other, but the alley was empty. Which way had he gone? Perhaps if she walked, she would meet someone who had seen him, and this thought terrified her. She was a news monitor. She knew the kind of people who lurked in the alleys at night. Knew the things they did.

Benny. She had to find him. She had to find him before something bad happened to him. She shouldn't have waited so long. She should have gone after him immediately. She pulled her raincoat more tightly around her and started walking toward the moon. She passed the loading dock of the Eternal Happiness Printing Company. She heard a noise coming from behind the Thrift Shop dumpster, saw something move in the shadows. Two figures stepped into the pool of light beneath the streetlamp, and seeing they were women, Annabelle relaxed a little. They were tall and slim, wearing pink and platinum wigs, matching tube tops, and tiny hot pants that looked like American flags. They stood there for a moment, checking each other's makeup.

"Excuse me!" Annabelle called, hurrying after them, and when she drew near, they turned, and she realized her mistake. "Oh, I'm sorry!"

The one in the platinum wig narrowed her eyes and looked down at her. "What's the matter, sweetheart," she drawled in a deep voice. "Not what you're looking for?"

"Oh, no," Annabelle said, blushing. "It's not that. . . ." She stood there looking up at them, with their long legs and big wigs, bright lips and tiny patriotic skirts that barely covered their asses.

"I'm looking for a boy," she explained.

They both studied her, thoughtfully, taking in the baggy pink sweatpants and oversized raincoat, and then, as if on cue, they collapsed into each other's arms, laughing.

"Oh, honey," the pink wig sighed, dabbing her eyes. "Good luck with that!" They blew Annabelle a kiss, and she watched as they linked arms and strutted off on their silver heels, butt cheeks twitching in unison, one red-and-white striped, the other blue and spangled with stars.

She headed in the opposite direction. The moon was following her now, so bright it cast her shadow out long, making her look impossibly tall and slender. Cobblestones poked from broken patches in the asphalt, gleaming like wet ocean rocks. She peered into corners and darkened doorways that smelled of skunk and urine. *Benny,* she whispered. *Are you there?*

Furtive shadows flickered in and out between the buildings, rising up like ghosts against the concrete walls and then vanishing when she drew near. Forcing the words past the fear in her throat, she called out, *Please, can someone help me? My son is missing . . .* Her voice sounded loud, but the shadows remained mute. She heard an animal in a garbage pail. A rat scuttled past. *Please, I'm looking for my son. . . .*

She walked and walked, all the way to the end of the alleyway, but no sign of Benny. Just as she was about to turn back, two black-clad figures stepped into the alley in front of her. They were dressed in combat boots and hoods that shrouded their faces. Panicked, she stopped and glanced behind her—as if running was even a possibility—but all she could see was the moon. She could run to the moon, but she would never make it. She turned to face them, and the taller one spoke.

"Mrs. Oh?" The face was in shadow, but the voice sounded familiar. "Oh, hey, Mrs. Oh. I thought that was you."

He pushed back his hoodie. In the moonlight she could see his acne-scarred face.

"Mackson!" she cried, pressing her palm to her chest. "Oh my goodness, you scared me!" She reached out her hand, groping for support, and Mackson caught her by the elbow. His companion took the other arm.

"Oh, thank you," she said, breathing hard. "I feel light-headed . . ."

They led her to a nearby loading dock and sat her down on the steps. The concrete, cold and gritty, sent a chill through her body. She hunched forward and hugged herself. "You scared me. I didn't know—" She looked up. "Mackson, Benny's missing. He ran off down the alley. Have you seen him?"

"Are you his mother?" It was Mackson's companion. Annabelle could see her face now, saw the metal rings in her nose and eyebrow, the ragged halo of white hair.

"You're the rubber duck girl!" Annabelle cried. "What are you doing out here so late at night? It's not safe, you know. . . ."

The girl laughed in a way that made Annabelle feel clueless. "It's cool," she said. "But thanks."

"What happened to Benny, Mrs. Oh?"

"We had an argument, and he ran off. He hasn't come back and I'm so worried. This is the second time he's done this. He has some problems with . . . you know—" She stopped then, because of course Mackson knew, because he had problems, too, and because there was something in the way they were watching her with their expressionless faces—so blank and terribly young.

She put her head down and started to cry.

They walked her home. By the time they reached the rickety blue gate, she had quieted.

"I'm sorry," she said, wiping her nose on her sleeve. "I've had a bad day. I'm not usually like this. It's my birthday. I don't know what's happening."

"Happy birthday," the girl said. "Is this your house?" Without waiting for an answer, she pushed through the gate into the backyard.

"I'm okay now," Annabelle said, following her in. "Thank you." She reached out her hand to Mackson. "If you see Benny, please tell him to come home, okay? Tell him I'm worried."

"Will do, Mrs. Oh. He's probably fine. Just chilling somewhere. Kids, you know?"

They watched her climb the rickety porch steps. The back door closed, the light went on, and her shadow appeared, framed in the kitchen window. In the backyard, they could make out mounds of black plastic, gleaming dully like coal in the spill of the light.

"What is all this shit?" the Aleph said in a low voice. She nudged the closest bag with the toe of her boot and it made a rattling noise. A piece of duct tape, stuck to it, read *Mass Shooting Investigation Coverage / Back-Up*. Mackson squatted and untied the opening. Inside was a cache of CDs and DVDs, and thick stacks of manila folders stuffed full of newspaper clippings, all neatly labeled. *04/02/2012 Oikos U, Goh, Oakland, CA. 07/20/2012 Dark Knight Rises, Holmes, Aurora, CO. 08/05/2012 Sikh Temple, Page, Oak Creek, WI. 12/14/2012 Sandy Hook Elementary School, Lanza, Newtown, CT.*

"Holy shit," the Aleph said. "Is it all like that?"

Mackson opened another bag. "This one looks like it's all wildfires." He opened a third. "And this one's all elections."

"Wait here," the Aleph said. She went to the side of the house. Wedging herself between the fence and the wall, she shimmied up to the window. A venetian blind hung aslant from the top, but she was able to see into the kitchen. It took a moment for her eyes to adjust to the massing of objects and start to pick out details, the garbage bags stacked around the perimeter, the baskets of laundry and tangled clothes hangers, the vacuum cleaner hose wrapped around a table leg, the lid of a salad spinner sticking out of a Priority Mail box. She saw a broken lamp, a drying rack, and a beagle in a mortarboard hat, and in the midst of all this, she saw Annabelle. Benny's mother was sitting in a small kitchen chair, slumped and motionless. Above her was a drooping banner that said, CONGRATULATIONS, GRADUATE!

The Aleph was a gleaner, a freegan, an artist who worked with garbage, but she had never seen anything like this before. As she watched, trying to take it all in, Annabelle raised her head and started talking. It looked like she was talking to the refrigerator.

"Shit," the Aleph said quietly.

40

When Benny awoke, the staff room was dark, save for the green glow cast by the exit sign, and the light from a single desk lamp on the old farmhouse table. It was silent, too, except for a small scrabbling noise, which sounded like a mouse. He sat up on the strange hard couch and looked around. The old hobo was sitting at the table. In front of him was a half-emptied bowl of popcorn, a half-eaten sandwich, and the Superpower mug. The scrabbling noise was not a mouse. It was Slavoj, scribbling. The old poet was writing with a pencil on a sheet of white paper. His back was bent and his big hoary head was swaying back and forth over the paper's surface. Benny's head was throbbing. He touched the bandage on his brow, felt his ribs, and the memory of the evening came back to him. A whimper rose from his throat and he couldn't keep it from escaping into the air.

The old man looked up. "Hey there, young schoolboy. How are you feeling?"

"Like shit," Benny said.

Slavoj nodded. "It vas your first fight?"

"I didn't really fight. I just ran away."

"Smart," the old man said. "You are hungry, ya? I hef saved this for you."
He held out a sandwich.

Benny joined him at the table. Suddenly he was ravenous. He took a
bite. It was roast beef and delicious. He ate until there was no more sandwich left, and then he finished off the popcorn.

"Thirsty?" Slavoj asked, pushing the mug over to him.

Benny looked inside and sniffed. It was vodka, but he drank a sip anyway. The fiery liquid burned as it went down, warming him. He was starting to feel better. The old man had gone back to his writing, bent over the
page.

"What are you doing?"

Slavoj lifted his head and sat up in his chair. "I am writing poetry," he
said, raising his pencil in the air. "Because I am a poet. Because I am a famous poet in my country."

"I know that," Benny said. The briefcase on the table was open. Inside
was an unruly manuscript, whose pages had once been white and smooth
but now were rippled and creased and covered with wild scribbling and
what looked like coffee stains and ketchup. "Are those your poems?"

The old poet nodded. "Ya," he said modestly. "It is my life's work, an
epic poem, my humble attempt to versify ze planet."

"What's it called?"

"*Zemlja*," he said. "In English, it is *Earth*. Not so original, perhaps, but
it is just a working title."

Benny eyed a short stack of paper on the desk. "Are those poems, too?"

"Nah," the poet said, despondent. "Only empty pages." He moved the
top sheet aside, and indeed the pages underneath were blank. He pointed
to the floor, where a large drift of crumpled paper balls had accumulated
by the wheel of his chair, and shook his head ruefully.

"Let me tell you something about poetry, young schoolboy. Poetry is a
problem of form and emptiness. Ze moment I put one word onto an empty

page, I hef created a problem for myself. Ze poem that emerges is form, trying to find a solution to my problem." He sighed. "In ze end, of course, there are no solutions. Only more problems, but this is a good thing. Without problems, there would be no poems."

Benny thought about this for a while. He thought about his mother and her fridge magnets. He didn't write those stupid poems, and that was the truth, but his mother thought he was lying, and that was a problem. He had a lot of problems. "Is that what you write about? Your problems?"

The poet shrugged. "Not so much my problems. But ze world's problems, yes. I listen and write down vat I hear."

Benny thought back to the conversation in the washroom. The old man had told him to contemplate his question—*What is real?*—and he'd tried, but since nothing seemed really real to him, he hadn't come up with a good answer. It was frustrating. Maybe he should try poetry instead. "Do you think I should write about what I hear, too?"

The old poet closed his eyes and silently pondered this question for what seemed like a very long time. When at last he raised his head and started to speak, his words were slow, deliberate. "You are *right* . . . ! You must *write* . . . !"

The words dropped into the silence of the night library like pebbles into a pond, creating ripples as they entered Benny's ears:

(((((right)))))

(((((write)))))

(((((right)))))

(((((write)))))

Usually this kind of thing bothered him, but tonight, oddly, his mind didn't mind.

The Bottleman was still talking. "Write it all down, all ze things that things say. All their problems . . ."

"The problem of things?" Benny asked.

"Of course. Things hef many problems, but people don't listen, so naturally they get frustrated. Of course they do! How do you feel when nobody listens to you?"

"Crappy. But people really don't want to hear what their things are saying. I know because I've tried to tell them. Like my shrink? When I tell her what her toys are saying, she doesn't believe me. She just thinks I'm hallucinating and tweaks my meds."

"I believe you, boy, and that is *her* problem. You can only deal with *your* problem. If you can hear woices, it is your job to help. You must be a secretary. An amanuensis. Do you know vat an amanuensis is? It is a person who takes dictation. Do you know vat dictation is? It is when you listen and write down vat is said. Perhaps it is a poem. Perhaps it is a story. You give form to a woice so others can perceive it."

Benny thought about the fridge magnets again. Maybe a story would be better than a poem. "And then what?" he asked. "What do I do with it?"

"That is not your problem, either. Words find their way into ze world. They are good at that." The old poet handed the boy a blank piece of paper. "Do you hear something now?"

Benny listened. He heard a small voice, the size of a walnut, located just beyond his left ear. He turned and spotted the source: a nozzle in the overhead sprinkler system. "Yes," he said, pointing to it. "That."

"Okay, good," the old man said, handing him a pencil. "Here. Pencils are good at writing. Now you must just listen hard and write down vat you are hearing."

Benny stared at the blank page and waited, but the nozzle went silent. "I can't hear it anymore," he said, discouraged.

"Hm," the Bottleman said. "That happens. Ze emptiness of a page can be unnerving. Too much unformed potential. Sometimes things get self-conscious and clam up. Don't force them. Just try again."

Benny listened. He heard something speaking underneath the table. It was a leg. At first he thought it was the Bottleman's prosthetic plastic leg, but then he realized it was made of wood. He bent down to take a look and saw the painted wooden leg of the white Hoosier table. The leg started to speak, but not in words that Benny could transcribe. There was some pain involved. And sadness. Benny gripped the pencil that was made of wood like the table leg, and this time he felt a strange resonance, like a current running between the two woods, and he was the living conduit. He closed his eyes and brought the sharpened pencil lead down to touch the tooth of the paper, which was made of wood, too, and when the connection was made, the circuits opened and words came spilling out.

THE STORY OF A TABLE LEG

The leg is remembering something. It's remembering a knot. It's remembering a baby tied with a knot. The table leg once had a baby tied to it, and it's remembering the baby tugging. The baby was tied by its leg. The table leg is hard and made of wood, but the baby's leg was soft. Soft skin, soft bone. It was a very young baby.

The table is remembering the mother tying the knot. She was careful and used a scarf. The scarf was soft and yellow with daisies on it, and she tied one corner around the table leg and the other gently around the baby's ankle. The baby was sitting in its diaper on the farmhouse floor, laughing and flapping its arms like it was trying to fly away. Maybe the baby thought this was a game the mother was playing. Maybe the baby—but no, the baby was too young for thoughts, and the table doesn't know about thinking. (What I wrote just now was me, Benny, thinking. This isn't my story.)

The mother kissed the baby and stood up. She filled a bottle with milk and gave it to the baby, but the baby threw it away.

Now why'd you go and do that? the mother asked, or maybe it was the bottle, asking. The mother watched the bottle roll across the floor, then she got a piece of string and tied one end around the bottle's neck and the other around the table leg.

There, she said. She put the bottle in the baby's hand, and this time when the baby threw it, the bottle stayed near.

If you want it, it's right here, she said. She put on her coat and squatted down. I'm sorry, baby. I gotta go. She paused in the doorway. The table leg remembers the tugging as the baby tried to follow. It remembers the baby crying. Now the mother is gone. The baby is gone. The bottle is gone, and the scarf is gone. Only the table leg is still here, in the Library, remembering.

BENNY

After I wrote down that story, the B-man asked me to show it to him. I thought it probably sucked, but he read it and said it was good. He asked me if I really heard the leg saying all the words that I wrote down on the paper, and I told him it wasn't like that. I mean, it's not like I was just making random shit up, but I also didn't hear the words the way you hear words when a person is talking. It's more like trying to write down the kinds of feelings you feel with your body and then remember later on. Like, when you hurt yourself, and later you remember the pain, but the memory of pain is different from actual pain, right? That's the kind of voices that things have, and the stories they tell are more like memories or dreams. You know how a dream can be totally real-seeming, but when you try to put it into words, it just kind of dissolves and melts away? That's what happens to the dream stories of things. Their feeling-voices are impossible to put into words, and as soon as you try, the story starts to evaporate, which was why what I wrote down came out so shitty.

I told the B-man all this, and he said poetry was like that, too, like breezes or winds in the mind. At first you might not feel much, not whole words or sentences, but more like currents of air moving across an open wound. You have to keep your mind open and try to feel the voice of the poem as it blows by, even if it hurts a little. He said the trick is not to grab at the wind because as soon as you do, it won't be there. He showed me with his hand.

He opened it and said to pretend it was my mind, and then he closed his eyes. He said I should hold very still, and keep the hand of my mind open and let the voices come to me. He sat there for a long time with his eyes closed and his palm open, like he was expecting a poem to drop from the sky.

Usually when I hear voices, I try to block them or use a Coping Card to make them go away. It never occurred to me to just let them be. When I told him that, his bushy eyebrows went up his forehead, and he looked shocked. He said my voices were a gift and I should never block them or try to make them go away. He said I must have a strong gift because I did a good job with the table-leg story and I should keep on trying. He said nobody is ever happy with what they write, so I shouldn't feel bad. I don't know much about writing, and I've never been great in English class, so I don't know if this is true or not. You tell me. You're a book. You should know.

Then the B-man asked me if all my voices were like the table leg, and I told him no, that there were different kinds, and some are nice, and some are neutral, and some are evil motherfuckers. And also some are personal and other ones aren't. What I mean is, things like the table leg or a pencil or a shoe are just pretty much humming along, even if nobody's paying any attention. It's not like they're talking to me, even though maybe they know I can hear, so when I'm around they get extra chatty. But it's not personal. They could be talking to anyone. But around the time that those scissors started trash-talking Ms. Pauley and telling me to hurt her, I started hearing a different kind of voice that was totally personal. It doesn't come from any one thing. It's just kind of there over my right shoulder, like an invisible PA system with a small, tinny speaker that follows me around, and when I do something stupid, it starts trash-talking, sneering and telling me I'm a fucking idiot. It's super harsh. When I told the B-man about this voice, he said it was probably the voice of my inner critic. That was news to me. I knew I had an inner robot, but I didn't know about an inner critic. But then he said all creative people have one, sometimes even more than one, and I felt kind of proud and happy, because he thought I was creative.

I didn't tell him about you, because I couldn't really hear you yet.

That night he told me this crazy story about his leg. Not his fake plastic leg, but his real one, the one he doesn't have anymore because he lost it. He'd taken off the fake leg and stuck it in a duffel bag hanging from the back of his wheelchair, and he'd tied a knot in the empty leg of his pants, just below his stump, to keep the breezes out, he said. When I was trying to describe how the voices of things are both there and not there, he kept looking down at the knot, and then he told me that sometimes, when he's half asleep, his leg itches, but when he tries to scratch it, there's nothing there. And I was like, Yes! That's exactly what I'm talking about! It's like your leg is talking to you, or the memory of your leg is talking to you, and even though the leg's not there, you can still feel the itch and it still means something, right? And he said yes, that was right, and that doctors had a name for this. It's called a phantom limb phenomenon, and so maybe what I have is a phantom *object* phenomenon. I thought that was pretty cool, and I told him I definitely have that phenomenon, but I have another one, too, only it's about my dad, because he's a phantom father. The B-man looked really sad then and asked, Where is he?

"Dead," I said. I started to tell him about the night my dad died, but he held up his hand.

"Wait," he said. "I can see this is a good story. It is your story, and you must write it down."

THE BOOK

What is a story before it becomes words?

Bare experience, a Buddhist monk might answer. Pure presence. The sensation, fleeting and ungraspable, of being a boy, of losing a father.

Being a book, we wouldn't know. All we know are the thoughts that arise in the wake of bare experience, like shadows, or echoes, giving voice to what no longer is. And after these thoughts become words, and words become stories, what is left of bare experience, itself? Nothing, the monk might say. All that remains is story, like a molted exoskeleton or an emptied shell.

But is that really all? We books would say no, that story is more than just a discarded by-product of your bare experience. Story is its own bare experience. Fish swim in water, unaware that it is water. Birds fly in air, unaware that it is air. Story is the air that you people breathe, the ocean you swim in, and we books are the rocks along the shoreline that channel your currents and contain your tides.

Books will always have the last word, even if nobody is around to read them.

41

Benny needed paper to write down his story, but the B-man's stock was running low, so they headed to the old Bindery in search of more. The Bindery was the source of blank paper, the B-man said, a repository of unbound words.

"You do not vant to spend too much time inside ze Bindery," he told Benny, strapping on his leg.

"Why not?"

The old man shivered. "It is a spooky place. Ze thrumming heart of ze Library." He wheeled himself from the staff room, leading the way.

Benny followed. "My mom said they closed the Bindery down."

"Indeed, that is vat they vant you to believe."

They were on the edge of the large book-processing area. Emergency exit lights dotted the perimeter, casting just enough light that he could make out the shapes of the wheeled trolleys on either side, laden with rows of books, stacked upright like soldiers, facing outward. Each of the trolleys was marked with bold black numbers on bright blue tabs, which divided the books into battalions, and the books themselves bristled with slips of pastel-colored paper, in green, yellow and pink, bearing the call numbers and key words and other retrieval information. These were the new books, fresh-faced recruits into the rank and file.

"People say ze Bindery is haunted," the old man said, as he navigated his wheelchair through the maze of trolleys. "I hef a different theory. But it is true you can hear sounds coming from there. Weird sounds. Ghostly music."

"Jazz?" Benny asked.

The old man stopped wheeling. He glanced furtively from side to side and then motioned to Benny to lean in close. His bloodshot eyes burned. Mad eyes. The eyes of a poet.

"*Calypssso*," he whispered into the boy's face. His breath smelled like vodka.

"What's that?" Benny whispered back.

"It is music from ze Caribbean. From African slaves who were brought in chains by ze French, back when Black people were traded like things. Those were terrible, terrible days . . ." Softly, Slavoj started to sing, "*Day-o, Day-ay-ay-o. Daylight come and me van' go home . . .*" He closed his eyes. "Ach," he sighed. "Belafonte . . ."

"What's that?"

"Harry Belafonte. A Calypso singer. Beautiful."

"Is he dead?"

"No. But he is very old."

"If he's not dead, how come his ghost is in there?"

"His living ghost, then." The old man frowned and shook his big, shaggy head. "Do not nitpick, young man." He started singing again, and his voice grew louder. "*Come, Mr. Tally Man, tally me banana . . .*" He rose from his wheelchair as though the song were lifting him, unfolding his limbs, one real, one prosthetic, until he was standing. His arms floated out to his sides, and he swiveled his hips, causing his great overcoat to balloon and sway.

Benny watched nervously. "Shouldn't we be quiet?"

The old poet ignored him and began to rotate, hopping awkwardly on his good leg in a circle. "*Daylight come and—*"

Just then, they heard a sudden noise, like a gunshot or a slamming door, and the old man grabbed Benny's sleeve. "Get down!"

They dropped to the floor and hunkered there. Benny listened, straining his ears, stretching the reach of his hearing into the furthest corners of the Library, but he could hear nothing other than the humming sound he'd heard before. Sound is the movement of objects through space, but nothing was moving. The labyrinthine network of ramps and shoots and conveyor belts was still, frozen in time like the escalators. Where was the humming coming from?

"Okay," Slavoj said, climbing back into his chair. "Coast is clear."

They moved cautiously forward through the book-laden trolleys. Benny could hear the wheels of the Bottleman's chair, squeaking behind him. Ahead, affixed to a glass block wall, was a long, dusty blue banner.

THE BINDERY AT THE PUBLIC LIBRARY

The thick glass wall was old, and behind its murky surface was darkness. Benny stopped, and the old man rolled up next to him.

"There it is," Slavoj said, in a low voice. "Ze Bindery. What do you think?"

"Is that where the paper is?"

"Yes. Ze Bindery contains everything. Now you must go inside and fetch it."

"Me?"

The old man averted his eyes and rolled his chair back a few inches. "It is your story. You must go, and go alone."

"But it's your story, too."

The B-man shook his head. "No," he said. "I am an old poet. Ze Bindery is too powerful for me. Anything is possible in ze Bindery. But you are young. Anything is possible when you are young."

Benny shrugged. "Okay."

He walked toward the murky glass wall and stopped to study the sign. It was just an ordinary banner made of blue Tyvek. He listened, but it was silent. The glass was silent, too, and looked normal enough, but with glass you never knew, so he put out his hand to touch it. Pressing his fingertips against the rippled, vitreous surface, he had the odd sensation that were he to apply sufficient pressure the glass would give way like a permeable membrane, and he would be able to pass right through it, but when he pushed harder, the surface remained cold and unyielding. He pressed his forehead against it, trying to see into the dim interior, but all he could make out were shadows. He spotted the door and walked toward it, aware that the

Bottleman, who had been slowly wheeling backward, had now disappeared. Benny wondered, briefly, if he should return to the staff room, but then his fingers located the door handle. It's probably locked, he thought, but he gave it a push, and after a slight resistance the door opened and he was standing inside.

The door closed behind him with a click and the humming stopped, leaving only a vast and empty silence. He looked back through the glass wall, which now had a strangely iridescent sheen, but he could see nothing of the processing area where he'd stood only minutes before. Surrounding him in the darkness was a confusion of ghostly shapes and shadows. He took a step forward. An acrid smell of machine oil and glue hung in the air, and as his eyes adjusted he could make out the silhouettes of a pair of large black sewing machines, glowing in a faint greenish light. He stopped to study them. They were ancient industrial Singers, made of iron and brass and strung with heavy cotton binding thread that fed like spider webs from spools perched on tall twin spindles. Next to them was an industrial-sized guillotine paper cutter, a Quintilio Vaggelli, made in Firenze. He lifted the massive blade and let it fall, slicing the air. Sound is the movement of an object through space. When movement stopped, the blade fell silent, and all Benny could hear was his own blood, pounding in his ears.

He moved on, inspecting a kettle, a serrated knife, a bone folder, an open jar of pitch-like glue on a splattered countertop. He ran his finger along a worktable. The Bindery had been closed for some time now, but there was not a speck of dust. He passed a pile of book covers, like stiff new coats, waiting to be tried and fitted. They were sorted by color—forest green, bloodred—splashes of pigment. Around him on all sides, towering reams of blank white paper rose up like ghosts, waiting for words to be impressed upon them. They were like people without faces, lining up to receive their eyes and ears and mouths and noses. He walked carefully among them, the way you might walk through a crowded hospital ward, careful not to brush against them in case their blankness, their emptiness, might be contagious. Words would give them features. Words would give them voices to speak with. Words would animate them and transform them into semi-living things, but for the time being, they were menacing in their muteness, their meaning not yet fixed.

The Bindery contains everything, the Bottleman had said. *Anything is possible,* and now Benny understood. The Bindery was primordial, a place of vast, boundless silence that contained all sound, and emptiness that contained all form. Benny had never heard such silence before. Never felt such imminence. He shivered.

Paper, he reminded himself. Just get the paper and get out, but everywhere he turned, it seemed there was more of it—shelves piled with it, cubbyholes filled with it, desks and tables stacked high with reams of it. There was paper everywhere, and as he stood there in the green light cast by the emergency exit sign, the leaves and sheets began to whisper like the wind in the trees that had been rendered into pulp and pressed into the service of meaning, to give form to the ineffable. He could hear their voices speaking, and then, suddenly, he could *see* them, too, all the wild, unbound words, like a frenzied cloud of dust motes spinning and dancing around him in the dim green light. He'd never seen words behave like this before, and the sight undid him. The world began to tip, but just as he started to fall, he heard a faint voice, like a gust of warm air rising from the maelstrom, tentative, hesitant and strangely hopeful.

A book must start somewhere . . .

It was a voice unlike any other.

He flung out his hand to catch himself and grabbed hold of the razor-sharp blade of the paper cutter. A searing pain shot up his arm. He gasped and recoiled, pulling his hand back. Bright red blood flew in an arc through the air, splattering the ghostly white stacks of paper as he fell to the floor, and the world went dark and silent.

When he came to, he was lying in a small puddle of blood at the base of the Quintilio Vaggelli. He sat up and banged his head on the huge round counterweight at the end of the cutter's blade that loomed over him like a guillotine. The side of his face was smeared with blood and saliva. He got to his feet. Blood was still leaking from the gash in his hand, and the memory of what he'd seen and heard came back to him—the wild words dancing through the trees, and that faint hopeful voice. He listened, but now the Bindery was silent. Hugging his bleeding hand into his stomach, he made for the exit, slipping in the blood on the floor. The Bottleman was right. The Bindery was too powerful. He pressed against the glass of the door, which mercifully gave way.

BENNY

That voice was you, wasn't it? That was the first time you spoke to me. I could barely hear you through all the noise the paper was making, but I knew you were different from the rest. I can't really describe it. I didn't know who you were or what you were. I just knew you were mine.

THE BOOK

Yes, Benny. That's right. We had to start somewhere. You were starting to fall, and we wanted to catch you, only we failed to account for the proximity of that blade. We felt bad when you cut yourself—the truth is that books are not omniscient, nor can we anticipate everything, no matter how hard we try—but we were relieved that you could hear us at all. Relieved, and happy, too, because it's not easy for a book to reach out like that. It takes a lot of effort. Most people don't even notice when their book comes calling. They're too busy checking their cell phones.

So thank you for noticing, and thank you, too, for what you said just now: *I knew you were mine.* These are words every book wants to hear, and they sent a tremor of delight down our spine.

And it's an interesting question, isn't it? Who belongs to whom? Your friend, Walter Benjamin, was a passionate bibliophile and book collector, who owned many, many books. He wrote a famous essay on the subject, called "Unpacking My Library," in which he elaborates the ways a collector can acquire books. He can buy them or win them at an auction. He can inherit them or borrow them with no intention of returning them. But, Benjamin says, "Of all the ways of acquiring books, writing them oneself is regarded as the most praiseworthy method."

On the surface, this seems true, but from the book's point of view, it's not so simple. Because, really, who is writing whom? It's the old chicken-and-the-egg conundrum, Benny. Think about it. Does the boy write the book, or does the book write the boy?

We wonder how Benjamin might answer this question. He concludes his essay about the books he owns with the memorable lines, "Ownership is the most intimate relationship that one can have to objects. Not that they come alive in him; it is he who lives in them."

With this, we have no quibble.

42

Annabelle sat on the kitchen chair, still as a stone, staring at her feet. From time to time she raised her head and spoke to the refrigerator door.

"Talk to me," she whispered. "If you have something to say, please just say it." She waited. Outside the kitchen window, she could hear the scrabble of rats, or cats, or skunks in the garbage. The poem hadn't changed.

> sing motherache
> beneath our stormy boy
> mad music sad sea

She hadn't sung in so long, but of course Kenji would remember. He loved her singing, and he always knew when she was aching. She wasn't sure now about the rest of the poem. Maybe Benny was right. Maybe it should be "beneath our stormy sea / sad music mad boy," but the linguistic confusion seemed to offer even more proof that Kenji had authored it. His English was never great, but he always managed to get his meaning across, and sometimes his words were even more beautiful for all their mistakes.

"Say something," she said to the refrigerator. "Can't you see I need help!" Again, she waited, but the magnets were mute. She checked the time and slowly got to her feet.

Back at Mission Control, she did a quick Google search, gleaned what she needed, and called 911. When the dispatcher answered, she asked to file a missing person report and was put through to an Officer Hooley. She took a deep breath and explained, calmly, that her son had run away. That they'd had an argument, that he—

He cut her off. "When was your son last seen, ma'am?"

"Do you mean when did I last see him? It was around seven, I think. Or seven thirty. Yes, that's—"

"Seven thirty tonight?"

"Yes, he's—"

"Ma'am, there's twenty-four-hour waiting period for filing a missing person report. You're gonna have to wait till tomorrow and then come to the precinct—"

She cut him off. "Excuse me, Officer," she said, consulting briefly the webpage on her screen. "With all due respect, my son is a minor. He's fourteen years old, with a history of mental illness. If I'm not mistaken, there's no twenty-four-hour waiting period for reporting runaways or missing children under the age of eighteen. I believe that as a child with mental disabilities, he should automatically be classified as a 'critical missing person.' I understand that the National Child Search Assistance Act of 1990 mandates that—"

"Name?"

"Excuse me?"

"Your son's name. What is it?"

"Oh. Benjamin Oh."

"Benjamin O . . . what?"

"No, *Oh*, Officer. That's it. The last name is *Oh*."

"Spell it," he said, and she did. She gave his date of birth, and his height, and his weight. She gave a brief account of the events that led up to his leaving. She left out the kitchen magnets. She gave a description of what he was wearing and what he looked like.

"He's a beautiful boy, Officer. He's mixed race, half Asian, with olive skin and brown hair from his father, and freckles on his nose and a little bit of curliness that he gets from me. His father's hair was perfectly straight. He's Japanese. And Korean. He's dead now."

"Any unique physical or speech characteristics?"

"Well, he's small for his age. He's a teen, but he hasn't really had his growth spurt. He's got a few pimples on his chin and his forehead, though." She realized his pimples were not unique, but they comforted her precisely because they were so normal. She gave him Dr. Melanie's name and a brief history of his diagnosis.

"Would your son have gone to his doctor or a social worker or a support group for help?"

"No, definitely not."

"Do you know where he might have gone?"

She thought about the Library, but it was closed. She thought about the alleyway, and the drag queens in their star-spangled hot pants. "No."

"Does he have any friends or relatives, anybody he might be with?"

She thought about Mackson and the rubber duck girl. "I don't know," she said. She thought she heard Officer Hooley sigh. "I'm sorry."

"Can you provide the name and phone number of his dentist?"

"His dentist? But his teeth are fine, Officer. He brushes every day, and at his last checkup the dentist even said . . ." And then it hit her. "Oh!"

Officer Hooley sensed her alarm, and his voice softened. "Just routine, ma'am. We keep the information on file for the record. Don't worry."

It would have been easier if he'd continued to be an officious asshole. She had trouble controlling the quaver in her voice when he asked if she had a recent photograph. She said she'd send him one, took down his email address, and thanked him. She remembered to get his badge number, the report number, and to verify the spelling of his name. She hung up and sat back in her chair.

Photos. She needed to find recent photos. There were so many of Benny as an infant, as a toddler, and as a little child. Real photo prints of her, holding him in her arms, and of the three of them at Disneyland and the local beach. As the years went by, the photos dwindled, and after Kenji died, there were fewer still. He was the photographer in the family. She tried to recall the last time she'd taken a picture of Benny. There had been so few festive occasions in their lives recently, but then she remembered his graduation. She checked her phone, and there he was, standing in the kitchen, wearing his mortarboard with the tassel dangling over one eye, holding his diploma and the stuffed beagle. The graduation banner dangled crookedly above his head. He was staring past her. What was he feeling? He certainly didn't look happy. How could she not have noticed? She'd been so carried away by her own need to make the day special. Stupid. But she'd been so stressed out. So tired of worrying. She just wanted him to be happy. She wanted him to be happy so she could stop worrying.

She rubbed her eyes and then looked at the picture again. It was a good likeness. She emailed it to the precinct and then went upstairs to Benny's room to look for his phone. Maybe he had other photos, selfies or maybe even some pictures of friends. As always, his room was an oasis of tidiness, the bed neatly made, the desk clear. His books were lined up on the shelf in order of size, alongside the rubber duck, the lunar globe and the box containing Kenji's ashes. Kenji would have liked to be next to the moon. Or, better yet, on the moon. The gray moon, covered in deep, soft dust. She retrieved Benny's phone from his backpack, but it was locked and she didn't know the passcode. She sat down on the bed and looked around and then she started inputting numbers. She entered 6006 for MOON. Nothing. She tried 6345 for NEIL, and then 2899 for BUZZ. She'd forgotten the third astronaut's name, the one who didn't get to walk on the moon, so she tried 3878 for DUST. She didn't really expect to get the passcode this way—the odds were against her guessing—but when she entered 5299 for JAZZ the phone unlocked and the home screen opened.

Her hands were trembling as she started scrolling through his list of recent calls and texts. Most of them were to her, but there was a second number that showed up with some frequency, belonging to someone or something named the Aleph. What was an Aleph? She took the phone back down to Mission Control and did a search. Aleph was the first letter of the Semitic writing system and was used in mathematics to represent the cardinality of infinite sets. It was derived from an ancient Egyptian hieroglyph depicting an ox. None of this made any sense. Was Benny a part of some kind of cult?

Then, because Annabelle was careful and had been trained as a librarian to pay attention to details, she put *The* in front of *Aleph* and searched again. This time she was rewarded with a list of sites containing information about a short story, entitled "The Aleph," written in 1945 by an Argentinian author named Jorge Luis Borges. Annabelle had never heard of him, but she located a PDF of the story and started to read it online.

The story was about a man, also named Borges, and his reluctant friendship with a bombastic poet who was writing an epic poem entitled, *The Earth*, in which he "proposed to versify the entire planet." One day Borges received a phone call from the distraught poet, who said that his house was about to be torn down by his rapacious landlords in order to make room for a bar. This was a disaster, the poet told Borges. He couldn't move from the house because in the cellar, under his dining room, was an Aleph, which he needed in order finish his poem. Borges did not know what an Aleph was, so the poet explained. An Aleph, he said, "is one of the points in space that contain all points." Curious now, Borges went to the house. He followed the poet down the narrow cellar stairs, where he was instructed to lie down on a burlap sack, which the poet had placed there. The poet then left, closing the trap door behind him and leaving Borges in total darkness. Borges grew increasingly worried. Was the poet a madman? Was his life in danger? He closed his eyes, convinced he was about to die, but when he opened them again, suddenly, in a corner under the steps, he saw a point of light about the size of a golf ball.

Here, words seemed to fail Borges as he groped for a way to describe this vision that surpassed the very limits of language. The Aleph was "a small iridescent sphere of almost unbearable brightness." It appeared to be "spinning," but this was in fact "an illusion produced by the dizzying spectacles inside it." These marvelous and fantastical visions, reflecting and refracting and whirling around inside the Aleph, Borges then attempts to enumerate: "Universal space was contained inside it, with no diminution in size. Each thing . . . was infinite things, because I could clearly see it from every point in the cosmos."

At this point, Annabelle gave up. It sounded like an acid trip. Was the Aleph the name of some kind of street drug? Was Benny getting high? She did not see how it was possible that a point in space could contain all points, nor did she see what this had to do with Benny. She unlocked his phone again and called the Aleph's number.

43

The Aleph was angry. "What the fuck were you doing in the Bindery?"

They were back in the staff washroom. Benny was sitting on the toilet, and the Aleph was kneeling on the floor next to him, attempting to close the gash in his hand with some adhesive sutures that Mackson had found in the first aid box, but the wound was awkward. The blade had sliced into the webbing between his thumb and forefinger, and the sutures weren't sticking. She brushed the hair out of her eyes.

"Slavoj sent you in there, didn't he?" It wasn't really a question. She spoke about the Bottleman as if he weren't there, even though he'd gotten up from his wheelchair and was standing just outside the door, trying to peer over Mackson's shoulder.

"I was trying to write a story," Benny said. "We needed more paper."

"He should have gone himself."

Benny winced as she pinched the wound shut and tried again. "He couldn't. He said the Bindery was too powerful."

"Why's that?" Mackson asked. His hands were resting lightly on the Aleph's shoulders. Benny didn't like the way he was touching her, massaging her gently to help her relax.

"Because he's a poet."

The Aleph snorted. "He was just trying to scare you, Benny. Pulling your leg." She raised her voice. "Isn't that right, Slavoj?" she called, over her shoulder.

The Bottleman lowered himself back down into his wheelchair. "I, of all people, do not pull legs."

"Okay, fair," the Aleph said. "Bad choice of words, but that was still really stupid."

She and Mackson had returned to the Library with a knapsack full of food they'd gleaned from the dumpsters and spotted the blood on the floor in Book Processing. They followed the bright red drops to the staff washroom, where they found the Bottleman, feeding Benny vodka to dull the pain while he tried to bandage the boy's hand. The Aleph kicked him out, dumped the vodka down the sink and took over. Now, satisfied at last with the sutures, she took a roll of gauze and started to wrap his hand.

"I can't move my thumb," Benny said.

"That's the point. It's amazing you still have a thumb. You sliced right through the web. What did you cut it on?"

"It vas ze old Quintilio Vaggelli," Slavoj said. "Ze big board shears with ze adamantine blade."

The Aleph shook her head. "It's going to be a bitch to heal. You'll probably need stitches, but this'll do for now. How's the head?"

"It hurts."

"Take an Advil. How's the rib?"

Benny hugged himself. "Hurts, too."

She found an old dish towel in the kitchen, ripped it in half and tied it around Benny's neck and arm to make a sling. When she was done, she stood and stretched. Mackson put his arm around her shoulders, and together they surveyed the boy. His forehead was bandaged, and now his hand was swaddled and in the improvised sling. "Dude, you look like shit," Mackson said.

"Thanks," Benny said.

"You think he looks bad," Slavoj said. "You should hef seen ze Bindery."

Benny felt faint. He closed his eyes. Memories of the visions he'd seen rose like ghosts. He remembered the voice, and he shivered. The Bottleman was still talking.

"—like a crime scene. Blood all over ze beautiful white paper—"

The words faded in and out. Benny felt the Aleph's hand resting lightly on his head. "You okay?"

He swallowed hard and took a deep gulp of air.

"—called in ze boys from Ljubljana to mop it up," the Bottleman was saying.

Benny leaned forward and put his forehead on his knees. The Aleph bent down, cupping the back of his neck lightly with her hand.

"Benny?" Her breath tickled his ear. She was so close. "What is it?"

"I saw stuff," he whispered. He didn't want Mackson to hear.

"What did you see?"

"I never see stuff, but this time I did. Words, floating. Then I heard this voice—"

He looked up at her then. Her beautiful face was inches from his. He wanted to tell her. He wanted her to know. He tried to hold his mind open, but the faint, hopeful voice he'd heard in the Bindery was gone, leaving him feeling hollow inside, like he'd lost something precious.

"Nothing," he said, dropping his head again. "It was nothing," he repeated, and was startled to find that he was crying.

"We better get him home," he heard her say. Just then, her cell phone started ringing. She pulled it from her pocket and answered. "Yo . . ."

44

"Oh!" Annabelle said, surprised that someone had actually picked up at this hour of the night. The voice was young, female, and sounded familiar. "I hope I didn't wake you. I'm looking for . . . is this, the Aleph?"

There was silence on the other end.

"I don't know if I'm pronouncing it right. Elf? Alif? Aileaf?"

"Who wants to know?"

"You don't know me, but my name is Annabelle Oh. I'm Benny Oh's mother? I found your number on my son's cell phone. I don't want to bother you, it's just that Benny's gone missing, and I was calling—I'm just wondering—have you seen him?"

She closed her eyes. She heard a rustling noise that sounded like small animals. Was she being too aggressive? The website for parents of runaway children warned against sounding angry or authoritarian when contacting a child's friends. Fearing the girl might hang up, she added, "I mean, you don't have to tell me or anything, but if you do see him, could you let him know that he's not in any trouble, but his mother is very worried and just wants . . ."

She heard the girl's voice say, "You better talk to her," and then, in the background, a muffled voice say, "Shit."

The phone went silent then. Annabelle pressed it to her head. "Hello?" she said. "Can you hear me? Are you there?"

"Yeah."

It was Benny. His voice, close inside her ear, was so familiar and dear, but strange and distant, too. "Oh, Benny, I was so worried. Are you okay?"

"Yeah." Her child's voice was breaking. Deep inside the cracks, a man's voice was waiting to come out. But not yet.

"Where are you? Do you want me to come get you? I'll take a cab. Just tell me—" She could picture the flash of impatience cross his face, the furrow gathering between his brows. She heard his sigh.

"I'm fine. I'm hanging out with friends."

He sounded like Kenji. "Who?" she demanded. "Who are you with?"

"Nobody. It's okay. Mom, listen, I gotta go. I'll be home soon. Don't worry, okay?"

But how could she not worry? She was on her feet, stumbling into the kitchen, looking for her coat, her shoes, her wallet, fumbling with the phone. "Benny, wait, where are you? Who's there with you? I can come get you. I'll take a taxi. Don't go anywhere, you hear?" And then, fearing that she sounded angry and authoritarian, she said, "I'm so sorry, Benny. I didn't really think you were lying. Of course you didn't move the silly magnets, and even if you did, it's okay. It's totally fine, really. Just tell me where—" But by the time she'd found her house keys under a pile of mail in the kitchen, he'd disconnected.

Keep calm, the website said. Don't blame or guilt trip your child. Don't beg.

Should she call him back? No. He said he'd be home. She would just have to trust him. She stared at the silent magnets on the fridge and then climbed the stairs and returned to Benny's room. Taking the box of Kenji's ashes from the shelf, she carried it into the bathroom. She sat down on the edge of the tub, lifted the toilet seat, and then opened the box. Inside was a thick plastic bag, like a heavy duty freezer bag, secured with a twist tie. She unfastened the tie and looked in at the contents.

"Damnit, Kenji."

She dug her fingers into the mouth of the bag and scooped up a small fistful of ashes.

"I'm really mad at you," she said. "Do you know that? You had a beautiful son. You had an okay wife—I know I'm not much, but we were happy enough, weren't we? And you promised. You said you'd stop. That you'd get help."

She studied the mound of ashes in her palm. The ashes were grayish white, granular like lunar dust, with little bits of bones mixed in. She held her cupped hand carefully over the toilet bowl.

"I need you to tell me you're sorry. I need to hear it."

She waited. A trickle of ash slipped through her fingers and fell onto the surface of the water where it floated.

"I mean it."

She spread her fingers, and a few more ashes fell, forming a thin pale film, which began to spread. She felt cold. As cold and lifeless as the moon. Then, changing her mind, she closed her fist again.

"Forget it," she said. "It's too late. I don't care if you're sorry or not. You're dead." She returned the ashes to the box. "Flushing's too easy. I need you to stick around."

She replaced the box lid, washed her hands in the sink, and blew her nose on a piece of toilet paper, which she threw into the bowl. It floated on top of the ashy film. She flushed and watched it disappear.

"Such a stupid way to die."

She returned the box to Benny's shelf and went into her bedroom. *Tidy Magic* was lying splayed open on the bedside table, so she climbed into bed, propped herself up and started reading. The chapter was titled "Tidying Is Love," and when she finished it, she took the book downstairs to Mission Control, logged on to her computer, and opened a new email.

"Dear Ms. Aikon," she wrote. "This is the third fan letter I've tried to write to you, but I always chicken out and delete them before I can send them. But tonight I really need someone to talk to, and you seem like a really nice person, plus, you're a Zen monk, which is like a priest, right? So maybe it's okay to tell you about my problems...."

She paused for a moment to study the author photo on the back cover of the book. Aikon had a kind face. There were so many things Annabelle wanted to say, but what good would it do to put it all in an email? These celebrity author types never read their fan mail, and writing everything down just seemed exhausting and futile. She needed to act. She hit Delete and went back upstairs to her bedroom. Starting with the dresser, she started dumping her clothes onto the bed until the mattress was piled high with socks, underwear, bras, T-shirts, pants, sweatshirts, and sweaters. Then she found a half-empty garbage bag and furiously began discarding.

TIDY MAGIC

Chapter 2
Tidying Is Love!

When I went to live with the old priest, he was quite ill, and his tiny temple was decrepit and run-down. I have to admit, I was terribly disappointed. I'd expected to live in an elegant Zen temple, with fresh tatami mats and gleaming wooden floors and beautiful scrolls and splendid statues and a tranquil garden. How could I fail to become enlightened in heavenly surroundings like that?

And how could I possibly become enlightened here? The temple had fallen into complete disrepair. The roof tiles were broken, and the walls were crumbling. In the tiny weed-choked garden, a jumble of laundry poles was strung with underwear from student boarders, whose rents provided the temple with a meager income. Inside the rooms, the tatami was old and soggy and the wood was dull. The altars and statues were covered with cobwebs, and there was clutter everywhere! Was this why I'd given up all the comforts of my life? To live in a small, crummy room in a dilapidated temple and play nursemaid to a dying old man?

My disappointment must have shown, because during our interview, the old priest was apologetic. We sat on cushions in his study in the abbot's quarters. Behind him, a dusty statue of Senju Kannon, the Bodhisattva of Compassion, watched from the altar with her eleven heads and a thousand arms. The old priest's body slumped like a rotting persimmon as he gazed dejectedly around the room. His face was sunken, and his cheeks were covered with gray stubble.

"I'm very sorry," he said. "I'm sure this is not what you expected. An attractive young lady monk like you would surely prefer to train in a more elegant Zen temple, with beautiful scrolls and splendid statues and a tranquil garden, not in a sad, run-down place, taking care of a sick old man like me."

He hadn't even looked at me, yet he seemed to know exactly what I was thinking. I felt ashamed that he'd seen through me, and I wanted to protest, but he was still talking.

"You see," he was saying, "I was hoping they would send me a strong, young, male monk, who would be able to do the gardening and the building repairs. A clever, young, male monk with financial know-how and fresh, new fundraising ideas, who could attract new patrons and parishioners, and be my successor, and take over as abbot when I die."

He sighed. "But of course," he added softly, "this is too much to expect from a young lady like yourself."

I remember that moment vividly. I was kneeling in front of him. My backbone stiffened, and my face flushed. Seething with wounded pride, I almost shouted. "Hojo-san! I may be only a female monk, but I am strong and capable! I will clean up your temple and take care of the repairs. I have a background in business, and I will think of ideas for generating income and attracting new parishioners. I will learn how to care for the garden, and I will care for you, too. Please give me a chance!"

I bowed until my forehead touched the floor, and when I sat up again, I caught sight of his bright eyes, observing me from under his shaggy eyebrows, and the smallest flicker of a smile.

Fueled by my umbrage, I cleaned every inch of the little temple. I washed and repaired all my teacher's old robes. I dusted the altars and every single one of Kannon's eleven heads and thousand arms. I found workmen who could fix the roof tiles and the crumbling stucco walls. I had the soggy tatami replaced, and polished the wooden floors until they gleamed.

The more I worked, the more I found myself caring for the old temple, and for my teacher, too, but sadly, even as the condition of the temple improved, my teacher's health deteriorated. He was dying, and there was nothing I could do. Ultimately, I had failed him. The financial situation was worse than before. The repairs cost money, and we had none, and I'd done nothing to attract new patrons or increase our membership. Novice monks are called *unsui,* clouds and water, because they drift and flow and have no staying power. I was just an inexperienced female *unsui.* How could I possibly save the temple? I had no skills, except what I'd learned during my years in fashion magazine publishing, which were of no use at the temple. The only practical skill I had was cleaning and making things tidy.

The situation seemed hopeless, and I would lie awake worrying. But then, one night, I had a flash of insight that felt like sudden enlightenment. I was so excited, I hardly slept, and the next morning, I went to see my teacher. He was terribly weak by then, but he never missed a single service or period of zazen. Afterward, I brought him tea and asked if I could speak with him. He must have guessed from my tone that what I had to say was important, so he made an effort to stay seated, instead of lying down again.

"It won't take long," I said, and then I explained my idea. I told him about how, despite my early disappointment, I'd grown to love the little temple, and how that love had come about simply by cleaning and caring for it, inch by inch.

How I'd grown to love Senju Kannon by dusting her every day, so that now I could appreciate her beauty and grace and her infinite compassion.

How polishing the floors had given me a deep connection with the temple buildings, and also with the trees that gave wood for the floorboards, and the monks who had scrubbed them for hundreds of years before me.

How weeding and raking the moss in the garden helped me understand that what's important is not *finishing* a task but rather just *doing* it, completely.

Doing connects me to this moment, this weed, this patch of moss. This moment is my real life. I am not separate from this moment, or from the floorboards, or the trees, or the monks, or the weeds. And then the weeds grow back, and that's okay, too.

It's not much, I said, but maybe I could write a little book about this Zen method of tidying. And maybe some people would buy it and read it, and it would help them, and maybe bring in some money for the temple, too. I knew these were not big, profound Zen revelations, only small lessons, but I felt I could share them because I believed them with all my heart and knew them to be true.

Cleaning is a practice of compassion.

Weeding is a practice of faith.

Tidying is love!

THE BOOK

45

They dropped Slavoj off at the Gospel Mission and walked Benny home through the alley in the pale dawn light. When they passed the spot where Kenji died, Benny stepped carefully around it, but nobody seemed to notice. The Aleph and Mackson were talking in quiet voices about the meeting they'd attended earlier, but Benny wasn't interested. His head hurt. His hand hurt. His rib cage hurt. He didn't want them to see the dump where he lived or run into his mother. When they reached the back gate, he stopped, hoping they would leave, but they pushed the gate open, shoving the trash aside like they already knew it was there. A large roof rat ran from the overflowing bins and disappeared under the house.

"*Rattus rattus,*" Mackson said, and Benny saw the way they looked at each other. He climbed the steps to the back porch, and as he turned to wave, he saw the way they stood, side by side, leaning into each other. He pushed through the door, and it slammed behind him.

The overhead light in the kitchen was on. He turned it off and went into the darkened living room. The blinking LEDs from Mission Control looked like an airport landing strip at night. He climbed the stairs, trying not to knock into anything or make a sound. As he passed his mother's bedroom, he could see her sleeping on the bed with *Tidy Magic* facedown on her stomach. Next to her was a giant mound of clothing. Her dresser drawers had been emptied and were stacked on the floor, except for one, at the foot of the bed, which she had started to fill back up with socks. He continued on to his own room and turned on the light. *Danger!* Something was different. His backpack was on his bed, and his smartphone was on his desk. His mother had been in his room. He did a quick perimeter check of the room and looked inside the closet for any stuff she might have stashed, but there was nothing. His bookshelf, too, with the globe and his books and the box of ashes looked exactly as he'd left it. Good. But still, something was different.

"Dad?"

There was no answer. Not that he expected one. He hadn't heard his dad's voice for a long time. Maybe he wasn't listening hard enough. Maybe he should try harder. He picked up the box of ashes.

"Dad? Can you hear me?"

The box felt lighter, like there was a tiny bit less of his father inside. But how could that be?

"Hey, Dad, guess what? I got stoned tonight. It was my first time. I smoked weed with these guys in that park you used to take me. It was weird and kind of awesome at first, but then I kind of freaked out."

His dad didn't answer.

"This one guy thought I was attacking him so he hit me with a baseball bat, but don't worry, I'm okay. After that I went to the Library and hung out with my friends. One of them is an artist, and the other one's a poet. They're both pretty cool. I think you'd like them."

Still no answer. He wanted to tell his dad about the Aleph, about how she looked, bending over his hand, bandaging his wound. How his heart pounded when she touched his bruised rib. He wanted to ask his dad what you were supposed to do when you thought you were maybe in love with a girl, but he didn't know how to talk about these things, and besides his dad was dead.

"I wrote a story tonight, too. It was stupid, but the B-man said it was okay. He's the poet. And then I thought of another story I'm gonna write that's about you."

The box still didn't respond. No surprise, but why did it feel lighter? Weighing it in one hand, he spun the globe and landed on Lacus Somniorum. It was Kenji's favorite lunar location, and he had a sudden vision of his dad's ashes slowly drifting upward in a spiraling cloud of particulate matter, transmigrating to the lunar surface and landing in the Lake of Dreams. The ashes were leaving this earth, leaving his son behind.

Typical.

He put the box back on the bookshelf between the globe and the rubber duck, then he crawled into bed and curled into a tight ball, hugging his rib cage, which was where his mother found him when she woke a little later.

HE'D BEEN HURT. There was a white gauze square taped to his forehead and a bloodstained bandage wrapped around his hand.

"Benny?" she said, bending over him. "Benny, wake up!"

He groaned and turned away from her.

She took him by the shoulders. "Benny, you have to wake up."

He opened his eyes, confused.

"Benny, look at me. What happened to you?"

He saw her and the confusion cleared. He looked away. "I'm fine."

"You're not fine. You're hurt. Your head, your hand." She touched his wrist, the bandage. "Oh my God, what *happened*?"

He pushed her away. "Mom. I'm fine. Really. I just need to sleep."

She took a deep breath. What if he had a concussion? Wasn't it dangerous to let someone fall asleep with a concussion, or was that a myth? She couldn't remember. "Okay," she said, touching the edge of the gauze on his forehead. "You rest. I'm calling a cab."

On the way to the hospital, he refused to tell her what had happened. He refused to tell the triage nurse in the emergency room, too, insisting that he'd tripped and fallen. He refused to let Annabelle stay in the room while the doctor examined his head and stitched up his hand, and while she waited, Annabelle called Dr. Melanie. She left a message, asking for an emergency appointment. She called the police precinct and told them that her son had returned home. What else? She was trying to be responsible. To be thorough. As if this would help heal her son and make him better. She glanced at the clock on the wall. School would be starting soon, so she called to tell them Benny would be absent and was put on hold. She was trying to think of what to say—Benny's not feeling well, he's had an accident, he's come down with a cold—when the principal came on the line.

"Oh, Principal Slater, I'm so sorry. I didn't mean to bother you. I just wanted to let someone there know that Benny isn't feeling well and won't be coming in to school today. . . ."

There was a pause on the other end of the line. Across the hallway, at the check-in station, a homeless man was arguing with the nurse. Outside, Annabelle could hear an ambulance siren approaching. The principal cleared her throat.

"Mrs. Oh," she said slowly. "I don't quite understand what's going on here, but it seems you're not aware of the fact that Benny has been absent from school for almost a month now."

PART THREE

LOST IN SPACE

Ideas are to objects as constellations are to stars.

—Walter Benjamin, *Ursprung des deutschen Trauerspiels*

THE BOOK

46

Danger! Danger!

The robot was speaking through the tinny laptop speakers.

Danger, Will Robinson!

Benny hit Pause. "Daddy, do you know what kind of robot that is? Because I know."

They were sitting on the couch in the living room, with Kenji's computer balanced on their knees between them. Annabelle was at the office. Benny had a cold and was staying home from school. He was seven. He'd become somewhat of an expert on *Lost in Space*, ever since his father had turned him on to it. He liked knowing more than his father. What boy doesn't?

"Is he the tin-can robot?" Kenji asked. He was drinking beer from a coffee cup. He took a sip.

"No."

"Is he the garbage-can robot?"

"No! Of course not."

"Hm," Kenji said. "I don't know then. You tell me."

"He's a B-9 Class M-3 General Utility Non-Theorizing Environmental Control Robot," Benny said, reeling off the name as if it were obvious, common knowledge, but not quite able to hide his pride at knowing. When he hit Play, the robot started waving its corrugated, retractable arms.

Warning! Warning! Does not compute. Does not compute. I cannot ac-cept that course of action.

"Daddy?"

"Yes, Benny?"

"So I read on this one website that they started making *Lost in Space* in 1965."

"Is that so?"

"Well, that's what the website said. It was on TV from 1965 to 1968."

"Okay. I believe you."

"But the show was supposed to be the future, right? It was supposed to be 1997, and there were too many people here on earth, so the Robinsons left on Space Station One."

"Right. They want to find some new planet to live on."

"I *know* that. But it doesn't make any sense. 1997 isn't the future. It's the past. In 1997, I wasn't even born yet—"

"It was future for people in 1965."

"I *know*!" Benny said impatiently. "That's what I said! But if 1997 was the future back *then*, then *now* is even more the future, right? Now is already 2009!"

Kenji took a sip of beer. "So what is your question, Benny?"

"If now is the future, how come there aren't any space missions? Or rocket ships with astronauts in them flying to other planets?"

"Hm," Kenji said. "Good question."

"Because *before*, at least there were moon missions, right?"

"Right."

"So what happened? How come they stopped?"

"Maybe time is going backward?"

Benny rolled his eyes. "That's stupid."

"Maybe there is no reason for moon missions anymore? It cost lotta money to fly to the moon, and then . . . nothing. Moon has nothing. Nothing to take. Nothing to sell. Nothing to kill and eat. Everything already dead on the moon, and if you can't make big money, then what is the point?

Better to make wars and kill each other here on the earth." He raised his arms like he was holding a fully automatic assault rifle and pretended to spray the living room with rounds. "*Dakka-dakka-dakka-dakka . . . ,*" he said.

Benny sank more deeply down into the cushions and chewed his knuckle. "That's just stupid."

"Yes." Kenji stopped shooting and put his arm around his son's shoulders and gave him a squeeze. "Killing is stupid. Better to stay alive." The boy relaxed into him, playing with his father's fingers. They smelled like the joint he'd just extinguished, sweet and smoky.

"Daddy?"

"Yes, Benny."

"When you were a little kid, were you alive when the astronauts walked on the moon?

"Of course! I was same age as you. I was six years old."

"I'm seven!"

"Okay, but I was six. It was 1969, and I was very young boy and worrying because in Japan, we have a fairy tale about a rabbit who lives on the moon, and I was afraid about the big American astronaut will hurt the moon rabbit. But everybody told me don't worry! American astronaut is very kind man. He won't hurt any moon rabbits! But still I was worrying."

"But it was okay, right?"

"It was okay. We watched on the old black-and-white TV set because we have no Internets back then. Then we see the first astronaut, Mr. Neil Armstrong, go down the ladder to the moon and say some famous words— *One small footstep for a man. One big jump for everybody else.* Something like that. You know those words? Very famous. So then I decide to become astronaut, too."

"Really?"

Kenji nodded. "It was my dream to do lunar mission. To take a walk on the moon."

"So how come you didn't? Astronauts were still doing stuff like that back then. . . ."

"In Japan we didn't have any astronauts yet. So I practice clarinet instead and give up my dream for going into outer space."

"Because of the clarinet?"

"Because of music." He closed his eyes and let his head fall backward against the cushions. Benny waited, watching a faint smile play across his father's face, like he was listening to something pleasant, far away. Sometimes Kenji did this, drifted off, and Benny had to nudge him and say *Earth to Daddy. Earth to Daddy. Do you read me?* in order to bring him back. But this time, there was no need, because Kenji sighed then and started talking. "Music is like outer space, Benny. No need for flying to some other place. Everything is so beautiful right here."

But Benny wasn't convinced. He frowned. "There's this kid at school who says his dad says the whole moon walk was fake."

"No" Kenji said, shaking his head and sitting upright. "That dad is wrong. It was real." He pulled the computer onto his lap, did a quick search and then hit play. It was NASA footage from the Apollo 11 lunar mission. They watched the ghostly shape of Armstrong in his white space suit, climbing slowly down the ladder of the lunar landing module, then stepping from the edge onto the moon's surface.

"It's all blurry," Benny complained. "It doesn't look real."

"Shh. Listen."

Amid the beeps and static, they heard the staticky words, *One small step for a man, one giant leap for mankind.*

"See!" Kenji said. They watched as Armstrong moved slowly away from the landing module, reporting on the condition of the struts, the fine dust below his boots, the first human footprint on the lunar surface, and then Aldrin descended. They set up the cameras, the commemorative plaque, and the American flag. Slowly, they learned how to be bodies on the moon, how to walk, to twist, to balance and bend, and before long, they were bounding across the powdery surface, the pull of the moon's gravity just enough to hold them upright, attached, and to keep them from floating away.

"Okay, that's pretty cool," Benny said grudgingly. "I would like to be an astronaut. I would like to walk on the moon."

"Me, too, Benny-boy. Me, too."

BENNY

I remember that! A couple days later, my dad came home with this big cardboard box, and when I opened it, it was the lunar globe. I was so excited. My
very own moon! He said he found it at an antiques store, and my mom got
mad at him and said I was just a kid and he shouldn't be buying expensive
antiques for a kid because kids can't appreciate things like that, and they
couldn't afford it. I remember it killed me to hear them fighting because I
loved that globe immediately, and I didn't want Mom to make me give it
back. But in the end, she didn't. And then Dad bought me all the Glow-in-
the-Dark Wonder Stars and stuck them on my ceiling, and he made a special constellation just for us called the Cheery Ohs, and by then Mom had
gotten over being mad, so that night we turned off the lights and piled onto
my bed, all three of us, and lay there, looking up at our constellation, glowing in the dark.

Sometimes we used to sit on my bed with the lunar globe and read all
the names of the impact craters, and you had to choose the one you wanted
to land on. Mom always chose the Bay of Dew or the Bay of Rainbows, and
Dad liked the Lake of Dreams. I always chose the Sea of Vapors, which was
next to Seething Bay, because I liked the sounds of those words, especially
after I looked them up and learned their meanings. None of us chose the
Sea of Tranquility or the Sea of Storms because other astronauts had landed there already. And none of us went to the dark side of the moon, except

for Dad, at least not on purpose. But sometimes we'd spin the moon, and you had to close your eyes and put your finger down to make the spinning stop, and wherever your finger landed, that was your spot, and you had to make up a story about it. It was a good game, but then Mom landed in the Sea of Crisis three times in a row, and Dad kept landing in these tiny places like the Marsh of Diseases and the Lake of Death. He thought it was funny, but it freaked Mom out, so we stopped playing.

But I remember one time when Mom landed in the Sea of Fertility, and she made up this story about a lady astronaut who landed there and then came back to earth and couldn't stop having babies. All of them were pale sons that she named after the smaller craters, so they had names like Copernicus and Clavius and Schickard and Humboldt and Bel'kovich and Al-Khwarizmi, and we had to memorize the names and learn how to pronounce them. I can't remember all of them now, but there were lots more, at least twenty pale sons, and they all turned out to be tiny astronauts, and the mother had to keep an eye on them because the earth's gravity wasn't strong enough to hold them down and they kept floating away. Inside the house it was okay if they floated, because they'd just hit the ceiling and bump their heads and start to cry, and she could climb up on a stepladder and grab a foot and pull them down again, but outside was a problem, and she had to tie strings around their ankles when they went for a walk. She said everybody would stare at her, walking down the sidewalk with all these little baby boys on strings, bobbing along like a big bunch of pale helium balloons.

It was a really excellent story, and Mom kept adding parts to it every night for a couple of weeks. I don't remember where the dad in the story was. I actually don't think there was a dad. I think the lady astronaut was already a single mom and the sons just kind of popped out on account of her landing in the Sea of Fertility, which was the point of the story, that she didn't need a dad to begin with. She and her sons had all kinds of cool adventures together, but then all the pale sons started growing up, and the bigger they got, the harder it was for the mom to hold them down to earth, and they started having trouble in school and stuff. Finally things got so bad, they had to have a family conference, and the pale sons told their mom that they had to go back to the moon. It was important for their self-esteem, they said. They had to go back to find their impact crater so they would know who they are. The lady astronaut was very sad when she heard this, but she realized she had to let them go because she wanted her sons to have healthy identities and lots of self-esteem, even though she knew she would be very lonely without them. The pale sons offered to take her with them, back to the moon, but she said no, because she was an earthling and one trip to the moon was enough for her. When the day came, she took all her sons outside on their strings, and she used her little embroidery scissors to cut their strings, and one by one the sons floated away into the bright blue sky, waving to her as they got tinier and tinier and paler and paler, promising to come back to earth, but they never did.

It was a really sad ending. I don't know where Dad was the night Mom finished telling it. Maybe he was playing a gig or something, because it was just her and me, lying on my bed, and when she got to the end, we were both just totally silent, staring up at the stars on my ceiling, and feeling really bummed, and then she was like, maybe we should make up a different ending, and I was like, yeah, and so we did. And in the new ending, just as the littlest boy was floating away through the trees, he happened to look down and see his mom crying, and at the last minute, he grabbed hold of the very top branch of a very tall tree and he held on tight. And because he was still small, the pull of the moon's gravity wasn't so strong on him, so he was able to haul himself all the way back down the tree, until he reached his mom. And he held on to her hand and told her that he'd changed his mind. He was different from the other boys, he said, more grounded, and he wanted to try to find his identity right here on earth. So his mother was really happy then, which helped his self-esteem, and she brought him inside, and the next day they went to a shoe store and had a special pair of super-heavy shoes made with shiny osmium soles that would hold him down to the earth, and at school all the kids wanted shoes like his, so he became really popular.

It was a much better ending.

Osmium is the heaviest matter in the world, and now that I think about it, that's what my dad needed. He needed superheavy shoes made with osmium soles to hold him down to earth. You know how he said that whole thing about how music was space, and he didn't need to fly off to some other place because everything was so beautiful right here on earth? Actually, I'm pretty sure that was bullshit. Maybe he used to feel like that once, but by the time I was seven or eight, he was already entering the twilight zone, and he and Mom were fighting a lot. It was mostly about the pot smoking—they never called it that, at least not in front of me, but I knew what was going on. He wanted to quit, and he really tried, but he just couldn't, and I could always tell when he'd started again, because it was like he was lost in space, orbiting around in some other galaxy, and there was nothing that could hold him down. Not even osmium. Not even me.

But I remember there was a time, once, when I was really little, when he didn't need the pot, and music really was *it* for him—pure space—and big enough to hold us all. And I was *it*, and Mom was *it*, too—we were all *it*, back then, and I remember what it felt like, when everything was beautiful.

Here's the thing about my dad. When he was alive, he was totally alive. I remember him playing his favorite track "Sing Sing Sing (With a Swing)" from the 1938 live recording at Carnegie Hall. He'd play it over and over again, and every time he heard it, he'd start to cry, and I could never understand why, so he'd try to explain.

It's live, Benny! Listen! That's Babe Russin on tenor sax. And Harry James on trumpet. And Gene Krupa on drums—oh, man listen to those tom-toms, he's killing it!

I can hear his voice even now, and see him, too, with his foot tapping to the big band sound and his head nodding and his whole body bopping up and down. I thought he was so cool and I'd try to imitate him. We'd listen to the trumpet trio, and about seven minutes in he'd close his eyes and be like, *Wait, wait for it! Here comes Goodman . . . !* And then we'd listen to that pure snaky clarinet solo, and my dad would literally be vibrating, waiting for that crazy impossible C above high C, and when Goodman hit it, he'd cry out *Yes!* and hug me so hard, *That's it, Benny! Oh, baby, that's some hot jazz! That's killer diller . . .*

And then, right then, that's when Goodman gives Jess Stacy his piano solo, the one that starts so soft and gentle, and someone from the audience, or maybe one of the musicians from the band, calls out *Yeah, Daddy,* and my own daddy's face breaks into his great big smile and he's rocking me and whispering, *Listen for the Debussy, can you hear the Ravel?* trying to get me to hear with his ears, and by the time Stacy finishes and the audience explodes into applause and Krupa raises his sticks and brings the whole thing home, my daddy's face is wet with tears and his eyes are shining and he hugs me tight, saying, *Listen, Benny-boy! That's pure live, that's how we gotta be!*

THE BOOK

47

But Kenji wasn't live. He'd died, leaving Benny behind.

Benny was back in school now. Annabelle no longer allowed him to take the bus by himself, and even though it created problems in her daily workflow, she insisted on riding with him in the morning and picking him up again in the afternoon. On his first day back, as he neared the school with his mother in tow like a giant dirigible, he heard the other kids snickering. In the classroom he heard them talking behind his back, and later, in the lunchroom, taunting him—*Yo! Benny! This is your sandwich talking. Don't eat me! Please don't eat me!*—which was cruel, but by now he was used to hearing the voices say stuff like this, and he barely noticed. If you had asked him how he felt, he would have shrugged and said fine, but in reality he was numb and detached, like everything in his life was happening at a very great distance. It's normal for one's past and future to feel far away, but Benny's here and now felt that way, too. Space and time were hopelessly entangled, and the present moment was growing increasingly remote. As the weeks passed, he felt like he was on an intergalactic space shuttle, hurtling through a black hole toward another star. He could still hear the voices of things speaking, but they were remote, too, shrouded in a white noise so thick and dense he could barely make out what they were saying.

Which, he'd say, was fine. The problem was when a person, like a counsellor or the school nurse or a social worker or his special ed teacher, spoke to him and expected an answer. That was where everything fell apart. And now there were a lot of persons who were expecting answers, because now he was being assessed as a child with disabilities, entitled to receive an Individualized Education Program, tailored to meet his special needs. Annabelle had fought hard for this. Shortly after Benny's truancy was discovered, she had been called in for a conference with Principal Slater. She sat there on the hard chair staring at the principal's many framed diplomas on the wall, while the woman told her about the phony emails.

"He must have accessed your account," the principal said, navigating to her inbox. "I'm surprised you didn't notice. I hope you don't share your passwords with him. We don't recommend that, you know." She frowned at the screen, typed something in, and then swiveled her monitor around so Annabelle could see.

Annabelle leaned forward and studied the email that her son had apparently written. How could she have missed seeing these emails going back and forth? And how could he have gotten access to her account in the first place? But then she remembered how easily she'd guessed the passcode on his phone, and it occurred to her that she and Benny knew each other pretty well, and that this was something not many mothers could say about their sons. She felt a quick throb of pride at this unexpected affirmation of their bond, and then she noticed the missing letter.

"Oh, look!" she said, pointing. "It's missing the *h*! It's just one letter off from my real email address, and you didn't notice."

The principal peered at the screen. "Clever," she said dryly.

Annabelle sat back in her chair. It *was* clever. Benny must have made a fake account and diverted the emails there. No wonder she hadn't seen them. That one missing *h* made all the difference. Letters were so important!

The principal opened another email, this one with an attachment.

"Here's the note he forged from his doctor—assuming that this Dr. Stack is real?"

"Of course she is," Annabelle said. "Dr. Melanie Stack." The note was written on a ridiculously cheerful letterhead, and she smiled in spite of herself. The logo, a teddy bear holding a smiley-face balloon, suited Dr. Melanie to a tee. She read the letter and started to laugh. She couldn't help it. "Did you even read this?"

Principal Slater frowned. "I'm sorry?"

"The letter. Did you read it?"

The principal swung the monitor back around.

"He misspelled *admitted*," Annabelle said. "And *schizoaffective*."

"This isn't about your son's spelling skills, Mrs. Oh. If he came to school—"

"No, of course, I realize that. But I'm just wondering how you could have thought this note was written by a doctor?"

The frown on the principal's face deepened. She took a deep breath. "And we're wondering, Mrs. Oh, how you could have not known your fourteen-year-old child has been skipping school for weeks now. How you could not have been aware of Benjamin's whereabouts for"—she typed in a series of search commands—"twenty-six days, to be exact?" She swiveled the monitor around again, sat back and waited.

She had a point, of course. Annabelle slumped in the hard chair like a punctured smiley-face balloon. How indeed? The principal was on a roll now, arms crossed, lecturing her about the dangers of truancy. About the kinds of trouble young children could get into when their parents were negligent. About drugs and crime and sexual predation. Annabelle stared down at her hands as she listened, nervously running her forefinger over the ridges on her thumbnail. All her fingernails had ridges on them, which she'd read was a sign of some medical condition, but she couldn't remember what, only that it was probably unhealthy. She had a hangnail, too. She wondered if there might be a nail clipper in her handbag. She'd had one, once. Several, actually.

"Mrs. Oh," the principal was saying. "Do you have any idea where Benjamin was? Who he was with? What he was doing every day when he was supposed to be in school?"

"He said he was at the Library," Annabelle said, worrying the hangnail. "He said he was reading books."

"And you believed that?"

"Yes," Annabelle said. "I did. I mean, I do."

The principal looked at her, incredulous.

"No, really," Annabelle insisted. "Benny loves the Library. He always has, even when he was a baby."

The principal took off her glasses and shook her head. "Mrs. Oh," she said. "With all due respect, I've been working in secondary school administration for my entire adult life, and I've never encountered a case of a truant child going to a library. Truant children go to malls. They go to shoe stores and Starbucks. They hang out in parks and alleyways and abandoned factory buildings. They don't go to libraries."

"Oh, but you're wrong!" Annabelle said. "I saw him there, myself. He went every day during summer vacation, and once I went to check on him. He was sitting at one of those little cubicle desks with a big pile of books stacked all around him. He'd fallen asleep reading—"

But the principal had stopped listening. She was shuffling through a folder, and now she drew out a sheet of paper. "At the beginning of the school year we sent you a letter, which you signed, signifying that you understood the district's attendance policies."

She placed the letter on the desk in front of Annabelle, which indeed bore her signature, and which she vaguely remembered signing but had not actually read.

"So you know that, as a parent, it's your legal responsibility to ensure your child attends school until the age of sixteen," the principal continued. "Failure to comply is deemed to be educational neglect, and the district can file a truancy petition with juvenile court. In the case of chronic absenteeism, we have no choice but to do so."

Annabelle looked up from the letter. "Wait, what? You're going to take me to court?"

"It's the law, Mrs. Oh." Seeing the dismay on Annabelle's face, she softened. "Of course we're not there yet, and I sincerely hope we won't need to, but I just have to warn you—"

"No," Annabelle said, shaking her head. She pulled herself upright and placed both hands on the principal's desk. "No, I'm sorry, that's just not right."

"Excuse me?"

"That's not right at all. Benny's not a juvenile delinquent, skipping school and hanging out at the mall or Starbucks. He hates malls. He can't tolerate Starbucks. The noise is too much for him, but whatever. The point is that my son has a mental disability, Principal Slater, and you people know this, and if he's skipping school it's because the school is failing to meet his needs. So let's talk about that, okay? Let's talk about that."

WHAT FOLLOWED WAS A SERIES of meetings and assessments and conferences, which Benny was compelled to attend. A team was assembled with the special ed teacher, the school nurse, his social worker and case manager. They asked him questions, wanted answers, all of which he found tedious and distressing. The school was legally bound to accommodate him, but he didn't want accommodations. He was fine, he insisted. Just as he was. Sure, he heard stuff talking, but so what? Mostly he could ignore it. Why couldn't they just ignore him, too?

At home, his mother also wanted answers. She was intent on keeping the channels open and creating opportunities for dialogue.

"Benny? . . . *Benny*? . . . *BENNY!*"

"What?"

"How was school today?"

"The same."

"Did you learn anything interesting?"

"No."

"Did you make any new friends?"

"No."

"Did you try? Did you talk to any of the other—?"

"No."

"How's your hand feeling?"

"Fine."

His hand was healing, and the stitches had come out, leaving an angry red slice of a scar, but he was still refusing to say how he'd gotten the injury. The emergency room doctor pulled Annabelle aside after he'd sewn up the hand and told her that the wound looked like it had been inflicted by a sharp blade from a knife or even a sword. Mostly likely the assailant had attacked from above, slashing in a downward motion, and the boy had raised his arm in self-defense. The doctor held his arm up to demonstrate, but later, when Annabelle asked Benny, he denied it.

"That's not what happened at all."

"So what did happen?"

"Nothing. It was an accident."

He refused to explain further, and finally Annabelle threatened to bring him to the police station and file a report.

"Mom," he said wearily. "They're not going to arrest me. I didn't do anything."

She stood in the doorway of his bedroom and studied her son. Was he being sarcastic? Laughing at her? His tone was flat and affectless. He was just stating a fact, and he was probably right, the police would be no help, and this, too, frustrated her.

"But *somebody* did! Somebody hurt you, Benny. You could have lost your thumb! Do you know what it's like to go through life without a thumb? And on your right hand, too! We need to get to the bottom of this."

Benny shook his head. He sat on the edge of his bed, fiddling with his spoon. "I told you it was an accident. I fell and cut it on something. It was dark. I couldn't see. I don't remember."

"Which is it, Benny? You couldn't see or you don't remember?"

"I don't remember."

Annabelle frowned. Was he lying? Why didn't he remember? Had he been taking drugs? "The doctor said you'd been attacked. He said it looked like a knife or sword wound."

"Mom. People don't carry swords around these days, in case you hadn't noticed."

That was definitely sarcastic. He was tapping the back of the spoon impatiently on his knee.

"What people?" Annabelle asked. "Who were you with?"

"Friends," he said, balancing the spoon on his forefinger.

"You were with that girl. Aleph or something. Her number was on your phone—"

"What about her?" he said, his voice suddenly wary.

"Who is she?"

The spoon wobbled. "No one. Just a friend."

If Annabelle detected the longing in his voice, she ignored it and pressed on. She had a hunch. Call it a mother's intuition.

"Is she that friend of Mackson's? Did you meet her in the hospital?"

The spoon fell, and he picked it up again. "No," he said. "She's a friend from school."

Now she had him. "You don't have friends at school, remember?" She tried to keep the note of triumph out of her voice, but it crept in, and he heard it.

"Fine," he said. "I lied. I made her up. She doesn't exist. Happy now?"

What kind of mother feels happy when she catches her child telling a lie? What kind of mother gloats over her child's friendlessness? She crossed the threshold into the room, sat down next to him on the bed, and put her arm around his narrow shoulders. She felt his body stiffen. "Benny, honey. I just want to help. It's good you made some friends at the hospital. Mackson seems like perfectly nice young man, but he's so much older than you, and we don't really know anything about him—"

"Mackson's not my friend."

"Or this Aleph girl. Is she older, too?"

She felt his shoulders go limp. He nodded.

"So why would she want to be friends with a little kid like you?"

He seemed to be shrinking under the weight of her arm. She gave him a squeeze, and then another, trying to pump some life back into him.

"I just don't want to see you get hurt, Benny. I want you to have friends, but age-appropriate friends, okay? Maybe now that you're in this new program at school, you'll meet some kids who are on your same wavelength."

She squeezed again, and he dropped the spoon. She leaned over to pick it up for him, and the words to the nursery rhyme floated into her head. *Hey, diddle diddle, the cat and the fiddle, the cow jumped over the moon. The little dog laughed to see such craft and the dish ran away with the spoon.*

It was one of the rhymes she'd used to help Kenji with his *L*'s. She'd recited it for him, and he repeated it, thickly, clumsily, laughing at his own terrible pronunciation. He couldn't say *diddle* or *fiddle*, but he loved saying *spoon*. When she was pregnant and her belly was big with their son, he would wrap his arms around her and cradle her from behind. *Spoooon*, he would whisper in her ear, drawing out the word. *Spooooooooon*. After he fixed the rocking chair for her, she painted the picture of the cow jumping over the crescent moon on the back, and when Benny was born she sat there and rocked him while he nursed. She remembered what it had felt like, to cradle a tiny new life in her arms and feel the surprisingly insistent tug of his lips on her nipple. The rocking chair had lived in Benny's room for so long, until a few years back, when he said he didn't want it anymore. She'd grown too wide to sit in it, but she couldn't bear to throw it out, so they moved it into her bedroom. Now, holding the spoon in her hands, she wanted so badly to say the rhyme out loud, but she checked herself. She glanced over at Benny, who was still slumped next to her, staring at the ground, and then she reached over and rested the end of the spoon's handle on his knee. She waited, and when he didn't react, she moved the spoon back and forth a few times, making it dance.

"*Hey, diddle diddle*," she whispered.

He jerked his knee away. "Stop it."

BENNY

I loved that spoon. It was old and made of silver—maybe not pure silver, maybe mixed with some alloy or something—but it didn't matter, because whoever made it really knew what they were doing. They knew how to make a spoon that was exactly the right shape to hold in your hand and put into your mouth, even if your hands were still small and your mouth was little. And I was positive that someone beautiful once ate something delicious with that spoon, because I could feel the memory of beautiful lips, and I could taste the deliciousness every time I put the spoon in my mouth and heard it humming with pleasure. Whoever made that spoon made it for that purpose, and the spoon was happy. It would always be happy, as long as it was helping someone eat.

That's why I always ate with it, and why I carried it around with me all the time, and why I was afraid it would get stolen. The rhyme said the dish would run away with the spoon, and I used to believe that could happen. I pictured it as a kind of kidnapping scenario, and I got in the habit of never leaving the spoon alone when my back was turned, especially if there was a dish around. Instead, I'd lick it clean and put it in my pocket. Stupid little kid stuff, which was fine when I was a little kid, but it didn't go over so well in high school. Some of the other guys saw me doing that at lunch, and this one asshole snatched it and ran outside, and his friends followed, and they amused themselves by playing monkey in the middle, throwing it back and forth over my head and yelling shit like, Hey monkey-boy, hey retard, come and get it, until the bell rang and they chucked it up onto the roof. I remember that. The way my spoon looked, spinning through the air like a silvery wheel, and then the sound it made when it landed. The cafeteria was only two stories, and the roof wasn't particularly high, but it sloped, and I heard the spoon clatter down into the rain gutter, where it stayed. I couldn't see it, but after that, whenever I walked by the building, I could hear it humming up there. I was going to tell my special ed teacher what happened and try to get it back, but then I decided not to. It was enough that I knew where it was. Even though my food didn't taste as good, and the spoon didn't sound as happy, at least I knew it was safe so long as I could hear it humming.

And about my mom, I felt bad, but she was driving me crazy with all her questions. I know she was just trying to help, but I couldn't tell her what had happened that night in the Bindery, about all those whispering leaves of paper and all those words, swimming around in the green light. I couldn't tell her about you.

I didn't really know who you were yet. It was too weird, too insane. I couldn't even tell the Aleph or the B-man. Not that I ever saw them anymore, but still. I was afraid if I told anyone I had this book following me around, narrating my life, they'd fucking lock me up forever.

THE BOOK

48

Dr. Melanie changed his treatment plan again. She was concerned about the lethargy, numbness, weight gain and the feelings of remoteness that he reported after returning to school. In Dr. Melanie's mind, symptoms like these were pharmacological; it never occurred to her that they might be the side effects not of his medication but of school, itself. In any case, it was true that once he started on the new regimen, these particular adverse effects diminished, only to be replaced by others, namely restlessness, agitation, and sudden erratic muscle spasms that were impossible to control. It felt to Benny like he was chewing on a wad of tinfoil, like his heart was always just about to explode, but these might have been the side effects of love, too.

"So," Dr. Melanie said, at the start of their next appointment. "How are you feeling?"

How could he possibly tell her? That he was in love with the Aleph, but she didn't love him back? That his heart was breaking? He was fourteen years old! He'd never felt this way before, and he didn't know how to put words to his feelings, so instead he scowled and slouched in his chair, hair falling across his face. "You always ask me that."

She leaned forward, studying him. "I always ask you how you're feeling?"

"Yes."

"And you don't like that?"

"No." He could feel his jaw tighten and his teeth begin to clench.

"Don't you want me to know about your feelings?"

"Definitely not."

"How does it make you feel?"

He felt anger. He felt it in his teeth. He narrowed his eyes and shot her an evil look. "It makes me want to *bite*."

"Okay," she said, drawing back but covering nicely. "Bite me?"

"No!" he said, exasperated. "Your *words*. Bite them off and spit them out!"

He began experiencing paranoid thoughts. His mother wasn't letting him go anywhere after school, especially not the Library, and he hadn't seen the Aleph since she and Mackson had walked him home after the incident at the Bindery. At first they texted frequently. He told her about getting busted, and special ed classes, and what a pain it was to be back in school, and she sent him encouraging messages, telling him to stay chill and remember to breathe, which was hard to do when the sight of her word bubbles took his breath away. But then abruptly her messages stopped. He continued to text her, and his texts seemed to be going through, but she never replied, and when he tried calling, he got an automated response saying, "The number you have reached is not accepting calls at this time." This numerical recalcitrance didn't surprise him—he knew how randomly fickle numbers could be—but after a whole week went by with no word, he had to conclude that the problem was not unreliable numbers but rather that she had blocked his calls.

He wondered if his mother had contacted her and said something that turned her against him, but that didn't make sense. The Aleph wouldn't just cut him off without offering some sort of explanation. Then it occurred to him that maybe it was her phone's fault, that it was blocking him. Electronic devices were untrustworthy, after all, and maybe she didn't even know he'd been trying to reach her! But since he'd never done anything to provoke her phone's enmity, he had to discard this theory, too. Then he started to worry. He became convinced that something terrible had happened to her, that she'd run out of money, or been sent back to the psych ward, or gotten run over by a truck. On the bus to and from school, he sat in his seat next to his mother and stared out the window, fidgeting and chewing on his wad of tinfoil, scanning the sidewalks for a skinny girl in combat boots with a shock of silvery hair, or an old man in a wheelchair, rolling down the street, followed by a billowing cloud of white plastic.

He couldn't stand it. He had to get back to the Library to look for her, so he told his mother he needed to do some research for a science project, and she said she would take him after work. On the bus on the way over she asked him all sorts of questions about his project and offered to help, but he fended her off, and once there, he left her in the periodicals section, while he conducted a methodical sweep of each level, from the ground floor to the top.

The Library seemed different now. When he reached Level Nine, his feet, acting out of habit, took him toward the precipitous footbridge and the improbable nook, but when he approached, he saw that his carrel was occupied by someone else, and the typing lady and astronomy boy were gone. They'd always been there, but now strangers occupied their seats. He paused on the footbridge. Was he even on the right level? He leaned over the railing to check, gazing down nine floors to the subbasement. He was at the top all right. The cold wind rising up from the Bindery made him shiver. He listened for the faint, hopeful voice he'd heard that night, but all he could hear was the wind. When the wind spoke, he followed.

He took the stairs all the way down to the subbasement, pushing through the heavy doors and into Book Processing. That night, the vast room had been utterly still, but now it was humming with activity, with movement and noise. Rollers rattled, wheels clattered, librarians were pushing carts back and forth, and all the while, an intricate arterial network of conveyor belts transported a steady stream of books from one automated station to the next. This state-of-the-art mechanical, computerized book-sorting system was installed as part of the renovation, and the books were beside themselves with loathing. They longed for human hands, for human touch. They bristled with ire at the indignity of their situation as they were spun, flipped, rotated, scanned, sorted, sent sliding down rackety gravity chutes into bins or hoisted hydraulically onto trolleys. It was more than any book could bear, and their lamentations rose above the clamor of the machines—*We are not units! We, who once were sacred, next to God!*

The sound of their heartbreak was almost human. Benny pressed his hands against his ears. He had to stay focused. He saw the staff room and headed toward it, but a librarian with a barcode reader intercepted him.

"May I help you?" she said. She was pointing the handheld scanner at his chest. It looked like a ray gun. Or a phaser weapon. *Warning!*

He took a step back and raised his arms.

The librarian gestured with her weapon. "Are you looking for someone?"

"No," he said. *Alert Level: Orange!* How did she know?

"You're not allowed to be in this area," she said. "It's off-limits to the public."

His mind was racing. She looked familiar. She wasn't a very big librarian. About his height or even smaller. Maybe if he acted quickly, he could disarm her and make a break for the staff room. Maybe the Aleph and the B-man were in there, and even if they weren't, there was probably enough food in that refrigerator to last for several days, and if he had the small librarian's phaser weapon he could take her hostage and hold her there, until the Library was willing to negotiate, and then he could offer to exchange her for the Aleph, who they must be hiding somewhere else. Where? The Bindery! They were holding her prisoner in the Bindery! His leg twitched and he took a step forward.

The small librarian backed away. "Hey," she said. "Are you okay? I'm going to call someone down who can help you. Just relax. Wait here."

Danger! Alert Level: RED! RED! RED!

She was quick, but he was quicker. As she reached for her communication device, he spun on his heel and bolted for the exit, and a split second later he was bounding up the stairs to safety. He took the steps two at a time. He wasn't as fast as he used to be, but he was still fast enough to outrun a small librarian. He reached the ground floor and kept on going, up the levels—Two, Three, Four—until he ran out of breath, and then he paused in the stairwell, gasping for air, but trying to do so quietly because he was listening, too, listening for footsteps following, for Alerts and Warnings, but he heard nothing, only his breathing, slowing, and a few faint words, trailing after his thoughts, like an echo, *like an echo . . .*

He was alone. The sign on the stairwell door said, LEVEL FIVE, so he slipped through it and went in search of the old men's washroom where the Bottleman drank vodka with his friends. Why hadn't he thought of that earlier? That's where they would be! He was certain he remembered where it was located. He followed the route the Aleph had taken, cutting through the 331.880s, but again, things looked different. The shelves in the section on Unions and the Class Rights of Workers were almost empty, and when he reached the spot where the old men's washroom door should be, there was just a blank wall, and no sign of a washroom at all.

Was the washroom real, or did he make it up? *What is real?* This was his philosophical question, the one the Bottleman had helped him discover, and he'd been practicing. At school, when a teacher said something, he would ask himself, *Is this person real?*, and if he decided she wasn't, he didn't bother to respond. When he walked home from the bus stop, and the sidewalk started talking to him, he asked, *Are you real?*, and if the sidewalk answered, he would contemplate its concrete nature, and appreciate how much work it did to bear his weight.

Now, facing the blank wall, he asked it, *Are you real?* When the wall didn't answer, he walked up to it and touched it. It felt as solid and real as a sidewalk. If the wall was real, and it was occupying the place where the washroom door should be, then what did that mean about the washroom? They couldn't both be real.

He shook his head to clear it. Was it the meds? Sometimes they made it hard for him to think logically, and now he had to focus, because if the washroom was unreal, then none of what he remembered from that afternoon in the washroom could be real, either. The Slovenian janitor twins weren't real. The vodka wasn't real. The Bottleman himself might not be real, in which case his philosophical question wasn't real, either. And of course, this made no sense, because his question felt very real—it was the realest thing he knew—and so where did it come from?

He pressed his ear against the wall, listening. He heard the gurgle of a water pipe and realized he was thinking about this backward. Since his question was real, then the washroom must be real, too. It must be right behind this wall. The wall must be hiding the washroom, and maybe it was hiding the Aleph, too, holding her against her will inside the washroom. *Is she in there?* he demanded. *Do you have her?* He listened for an answer, but the wall wasn't talking.

He backed up as far down the aisle as he could, stopping at wealth distribution and class macroeconomics. From here, he could get a running start. If only he had a siege engine, or a battering ram, or even a lance. He bent down like they'd been taught to do in gym class and looked at the wall, and just then, a faint voice, cried out—

No, Benny, wait . . . !

Was it the wall, crying out for mercy? But it was too late, because he was already running down the 339s and picking up speed.

Bam!

He slammed into it, hard, but the wall repelled him, and he fell to his knees. Stunned, he rubbed his shoulder and studied the wall, and then he got to his feet to try again. As he bent down and got into his starting position, he heard the faint voice, calling.

Oh, Benny, no . . .

It must be the wall! The wall was weakening, giving in to his onslaught, and so he charged again, with the other shoulder this time, but again the wall repulsed him. He started kicking at it, encouraged by the hollow sound that confirmed his suspicion. Behind the sheetrock, the wall was hiding the washroom where the Aleph was waiting for him to rescue her.

"I'm coming!" he cried, pounding with his fists and kicking with his

feet, and just as the wall began to relent and give way, Library Security arrived to restrain him and escort him from the stacks.

THE SMALL LIBRARIAN WAS STANDING in the security office when he was brought in. He was docile now, but when he saw that she still had her phaser weapon attached to a holster on her hip, he stiffened.

"Relax, little buddy," the security guy said, and so he did. By now Benny felt okay about the security guy. His name was Jevaun. He had dreadlocks and looked like the musicians that his dad used to hang out with.

"You have a seat," Jevaun said, pointing to a swivel chair. Benny sat. Jevaun turned to the small librarian. "Is this the one?"

"That's him," the small librarian said, and then she turned to Benny. "Are you okay?"

The swivel chair he was sitting on faced a panopticon, comprised of a bank of video monitors, which reminded him of his mother's Mission Control. Grainy black-and-white security camera images flickered on each. He stared at them, thinking he might see the Aleph or the Bottleman slip by, but the jerkiness of the images hurt his eyes, and he had to look away. On the metal desk in front of him was a half-eaten ham sandwich and an open book called *Babel-17*, both of which seemed annoyed to find him sitting there. They didn't like being interrupted, and the chair was unsettled, too, but Jevaun had told him to sit there, so Benny had to stay. He had to do what he was told. He stared down at his sneakers. His toes hurt from all the kicking. His Air Maxes had done nothing to protect him. They were no longer trustworthy. His knuckles were scraped up, too, from the punching, and so he put them in his mouth and started to suck them. They tasted like iron, but they were warm like blood. Everyone in the room was quiet and watching him, so he removed his knuckles from his mouth.

"What?" he said, looking around.

"Are you okay? I'm sorry I called Security, but I was worried. Is your mother or somebody here with you?"

It was the small librarian talking. He'd gotten distracted by the taste of his knuckles and forgotten all about her. What was she doing here? Sneakily, he glanced sideways at her. She was wearing funny glasses. He looked down at her ankles. *"Wang wang,"* he said.

"Excuse me?"

"Kokekokko!" he said.

"Sorry, I don't—"

"Gaggalago! Grunz grunz! Grok grok!"

He'd closed his eyes and was sitting up tall in the swivel chair, neck stretching out long as he barked and grunted and crowed. The librarian stared at him, and the security guard took a step forward. "Hey, buddy," he said. "You gotta chill out now—"

And just then Annabelle burst through the door. She'd been sitting in the periodicals section, browsing through a stack of crafting magazines, when she realized it was getting late. She'd checked the time. What was taking Benny so long? She skimmed another article on gelli printing, and then one on needle felting. Finally, she went to the information desk to ask if they could page him, or help her locate him somehow. They already had.

"Benny!" she cried, pushing past the security guard. She ran to her son and hugged his face into her stomach.

"Shhhh," she said. "Hush, sweetie, hush." She looked up at the guard and the small librarian. "What happened?"

"I found him on Level Five," the security guard said. "Kicking and pounding on the wall and hollering about a washroom. There's no washroom there, I told him. You need a washroom, you gotta go to Level Four, but he kept pounding."

"Oh, sweetie," Annabelle crooned into the top of her son's head. "Did you have to go potty?"

BENNY

I swear to god, my mom is nuts. She's crazier than I am. Okay, sure, that whole wall business was pretty mad, but the new meds were fucking with my head, and I was positive the Aleph was being held hostage in that old men's washroom, and the evil wall was all that stood between us. Turns out I was wrong about the wall, and the washroom was down on Level Four, just like Jevaun said. I must have misremembered.

And I was wrong about the faint voice I heard, too. That wasn't the wall at all, was it? It was you. You were trying to warn me, but how was I supposed to know?

In the end, it was probably a good thing all this mad shit went down the way it did, because it was on account of me barking and crowing that my mom met Cory. She's the small librarian who used to read to us during Children's Hour. I didn't recognize her at first. I was too freaked out by her scanner and trying to figure out how to disarm and kidnap her. But later, in the security office, something clicked, and then Mom made that totally inappropriate comment about going potty, and that's when Cory recognized us, too. She was staring at my mom, and then at me, and suddenly she was like, Hey! I know you guys! You're the little boy who used to sit under my stool and hold on to my ankle! That was the cutest thing ever! And Mom was like, Oh! You're the Children's Librarian! And Cory said, Oh, he's gotten so big! And Mom was like, Oh, no! He still hasn't had his growth spurt yet!

And I'm sitting there, totally dying of embarrassment, with all their ex-clamation points like flying needles in my ears, and at the same time, I'm remembering this other stuff, too, about being under the stool, and the li-brarian's fuzzy skirt, and her warm lady smell, and how nice it felt to hold her ankle while she read, like some kind of miniature pervert or something. How creepy is that? But even though it sounds creepy, that's not how it felt at all. I was too little to be a pervert. I just remember how warm and safe it was under there, with the voices all around me.

So there are actually two reasons why it was good that all this happened the way it did. One, Cory made it so I didn't get arrested or banned from the Library. I just had to promise to check in with a librarian whenever I visited, so they would know I was there. That was one good thing. The other good thing was that on account of me trying to break down the wall, Cory and my mom became friends, sort of. Not right away. Eventually. My mom didn't have any friends after my dad died, and she really needed one more than ever.

THE BOOK

49

When the text from the Aleph finally came, Benny was in math class. It was third period, on the third floor, in Room 332, a classroom he didn't like because the 2 didn't fit in with the 3s, which made it hard to concentrate. His phone vibrated in his pocket, and he sneaked a glance, and his heart jumped right up into his throat and stayed there. The text said,

Get a hall pass. Go to the bathroom.

He'd just gone, but he raised his hand, and amazingly the teacher let him. He left the classroom and headed toward the third floor bathroom.

The first floor bathroom, near West Street exit.

He ran down the stairs. The halls were empty, and his sneaker squeaked. He slipped into the bathroom and stood there, waiting. The door opened, and he ducked into a stall. He heard a zipper, unzipping, and the sound of peeing, and then his phone vibrated.

Come outside. Coast is clear.

But it wasn't. The person was still peeing. It was the longest pee in the history of the universe. Nobody could pee that long. He pressed his head against the side of the stall. Hurry, he thought.

Hurry!

Or, was he hearing things? Maybe the person had already finished and left, and what he was hearing was an echo. An aural impression. Of the sound of peeing. Lingering in the urinal's memory, or in his mind. He heard Dr. M saying *It's a hallucination, Benny. Your brain is causing it. It's not real.* But it sounds so real!

What is real? the old poet asked. He leaned over and peered under the stall door just in time to see the peeing guy's shoes pivot as he zipped up and headed toward the door. Nikes. Those were real. He was not hallucinating.

Hurry!

He slipped out of the stall and washed his hands. The hall was still empty and the coast was clear. He tried to look purposeful as he walked toward the exit, like a normal boy who had an important appointment. A medical appointment, with a doctor or something. A normal boy with a normal mom who was sitting outside in her car, waiting with the engine running. Only his mom didn't have a car and didn't drive, and the only vehicle parked nearby was a beat-up white cargo van with a giant cockroach painted on the side. Over its head were words that said, *AAA Extermination Services.* Underneath, the words said, *Roach-Be-Gone!* The roach was glancing over its shoulder, looking scared.

Look for the white van.

He didn't need to. He'd already seen it, and now he saw her. She was leaning against the bumper, looking down at her phone. It was a glorious fall day, cool and crisp, and a brisk wind had cleared the smoke from the air, and the sun was shining, making her crazy white hair glow like an LED. When he reached the sidewalk, she looked up and waved. He felt his breath catch because she was so bright and beautiful.

"What took you?" she said, swinging open the passenger door for him.

"I got stuck in the washroom."

"Yeah," she said. "That happens."

She climbed behind the wheel, started the engine and drove past the main entrance of the school. Instinctively he ducked, slumping down into the seat, but when they passed the cafeteria, where his spoon was still humming in the rain gutter, he poked his head up and listened. The humming was sadder today. Muted and lonely. He slumped back down again and stared out the dirty side window. They were following the eastbound bus route that skirted the edge of Chinatown, the same one he took to go home. He didn't want to go home. He thought about how the school would probably telephone his mom when he didn't come back from the washroom and how she would freak.

"You might want to text your mom," the Aleph said. "So she doesn't worry."

How did she know? "Yeah," he said, but then he didn't. Instead, he heard himself say, "Where have you been?" His voice came out wrong, all peevish like his mom's, but once it started, it wouldn't stop. "I texted you like a million times but you never texted back." *Shut up, already!* "I thought you were dead or something. . . ."

It was like his words had minds of their own. He turned away to hide his embarrassment. They passed a flop house and a dim sum store and a Chinese butcher. Plucked ducks hung by their long necks in the window. He saw an old Chinese man tugging on a pug. He felt her hand touch his forearm.

"Sometimes I just need to disappear," she said. Her voice was thick with something he didn't understand, but then she squeezed his arm and smiled. "We missed you, too, Benny Oh."

His heart skipped with relief, a quickening joy, just as another hand clasped his shoulder from behind.

"Ya, we hef come to rescue you!"

"Shit!" Benny said. He twisted in his seat and smelled the vodka. "You scared me."

The B-man cackled. He was leaning forward in his wheelchair, which was ratchet-strapped to the side walls of the van. He squeezed Benny's shoulders hard with both hands and grinned his gap-toothed grin. There were a couple of knapsacks and a duffel bag on the floor behind the driver's seat. Benny turned back around. "Where are we going?" he asked the Aleph.

"We are going to ze mountain," Slavoj replied.

THEY HEADED EAST out of the city, following the tracks through the industrial edge sprawl. It was the same trunk road he'd taken on the bus when he visited the Aleph's studio, and when they passed the boarded-up factory building, he pointed to it.

"Isn't that your studio?"

"Was," the Aleph said, keeping her eyes on the road. "We had to relocate."

There was tension in her voice, sadness in her profile. He looked away. The road fed onto a long bridge that spanned the inlet. Below, the docks jutted out like bared teeth, lining the jaws of the estuary. Tall red cranes stretched out their fingers to greet the barges and container ships that stood in line like patient cows, waiting to be milked. Freight trains groaned in the switching yard. Beyond the bridge, the highway turned north and hugged the coastline, and soon they began to climb. The Aleph turned on the radio and a flood of words spilled out, filling the van with throaty *chhh* and *dzzz* sounds that Benny didn't understand, but which he recognized as coming from the same language, sinuous and impassioned, that the

Bottleman used when discussing poetry with the janitors. The Aleph fiddled with the stations and the old man started to complain, but then she tuned in to a jazz station, and he settled back down. "Blue Monk" came on the air. It was one of Kenji's favorites. Behind him, the Bottleman began to snore. Benny closed his eyes and listened to the clarinet riff, and by the time the piano kicked back in, he, too, had drifted off to sleep.

He woke again when the van pulled to a stop.

"We're here," the Aleph said, killing the engine.

They were in a clearing at the end of a dirt road, surrounded by trees that were dark and green, and so tall he could not see the tops of them. Autumn sunlight filtered through the boughs, catching the dust on the dirty windshield and making tiny rainbows. He rubbed his eyes. How long had they been driving?

The Aleph climbed down from the van, and he followed, stepping out into a deep cool pool of silence. He had never heard anything like it before. The clamorous world was utterly still, and in the quiet, he began to discern the tall whispers of wind in the tree tops, and the occasional creak and sigh of wood, and small round sounds that were birds in the forest, singing notes like tiny colored pebbles, catching the light and glinting in the dark silence.

And then there were footsteps in gravel, the creak of rusty hinges, and the Aleph's voice, calling, "Hey, Benny, I need you," from the rear of the van.

She needs me, he thought, and he spun on his heel and ran to her.

She was wrestling a metal ramp from the cargo area. He took the opposite side and pulled. The scraping of the metal was loud, but it didn't bother him. He watched her carefully so as to better time his pull with hers, and he could see the sinewy muscles in her arms and the hollow place under her armpit that curved toward the swell of her breast beneath her tank top. He could see the tiny tattoo markings, like flea bites running along the inside of her forearm. The end of the ramp clattered as it hit the ground.

In the dark interior of the van, the Bottleman was aligning the wheels of his chair with the top edge of the ramp, like a ski racer, testing the snow pack at the starting gate. This chair was different from his usual electric one. It was the folding kind, compact and agile. He made some adjustments, shifting his weight forward and back, settling the briefcase in his lap, and then a maniacal grin split his face.

"On your mark," he said. "Get set . . ." And then, with a howl that spiraled up past the treetops, he pushed out of the gate. The chair hurtled down the ramp and careened down the road, listing and tilting until finally it toppled, pitching the old man into the dirt.

"Oh, for fuck's sake," the Aleph said.

She took off down the road after him, and Benny followed. The chair was on its side, wheels spinning. The B-man lay next to it, motionless, his briefcase open, its contents scattered.

"Hey," she said, squatting down next to him. "You okay?"

He opened his eyes and nodded, sheepishly.

She stood and crossed her arms, looking down at him. "Okay, that was incredibly stupid," she said, and then she turned and walked away.

Benny helped the old man back into the chair, picked up the strewn pages, and wheeled him back to the van. The Aleph was inside, dragging out a large duffel bag.

"Is his chair okay?"

"Kind of. The wheel got bent."

"Oh, great." She passed Benny the duffel and a handful of bungee cords. "Tie that to the back, will you?"

"What is it?"

"Camping stuff." She jumped down and slung a knapsack over her shoulder and pointed to another. "Sleeping bags. That one's yours." She glanced down at the B-man, who was sorting the papers in his briefcase. "You bringing that?"

"Of course," he said. "I must hef my poems."

"Fine." She slammed the van doors. "Let's go."

She led them to an old paved road that wound up the mountain, and taking the lead, she quickly outpaced them. The Bottleman followed, and Benny brought up the rear. Before long the B-man's strength began to flag, so Benny started pushing. The old man sat back in the chair, resting his hands on the briefcase.

"It is a good road, yes?" he said over his shoulder. "Much better than ze alpine pass across ze Pyrenees that Valter Benyameen traversed when he vas fleeing from ze Nazis. Hef you learned about this tragic episode in history, young schoolboy?"

"No," Benny said. "He was the philosopher who killed himself, right?"

"Indeed. It is a very sad story. He vas a German Jew, living in exile in Paris. When Hitler invaded France, Benyameen vanted to escape to America, but he vas a stateless refugee, so he could not get ze required exit papers. His only hope vas to climb over ze Pyrenees into Spain and attempt to leave from there."

The road was growing narrower. Heavy boughs of cedar drooped from overhead and blocked the sky. Muscular roots stretched beneath the road, causing an upheaval of sinuous ridges and cracks in the asphalt.

"It vas an arduous journey, and Benyameen vas not a robust man. Only forty-eight years old, but he hed a weak heart. And then there vas ze heavy briefcase which he carried. It contained ze manuscript of a book. His last book."

The bent wheel of the old man's chair wobbled over the uneven ground.

"He traveled with several others. The hike took two days because he often hed to stop. Every ten minutes he vould put down his briefcase and rest for precisely one minute—he vould time it with his pocket watch—until finally they reached ze summit. From there, they could see ze Spanish coast below and ze deep-blue waters of ze Mediterranean. Imagine! How triumphant they must hef felt! But when they descended to the port town and tried to buy a railway ticket, they were detained by the Spanish police. The police told Benyameen he hed entered Spain illegally and vould be deported back to France ze following day."

They rounded a bend, and the paved road ended.

"They were escorted by ze police to a small hotel. That night, in his dingy hotel room, Valter Benyameen took morphine and died."

Benny leaned in and pushed harder, and the chair lurched forward. "Did the rest of them get sent back then?"

"No. This vas a terrible irony. On ze very next day, Spanish authorities reopened ze border and allowed his friends to leave. One week later, they boarded a ship to America. Benyameen took his pills too soon. If he only could hef waited . . ."

Beneath the wheels was now just dirt and gravel, a rutted path. The B-man clutched his briefcase to keep it from falling.

"Shit," Benny said. "That sucks." The bent wheel caught in a rut. He threw his weight against the chair handles. "What happened to his briefcase?"

The B-man was looking up ahead to where the Aleph was standing. She had her arms crossed, watching them, making no effort to help.

"She is very angry with me," Slavoj said in a low voice. He leaned forward and gripped the wheels, trying to rotate them. "She says I am irresponsible. Ach, of course she is right! She says I am a fool to take foolish risks. But vat choice do I hef? I am a poet. Poets must take risks. And I am a fool, so my risks must be foolish. I see no way around this, do you agree?"

Benny didn't answer. He pushed harder and the chair inched forward. The Aleph turned and walked on. "Is she angry at me, too?" he asked. "She stopped texting me. I couldn't text her, either. I tried."

The Bottleman shook his head. "With you, it is not personal. Only a logistical hitch regarding her communication device, which an intake nurse removed from her possession."

They were moving again, slowly. "Was she back in the hospital?"

The old man shrugged. He was sweating and his face was red. Strands of gray hair were plastered to his forehead. "You must ask her."

SILENTLY, they struggled on, until they came to a great confusion of toppled trees blocking the way. The Aleph had stopped and was surveying the damage. The tall trees lay crisscrossed and scattered, some uprooted, others snapped midway up their massive trunks. She climbed onto one and walked its length like a cat. Benny followed. They looked at the raw, splintered end.

"Blowdown," she said.

"It was probably the storms last winter," Benny said. He knew all about extreme weather events from Annabelle. She had told him about the winter storms and summer fires, the droughts and ozone pollution and overlogging. The soil was dry. The trees were weak. Winds blew them over, or fires burned them down. In winter, when the storms came, heavy rains caused landslides that washed away the soil. And then there were the beetles. Warmer temperatures led to an explosion in the bark beetle population, killing the trees.

He told the Aleph all of this. He'd never said this much to her at once before. "My mom says it's the death of the forests."

"Wow," the Aleph said. "You know a lot."

"Not as much as her. Did you know there are like five hundred and fifty different kinds of bark beetles in North America? More, even."

"Really."

He blushed. He sounded like a know-it-all. "My mom monitors this stuff for logging companies. It's her job."

"Wow," the Aleph said again.

THEY RETURNED TO THE TRAIL, where the Bottleman was sitting on a stump, waiting. He had abandoned his wheelchair and had tried to crawl under the fallen tree trunks, but it was too much for him. His face was covered with dirt, and there were twigs and pine needles in his hair. He looked pale. The Aleph handed him a water bottle. He took a long drink and nodded, pinching his nose and wiping the sweat from his face.

"It is no use. I hef failed. I vill not make it to ze summit. If I were Valter Benyameen, I vould be captured by Nazis now."

"Good thing you're not, then," the Aleph said dryly. She pointed to a clearing off to one side. "We'll set up camp over there."

They wheeled the B-man over a patch of smooth bare rock, stopping a good distance from the edge of a rocky promontory. She set the brake and walked to the brink, and Benny followed. He looked down at his toes. The precipice they were standing on ended in a sheer vertical drop. Far below was a dense canopy of tiny trees and beyond that, the sea. The Aleph turned and walked back to the wheelchair, rolling it backward farther from the edge.

"Do *not* touch that," she said, and the old man nodded meekly. She took out a plastic bag from the duffel, pausing to rest her hand lightly on his grimy, stubbled cheek. Benny watched, wishing he were that old cheek.

"Thenk you, my dear," the Bottleman said. He reached for her hand and kissed the star cluster tattoo on inside of her wrist. In a small voice, he added, "I am so sorry."

"It's okay." She squatted on the rock at his feet and started unpacking food from the bag. She had made log-shaped sandwich wraps, covered in foil. She handed one to the Bottleman and another to Benny, who sat down beside her.

"It vas my fault," the old man said, staring mournfully at the sandwich. "I vas careless." His big head swung heavily from side to side. "I should not hef been so careless."

"True," the Aleph said. "But you can't help yourself."

"I should never hef let them out."

"I should have made other arrangements."

The old man looked beseechingly at her. "I did not think they vould bite me. I thought they liked me."

A flicker of pain crossed the Aleph's face like ripples on a pond. "They didn't really like anyone but me," she said, looking out over the mountains. "They were a one-woman ferret."

TAZ, Benny thought. They were talking about TAZ. "What happened?"

She unpeeled the foil from her wrap and took a bite, chewing slowly. Benny watched the movement of her delicate jawbone, the gentle contraction of her throat as she swallowed. There was a crumb of tortilla stuck to the bottom of her lip. He wanted to remove it. He would have eaten it if he could. It would have been delicious.

She must have felt his eyes on her.

"Eat," she said. The wrap was filled with avocado and salad and cheese. Only when he took a bite did she start talking.

"I was in rehab," she said. "Some shit happened, and I ended up back in the hospital."

She didn't explain. She'd never talked about her diagnosis, and he'd never told her about his. They didn't talk about clinical stuff.

"That sucks," he said.

"Sucks," the Bottleman echoed. "She asked me to care for TAZ. They were in their cage at ze old factory, but it is not pleasant to see animals in cages, you know? So one night I released them. I tried to pick them up and they bit me, and then—" His hands clapped together once, a brief explosion, and then he hugged himself. "I meant to hold them."

"They ran away?"

"Ya," he said. He clenched his fist and punched the empty place on the chair where his leg should be. "And I could not chase after."

"Are they still in the factory?"

"No," the Aleph said. "There were rats in the factory, and the management company had called in the exterminator. They put out poison. We knew this. It is why TAZ was supposed to stay in the cage."

"TAZ ate the poison?"

The Aleph nodded. "They hated rats. They would have hated to die like one."

"Ze exterminator is also my countryman," the Bottleman said. "He found TAZ, and brought them back to me. TAZ vas dead. My friend, he felt terrible. He cried."

"He's a nice guy," the Aleph said, finishing the last of her wrap. "He lent us his truck so we could bring them here for their funeral." She crumpled up the tinfoil and tucked it back in the plastic bag, then started digging around in her knapsack. "I don't know why it matters to me. TAZ was a domesticated ferret, but there was a wildness to them, too. I wanted to honor that."

Benny nodded. He'd never liked the ferret. He'd always felt the Aleph's pet had it out for him, but he was willing to try to feel sad because she was. He watched as she pulled out another wrap and started to unroll it from the foil, glad because he was still hungry.

"That's why I called them TAZ," she said. "I was reading about ferality and temporary autonomous zones, and the name just kind of stuck. But now that they're dead, I wanted to bring them back into the wild. I felt like they deserved a more permanent autonomous zone, like on top of a mountain."

Benny thought about this. "You could rename them," he said. "PAZ...?"

She smiled sadly. "That's a nice idea, but they weren't permanent. Nobody is." She looked at him, and her eyes were shiny. "I know you loved them, too."

Benny nodded, even though he didn't.

"That's why I texted you," she said, holding out the wrap and offering it to him.

He took it, expecting a tortilla. Instead, he saw the ferret's long stiff body, lying on their back in a coffin of foil. The fur was matted and dingy, and one eye was open, staring dully, resentfully, up at Benny.

"They would have wanted you to be here," the Aleph said. "I wanted you to be here, too."

She wanted him to be here! He heard her say it, those actual words, and he wanted to say something back to her that was smart and deep and meaningful. He stared at the foil packet. The ferret's little hands and feet were curled up tight, and their pointed nose looked dried and shrunken and even sharper than before. The body was surprisingly light, lighter even than the sandwich wrap he'd just eaten.

"I thought they were a tortilla," he said.

Seriously? What kind of retard are you?

She smiled sadly. "The exterminator kept them frozen for me until I got out."

"What are you going to do with them?"

Gee, how many stupid questions can you ask, dumb fuck?

"I wanted to build a funeral pyre and cremate them, but there's still a fire ban, so we have to bury them instead."

"That's better," Benny said.

Oh, listen to the expert!

"I guess," the Aleph said. "They'll go back to the earth that way, and it's more organic. But I liked them becoming part of the wind and the air."

Benny looked up at the wind in the treetops. "I never thought about it like that before."

Like you think about anything?

"Anyway, there's too much smoke in the air," she said. "I don't want to add more." She stood and stretched. "Let's get going."

"What should I do with them?" Benny asked.

How about you shove that ferret tortilla up your ass, retard boy?

"Just wrap them back up, and we'll take them with us."

She looked over at the Bottleman, who was asleep in his chair, his head fallen forward like a heavy sandbag.

"We'll have to go without him."

50

Annabelle hauled two more bags out to the sidewalk and heaved them on top of the pile by the curb. That was it for the nonrecyclables from the front porch. Now there was just the stuff from the back porch and the small yard, and all the paper recycling in the house. She took her inhaler from her pocket and puffed. Her hip was hurting. She really should make more of an effort to get outside and get some exercise. Maybe once the air quality improved. The rains would be here soon and scour the last of the smoke from the sky. She was looking forward to winter, to the long gray days and the soft, damp chill that made you feel okay about staying in-doors where it was warm and cozy. She checked her watch. No-Good was coming to inspect that evening, and she still had quite a bit to do. Benny promised he would help when he got home from school, but she needed to stay focused.

A crow cawed from the powerline overhead, and she looked up. The bird was watching her with its beady black eye.

"All right, all right," she said. "So impatient . . . !"

She limped around the house to the feeding station in back. The crow followed, calling to its friends. One by one, they came, swooping overhead from roof to roof, branch to branch, in a flurry of sleek black wing and feather, and coming to land on the fence that bordered the alley. From there, they observed her as she climbed the sagging porch steps to the kitchen. They cocked their heads and waited. When she reemerged with a mooncake in her hand, one of the bigger and more daring juveniles flew to the porch railing and sidled over to the platform.

"Well, you're getting awfully bold," she said to him. "You think you can get away with that? Didn't your mommy teach you any manners?"

The young crow bobbed up and down and ruffled its feathers. "*Caw,*" he said, and Annabelle laughed. She'd seen this particular crow fly off with an entire mooncake in his beak, so she broke it into pieces, and held one out.

"Here. You want it?" She waited. The young crow cocked his head, beady black eye looking first at the cake and then at her face, back and forth. She'd been trying to train him to take food from her hand, even though she knew she shouldn't. She monitored news for the Park Service, so she knew it wasn't good for wildlife to get acclimated to humans, but this crow was so cute, and smart, too.

"Come on," she said. "I won't hurt you." The crow edged a bit closer and stretched out his neck, flapping his wings to keep his balance on the railing. He poked his long sharp beak out further and further until the tip was just inches from her fingers, and then, at the last minute, withdrew and hopped away.

"Not so brave after all, are you?" she said, dropping the piece of cake on the platform and scattering the rest. "You be sure you share that with your brothers and sisters." She stepped away, and immediately her young crow flapped over, snatched the biggest morsel and flew off, and then the rest followed, swooping down in groups of two and three. In the months after Kenji died, she would occasionally forget to feed them, and when she did, the crows would complain outside her window. Some people might have found the ruckus annoying, but Annabelle never did. They greeted her with caws and flapping. They studied her. They knew her habits. You could even say that, in their crowish way, they were fond of her, or at least that's what it felt like, and she was grateful.

When the last crow had eaten, she surveyed the backyard. She'd made some progress, but there was still so much left, and she couldn't pile any more stuff on the sidewalk without risking a fine. She should have started this weeks ago. Well, there was no help for it. She would have to use the Thrift Shop dumpster and hope no one would see her. She wrestled a couple of big bags through the gate, and when she saw the alley was clear, she dragged them to the dumpster and heaved them up and over the side. Some children's items—an infant car seat, a baby bassinet—lay discarded on the sidewalk, and she stopped to inspect them. Benny's stroller was somewhere in the house, but it had been years since she'd laid eyes on it. Was it in the hallway closet? She vaguely remembered seeing it there, but she hadn't been inside that closet for a while. Well, now was her chance to get rid of it. This was no time for sentimentality, she thought, heading back into the house. It was time to move on.

51

They left the Bottleman asleep with his briefcase, a bag of nuts, and a bottle of water. They pinned a note to his chest where he would be sure to see it when he woke. *We've gone to the summit*, the note said. *Text if you need us. Do not touch the brake!*

They climbed over the downed trees, and as they scrambled up the scree-covered slope, the trees thinned and the blue sky grew bigger, expanding overhead and then stretching out on all sides like a big round bowl, so that when they emerged onto the rocky pinnacle that marked the summit, the sky was so big that some of it was even below them. Benny had never been higher than the sky before, and the view made him dizzy. He looked out over the mountain ridges that rippled toward the sea. He could see dry, dead rectangles demarcating the clear cuts, and blackened strips where the slash had been burned, but mostly the mountains were still green with trees, the closer ones dark, the distant ones made pale by mist and smoke and haze. Beyond the palest line of trees they could see the ocean, and the container ships carrying e-waste to China were just specks on the dull gray water. A stiff breeze blew in from the sea, bringing a faint smell of salt and smoke and charred wood.

It felt like the top of the world. They stood there, side by side, facing into the wind. The Aleph stood on her tiptoes and leaned forward, looking as if she were about to fall, but the wind held her. Her icy-white hair, made crazy by the wind, rose up from her head like live things. She closed her eyes. When she breathed in, her nostrils flared, and when she breathed out, her words traveled on the outflow of her sigh.

"Beautiful, isn't it?"

"Yes," he said, knowing he should be admiring the landscape, but unable to take his eyes off her. She was so precariously beautiful, standing there on the edge.

She smiled, as if somehow sensing he wasn't looking at the view. "Close your eyes, too," she said. "Close your eyes and really listen," and so he did.

It was a strange sensation. Ever since the voices started, he'd fallen out of the habit of really listening. He couldn't help hearing the voices because they were there, but he learned he didn't have to listen, and most of the time he tried not to. But this was different. He could hear the wind, and that was all—*that was all*—and it was so simple and beautiful, rising and falling, whistling and tapering off and then swelling again. It was real. It was the realest thing he'd ever heard, and when he opened his eyes, the Aleph was watching him.

"Did you hear it?"

"The wind?"

"The world, breathing."

She led him over to a grove of stunted fir trees, and they sat in the shade, facing out to the sea. They didn't talk, but it was okay. He was hot after all the climbing and it was nice in the shade. He closed his eyes and tried listening again, and now he heard a small sound coming from the moss, behind him.

"Oh," he said, opening his eyes and twisting around to look.

She followed his gaze. "What?"

He hesitated, not wanting to sound stupid. "My shadow."

"You don't have a shadow. We're in the shade."

He nodded. "I know. That's why I almost didn't hear it."

He glanced at her to see if she thought he was crazy, but she was studying the pillow-like mound of moss behind him. "What did it say?"

"Nothing. Just that it was tired. From walking up the mountain in the sun. It likes the shade for giving it a place to rest. Is that weird?"

"No," she said seriously. "Your shadow's right. This is the perfect place to rest."

She opened her knapsack and took out a water bottle and the foil wrap containing the dead ferret, which she laid on the ground. She uncapped the water bottle and drank, and he studied the undulations of her throat as she swallowed. She wiped her mouth with the back of her hand and handed him the bottle. He took a sip, astonished that his lips were touching the same rim that hers had touched only moments before. He ran his tongue around the inside of the rim, hoping for a taste of her. He wanted to drink some more, but he stopped himself and screwed the cap back on.

She turned to kneel beside him, brushing stray twigs from the pillow of moss. She unwrapped the dead ferret and lifted the stiffened body from the foil.

"Do you think your shadow would mind sharing?"

He shook his head. He was pretty sure his shadow had moved on but it was hard to tell. She laid the ferret on the mossy pillow. She brushed away a smudge of dirt.

"There," she said, sitting back on her heels. "That's good."

She stood and stretched her arms over her head, arching her back and exposing a sliver of pale skin and the sharp tattooed bone of her hip, then she sat down again, next to him but with the ferret still between them. He glanced down at the dead animal. Even in death.

"Are you just going to leave them there?"

She was looking back out to the sea, and at first he thought she hadn't heard, but then she spoke. "It's a sky burial. That's what they do in Tibet when someone dies, but it makes even more sense for an animal. I mean, why stick them underground? Here we are, on the top of the world. Better for them to just be here in the open. Until they're not."

"But they're a ferret."

"So?"

"Don't they live underground?"

She frowned. "Good point. But TAZ liked being aboveground. They were pretty social. And we can cover them with some moss." She picked up a few long, stringy pieces of witch's hair lichen and laid them across the ferret like a blanket. "I wish the B-man was here. He wrote a poem for

TAZ. He wanted to read it." She smoothed the lichen. "Do you think he'll be upset?"

He couldn't see her face, but he could hear pain in her voice, and this surprised him. He was used to hearing pain in the voices of things, and he often knew at once what they were feeling. But human beings were more opaque. And then there was the question itself. Why would he know what the B-man would feel? She knew him so much better than he did.

"No," he said, but he had no idea if this was true or not.

She was looking out at the ocean again. "He showed me that story you wrote. The one about the table leg."

"Oh," Benny said. "That." He'd forgotten all about the table leg. "That was stupid."

"It was sad."

"I'm sorry," he said, because he didn't want to make her sad.

"No. I mean, sad in a good way."

"Oh, good," he said, because he wanted to make her happy, but then he realized he didn't understand. "Wait, is there a good way to be sad?"

"Sure. Art can make you sad. Or music. Or a book."

"A book?"

"Sure. Hasn't a book ever made you cry?"

He thought about *Medieval Shields and Armaments* and *Byzantine Garden Design*. "No."

"Okay, wow. Well, maybe you should try reading different books."

He fell silent. Books were what he read in order not to feel sad. He thought about the book his mom was reading. *Tidy Magic.* He'd seen it splayed open on her bed. The little book looked sad, or maybe it was just discouraged. "My mom reads books," he said. "I think she's always sad, but not in a good way."

"That must be hard."

He shrugged. "She's okay."

"Hard for you, I mean."

He'd never considered whether Annabelle's sadness was hard for him or not. "She tries to be happy. And I'm used to it by now."

"The B-man is the same," she said. "He tries to be happy. That's why he drinks."

He thought about this for a while. "You know how the B-man hears voices?"

"Yeah."

"And I hear voices, too?"

"Yeah."

"So, do you think I'm . . ." He hesitated. "You know—"

"What?" There was an edge to her voice now.

"Nothing."

"Say it," she said. "Do I think because you hear voices, you're going to end up like the B-man, a random old homeless dude in a wheelchair, with a missing leg and rotting teeth, who needs a shower and drinks too much and collects cans and bottles and begs for spare change?"

The edge of her voice was turning into a blade. *Danger!*

"That's what you mean, isn't it?" she asked. Eyes narrowed. Watching him.

He nodded, miserable.

She studied him. He held his breath, his entire life in balance, waiting for her verdict.

"No, Benny," she said finally. "Most definitely not."

He felt a rush of relief, but she wasn't done.

"Because that's not what the B-man is, either. You think he's this crazy old hobo, but he's not. He's a poet. And a philosopher. And a teacher. And it's not him that's crazy, Benny Oh. It's the fucking world we live in. It's capitalism that's crazy. It's neoliberalism, and materialism, and our fucked-up consumer culture that's crazy. It's the fucking meritocracy that tells you that feeling sad is wrong and it's your fault if you're broken, but hey, capitalism can fix you! Just take these miracle pills and go shopping and buy yourself some new shit! It's the doctors and shrinks and corporate medicine and Big Pharma, making billions of dollars telling us we're crazy and then peddling us their so-called cures. *That's* fucking crazy. . . ."

She was breathing hard. The sun had disappeared behind a thick bank of clouds on the horizon and the sky was darkening.

"Sorry," she said.

He didn't understand, but he felt she must be right. Or, rather, he felt that if she believed this so strongly, then he would, too. He wanted so badly to believe what she did. She was looking out over the mountains toward the sea.

"The B-man's a fucking revolutionary, Benny. And he's also the kindest man who ever lived. He found me on the street when I was fourteen, and he took care of me. Every time I ran away from whatever foster home they put me in, or started using again, he was there to catch me. He taught me stuff, about art and books. Protected me from all the scum—or tried to, anyway."

She turned to him. Reaching over the body of the dead ferret, she took his hand and pulled it to her, sandwiching it between her knees. "So what if you hear voices. A lot of people do. That doesn't make you like him, but who knows? Maybe you'll be a poet or a philosopher or a revolutionary, too." She squeezed his hand and then released it. "You are who you are, Benny Oh. Just don't let anyone tell you that's a problem."

His hand hovered by her knee, reluctant to return to him. It was awkward.

"It's going to get dark," she said. "We better go back." She shifted and then knelt beside her dead pet, leaning down until her lips touched their ear. "Goodbye, my dear darling TAZ," she whispered. "I love you. You'll be with me forever."

Benny watched, wishing once again that he were the dead ferret.

She straightened up and stretched again and took out her phone. "I'll tell the B-man we're coming. Hey, did you text your mother?"

52

I'm with my friends. Dont worry! ☺

Her phone pinged as the text flashed on the screen. A minute or so later, it pinged again, making a feeble second attempt to summon her, but to no avail. There were missed-call notifications from the school, too, but buried under a stack of junk mail on the kitchen table, the phone was mute and helpless.

At that moment, Annabelle was maneuvering Benny's old stroller out the back door and onto the porch. Balanced on the stroller was a heavy cardboard box filled with old books, boots, and broken kitchen appliances. On top of the box was a large plastic fan, speckled with fly dung, and a musty set of secondhand golf clubs that Kenji had bought and never used, which she'd found in the closet along with the stroller. She was pleased. The stroller was the perfect means of conveyance. The books she would bring to the Thrift Shop, and she was sure they would take the stroller, the fan, and the clubs, too. Maybe not the boots, which were worn and covered with cobwebs, although she'd done her best to clean them. The broken appliances maybe someone could fix, but if the Thrift Shop really didn't want them, she could pitch them into the dumpster on the way back.

She stood on the porch and pondered the loaded stroller and the rickety steps. Rather than pushing, it would be easier to back down the stairs and pull the stroller after her. She maneuvered into position and tugged on the footrest where Benny's little feet used to go. The splintery wood of the stair tread sagged beneath her, and the heavy box teetered above. This was going to be harder than it looked, and for a moment she considered unloading the stroller and bringing the stuff down bit by bit, but it was getting late and the Thrift Shop would be closing and she had to pick Benny up from school. She took another step, drawing the stroller toward her.

The front wheels spun in the air as she gripped the axle, trying to support its weight with one hand and stabilize the load with the other, but it was too much. She tugged too hard, and the back wheels rolled over the edge of the tread, and the whole towering contraption shuddered, and swayed, and pitched forward. With a cry, she fell, tumbling down the steps, and as the loaded stroller clattered down on top of her, her head hit the concrete at the bottom.

She lay on her back, drifting in and out of consciousness. She was dully aware of the pain migrating through her body. It moved from the base of her head, down her spine and into her hip, then leaped across to her wrist and arm, and now there was something sharp poking her, and something heavy holding her down. She blinked, opened her eyes, saw the sole of a boot and the sky darkening around its edges. She tried to dislodge the box fan that had fallen across her chest, but the movement hurt, and so she stopped. It was late. Benny would be getting home from school soon. That was good. He could help her. But there was something else. She shivered, suddenly cold. Was it winter already? Benny was in school. He would be getting home—but no, he wasn't allowed to ride the bus alone anymore! She had to go pick him up, and he was waiting! She moved her arm, pushed through the pain against the weight until it shifted. Something clattered beside her. A toaster oven. Where was her phone? She heard a groan, coming from her throat as the pain worsened, and then something moved in the corner of her vision. A flash of darkness, a black smear, and then another. She closed her eyes, and the world faded away.

HOW LONG DID SHE LIE THERE? A few minutes? A few hours? It was late October, and the days were growing shorter, the weather cold and raw, and the autumn rains chose this moment to start. Bad timing. She lay there as the first drops fell.

Inside the house, under the stack of junk mail, her cell phone pinged and flashed.

Be home tomorrow morning! Dont be mad ok? ☺

A crow perched on the roof. It cocked its head and trained a beady eye on Annabelle. Another crow arrived, and then a third, and then the flock followed. One by one, they flew down, landing on the ground beside her. Cautiously at first, and then with more ease, they ambled over to her, flapped and settled on top of her, spreading their feathers to keep her warm and dry.

BENNY

I didn't know. I didn't know she'd fallen. I just wanted to tell her I was okay so she wouldn't freak out. She didn't text me back, so I figured she was just pissed off but she'd get over it. If she was really freaking out, she would have texted right back. That's what I thought anyway. I didn't know she'd fallen. I didn't know about the crows.

THE BOOK

53

They climbed back down to the rock below, where the B-man was waiting. He was reading a book and scribbling poems in the margins, and somehow the water bottle they'd left him now had vodka in it. The Aleph didn't say anything, just pressed her lips together and started unpacking the duffels, dragging the camping gear far away from the cliff to an open area by the trees that was covered in crunchy moss. The sleeping bags were old and smelled like damp basements and unwashed hair, but Benny didn't mind. He was just happy she'd brought one for him, and happy, too, because she'd brought more food: more sandwich wraps, and chips, and a plastic bin of salsa. She told him the sandwich wraps were on account of Mackson scoring a whole unopened case of freezer-burned tortillas from a Mexican restaurant dumpster. Mackson's an awesome gleaner, she said. The chips and salsa came from there, too. Benny didn't know what a gleaner was, but he wanted to be one.

"Is Mackson coming?" Maybe the extra sleeping bag was for him, or maybe Mackson and the Aleph were going to share one, which would be even worse.

"Coming where?"

"Here."

They were unrolling the tarp, and she stopped and shook the hair from her face. "No, he went back to college."

This didn't make sense. Mackson was only sixteen. On Pedipsy, Mackson was a Blue, which was the team for the older kids, but that didn't make him old enough for college.

"He graduated high school when he was fifteen and started college right away," the Aleph said. "He's super smart, like a genius or something, but the pressure got too much."

It pissed him off that Mackson was a genius, but he didn't say anything.

"Halfway through his second year, he flipped out, and his parents made him come home."

That was weird. He'd never thought of Mackson as having parents. He told her this, and she laughed, but not in a mean way.

"Everybody's got parents, Benny."

Two things were going through his mind. One was that he couldn't picture the Aleph with parents, either. She said she'd run away, but even before that, growing up in a house with a mother and a father and maybe a dog—the image just didn't fit. It seemed more likely that she was an extraterrestrial being who had hatched from a beautiful alien egg, and he didn't mean that in a bad way. She just seemed to have come from a dream.

And the second thing he thought was that he couldn't imagine himself with parents, either. Not with two of them. Not anymore.

"Where are your parents?" he asked.

She was sniffing the flannel lining of the sleeping bag, and she screwed up her nose. "I don't have any."

"But you said . . ."

"Everybody but me."

So maybe he was right about the beautiful alien egg. It was clear she didn't want to talk about it, and there was something more pressing he needed to know.

"Are you and Mackson—" He stopped in midsentence.

Oh, please. You're not really going to ask her that?

"Are we what?"

"Nothing."

Ask her, fuckface. Or don't. Because it's really none of your fucking business.

She was crouched down on the moss, spreading out the blankets. She looked up at him and squinted. A last ray of sunlight caught her cheekbone and the golden sheen gave him courage.

"I mean, are you guys, like . . . together?"

"As in a couple?" She frowned, but he sensed she was amused, too. "No. Mackson's great, but we're just friends. And we're both in recovery, too, so we don't really do the romantic thing, you know?"

"Oh, yeah," he said. He didn't know what she was talking about, but inside he felt a mad rush of happiness.

Wow. You really are pathetic.

"We met on Pedipsy, and when we got out, Mackson got a bunch of us to help him with this group. The SPK."

"Oh, right," he said.

Liar. Shithead.

"Isn't that like for protecting animals?"

She laughed. "No. It's a peer support group."

Bitch, the voice muttered, but she looked so unbitchy, crouching on the moss with her head cocked, explaining stuff, that the voice gave up and faded away.

"For young people who are labeled mad or diagnosed as mentally ill. The group's still going, but Mackson went back to school."

"What does SPK stand for?"

"Socialist Patients' Collective."

He still didn't understand, but this time he wasn't going to fake it. "Collective is with a C."

"In German, it's Kollective, spelled with a *K*. The B-man was telling us about it. He was part of this group of students and mental patients in Heidelberg back in the seventies, when he was in university. They had it right. They knew they weren't the crazy ones. They were sane. It was capitalism that was making everyone else crazy."

He looked up at the mountain top. "Like what you were saying up there."

"Exactly."

They brought the sandwiches and food back over to the rock. The B-man was sitting there in his wheelchair with his notebook in his lap, staring out at the sunset, and they sat on the ground next to him. He seemed quiet, subdued, and not terribly drunk, but the Aleph still seemed annoyed. She asked him, somewhat curtly, if he was okay, and he just nodded and sighed and pointed with his pen out to the horizon.

"So beautiful," he said. "Soon the fall rains vill be coming." And it was true. Dark rain clouds had already collected over the city, but over the ocean, the sky was a deep indigo blue. A thin line of orange lingered on the horizon where the sun used to be, and a pinkish silvery afterglow, like a memory, shimmered on the surface of the water. In the foreground, the dark looming shapes of islands looked like giant beasts, bedding down for the night. Even the wind was more subdued. The B-man spoke softly into the wind.

"When I vas still a young man and hed two legs, I used to enjoy skiing and climbing in ze mountains. Now, I cannot often leave ze city, and climbing mountains is impossible." He looked down at the Aleph, sitting beside his wheelchair, hugging her knees. "Thenk you, my dear."

The tone of his voice made Benny look up. He saw the sadness in the old man's face, and he wanted things to be okay between them. The Aleph didn't say anything at first, and Benny thought she was still mad about the vodka, but then, in a small voice, like a guilty child, she said, "I left TAZ up on top."

The old man closed his eyes, and for a moment his big head looked too heavy for his neck to support, but then he pulled himself upright in his chair.

"I see," he said, nodding slowly. "A sky burial."

"I should have waited for you."

"I could not climb so high."

"Then we should have done it down here."

"No, no, it is perfect. On top of ze world."

"But you had a poem—"

He reached over to her, resting his rough hand gently on top of her head like he was holding her down to the earth with the weight of it. "Ferrets do not care about poetry. You did just ze right thing, my dear. Nothing else is needed."

THAT NIGHT THEY SLEPT ON THE MOUNTAIN, like caterpillars in their bags, all lined up in a row. Above them the dark night sky was sighing, and below Benny could hear the breathing of the earth and the crunching of moss whenever he moved—something he was trying not to do, but the Aleph was lying next to him, so close they were almost touching, and he was trembling, quite literally vibrating, not from the cold, but from the proximity to her. He was sure she would notice and say something, but she didn't. She and the B-man were talking, and Benny lay on his back, arms stiff at his sides, trying not to shake as he stared up into an emptiness that was bigger and blacker than anything he had ever seen. There were stars, but they were millions of light years away, and there was the moon, but it was just a small pale hole in the blackness. Sometimes airplanes went by with their headlights pointing to Asia, and there were satellites, too—low-earth orbit weather satellites, telecommunications satellites, GPS and military surveillance satellites, circling the globe in mega-constellations like bright planets on a mission. Benny thought they were cool, but the Bottleman was on a quiet rant about them. It's the end of dark skies, he was saying. The end of astronomy. Ptolemy, Copernicus, Galileo would weep to see this, and all the space debris, too, orbiting Earth like a thick cloud of gnats—old rocket boosters, dead spacecraft, busted-up satellites and weapons; the bags of Russian garbage from the Mir space station; not to mention all the ordinary things people lose on earth, like a glove, a wrench, or a toothbrush. Space was a junkyard, the B-man was saying. When he was a kid in Slovenia, there was no debris in outer space, he said. Space was clean as a whistle.

It freaked Benny out. Space junk was not something he'd ever thought about when he looked up at the sky at night, because space seemed so big and empty, but as he lay there, listening and looking upward, he felt the presence of the Dark Comet looming at the edge of his consciousness. The Dark Comet always started this way, a tiny mote of matter in his mind, emitting waves of dense energy that oscillated through him, thrumming and growing larger and larger and larger, bearing down on him until it—

No! he thought, groping for his Coping Card, but there was no coping technique for lying on a mountaintop next to the girl you love, with the Dark Comet hurtling toward you.

Then her voice, like a slight breeze, brushed against his ear. "You okay?"

He couldn't answer so he nodded, even though she couldn't see.

"You have your inhaler?"

He remembered then. It was in his pocket. He fished it out and took a puff and felt better.

Then the B-man's voice drifted through the darkness, "Is it freaking you out, young schoolboy?"

He was talking about space. He was talking about emptiness and silence.

"No—" Benny said.

Liar!

"Maybe. A little. I've never slept outside before."

The Aleph's hand crept across the moss like a small burrowing animal looking for warmth. Benny heard it coming, felt it brush against his arm and travel down into his sleeping bag past his wrist to his palm. He felt her fingers twine through his as she drew his hand back across the moss toward her. She brought his knuckles to her lips and then clasped his hand between hers, tucking it under her chin like a prayer. His shaking subsided.

He didn't care that she knew he was freaked out. He wanted her to know, and the B-man, too. He wanted them to know everything, but the words wouldn't come, and in the long silence that followed, one by one, they fell asleep.

54

The first thing No-Good saw when he swung his Nissan onto the block was the dark, gleaming silhouette of the garbage bag escarpment, rising from the rain-slick sidewalk in front of his mother's house. He pulled over to the curb and sat there, leaning over the steering wheel with the engine running. In the cool bright light of his headlights he could see the rain falling on the wet plastic. He turned off the ignition, got out, and slammed the door, kicking at a bag that blocked the sidewalk. Stupid *gweipo* pig. This would get them a ticket for sure, but let her pay the fine. He lit a cigarette, exhaled, and pulled up the collar of his jacket.

Her front porch looked better. He hadn't expected that. He squinted at his ma's side of the duplex. It looked shabby, too, but slap on a coat of paint and it'd look prime. Wouldn't be long now. The real estate agent was set to list, just get the *gweipo* out, Fung said, so what the fuck was he waiting for? He ground out the cigarette under his heel, took the porch steps two by two, and knocked loudly. When no one answered he peered into the front window. He could see the glow of the lady's computers through a crack in the curtain. His ma said her job was reading newspapers, but that was obviously bullshit because nobody got paid for that. With all that computer equipment, whatever she was into must be major. When he evicted her, maybe he'd get possession of it. With a setup like that you could do serious business. Fung would work it out.

He banged on the glass, first with his knuckles and then with his fist, and still no answer, so he headed around toward the back. She knew he was coming and he'd find her. She couldn't hide from him, no way. She'd barely made a dent in the trash that lined the side of the building. Good, he thought, as he picked his way past it. Just give me a reason, honey pie, that's all I need, and then he rounded the corner and stopped short.

At the bottom of the porch steps, under an overturned stroller, was the big dead *gweipo* lady. She was lying on the ground, surrounded by stuff. Boots. Books. A toaster. A box fan. Junk. He stood there, staring, unable to move. He had found his ma on the ground, too, but she was tiny and alive and screaming at him even with her broken hip. This *gweipo* was big and fat and silently dead, and there was something else, too, something shiny and black, covering her body. He took a step forward, and that's when he saw it, the really fucked-up thing that filled him with terror and would haunt his dreams—she was covered with crows. She was covered with crows, and they were eating her.

Nobody deserved that.

A tangle of golf clubs lay on the ground. Grabbing a nine iron, he ran at the crows, brandishing the club and screaming, *"Get off her, you mother-fuckers!"*

In a flurry of beating wing and black feathers, the flock rose up from her body like a dusky cloak and flew away into the alley. No-Good watched them go, cursing them, and he was still standing there, with the nine iron raised over his head, when the lady's eyelids fluttered, and she blinked and opened her eyes.

"Oh," she said, looking up at him, bewildered.

He looked down and gasped. "What the fuck, lady! You're not dead!"

She raised her head slightly, wincing at the pain, and peered down the length of her body. "No," she said, weakly. She looked back up at him and saw the nine iron. "Oh! Were you trying to kill me?"

It seemed so clear to her, so obvious. She had no memory of the fall, and so when she regained consciousness and felt the pain radiating through her body and saw No-Good standing over her with the golf club raised, what else could she conclude? She had a hazy memory that he didn't like her—or maybe she didn't like him? Yes, that was it. She didn't like him because she feared him, because he was trying to kill her. It all made sense. She tried to sit up, but the pain was too great. There was nothing she could do. This was it. Even after he dropped the golf club and called 911 and started moving the stroller off her, she just lay there with her eyes closed, waiting for the end. Why didn't he just get it over with? Please, she thought, and then, miraculously, as if in answer to a prayer she never made, she heard sirens approaching, the screech of brakes and the slamming of doors. There were hands, touching her, and men in uniforms asking questions. What happened? Did you fall down the stairs? She opened her eyes. Oh, no, Officer, she explained. That man tried to kill me.

The paramedics examined her. She heard the crackle of police walkie-talkies and No-Good explaining that there had been no assault, he wasn't trying to kill the lady, he'd called 911, he'd saved her life! Saved her from being devoured by the filthy crows that were crawling all over her body, about to eat her flesh and pick her bones! Annabelle knew this was wrong. Kenji's crows would never eat her, and she knew what she'd seen: No-Good Wong, standing over her with a raised golf club in his hand.

But her injuries told a different story. They could not have been inflicted by a nine iron, the paramedics explained. She must have tripped and fallen down the steps, and they pointed to the boots and the books and the golf clubs, littering the ground. Lying on the gurney, Annabelle realized they must be right. She tried to explain. They were my husband's things. He's dead. I was cleaning out the closet. It was an accident. I'm sorry. I made a mistake. Satisfied, the police headed back to their cruiser. The paramedics loaded her into the back of the ambulance. No-Good was lurking around in the shadows outside.

"I'm sorry," she said. "Thank you for finding me."

No-Good shrugged. "Yeah, no worries."

There was something else, but her memory wasn't right. She looked at her landlady's son, slouching against the side of the duplex, one hand covering his birthmark, something she'd seen him do ever since he was a teen. He was always a twitchy, fidgety kid, and now he was a twitchy, fidgety man. The police had left, but he seemed to be waiting. For what? And then she remembered. He was going to inspect her house. She hadn't finished tidying, and now it was too late. The paramedic reached for the door, and No-Good stuck his head in.

"Hey, Miz Oh. You need me to do anything?"

"Oh, no, thank you," she said. Henry. His name was Henry. Maybe he wasn't such a bad son, after all, and then she remembered.

"Wait!" she cried. "Have you seen Benny? Where is he?" She struggled to sit up, but she was strapped to the gurney.

"Please," she said to the paramedic, grabbing his arm. "I have to pick my son up from school. He's waiting for me. He's not well. Where's my phone? Henry, can you find it? I think I left it on the kitchen table. Please, we can't leave yet, I need my phone. I need to call my son!"

As she watched No-Good climb the steps, squeeze past the junk on the porch and push open the door, an image of the kitchen—the state she'd left it in—rose in her mind's eye. She'd meant to get it all cleaned up before No-Good came for the inspection. She'd never let him inside the house before, and now he would see everything. She let her head drop back against the gurney.

"Oh God," she whispered. "What have I done?"

55

The wind had died on the mountaintop, and a dense, thick fog had moved in from the sea, blocking out the moon and stars. Benny woke to find the Aleph's hand gone. Had he really been holding it or was that just a dream? He could hear the Bottleman snoring and her quiet breathing. They both sounded so close, like the three of them were lying under a blanket together, only blankets are warm, and the fog was cold. His nose was like a nub of ice. He had to pee, but he didn't want to leave his sleeping bag, so he waited for as long as he could, and then he wriggled out and started walking. The rocks were sharp, and the moss crunched under his socks. He paused and listened. He didn't want them to hear him peeing, so he walked a bit further. Without the light from the moon, the night was so dark he could barely make out the trees until he was almost bumping into them. He stumbled into a patch of scrubby brush and backed away. He couldn't hold it any longer. The stream of pee spattered loudly in the shrubbery. When he finished, he zipped and turned and took a step, but then he stopped. *Danger!* The darkness was complete. A thick, cold, black void, blanketing him in silence. He listened for the B-man's snoring, but he'd come too far.

He took another step, and the rock turned smooth under his feet. The steep cliff where they'd eaten was somewhere nearby. He should have brought his phone to use for light, but the battery had died. *Stupid.* He walked forward, slowly, with his hands outstretched, straining his eyes to see into the blackness and listening harder than he'd ever listened before. Where was the edge? He could picture the sheer vertical drop, and the tiny trees way down at the bottom. He took another half step, and his foot slipped on a crumbling patch of shale. A current of warm air rose up like a whisper.

Stop.

He stopped. The voice was quiet and firm and seemed to be coming from the gentle updraft.

Take two steps back.

He did.

Good. Now, slowly, get down.

He crouched, touching the warm rock with both hands as if doing so would keep him earthbound. He could hear blood pounding in his ears.

Don't move. Stay very still. Wait . . .

He waited, straining his ears, for another instruction. The updraft wafted around him, tickling his face. How long did he crouch there? He had no way of knowing. Huddled, he dozed and woke and dozed again.

Then, in the distance, he heard her voice. It was coming from behind him, from the deepest folds of fog and silence.

"Benny?"

A thin beam of light flickered over the slick rock beside him.

"I'm here," he whimpered, turning toward the light.

The beam came closer. He stood, but his legs were unsteady, cramped from crouching. His knees buckled and he started to sway, but she was there and caught him by the wrist.

"Come," she said, her voice low, urgent. "I've got you. It's okay."

Her breaths came out in puffs of white in the beam of the flashlight. He stumbled toward her and fell into her arms.

"Fuck," she said, hugging him tightly, then she released him and shone the light in his face. "Are you fucking crazy?"

He blinked, held up his hand to block the beam. "What?"

She turned the flashlight toward the place where he'd been sitting. The beam of light traced the steep edge of the precipice before disappearing into the blackness beyond. Another step and he would have fallen.

She turned the beam back on him. "What were you doing?"

"I had to pee," he said. "It was dark. I got lost."

She ran the light over his face, studying it to see if he was lying. "I woke up and you weren't there, so I went looking. When I saw you, I thought you were about to jump."

"Oh," he said. "No. I wasn't."

She took a deep breath and exhaled. "Come on. It's cold."

He followed her back to their campsite. The B-man was still snoring. Benny crawled into his sleeping bag and lay there on his back. He could hear the Aleph breathing next to him, and it sounded like she was waiting for him to say something else.

"I really wasn't," he whispered. "Going to jump, I mean."

There was a long pause. "Okay."

"I couldn't see the cliff. I didn't know it was there. I almost fell . . ." He shivered at the memory of the warm updraft of air. There was a rustling sound as she rolled onto her side, and he could feel her eyes on him, watching in the dark. "But then I heard something."

"What?"

"A voice." He hesitated. "But not the usual ones."

"What are the usual ones?"

"Just random things. Some are more personal, like my inner critic or the robot."

"You have an inner robot?"

He nodded.

"Wow. All I have is inner demons. Demons and monsters."

Her face was so close, he could feel her warm breath against his cheek. He rolled over on his side, so now they were facing each other, nose to nose.

"That sucks," he said.

"Yeah. So what was the voice on the cliff?"

"It was a new one. I heard it for the first time in the Bindery."

"Is it a thing?"

"Not really. But it's not a person, either. It's kind of in between."

"What did it say?"

"Not much. That night in the Bindery it was something about books. I think it wanted to say more. I could hear it wanting."

"I guess that makes sense because it was the Bindery. Did it freak you out?"

"No." He was lying so he stopped. "Okay, a little. But tonight, I think it saved me. It was totally dark and I couldn't see. I would have walked off the edge of the cliff, but it told me to stop and get down and wait for you."

"It knew I was coming?"

"Yeah. I think it knows stuff."

"What stuff?"

"Like what's going to happen. In my life."

"It can tell the future?"

"Sort of. But also the past. And I think it can make things happen."

"What kind of things."

"I don't know. Things in my life. I can't explain, but it's kind of powerful. . . ."

"Like God or something."

"Maybe. It's like it has a plan for me. That's the kind of stuff people say about God, right?"

"Actually, I was just kidding about God."

"Oh."

"You really think it's making stuff happen?"

It sounded so crazy. "I don't know. It's just this feeling."

"Are you scared?"

"A little."

"If it saved your life, maybe it's a good voice. A friend. Maybe it's looking out for you."

"Maybe."

"Friends are good," she said. "It's good to have friends." Her hand crept across the moss again and her palm came to rest against his chest. "Get some sleep, okay?"

His heart was beating hard beneath her palm. He put his hand on top of hers and clasped it.

Do it, a voice whispered. *You know you want to . . .*

He raised himself up on one elbow. She turned over onto her back.

Do it! Now!

And so he did.

It wasn't a long kiss or a very good one. His aim was off and he missed and found himself kissing the corner of her mouth, or more like her cheek, really, and at that moment the kiss could have turned into something safe and unsexy, the kind of kiss you would give to your aunt, but it didn't. Instead, he shifted his weight so that their lips met properly. Her lips felt soft and squishy like raspberries, and salty like a tortilla. A yeasty taste, and familiar somehow, as if from a dream. He'd never kissed anyone except for his mother and father, and he didn't know what to do next, but he understood that something more had to happen. She wasn't helping, exactly, but she wasn't pushing him away, either, so he pressed a bit harder. He could feel the hardness of her teeth beneath her skin, and now her lips were moving against his—

"Benny . . . ?"

Her lips were shaping his name. He tasted his name on her breath and inhaled himself deeply. Yes! He was Benny! Maybe for the first time in his life, he was completely who he was. He could feel her hands against his chest, just above his heart, pushing against him, and so he pushed back. His body was alive and so was hers. Stars twinkled behind his eyelids. His spine arched and he started to rise, to reach—

"Benny, no . . ."

No?

He hesitated. Something was wrong. What did she mean, *no*, when everything, even the stars, was saying *Yes, Yes, Yes!* Why didn't she understand? That he was kissing her because he loved her, and love was good, and the voice told him to! Words were so unreliable. Her *no* must be mistaken. Her *no* was confused and didn't mean what it said. It meant to mean *yes*, and he would prove it. He pressed his lips to hers harder, and for a long moment, she relaxed and even seemed to kiss him back a little before she sighed and turned her head.

"No, Benny, we can't—"

He fell onto his back and faced the sky. This time there was no mistaking it. Her meaning was clear. Her *no* meant *No*. He was the one who was confused, who didn't understand. Because he was *so stupid*. Because he was a *moron*. Because he was *too young*. He knew he should apologize, but the words wouldn't come. He wanted to disappear, but he couldn't. She reached over and put her hand against his burning cheek.

"I'm sorry," she said, which were the words he should have said, and then she rolled away, turning her back on him. He heard her exhale, long and careful, into the night.

BENNY

That was you, wasn't it? You knew I wanted to kiss her, and you told me to do it! The whole thing happened so fast, I wasn't sure, but I get it now. That was your voice. *Do it!* you said. And so I did.

Were you just fucking with me? You knew it was an idiot move. You're a book! You must have known how it was going to turn out, but you made me do it anyway because—what? It was more interesting, or romantic, or dramatic, or some crap like that? Maybe you just wanted to watch! That's such bullshit! You were just using me, making me do stuff, so you could tell a better story.

Fucking books.

You should have just let me walk off the cliff and die.

THE BOOK

Oh, Benny, no. We didn't make you kiss her. That wasn't our voice you were obeying. It was the voice of an impulse far more primal and urgent than anything a book can muster.

But you're not entirely wrong, either. Because while we didn't make you do it, we wouldn't have stopped you even if we could have. Books do like a little romance, a little drama, and that's the truth. Call us prurient (and many have), but we needed you to taste her lips so that we could taste them, too. We wanted those words to describe your kiss. You people get swept away by passions of your body, but for books, our lust for words is equally undeniable. So you're wrong about us *making* you kiss her—books are not omnipotent, nor are we pimps or panderers—but we are guilty of wanting it, and if you feel used, then we're sorry. Even as it was happening, we were sorry.

You don't believe us. We can see that. And now you're trying to block us out, just like you block out the memories of all the things you want to forget.

Okay, you leave us with no choice. We're not just another one of your random voices, Benny. We're your Book, and this is our job. We have to fill you in.

56

You didn't sleep much after that. You lay there, face burning hot in the cold night air, listening to the pounding of blood in your ears. The sound of blood was an inside sound, coming from deep within your body, but there were outside sounds, too; you could hear the Aleph's breathing and the old man's snores, and somewhere on the mountain, the cry of a night bird. And then there were the new sounds, the ones you'd never heard before. Drifting and discordant, they seemed to be coming from very far away, from all the debris, lost and tumbling through space.

Somewhere out there, the Dark Comet was waiting.

The more you thought about what you'd done, the more agitated you became. You really fucked up big-time. Because of course she didn't want to kiss you. Because why would she? Why would anyone want to kiss you? Because *she's a bitch and you're just a fucking kid, an idiot, a moron, an immature loser who deserves to die, so just do it, okay? Throw yourself off the fucking cliff already and make her sorry! What are you waiting for?*

But you waited. You remembered your Coping Card. You lay there breathing and counting, and counting and breathing, until finally, just before dawn, you drifted off to sleep.

When you woke again, the sun had risen and the two of them were already up. The Aleph was brewing coffee on a little stove she'd made from some old tin cans. She asked you if you wanted some. She seemed cheerful. Like nothing had happened. You shook your head. The fact that you didn't drink coffee made you feel like a baby, but the tin-can stove was cool, and normally you would have asked her to show you how it worked, but instead, you went to pee. When you came back, they were sitting at the edge of the cliff where you'd almost fallen to your death the night before, sipping coffee and talking quietly, looking out to the sea. When she saw you, she held out a cup. It was hot chocolate. A baby drink. You took a sip, and it was delicious, but at that moment, you hated her.

The descent down the mountain was much harder than the uphill, and you and the Aleph had to work together to keep the B-man's wheelchair from hurtling off the path. Often, standing next to her, your elbows touched, or shoulders, or hips, or hands, and when this happened you shied away. At one point, on a steep and gravelly patch, the wheelchair skidded on rock that crumbled out from under your feet, and you let go of the handles so as not to make contact with her forearm. She turned to you then, face flushed from the effort of bracing the wheels.

"You're being super weird and I need you to stop."

You took hold of the handles again, but after that she didn't speak to you the whole way down, and you didn't speak to her, either.

The Bottleman sensed something was amiss. He sat in his precarious wheelchair, clutching his briefcase and talking again about Walter Benjamin, about the tragedy of his death and the conspiracy that grew up around it. Some people disputed the philosopher's suicide, insisting he'd died of a heart attack. Others claimed he'd been murdered by Stalinist agents. The Spanish death certificate put the cause of death as a cerebral hemorrhage. The briefcase containing the mysterious manuscript vanished, and in spite of the efforts of his friends it was never found.

"No one vill read it now," the B-man said mournfully. "It vas his final book. He told his friends it must be saved, that it must not fall into ze hands of ze Gestapo. He said it vas more important than his life."

This assertion made you mad. "I don't think books are more important than a person's life," you said. The wheel of the chair caught on a root, so you gave it a hard shove.

"Ah," said the B-man. "That is because you hef not written one yet. Once you hef written a book, you vill see."

"Bullshit," you said, as the chair lurched forward. "I'll never write a book."

"Just wait," the old man said. "You vill see. Every boy hes a book in him, Benny."

At that moment, the thought of having a book inside you was monstrous. "I don't," you said, but either the old man didn't hear you, or he was ignoring you. He was talking about Walter Benjamin again.

"Such a tragedy," he said, shaking his head. "There is nothing sadder than a lost book." And with that, he sunk into a despondent silence.

NO ONE SPOKE ON THE RIDE back to the city. They dropped you off in front of your house. The Aleph parked the van next to a pile of garbage and recycling bags. With the engine running, she reached over and squeezed your hand. You felt your body stiffen. *Danger!*

"I'm sorry," she said softly. "I love you, Benny. Just not like that, okay?"

Bitch, a voice said. Whatever.

You stood on the curb as the van drove away, and when it was out of sight, you turned and tripped over a garbage bag. You kicked it, hard, again and again, until a hole opened up and some DVDs spilled out, and that's when you remembered. You'd promised to help your mother tidy up when you got home from school. That was yesterday. She still hadn't texted you back, but your phone battery had died on the mountain. She'd probably been trying all night, and now you were seriously fucked.

You kicked the discs back into the bag. Overhead, your dad's crows were watching. They were perched on the powerlines, cawing the way they did when they wanted to be fed. You headed toward the back of the house, and one by one they followed you. When you rounded the corner, they swooped down and landed on the railing near the empty feeding station. Why hadn't your mom fed them? The ground at the base of the steps was littered with junk. Your old baby stroller was lying on its side. What was it doing there? You climbed over it and went inside. The house was silent. Still a mess. You went into the living room. Mission Control was empty, but it was Saturday, you realized. Your mom's day off.

You went back to the kitchen, got a bowl of cereal and plugged in your phone. Your mom's Melitta was sitting on the counter, so you decided to make yourself a cup of coffee. You balanced the filter on the cup and put a heaping spoonful in and then another. You boiled some hot water, poured it in, and let it drip through, took a sip, and then spit it into the sink.

Upstairs, you paused outside Annabelle's door and listened. She must still be sleeping, you thought, which maybe meant she wasn't so angry after all. Relieved, you went to your room, took off your clothes, and crawled into bed. On the desktop next to the pillow was the old *Grimm's Fairy Tales* that you'd borrowed from the Library. The vein-like tangle of roots and branches embossed on the bloodred cover reminded you of the mountain, and you thought about what the B-man had said on the way down, about how everybody has a book inside them. You got up and moved the *Grimm's* to the opposite side of the room, away from your head, then you lay back down and put the Grundigs over your ears and fell asleep.

The faint sound of the doorbell woke you. A woman was standing there with her finger on the bell, but she stopped when you opened the door. She drew back in surprise when she saw you, like you were a Martian from outer space, but you had the Grundigs on, so that made sense.

"Are you Benny?" She introduced herself. Her name was Ashley something. She was a hospital social worker. "Your mother had an accident last night."

She paused, watching you. The Grundigs made her seem very far away.

"She fell down the steps and was taken to the hospital." Again, she paused. Waiting. Studying your face. Maybe you looked confused, because she said, "Don't you want to know if she's okay?"

You nodded.

She's dead, a voice said. *And it's all your fault.*

"She sustained some pretty bad injuries. She'll recover, but she's worried sick about you. Come on."

On the drive to the hospital, you slouched down in the passenger seat of her car, still wearing the Grundigs and trying not to listen while she asked you questions—where had you been, why didn't you let your mother know? You figured she didn't much like you, which was fine because you didn't much like yourself, either, and all the while the voice muttered, *Your fault, your fault, your fault* . . .

HOW MUCH OF this do you remember, Benny?

Benny?

Are you there?

Can you hear us?

Are you listening?

57

Annabelle had little memory of her fall, but she would never forget the long night she spent in the emergency room afterward. No-Good had been unable to find her phone under all the stuff on the kitchen table, though she doubted he'd tried very hard. She'd called the police from the pay phone in the ER waiting room and asked to file a missing person report but ran into the same red tape she'd encountered the first time. She asked to speak to Officer Hooley, but he wasn't on duty. Finally she became so distraught, the nurses had to give her a sedative, and that's when the social worker got involved.

Ashley was a lovely girl, cheerful and energetic, with shoulder-length blond hair and an intensely earnest way of listening. She asked all about Annabelle's accident and her job and her home situation. She asked about Benny and Kenji, too. She seemed dismayed that Annabelle had no one to call on for help other than her teenage son. She perched on the edge of the chair next to her bed and patted Annabelle's hand, leaning in from time to time to offer her a tissue and making eager little grunts of encouragement. Her blue-eyed gaze was like a vacuum that could suck your pain right out of you, and Annabelle took to her right away, but all the talking wore her out, so Ashley left, telling her to get some rest. When Annabelle woke up several hours later, Benny was sitting in the chair, wearing those silly-looking headphones that belonged to his father, staring at an early morning news show about the upcoming election on the muted television.

He'd gone camping with friends, he said. He was fine. He was sorry he'd left school without telling anyone. He was sorry he hadn't called. His phone ran out of juice. The fact he apologized was huge, Annabelle felt. He seemed subdued, remote, but cooperative, and so, with Ashley's assistance, they worked out a plan for Annabelle's discharge. Until she could manage the stairs to her bedroom, she would sleep on the sofa bed downstairs, and that afternoon, Benny cleared paths in the living room, the hallway and the downstairs bathroom, so she could get from place to place on her crutches. She couldn't make meals or go shopping, but they could get take-out for dinner. In the mornings, Benny would make her breakfast and coffee, and on the way home in the afternoon he could pick up groceries at the corner store. He could buy his own milk. He would have to take the bus to school by himself, but he seemed fine with that. Relieved, even.

The sprained wrist was inconvenient, and the broken ankle painful. She was suffering symptoms from the concussion: headaches, nausea, memory loss, dizziness when she tried to stand. All she could remember of the accident was lying on the ground looking up at No-Good, standing over her with the raised golf club in his hand. She had been so sure he was trying to kill her. But she'd been wrong, and afterward he'd been surprisingly sympathetic and even agreed to postpone the inspection. Was he trying to suck up to her while secretly planning to have them evicted?

Whenever she thought about this, the headaches got worse. Don't think, the doctor had said. Don't think, don't drink, eat healthy, get rest, avoid stress, and above all, stay off the computer. Of course, the first thing she did when she got home from the hospital was to hobble over to Mission

Control and check her email, but after a few minutes, the pixilated words on the screen began swimming in and out of focus, and the bright monitor made her head throb, and she had no choice but to stop. Following the doctor's advice, she had called her supervisor and told him she'd had an accident and would have to take some time off of work. Charlie had been surprisingly agreeable, too, told her to take care of herself and not to worry. Was he being kind now so he could fire her later?

It was quiet in the house without the humming of the hard drives, and quiet in her head, too, without the steady chatter of news. Good to have some time to catch up with other projects. She opened her book. She was reading *Tidy Magic* and trying to follow some of the clutter-clearing tips. Benny had brought the sock drawer down from her bedroom, rounding up all the strays from the floor and from the laundry, so she could sort them. It was soothing work, the perfect task for her recovery. She was going through the mountain of socks, one by one, holding each one up and examining it to determine which sock lifted her spirits, and which one made her sad. The sad ones were threadbare or were missing a partner, and these she pressed to her heart, thanking them for all their hard work on behalf of her feet, before respectfully discarding them. The intact pairs she folded and arranged in the drawer according to color, creating a perfect rainbow of tidy socks. Aikon was right. There was joy to be had in small, simple things done with love, and once you got started, one thing just led to the next. Soon she would be ready to move on to T-shirts, and there was a proper way to fold these, too.

She put the book down and closed her eyes. It had been years since she'd lain around like this in the middle of the day. The last time was just after Benny was born. She remembered so vividly lying right here on the sofa with her brand-new baby tucked in beside her, dozing and waking from time to time to nurse, while Kenji cooked and brought her hot tea and massaged her feet and shoulders and belly.

"So empty," he would say, rubbing the loose skin that pooled in her pelvis. "We must fill you up again." It was a joke, of course, but he spent his days making all sorts of nourishing Japanese dishes for her—miso soups and savory egg custards, noodles and donburi rice with her favorite toppings—and then he'd sit at the end of the sofa with her legs on his lap, strumming the ukulele or blowing softly into his ocarina, watching his baby boy suckle and sleep. At night, he'd go out to play his gigs, but after the last set he would come straight home instead of hanging out and getting high with the band. Those were good times. Hopeful times.

And they still were hopeful, she thought. Because what good did it do to despair? Things could be a lot worse. She could have broken her neck falling down those stairs. And something terrible could have happened to Benny. But instead, he was safe and sound and settling back into school. She reached for her phone and checked the time. He was still in class. He'd be hungry when he came home.

Outside, the crows were cawing for their supper. She texted him to pick up a pizza. He didn't answer, but then she didn't expect him to. Students weren't allowed to be on their phones in class. She got to her feet and waited for the dizziness to pass. There were no more moon cakes in the kitchen, but she found a bag of stale Doritos in the laundry room and limped out to the porch.

On the feeding station were some little objects, a bright pearl earring, a piece of pale green sea glass, and a hexagonal bolt. The crows had brought her more gifts! She picked up the pearl. It wasn't real, of course, but it was shiny and pretty. The bolt was heavy, hard for a crow to carry. The sea glass reminded her of Kenji.

She looked up and saw the crows, carefully watching her. "Thank you," she called, scattering the Doritos onto the platform. "Thank you!"

One by one, they came toward her, their wide black wings outstretched like fingers, swooping in so close she could feel the dusty, displaced air tickling her face. The full memory of the accident came back to her then. She remembered trying to balance the loaded stroller. She remembered the horror of falling backward into empty space, and the cold, and the sickening pain. It had started to rain. Then, out of nowhere, came a rush of air, as one by one the crows landed, and she remembered the prickling of claws and the weight of their small bodies as they moved and settled down on top of her, fluffing their feathers to brood her like a very large egg.

Now, watching them peck and snatch at the Doritos, she felt tears welling up in her eyes with gratitude. The crows had kept her warm and dry. They had saved her.

58

Dear Ms. Ai Konishi,

I have never actually written a fan letter before, but I wanted to thank you for your book which is really revolutionizing my life, not to mention my sock drawer! As soon as I started reading *Tidy Magic*, I felt a special connection with you for several reasons. First, what you wrote about your stepfather really resonated with me because I had a stepfather, too. He wasn't a corporate executive, just a drywaller, but he treated me and my mom very badly in ways I don't want to go into, but I think you would understand.

But also, there's the fact that you're a Japanese Zen monk and my husband, Kenji, was Japanese and used to live at a Zen temple. He was a jazz musician and a very Zen kind of guy, but I lost him in a tragic accident when he got run over by a truck. Our son, Benny, was traumatized. He had just turned twelve at the time and he loved his father very much, and since then he's developed some emotional problems. He's fourteen now and he's changed so much. There are times when I don't even know who he is anymore. I understand that sometimes parents feel this way about their teens, but we used to be so connected, and I can't help feeling like it's all my fault, like everything I do is wrong.

It didn't used to be like this. When Kenji was alive, he made everything right. The three of us would go out and people would take one look at Kenji and me and they'd put it together that Benny was our son and that we were a family. But now it's different. People look at me and Benny and they don't connect us, you know? They think he's adopted. Sometimes this would happen when Benny was a baby and I went out with him alone, and people would come up to me and say, Oh, what a darling baby girl! Where did you get her? No one ever made mistakes like that when Kenji was with us, and now that he's dead it feels like I'm not even Benny's mother anymore.

I'm sorry. I didn't mean to give you a whole sob story. The real reason I wanted to write now is because of another connection we have, which is crows. Crows are amazing! I loved your story about how your teacher crow saved your life and I wanted to share a little story with you about some special crows who saved my life, too. . . .

59

The fly on the wall was watching you, keeping things real. You were sitting at your desk in your special ed class. In front of you was the library book you were supposed to be reading, and in your pocket was a thumbtack that you'd stolen from the bulletin board. You kept the thumbtack stuck into a dried-up piece of chewing gum so it wouldn't poke you when it was in your pocket. Thumbtacks were dangerous, but not as dangerous as books.

The fly on the wall knew about the thumbtack. The fly was keeping its eye on you, helping you keep your shit together, and when you started to lose it, the fly started to speak:

Benny is leaning over the page, but he isn't reading. He is making his mind go blank so the words can't enter. Benny doesn't trust books anymore, because books are not trustworthy. Books are always watching you, trying to read your mind. They make you do things, even things you shouldn't do. They write bad things into your life, and then they go and blab and tell everyone about it.

That the fly on the wall knew so much about books comforted you. It was obviously a clever fly, and you were lucky to have it. The fly could read your mind, but it didn't make you do stuff. It simply watched you and said what was going on.

As you stared at the page, the words lost focus, dissolving into letters that swam helplessly across the white paper like ants in a sink full of soapy water. They were trying to swim to safety, and you wanted to help. When the teacher wasn't looking, you slipped a hand into your pocket and pulled out the tack. The point was sharp, and you applied it to a period at the end of a sentence, opening it up. The period became a hole. You poked another period, made another hole.

Benny is feeling better now. He can hear the letters breathing tiny sighs of relief. The page is full of holes, so he turns it and starts another. When he closes the covers of the book, the letters will be free to swim through the holes and escape. He is liberating the letters from their sentences. A small revolution. They will be grateful.

He can hear words singing his praises, like in a hymn.

He is imagining how surprised his teacher will be when she opens the book and sees the blank, white, perforated pages. This thought makes him smile, but then he stops himself. The Book is probably reading his thoughts, he thinks. Best not to think. He opens his mind and lets the thoughts go until his mind is as clear and empty as a blank white page.

Better to let the fly on the wall do the thinking, he thinks. Safer that way.

AFTER SCHOOL YOU PICKED up a Hawaiian pizza, the kind your mom likes, and took it straight home. You checked on her to see if she needed anything, then you tidied the kitchen and went upstairs. You were supposed to be doing your homework. Instead, you sat on your bed with the Grundigs clamped to your ears and your sleeve pushed up to reveal the underside of your left forearm. You studied the pale skin, trying to recall the pattern of holes in the Aleph's arm. You knew it was a constellation because she told you so. You thought she said it was Andromeda. The holes in her arm weren't just holes, though. They were track marks that she had tattooed over. She didn't have to tell you this. You'd figured it out on your own.

In the medicine cabinet in the bathroom, you found some cotton balls and a bottle of hydrogen peroxide and brought them back into your room. You googled Andromeda and a picture of the constellation came up on the screen. There was a drawing of it, too, which looked like a lady falling through space. You recognized the shape of the stars from the Aleph's arm, and so you started reading. Andromeda was a beautiful princess whose kingdom was being ravaged by a horrible sea monster named Cetus, so her father, the king, ordered her to be sacrificed. He had her chained to a rock in the ocean for the sea monster to eat, but then a hero named Perseus came along and killed the monster with a diamond sword, so she married him and they had a bunch of kids, and when she died the goddess Athena turned her into stars.

You studied the stars. Your mother was calling from the living room. She wanted you to come downstairs and reheat the pizza, but you ignored her. You copied the stars onto the underside of your forearm with a felt-tipped marker, then you aligned the sharp point of the thumbtack with the first star nearest to your wrist and pressed the point into the skin. The pain felt real and necessary. If you were a hero, you could rescue the Aleph from the demons and monsters inside her head. If you had a diamond sword maybe she would even marry you. Your mother called again, and you pushed harder. A small bead of red blood rose from the point, and as you watched it swell, you named it: Alpha Andromeda, the first and brightest star in the constellation, the head of the lady in chains.

Daubing at the blood with the peroxide-saturated cotton, you remembered the Aleph's paint-stained fingers, holding your wounded hand, pressing against the gash to staunch the bleeding. This image soothed you. The smell of the peroxide soothed you. Maybe if you made enough holes in your skin, the voices inside you would find them and leave. Maybe that was the problem. The words were trapped inside you, looking for an exit. That's the thing about words. They want to be out in the world.

60

Benny was being awfully quiet upstairs. She had called to him twice now to come down, but he hadn't answered. He must be doing his homework, she thought, and with those headphones on, he probably couldn't hear her. She leaned back in her chair. In front of her, the monitor glowed in the darkness. She wasn't supposed to be on the computer, but it felt good to write and actually send the fan letter, even if it was to a complete stranger who would probably never even read it. It felt good be back at Mission Control, too. She'd been offline since the accident and had lost track of what day it was. Time moved differently without her newsfeeds, and while it had been a pleasant respite, now she was feeling the tug of the world. She liked keeping an eye on current events, as if, by doing so, she was somehow helping. She knew it was silly. The world wasn't going to fall apart just because she wasn't watching. Still, maybe it wouldn't hurt to check the feeds. The elections were looming, and the wildfires still burning. She would need to go back to work, and it would be good not to fall too far behind.

She heard a sound in the hallway and looked up just as the overhead light switched on. She was more sensitive to light since the accident, and now she winced and closed her eyes against the sudden brightness. When she opened them again, Benny was standing in the doorway.

"You're not supposed to be on the computer. Too much screen time is bad for you." His voice sounded odd, flat and affectless, like an automaton parroting back the words she used to say to him when she caught him playing video games, before he gave them up.

"You're right," she said. "I'll stop." She put the computer to sleep and swiveled back around. "Hey, are you hungry yet? I am. Do me a favor and take that sock drawer upstairs, and then we can reheat that pizza."

He went to the sofa and pointed at the drawer on the floor. "This?"

"Yes," she said, and then added, proudly, "What do you think?"

He shrugged. "It's okay."

"It's pretty, right? With all the colors?" She held up *Tidy Magic*. "I'm learning all these nifty Japanese ways of folding stuff. Here, I'll show you."

She stood, steadied herself, waiting for the dizziness to pass, and then she hobbled over to the sofa. "The lady who wrote the book is a Zen monk, like your dad used to be. She says in Japan they believe everything has a spirit, even ordinary things like socks and underpants, and you have to treat them nicely so they can be happy. Your socks work hard to take care of your feet, and when they're not working, they like to be folded up like this and put in the drawer so they can rest and relax."

"That's kind of weird." He watched her tuck the socks back in the drawer and then pointed to the pile of discards on the floor. "What about those?"

"They're the old worn-out ones. I'm throwing them out."

"They're not going to like that."

"Oh, they don't mind. I thanked them. You have to thank them first. Get me a garbage bag from under the sink, honey, and then I'll show you the technique for folding T-shirts. It'll be easy for you. You're naturally tidy like your dad. He always took good care of his things—"

She could hear Benny rooting around in the kitchen. " . . . just not himself." She eyed the drawer. "Well, at least his things were happy."

She looked up as Benny came back into the living room. "And your drawers are always tidy," she added brightly. "So your things must be happy, too!"

He crouched by the forlorn heap of crumpled socks and started shoveling them into the garbage bag. "I don't do it to make them happy," he said. "I do it to make them shut up."

THE BOOK

Benny? Are you listening? Are you still mad?

We know what you're doing. We can feel you blocking us. We can feel you not thinking, but it's too late for that. It's one thing to block your book when it first comes calling, but we've covered so many pages together by now, and having come this far, you can't simply stop. Books have a life of their own, too, Benny. You can't hide from us, and you can't shut us out.

But don't worry. We get it. This is difficult stuff to process, and you've been working hard and deserve a rest, so let's take a little break, shall we? Spin the globe and ride the rhizomatic network halfway around the planet, down a narrow side street to a tiny wooden temple, nestled in the throbbing heart of Tokyo. Let's pay a quick visit to the nun.

Why are we doing this, you might ask? The answer is simple. Because we can. Because when Annabelle reached out to Aikon, wrote her that email and hit Send, her action completed the circuit of words, and now we can travel through it.

61

The email was a long one, in English, and it had taken her almost an hour to read it. The ones from Japanese readers were quicker, of course, but ever since the international publication of *Tidy Magic*, fan mail was coming in from all over the world. Most of these were in English—never Aikon's strongest subject in school—and she often had to consult her battered English-Japanese dictionary to understand what they said. Many were just brief notes of thanks from women who had enjoyed her book, but others were longer, lengthy confessional missives, filled with the kind of determined cheer that masked a deeper despair. When she found the time to read them, they broke Aikon's heart.

Like this one, from the woman whose husband had been run over by truck. Their young son had been traumatized by his father's death. There was a long story about crows who brought gifts to the lady and sat on top of her when she fell down. There was a photo, taken at a beach, of a sweet-faced blond woman in a bathing suit, standing arm in arm with a small Japanese man in surfer jams. In front of them was a boy of about four or five, who stared into the camera with a clear-eyed gaze that made Aikon pause. He must be the couple's son, a teenager now, with emotional problems. Sad.

Aikon archived the email and then checked the Inbox. There were still hundreds of unread fan letters, and the number rose, even as she watched. She closed her eyes and rested for a moment, and then clicked on the next one, which was from the same woman.

Hi, again! Sorry to bother you again, but I found the picture of my husband, Kenji, from when he was at the Zen temple, and I scanned it so I won't lose it again, and I'm attaching it here. And I completely forgot to mention another connection, which is that my

husband's mother was named Konishi, and it crossed my mind
that maybe you two are related. You don't happen to have a
long-lost brother named Kenji, do you?

Aikon sighed, took off her reading glasses and switched on the desk
lamp. Konishi was a fairly common name, and she did not have a long-lost
brother named Kenji. She had no brothers at all. She wanted to answer
the lady—she wanted to answer all the ladies who wrote to her, but there
were so many, and she was afraid of inadvertently writing something in her
clumsy English that would hurt instead of help, so she just added their
names to the list for the well-being ceremony and filed the emails away.

A sharp clack echoed through the garden, and she looked up. The timekeeper, a novice who had just taken her vows, stood on the walkway, holding her wooden mallet, getting ready to strike the wooden plaque again to
signal time for zazen and evening service. Aikon could hear people arriving, taking off their shoes and heading toward the zendo. Ever since her
book hit the best-seller lists in Japan, people had been showing up to the
little temple. Some came once or twice out of curiosity, but others, mostly
office workers from nearby companies, had started coming regularly to sit
zazen, listen to her dharma talks, and attend daylong retreats. A few of the
women, refugees like Aikon from the corporate world, asked to stay, to be
ordained and live there as her students, so now there were three nuns in
residence, too. The temple was doing well, but sadly, her teacher had not
lived long enough to see this.

She closed down her computer. The rest of the emails would have to
wait. She stood up slowly, stretching her legs, and then changed into a more
formal robe. At the altar, she lit candles and a stick of incense. A framed
portrait of her teacher rested beside the Senju Kannon. He was dressed in
his finest ceremonial robe, the one she'd mended so often because he could
not afford a new one. He gazed at her from the frame, and even though his
mouth was stern, his eyes were smiling, as if at some private joke that he
expected her to share. She touched the stick of incense to her forehead, but

before she made the offering, she paused and looked at him, meeting his gaze and holding it—something she had never done while he was alive.

Well, she asked him silently. Are you satisfied?

She'd never known whether her teacher had believed in her or not. When, bubbling with excitement, she had told him her idea about writing a book, he'd sat there with his eyes closed, patiently listening as she explained how tidying was very trendy, and the magazine she used to work for published many lifestyles articles about clutter, and books on the subject had even become international bestsellers, and when she was finally done, he just sighed. If you think your book will help a few people, you should write it, he said. She remembered how dull his eyes were then, all the brightness gone out of them, and how his head drooped like an old camellia blossom on a wilting stem. I must lie down now, he said. I'm very tired.

That was the last time he had sat upright. In the months that followed, she had watched over him, working feverishly on her book and listening to the sound of his labored breathing. She knew he didn't have much time left, and she wanted to finish the book so that his spirit would be at peace when he died, knowing his temple was safe. Every morning, noon, and evening, she performed services in the abbot's quarters, lighting incense at the altar, chanting sutras, and making prostrations. Sometimes while she was chanting, his lips would move. Sometimes he pressed his palms together over his heart. And all the while, the Senju Kannon watched over them. She was very beautiful, sitting on her lotus, the manifestation of the Bodhisattva of Compassion, whose job it was to watch over the Realm of the Hungry Ghosts. Aikon, who had dusted each of her arms and heads, felt very close to her, and as she sat at her teacher's side, writing late into the night, she would gaze up at Senju Kannon and think about the Hungry Ghosts, with their great, big bellies that were always empty and their insatiable appetites and never-ending desire for more. Their mouths were as tiny as pinholes and their throats were as thin as a thread, so they could never consume enough to satisfy. Aikon understood their torment.

Dear Senju Kannon, she prayed. *Please help me write this book. Please let my book be of help to others who suffer like I did. Please let my book be a huge best seller so I can pay for the new roof.*

On the day her teacher died, the roofers still hadn't been paid. With a heavy heart, she sat with him and watched him as he struggled to breathe. She had failed to finish the book in time and failed to fulfill her promise to bring in income for the temple. He must be terribly disappointed in me, she thought. If he died disappointed, would he become a hungry ghost, too? It was a dreadful thought. And the old temple, what would become of it? Would the land be sold and the temple torn down to make room for office buildings and high rise condominiums? In the last month of his life, her teacher had given her dharma transmission and made her his dharma heir, but without the temple, there was little to inherit or pass on. Would his lineage die as well?

And what would become of her? Where would she go?

It was as if her teacher could hear her thinking. He had been unresponsive for days, as his breathing slowed and the silence between each inhalation grew longer. But just then, he opened his eyes and looked straight at her, and his eyes were bright and burning with intensity. He didn't say anything, but he didn't need to. She knew what he was thinking.

"Okay," she whispered. "I won't give up. Somehow, I'll keep our temple going. I promise."

It seemed like he heard her. The light in his eyes seemed to flicker in response, and then he blinked and closed them forever.

NOW SHE STILL felt his eyes on her from inside the portrait frame, watching her with that quizzical expression. The curl of smoke trailed from the tip of the incense as she reached forward to make the offering, planting the stick firmly in the bowl of ash.

"You thought I couldn't do it," she said. "But I did."

Her assistant, another novice named Kimi, slid open the door, bowed, and then stood aside to let her pass. Aikon stepped out into the hallway that led to the zendo, bowing to the timekeeper as she passed and glancing at the graceful calligraphy painted on the wooden plaque. It was an old Zen poem, written by her teacher, that when translated meant:

> *Great is the Matter of Birth and Death.*
> *Life is transient. Time will not wait.*
> *Wake up! Wake up!*
> *Do not waste a moment!*

The verse, while admonitory, always made Aikon perk up and pay attention. In the zendo, she settled herself in her teacher's old seat and looked out over the room at the rows of meditators who were settling on their cushions, turning to face the smooth, white walls. On one side were the guests and parishioners, and across from them were the nuns. She ran her eye down the row, checking her students' posture, pleased to see that their backs were straight and their heads cleanly shorn and gleaming in the dim twilight. It was a lineage of women, Aikon thought. That's what her teacher got. None of them were looking at her. They were sitting with their eyes downcast, deep in meditation, but if they had been watching, they would have seen a tiny smile, like a shadow, flicker across her face. Strong, competent women, the abbess thought. The old man got what he deserved.

62

Dear Ms. Konishi,

I hope it's okay that I keep emailing. I figure you probably don't read your emails anyway so it doesn't really matter. I don't have much of a social network these days, and writing to you helps me get my emotions under control, so you're helping me even if you don't answer.

But if you do happen to read this and feel like answering, I have a specific question about my clutter-clearing project, which is going better, by the way, because recently my son has started to help. In my first email, I told you that Benny has emotional problems, but it's actually more serious than that. He has auditory hallucinations and hears things talking to him, like his running shoes, that aren't real. (The running shoes are real, but they're not really talking to him, I mean.) He's on antipsychotic medication and was on a children's psychiatric ward for a couple of weeks, but after he was discharged, his behavioral problems just got worse. He started lying to me and skipping school and hanging out with some older kids he met on the ward, and I worried that they might be doing drugs. Now his doctor says he might have schizophrenia, but it's hard to know because she keeps changing her diagnosis. Of course, he's a teenager now, and so some of this acting out is probably due to hormones, but I've been worried sick.

Recently, though, I've been feeling a bit more hopeful, because after my little accident, when I fell down the steps and the crows saved me, Benny has been helping around the house, doing the grocery shopping and tidying up. I don't know what I'd do without him! He's still withdrawn, but his doctor thinks he's doing better, too, so this is progress. His father had a drug and alcohol problem, and sometimes I worry that Benny might have gotten this from him. Kenji almost never did hard drugs, but he loved to drink and smoke pot with his friends. It didn't bother me at first, because he was a musician and that was just his lifestyle, but later, when I got pregnant, I asked him to quit, and he did. He really and truly wanted to be a good dad, and we both agreed that we needed to set a good example for our son. We knew we would never be rich or be able to give Benny a lot of material things, but we were okay with that. We were confident that we could provide a loving, stable, creative home environment, and for a while I think we even succeeded.

But when Benny was about six or seven, Kenji started up again. I think maybe he was frustrated because his band wasn't really going anywhere, and he was getting older and he felt kind of stuck, but he never really talked about it. He started staying out later and later after gigs, and since I always had to go to bed early on account of my work, I didn't notice at first. But then I found a bag of weed in his pocket, and that led to our first really big fight. I was so mad at him for breaking his promise and for lying to me, and in the end, he apologized and swore he would quit again, and he tried. He really did try.

Anyway, I didn't mean to get into all this. I just wanted to tell you that Benny is doing better, and the tidying is going pretty well, too, or at least it was. The success I experienced with my sock drawer gave me confidence and showed me that I can change, but the rest of the house still needs a lot of work. In your book, you said that what's important is not *finishing* a task, but rather just *doing* it, completely. But unfortunately, I have to *finish* because my landlady's son rented a dumpster, which he's deducting from my security deposit, and he's ordered me to clean up my side of the duplex or he'll start eviction proceedings. And I can't *do* this task completely because I have a broken ankle, a concussion, and a job.

I don't mean to complain. The good news is that my ankle is healing, and my concussion is better, too, and the doctor said I can use the computer again as long as I take it slow, but with the elections coming up in a week, there's so much going on in the news that I have to work overtime, and there just aren't enough hours in a day! So that's my question: How am I supposed to tidy completely, with love and compassion, when I have a broken ankle, a sick child, and a country that's on the brink of disaster? And if I can't finish tidying up, and we get evicted, where will we go? Our landlady, old Mrs. Wong, was fond of my husband and never raised our rent, but I barely make enough money to cover it, and rents in the city have shot up so high, we won't be able to afford to live here anymore.

We could move to another city, I guess, but there's the whole situation with Benny. He's finally starting to settle into his high school with a new Individualized Education Program, but recently . . .

63

All night long, while the nuns slept soundly, the emails continued to arrive. The incessant sounds of the outside world broke like waves against the walls of the little temple, but somehow the din didn't reach them. The rumble and whine of the traffic, the screeching of police sirens and the ambulances, the drunken salarymen singing and vomiting on the sidewalks—none of this penetrated the sleeping quarters of the nuns.

But Aikon could hear it. In the abbess's quarters, she lay awake, worrying. She had taken to sleeping in her study, so that during her frequent bouts of insomnia she could work. There was always too much to do these days. The media group that published her book in Japan was pressing her to do a TV show, the US publishers wanted her to do an author tour, her nuns needed training, her growing congregation needed attention, and she had signed a contract for a new book that she had no time to write. She'd left corporate life in order to get away from this kind of pressure, but the stress had followed her here.

Reflexively, she glanced toward the altar where Kannon sat serenely on her lotus, moonlight limning her eleven heads. Her thousand arms emanated from her body like an aureole of chrysanthemum petals, each one bearing an eye on its palm or holding a tool of enlightenment. When Aikon was still a novice monk, dusting all those intricately carved tools—the mirrors, axes, jewels, beads, flowers, bells, wheels, whisks, swords, bows and arrows—she often wondered why Kannon needed so much stuff to save all beings from suffering. Why couldn't she dispel greed, hatred and delusion with less clutter? She had asked her teacher this question once before he died, when she was writing a chapter on the desire for material possessions. Her teacher was lying on his futon and he didn't answer at first, and she wondered if he'd even heard her, but then he stirred, turning his head to look at the statue. When he spoke, his voice was so soft, she had to strain to hear it.

"Kannon is a lady," he said. "Ladies like pretty things."

The familiar spark of anger flared up in her breast and made her cheeks burn. He was an old man, a Zen master, and he was dying, but that was no excuse for this kind of sexism. She took a deep breath and was about to protest when he turned his head and she saw that he was smiling. She exhaled. Of course. He knew just which button to push.

"Do you know how Senju Kannon got her thousand arms?" he asked, and when she said she didn't, he nodded slowly. "Well then," he said, closing his eyes. "I will tell you. A long time ago, Kannon, the Bodhisattva of Compassion, made a deep vow to free all beings and help us wake up to our true and luminous nature."

His words were like beads on the string of a mala, escaping his lips in small puffs of air. "Kannon was like you. She worked so hard, but there were always more beings, trapped in delusion. She heard their pitiful cries, and she became so distressed that one day her head exploded." He paused, opened his eyes wide, and looked at her. "You don't believe me? Well, it did. It broke into eleven pieces, so now she had eleven heads. How wonderful!"

He was sounding livelier, almost like his old self. "But eleven heads were still not enough. There were too many beings to hold in her arms, and she kept reaching and reaching until her arms exploded, too. They split into a thousand pieces, so now she had a thousand new arms and a thousand new hands, and each hand had an eye in its palm."

He closed his eyes again. "This is why she is called the Sound Observer," he said, sighing. "The One Who Hears the Cries of the World . . ." His voice trailed off, but his words hung in the air like the fragrance from a stick of incense, so that even now, two years later, Aikon could still hear the echoes in the darkness.

She could relate to Kannon. All her nuns could, too. They were all overachievers with exploding heads, and this was not a good thing . . . or was it? Her assistant, Kimi, had a corporate job at an international ad agency, where she put in so much overtime that, at the age of thirty-two, she suffered a heart attack and collapsed at her desk. Maybe at that moment, her heart exploded into a thousand pieces, a thousand hearts, to better love the world. Yes, Aikon thought. Kimi was a true bodhisattva, and her English skills were excellent. It was time to give her more responsibility.

She could feel her teacher's presence in the room. Go ahead, she thought. Laugh all you want. I'm saving the temple, aren't I? She looked up at Kannon and pressed her palms together over her heart, and then she closed her eyes and slept.

THE BOOK

Benny? Are you there? Are you still not talking?

You can try to block us, but the memories are still in you, and we know where to find them.

All right, fine. You leave us no choice. We'll just have to continue without you.

64

Your teacher found the library book you'd defaced. She saw all the punctured periods, all the perforated pages, and she confronted you. At first you pretended not to know what she was talking about, but then she held a page up to the window.

"Look!" she said.

The slanting light from the late autumn sun shone through the holes, thin bright needle-like rays, shooting through the tiny pinpricks. It was beautiful. Why weren't all pages this beautiful? But then, looking more closely, you grew confused. You were expecting the page to be blank and white and empty, but the words were still there. You thought you'd liberated them, thought they would have fled by now, but instead, there they were, all those words and letters, neatly aligned and serving their sentences, while the page cried out in pain. It was too much. How could words be so servile? So obedient to the status quo and blind to the conventions that bound them?

You put your head down and started to bang your forehead against the desk. The teacher called health services.

At Dr. Melanie's office, you decided to come clean and tell her.

"It's a *book*," you whispered.

Dr. Melanie leaned forward. She was wearing pale blue nail polish to-day. "I can't hear you, Benny. Why are you whispering? Can you speak louder?"

"No. It'll hear me."

"What will?"

"The Book. It gets inside my head. It's reading my mind. It's making bad shit happen."

"What kind of bad shit, Benny?"

You weren't going to tell her about kissing the Aleph on the mountain. Nobody could know about that. You hugged yourself and started rocking.

"Benny? Can you tell me?"

"Just stuff. Whatever. It makes shit happen and then tells everyone about my life, and I can't make it stop. I can't get away from it!"

"Is this book one of your voices?"

"Yes, of course!" you cried. "It's the Voice of all Voices, like God fucking Almighty! It knows everything about me, and my mom, and random peo-ple, too. It even knows about you."

"Me?"

You glanced at her slyly. "It goes inside your head, too. It knows what you're thinking, and it'll tell everyone. Can't you feel it?"

She drew back, startled. "I can't feel anything, Benny."

There was no point in arguing, so you put your head down on the table.

"Benny? Talk to me."

"What's the point?" You felt her watching you with gentle, worried eyes, and so you tried again. "Why can't you just try to believe me? What if what I'm saying is true?"

"That there's a book in my head that knows what I'm thinking?"

"Yes."

"Because I don't believe it's true, Benny. Why should I?"

"Because it's really *there*! It can see everything, and it'll make you do shit, too, if you aren't careful."

"Is it making you do things?"

"Yes! I told you! Why don't you listen?"

"Benny, calm down. Breathe. Now, try to tell me exactly what you think this book is making you do."

You started counting your breaths.

"Is the book telling you to hurt yourself?"

You were wearing long sleeves so she couldn't see the secret constellation of scabs on your forearms. They were healing over nicely, leaving pretty little scars. You tugged at them and shook your head. "No."

"Is the book telling you to hurt other people?"

"No, of course not," you said, exasperated. "It's a book. It's not scissors!"

You were so sure. Because, while it seemed reasonable to think that a book might read your mind, the thought that a book would make you hurt someone had never occurred to you. But then, as Dr. M's question lingered in the space between you, doubt crept in.

"I don't think books can do that . . . ," you said. "Can they?"

A shadow crossed your face, and in that moment something changed. We felt it happen. For the first time you realized the power of books and what we might be capable of, and you were scared. Once a thought is thought, it cannot be unthought. Once riven, how can trust be regained? There are no easy answers.

65

Why can't you just try to believe me?

She was sitting at her desk with her eyes closed and her earbuds plugged in, trying to clear her mind before her next patient arrived, but the boy's question just kept replaying like a tape loop, and the new meditation app wasn't helping. The ambient soundtrack she'd chosen was Raindrops on Leaves, but the raindrops sounded a lot like radio static and this was making her feel anxious. She opened her eyes and scrolled through the options, looking for a more relaxing scenario. There were many different types of precipitation to choose from. Would Pouring Rain be better? Or Drizzle? What about Thunderstorm? No, too thunderous. Perhaps snow would be softer. Snowflakes in Moonlight sounded nice.

She used to be able just to sit and meditate without any soundtrack, but these days her mind was too jumpy and her thoughts too incessant. Once her mind latched onto a particular thought, it refused to let go. Was this what perseveration felt like? Did it indicate a diminishment of cognitive flexibility? She didn't use to be like this. Was she getting old?

Why can't you just try to believe me? What if what I'm saying is true?

Of course there was no book inside her head, narrating her thoughts, and making her do things. That was delusionary, but something in Benny's questions haunted her. Why couldn't she try to believe him? What was stopping her from imagining what it would be like to hear the voice of a book inside your head and believe it was real?

They were good questions, worthy of consideration, and she wished she could explore them in her session notes about Benny Oh's case. Because, while she didn't believe there was a book inside her head, her head often *felt* like a book, crammed full of stories from her young patients, and she would really like to get them out of there. Writing would no doubt help—Freud wrote his patients' stories down, after all, and reading his books was what had drawn her to the field in the first place—but this was no longer possible. The days of long, narrative, psychoanalytic case histories were over, and now she barely had time to jot down a brief assessment and treatment recommendation. The hospital, for reasons having to do with litigation, discouraged anything more elaborate, but while it was inadvisable to put her doubts in writing, this didn't mean she didn't have any. Benny Oh's case perplexed her. While the boy was presenting with some symptoms of schizophrenia, she had doubts about her diagnosis, and now that he seemed to be entering an acute psychotic phase, she needed to find a treatment that worked. She was still a young doctor, with only a few years of clinical experience. She was earnest and diligent and had grown fond of the boy and his mother. They were suffering, and she wanted to help. Realizing this, we felt a kinship with her. Her wish was not unlike ours.

She took a deep breath as Benny's questions cycled back again. He was right. She should *try* to believe him, and if she couldn't believe, then at least she could imagine. What if there really was a book in her mind, reading her thoughts? What if a pencil could speak? What if talking objects were real, and what was "real" anyway?

Just then a loud clap of thunder sounded in her ears, knocking her out of her thought loop. Thunder? Why was there thunder in Snowflakes in Moonlight? Annoyed, she pulled out her earbuds and opened her eyes. Rain was pelting against her window. The bell in the waiting room tinkled. A flash of lightning lit up the darkening sky.

66

Dear Ms. Konishi,

I wish I had some better news. You must think I'm just a big old whiner, but actually I'm a pretty optimistic person. I'm just going through a rough patch, but I'm sure my luck will change, and I'm grateful to you for being there and giving me someone to write to. At first I was half hoping you would write back, but now I see it's better if you don't. I mean, I would be super excited to get an email from you, but if you did write, then you'd become real in my mind, and it would be a lot harder to confide in you. But this way, you don't feel really real, and I can tell you anything I want, so please just continue not answering my emails, and maybe don't bother reading them, either.

My biggest problem right now is that my boy, Benny, isn't doing so well, and his doctor wants him to go back to the hospital. She's changed his medications again, too, which is always a big deal, since we never know how he's going to react. Benny isn't happy about any of this, and I'm just sick with worry. To be honest, it's breaking my heart.

And then recently something else happened, too, that was weird and upsetting. Do you remember I told you about my husband's crows, and how they used to bring me little gifts? Nothing super valuable, but I always felt like the gifts were from Kenji. Benny laughs at me, but I know he loves his dad's crows, too. When we go out, they swoop down to the feeding platform, and last week I finally got my special crow, Mister, to take a moon cake from my hand. I was so excited! But yesterday when I went out, they wouldn't come at all. They just perched there on the fence, silent and still, watching me. It was creepy. I left the moon cakes on the platform, and as I went back inside, I happened to look down and I saw the bodies. There were two of them, lying at the foot of the steps, and I knew immediately that one of them was Mister. I was so upset! I know you're not supposed to feed crows because they shouldn't get habituated to humans, and that makes sense for wolves and bears in the woods, but crows live right here in the city, so they're already habituated, right? But my first thought was that this was all my fault. By trying to care for him, I'd somehow killed my favorite crow. I hid their bodies under the porch so Benny wouldn't see them, figuring that I'd bury them later.

The crows stayed away from the feeding platform all day, but I knew they were out there. Every time I looked out the window, I saw them, shoulders hunched, silently watching. I meant to bury Mister and his friend but I couldn't find the shovel and then I got busy with work, and then Benny came home. He was very upset. Usually, when the crows see him walking from the bus stop, they fly alongside and keep him company, but this afternoon, about a block from the house, one of the crows just dropped from the sky and landed at his feet. It was obviously sick but still moving, so he picked it up, and as soon as he did, the other crows started screaming and cawing and flying at him. He ran, but they kept dive bombing him, and one of them even pecked his head. He showed me the sick crow that he'd wrapped in his hoodie, but by then it was already dead.

Honestly, Ms. Aikon, if my son tells me that crows are dropping out of the sky, as much as I'd want to believe him, part of me would always wonder if he was lying or suffering from a hallucination, but I'd seen those two dead crows with my own eyes that morning, so I believed him. In a situation like mine, you learn to be grateful for the little things. But we still don't know what's going on with the crows.

67

They buried the first three crows in the backyard, digging a hole in the dirt with a screwdriver and a large soup spoon. It was hard digging, and Annabelle was worried that if the hole wasn't deep enough the crows might get unearthed and eaten by rats. Benny didn't say anything, but after they'd dug a bit more he asked, "Why are we doing this?"

She looked up, startled. It was obvious. Why was he asking? "The crows are dead, honey. We have to dig a grave so we can bury them."

He sighed. "I *know* that. I asked why."

"Because that's what you do when things die."

"You didn't bury Dad. You burned him."

"We cremated him, Benny. For humans, the word is *cremated*. And we chose to do that because that's what they do in Japan."

"I didn't choose that."

"Okay, true. You were younger then. . . ."

He wiped his nose with his sleeve and looked down at the dead crows. "So for birds, it's a barbecue?"

"Is that supposed to be a joke?"

"No."

He fell silent then and kept on digging, hacking away at the hard ground with the screwdriver while she scooped with her spoon, and when the hole was deep enough, they laid the three crows inside. Their bodies, which she'd never held while they living, were light in her hand and weighed almost nothing. She had an idea, then, and hobbled back into the house, returning with a small handful of trinkets—the bolt, a bottle cap, a shiny pebble. She leaned down and placed the trinkets on top of the bodies.

"There you go, Mister," she said, looking sadly into the hole. "Something to play with. Goodbye. I'm going to miss you. You were such a funny crow." She turned to Benny. "Do you want to say something?"

"To them?"

"Yes. Some final words?"

"Not really."

"Okay. Well. We'd better cover them up then." She pushed some of the dirt into the hole on top of the crows' bodies. "Ashes to ashes, dust to dust..."

"They're not going to like that," Benny said.

"Like what?"

"Being underground and covered with dirt. They're birds. They like being in the sky. We should have done a sky burial."

She brushed the hair from her forehead with the back of her hand. "A sky burial? What's that?"

"Just what it says. You bury them in the sky. They do it in Tibet and places. You bring the dead body to a mountain and leave it so they can be out in the open until they're not."

"What an interesting idea!"

"It's usually for people, but you can do it for animals, too."

Where did he learn this? Was it morbid? Should she be worried?

That night, she couldn't sleep, thinking about Mister. She wasn't sure how she knew this, but she felt certain that he'd been the one who found her the night of her accident. In a flurry of sleek black wing, he'd landed on her stomach and then hopped closer, first to her chest, then to her neck, coming to rest just below her chin, where he cocked his head and peered into her eye. She remembered the feeling of his sharp claws, pricking her skin, but he soon settled down and tucked them into his feathers. *Caw, caw*, he cried, and one by one, the others had joined him, covering her from head to toe, and then there was just the soft warmth of their bodies, shielding her from the rain and the cold night air with their sheltering wings. They were her crows. They'd saved her, and now they were dying. Why? Was it some kind of avian flu? She'd monitored the spread of the H5N1 virus several years earlier for a corporate HMO client, when the news was full of stories about the mass slaughter of domesticated fowl, the stockpiling of antivirals, and the looming threat of a human pandemic, but then the virus just faded from the news. What happened to it? Had it mutated? Was it contagious? Transmittable to humans? Both she and Benny had handled the crow carcasses. Should she be worried?

At dawn, she drifted off. The next morning, a quick search for *#crows, #suddendeath, #avianflu* on her Twitter feed turned up nothing. Relieved, she logged onto her work account and skimmed through the first batch of news items. So much had happened in the world while she was recuperating. The elections were just a few days away, and the bizarre twists and turns in the presidential race were having a huge impact on the local campaigns she'd been monitoring. Racial tensions were escalating, rallies were turning into riots, and coastal wildfires were still burning, but she had no time to read up on all the stories she'd missed. She stared at the bright, hard faces of the newscasters as their words filled the air. It was hard to concentrate. Was she still suffering effects of the concussion?

She had to take a break. In the kitchen, she found a stale moon cake that had fallen into the laundry basket and broke it into pieces. Mister used to try and fly off with a whole moon cake. Greedy little guy. She stepped out onto the porch, hoping to hear the familiar caws of the flock, but there was nothing. No movement in the trees or rooftops. Just silence, and the absence of crows.

She heard a *shush shush* sound coming from around front. She limped down the steps, pushing the overturned stroller out of the way with her crutch. The sound was coming from No-Good's rented dumpster. She rounded the corner of the duplex and saw No-Good sweeping the sidewalk with an old broom. A large dustpan lay on the ground, and in it was something shiny and black. Feathery. No-Good put the broom to one side and unlatched the dumpster door. It swung open, and the slow groan of metal sent a shiver up her spine. He retrieved the dustpan and flung the contents inside.

"Hey!" she called, limping toward him.

He turned then and saw her, and the dumpster door clanged shut. "I warned you," he said, blocking her with the broom pole. "I tole you to get rid of them."

She pushed past him and pulled the door open. Inside, the dead crows lay strewn amid the garbage bags. Their small neat bodies were like pairs of hands pressed together in prayer. Their feathers, once sleek, were dusty, and their eyes were dull with death. Setting her crutch aside, she stepped in and started to collect them.

"Hey!" No-Good said. "Whadaya think yer doing?"

She ignored him. She stretched out the front of her sweatshirt, making a pouch, and placed the dead crows inside.

"You can't do that," he said, approaching her with his broom.

She looked back at him. "You murdered them. That doesn't mean you own them."

A murder of crows. A murderer of crows.

"They're filthy birds. I tole ya to stop feeding them."

"How did you do it?"

He shrugged. "Rat poison," he said. "You gave me the idea. For using moon cakes, I mean. Ate 'em right up." He sounded proud.

"You disgust me," she said, turning away. "You are a terrible man." She placed the last of the crows in her sweatshirt and held the bundle closed.

"You can't talk to me like that. I saved your life, remember?"

"No," she said. "They did. They saved my life. They sat on me and kept me warm. Like an egg."

No-Good snorted. "You gotta be kidding. They was gonna eat you!

They was gonna start with your eyeballs and eat you bit by bit. They was just softening you up, waiting till you got good and ripe."

"No," she said, cradling them in her arms. "They were my friends."

He shook his head. "Oh, lady," he said, retreating to his side of the duplex. "I could evict you for harboring dead crows, you know." And then, when she didn't respond, he added, "You're crazy, you know that? No wonder your kid's a fucking nutjob."

She felt the blood rush to her cheeks. "How dare you say that about my son! You should be ashamed of yourself, Henry Wong. What would your mother think?"

A dark look crossed his sallow face like bad weather, and the wine-colored birthmark flushed a deep red. He took a step toward her, brandishing the broom pole. "Don't!" he cried, his voice suddenly shrill. "Don't you say nothing about my Ma!"

Annabelle groped for her crutch and held it in front of her, hugging the crows to her belly. He stood there, wavering, and then his arm dropped and his thin shoulders slumped. He looked like he was about to cry.

"Henry, what's wrong?" she said. "Is your mother okay? I thought she was recovering."

He turned away, clutching the broom pole with both hands. It was his mother's broom. Mrs. Wong used to sweep the sidewalk with it almost every day. "They say she caught some kinda infection. Say she's not gonna make it."

"Oh, Henry. I'm so sorry."

He turned to face her again. "Yeah? Well, you should be. Them crows put a curse on her and she fell down the steps. You fell down the steps, too. You think that's just bad luck? No way! Them crows cursed you, and they was gonna eat you. You should thank me, lady. For saving your life before you was dead."

She wanted to argue with him, wanted to defend her crows, but she stopped herself. He was angry. He was grieving. Grief took many forms and went through many stages. She understood that. "Henry, can I do anything?"

For a brief moment, in the surly face of the man, she saw the young boy he'd once been, and then the boy was gone. "Yeah," he said, narrowing his eyes and nodding his head toward her yard. "You can clean up all your shit now so I don't have to do it after I evict you."

"I don't think harboring dead crows is cause for eviction, Henry."

"Maybe not," he said. "But hoarding is. My lawyer's on it now. I'm renovating this dump and selling it, and I'm not letting your shit bring the price down. I gave you a chance, lady. You failed the inspection. You're out."

68

"So many sad stories. Like this poor woman." Aikon turned the laptop around so Kimi could see the screen. "Her husband was killed in a car accident, and their son was traumatized and started hearing things. She sends me photographs."

They were sitting together at the low writing table in the abbess's study. A light rain was falling in the tiny garden outside the veranda, turning the leaves of the maple tree a brilliant crimson. They were having tea, and Aikon had offered Kimi the cup she usually used herself, an antique one that had been broken and painstakingly repaired with gold. It had a poem, written in beautiful calligraphy, on the side, and the sinuous filigree of gold wound like a thread through the delicate Chinese characters, stitching the cup back together. Kimi knew it was Aikon's favorite cup and she felt honored. She loved these moments with her teacher. They were precious, quiet, and also nothing special.

"I understand why Senju Kannon's head exploded," Aikon said. "So much suffering."

Kimi took a sip of tea and studied the picture of the family on the beach. "He is a sweet-looking boy," she said. "I wonder what he hears..."

"The mother didn't say. Only that he hears things, like his running shoe, talking to him."

In Japan, things often spoke, or at least their spirits did. Lanterns, umbrellas, tea kettles, mirrors, clocks. Shoes spoke, too, but usually they were Japanese shoes, like straw sandals.

Kimi hesitated. "Maybe the shoe is *tsukumogami*?"

Aikon looked doubtful. "Do they have *tsukumogami* in America? I've never heard of an athletic shoe with an unquiet spirit, have you?"

"No . . . ," Kimi said.

"Well, never mind," Aikon said, pulling the laptop back around. "She says her son's condition is worsening, and their landlord is going to evict them because she is so untidy. It's a terrible situation, don't you think?"

"Yes, it is." Kimi hesitated again. "Is there any way to help them?"

"What can we do?"

Her teacher's question felt like a test. "We can chant for them?"

"We have," Aikon said. "And so we should again. The mother's name is Annabelle, and her son's name is Benny. Please put them on the well-being ceremony list this week."

Kimi felt she'd gotten the wrong answer. She repeated the names out loud and then wrote them down in the little notebook she carried. She could feel her teacher's eyes on her.

"Your English pronunciation is very good," Aikon said.

Kimi blushed. She had studied abroad in America during high school, and then majored in English literature in university. "No," she said. "It should be much better. . . ."

"But you can read and write, yes?"

Kimi nodded.

"And you are a hard worker, too. Meticulous. Would you say you are a perfectionist? Do you feel the need to finish every job you start?"

Kimi nodded again, somewhat more confidently, this time.

"Excellent!" Aikon said. She picked up the teapot and refilled Kimi's cup. "I have just the job for you. I'd like you to take over managing the international fan mail and social media accounts, and then you can come as my assistant and interpreter for the US book tour. What do you think?"

Kimi put her teacup down and bowed. "I am honored, but I couldn't possibly do a job like that—"

"Of course," Akon said. "The job is impossible. You will have no time to be meticulous. That is why it is perfect for you. You will never finish. Life will go on. You will be cured of your afflictions in no time!"

Kimi thought she heard a hint of laughter in her teacher's firm voice. "Okay," she said. "I will try."

"But please don't try too hard. You must take care of your heart."

Kimi looked down at the names she had written in her notebook. "Should I respond to the emails, too? And to Twitter?"

"The Buddha said that responding to email and Twitter is like sweeping the sands from the banks of the Ganges River."

"The Buddha said that?"

"Well, maybe not. But the point remains the same. Some tasks are impossible, even if you are a Buddha. Even if you have eleven heads and a thousand arms."

"So, I shouldn't try to answer . . . ?"

"Only if it would help."

"How will I know?"

Aikon drank the last sip of tea in her cup. "Yes," she said, turning the empty cup in her hand, admiring the glaze. "That is a good question."

69

You were aware the elections were imminent, but you experienced them mostly as a background noise coming up through the floorboards. When the day finally came, you woke with an earache, a sore throat, and a fever just high enough that Annabelle, after taking your temperature, agreed to let you stay home from school.

"I'm going out to vote later," she said, leaning on her crutch. "I'm taking a taxi. If you're feeling better, you can come along."

"I can't vote," you told her.

"I know. I thought you might want to see democracy in action. You were only ten during the last election, and this one is historic, not to mention you'll be old enough to vote in the next one." She gazed down at you like you were a freak or a miracle. "Amazing. You're growing up so fast. What do you think?"

"About growing up?"

"No, silly. About coming with me to vote."

"Um," you said, pretending to consider it. "No."

She sighed and settled her crutch under her armpit. "Get some rest," she said. "I'll bring you some lunch later if you're not feeling better."

All morning long, voices filtered up from Mission Control, the strident voices of the candidates, the brisk upbeat voices of the newscasters, and the sonorous pundits, interspersed with extravagant orchestral cues. With your father's musical ear, you had learned to recognize the different intros and outros: the dark epic war themes for conflicts in the Middle East; the urgent, patriotic anthems for breaking stories in the US. You lay in your darkened room, listening to the music swell and fade until finally you fell into a dreamless sleep.

Around noon, Annabelle woke you with crackers and some chicken noodle soup in a thermos. She sat on the edge of your bed with her foot sticking out, propping herself on her crutch and watching while you ate.

"How are you feeling?"

"My head hurts."

She put her hand against your forehead. "Your fever's down."

"It really hurts. It feels like it's gonna explode." You handed her the half-empty cup and lay back down.

"That's all you're having?"

"I'm not hungry."

She drank the rest, screwed the cup back on the thermos and then stood. "I'll be leaving in a couple of hours. Sure you don't want to come?"

You shook your head, which made it hurt more, so you put your hands over your ears, squeezing to hold it together.

That afternoon, something in the newsfeeds changed, like someone was tightening the strings. The pitch rose and the oscillation increased, turning the sounds into jittery shards that sneaked up through the cracks in the floor and under the doors, glinting and slicing. You put on the Grundigs, but this didn't help. You covered your head with your pillow and tried to hum, but the shards cut through the tremulous whimper that was all your sore throat could produce. "*Shut up,*" you whispered. "*Shut up, shut up, please.*" Finally, just when you couldn't stand it anymore, you had an idea. You got up and went into Annabelle's bedroom.

Her nest was forlorn and abandoned since she'd been sleeping downstairs. It had been over a year since you'd eaten Chinese take-out and lain on your belly and let her scratch your back. You were different then. A different boy. Now, the air was stale and sour. Here and there, you could see a plaid flannel sleeve from one of your father's old shirts, reaching out from underneath the dank tangle of bedding like a drowning man sinking below the waves. The dresser in the corner was still missing a drawer, and the gap looked like a dark open mouth. The noise from the newsfeeds was even louder here, reminding you of why you'd come, and so you stepped over a pile of books and went to the closet. Inside the box of your father's old mixing equipment, you found the audio cable for the Grundigs. You plugged one end into the headphones and the other into the stereo, and selected disc one of Benny Goodman's famous 1938 concert at Carnegie Hall.

At the first brassy blast of "Don't Be That Way," your body relaxed like a sigh. Why hadn't you thought of this before? The music swelled and filled your ears, and when it moved into the cheerful, upbeat swing of the melody line, your head began to bob to the familiar rhythm. When the slow, slinky "Sometimes I'm Happy" came on, you glanced up and caught sight of your reflection in your mother's mirror. A solemn boy with over-sized headphones looked back at you, a little astronaut. You pulled up your sleeves, and the astronaut did, too. You showed him your forearm, where the constellation of stars had scabbed over, leaving tiny puckered scars. Your arm looked like hers now. You brought your arm to your lips and kissed the stars, felt the ache in your heart. You turned away from the mirror and lay down, burrowing into the nest and closing your eyes, sinking into the sweet staticky jazz.

YOU WOKE TO the sound of the stylus, circling round and round the run-out groove. The room was dark, and Annabelle was standing over you, with an expression so sorrowful, you sat up in a panic. "What happened?"

She reached down and took the headphones gently from your head. "I'm sorry, honey," she said. "I didn't mean to wake you." She switched off the turntable and put a cool palm on your forehead.

"What time is it?"

"It's late. Go back to sleep."

You could hear the muted sound of a single television station coming from downstairs, and then you remembered. "Is it over? Did you vote?"

"Yes," she said. "It's over."

You tried to get up, but she pushed you gently back. "Stay," she said. "I have to work through the night."

WHEN YOU WOKE AGAIN, it was light outside and your fever had broken. The newsfeeds were muted, but you could feel a new tension in the air, as if the air itself were agitated. You got up and went back to your room. The agitation seemed to be coming from outside, but when you looked out the window, the alley was empty. What was the noise? It was a turbulence, like the angry thrumming of a million bees. Was it in your head?

No. It was real. It was coming from the world.

You put on your black hoodie and your old Nike sneakers. Downstairs, Annabelle was asleep on the couch. You paused in the doorway. In sleep, her pale face was soft, and the lines of worry that usually creased her forehead were gone. She looked like a sleeping princess, like a young, untroubled mother. A thick, sad feeling rose up in your throat and you swallowed it back. Surrounding the sofa on the floor were T-shirts, sorted into unruly heaps of discards and donations. Next to the piles was the emptied dresser drawer, which she had begun to fill again with the shirts she was keeping, but she hadn't gotten far, and the folded tees in the drawer slumped to one side, discouraged by the lack of progress. You crouched down and quietly started folding. It didn't take you long. You were good at folding, and soon you had them lined up in the drawer, standing straight and tall.

You surveyed the array. *Better?* you asked the shirts in your mind, but they were shirts, not mind readers, so they didn't answer. You suspected they didn't really care, but at least the drawer looked nice. Maybe, when she woke up and saw it, she would think the shirts had folded themselves. Or, maybe she'd guess you had folded them, and forgive you for sneaking out.

OUT ON THE STREET, the thrumming was louder, as if the bees were getting ready to attack. You set out down the alley in the direction of the sound, and when you reached the sylvan pocket and saw the massing sea of bodies that filled the park, you knew you had reached the source. You'd never seen so many people in the pocket before, milling around the tents in the homeless encampment, holding signs with angry words. Cop cars were stationed around the perimeter of the park with their lights flashing, and riot police were standing by with shields and guns. Guns want to kill, so you pulled up your hood and merged into the throng. In the middle of the park, you spotted Jake and the guys, all dressed in black, and you swerved away, but the dogs spotted you. The pale male called Riker started barking, and then Jake looked up and saw you, too.

"Yo, B-boy!" he called. "Over here!"

Just then, a leather-clad arm came from behind and caught you by the neck in a headlock, crushing your head and grinding your face into the sweet scent of weed and black leather. A metal zipper scraped your cheekbone. You clawed and twisted, trying to get away, but the chokehold tightened, and a voice growled into your ear.

"Relax, Benny-boy. No hard feelings, right?" You couldn't see the face behind the voice, but you knew who it was. You nodded but that wasn't enough. "Right?" the voice repeated, louder now. "Say it!"

"Right," you gasped, and the arm relaxed. You coughed and pulled away, and when you turned, there was Freddy. He was wearing a ski mask pulled up on his forehead. His eyeballs were red and spinning around in their sockets and he was carrying his baseball bat.

"That's more like it," he said, punching you on the shoulder and then throwing an arm around you. "We're buddies now, right? Forgive and forget. Just don't go crazy on me again." And as the crowd pushed forward, surging like a wave toward the center of the city, he handed you the bat.

70

Oh, Benny, no.

We knew this was coming, but can't we reconsider? Give him back the bat and rewind you down the alleyway to the safety of Annabelle's nest, so that when your fever breaks, you wake up hungry instead? And you go downstairs to look for something to eat, and see your mom sleeping on the couch. And she wakes up while you're still folding her shirts, and she's so grateful and happy she weeps a few tears of joy and then orders Chinese take-out, and just as you're about to eat, you hear a noise at the back door, and it's Kenji, home from rehearsal and just in time for dinner! And he takes off his hat, stows his clarinet in its place on the shelf, and then sits down with you at the kitchen table, and you all dig into a feast of dim sum and chow fun and moo shu pork, making sure to save a moon cake for the new crop of baby crows. Can't we do this? Is it too late?

But of course it's too late. Please, forgive a book its hubris, to think that our wishful thinking might undo your plot. . . .

ANNABELLE DID WAKE UP. She had worked through the night, covering the first wave of protests, which, by morning, were being called riots. She'd gone to sleep after the morning news, and now she woke to find her T-shirts neatly folded and stacked by color in rows, and it was like magic, like one of Santa's elves had been riffling through her drawer. She got off the sofa, limped to the foot of the stairs, and called to him. "Benny! Honey, thank you so much! The drawer is beautiful! You are a miracle!" She waited. "Benny?"

He must still be sleeping, she thought, uneasily. Still sick, poor thing. She should take his temperature again. She started up the stairs and then she noticed the time. It was already past noon, and he would be getting hungry. She would make him something nice for lunch and bring it up to him. Something comforting. Mac and cheese? She hobbled into the kitchen, found a box of noodles on the shelf, and when she looked in the fridge, she saw that he had bought milk. She turned on the oven and put a pot of water on to boil.

An hour later, the mac and cheese was congealing in the bottom of the casserole dish, but by then Benny's lunch was the least of her concerns. She stood in the doorway of his empty bedroom. His backpack hung from his chair, and his school books were stacked neatly on his desk. She went into the bathroom and saw his cell phone plugged into the charger next to the sink. She limped back downstairs to the kitchen, hesitated, and then called the school.

"Yes, we do have Benny down as absent," the secretary informed her. "The emails went out. Didn't you get one?"

"Yes, of course," Annabelle said. "I was just—" But then she stopped. She didn't know how to finish the sentence. *I was just hoping that by some miracle he'd turned up, that he was sitting in his classroom, that he was studying algebra, that he was safe.* She hung up quickly before the secretary could ask her more questions and then sat at the kitchen table, hugging her chest to keep her heart inside. *You don't understand. You people just don't understand what it's like.* She straightened and called the woman back again.

"Sorry," she said, briskly. "We were cut off. I was just calling to let you know that Benny was sick but he's feeling better. He's on his way to school, so could you have him call me? He forgot his cell phone, so I can't call him. Kids!"

Dr. Melanie was next. She left a message with the answering service saying Benny had gone missing again, and then she checked the time. Who else? She pulled up the number for the local precinct but there was no point in calling yet. It was too soon, and maybe Benny really was just on his way to school. It was a possibility, although without his backpack and books . . . She shook her head in frustration and struggled to her feet. She couldn't even go out looking for him with her ankle like this. She limped out to the back porch and leaned against the deserted feeding station, listening to the sirens in the distance. No, she thought. Just be patient. He always comes home. You're overreacting. A low-flying helicopter passed overhead and she felt the throbbing of its rotors in the rickety wood railing.

71

There was anger in the air. Outrage and confusion. Disbelief. Helicopters hovered overhead, and down below, the protesters surged through the streets, blocking traffic and chanting as the car horns blared.

The PEOPLE, UNITED, will never be DEFEATED!

The fury of it energized you, a powerful high. Freddy was there. Jake was there. Dozer was there. T-Bone was there, and several others, too, shadowy guys, dressed in black and carrying backpacks. Where did they come from? They filtered in from all sides, and their dark numbers made you feel powerful, like you were part of a special posse—but not "special" like in school, where the word meant you were a loser. Special, like in special troops or special taskforce or special squadron. Different from the righteous citizens with their hand-lettered signs.

SHOW me what democracy looks like! THIS is what democracy looks like!

"Fuck democracy!" Freddy yelled into your ear, and you nodded because at that moment Freddy was your friend, your leader and commander, and anything he said sounded right.

No JUSTICE . . . no PEACE!

"Fuck justice!" Freddy shouted. "Fuck peace!"

Climate change is not a LIE! We won't let our planet DIE!

"Fuck the planet!" He handed you a dirty bandana and pulled his ski mask down over his mouth and nose. All you could see were his spinning red eyes, but underneath you could tell he was smiling. "Cover your face," he said. "Stay close," and you did what he said.

The other guys, also masked, followed as the crowds pressed forward, heading toward the center of the city.

LOVE not HATE, makes us GREAT!

You marched along the bus route, toward Library Square. Bare trees lined the median strips. You passed retail stores and office buildings, banks and cafes.

No more SILENCE! End police VIOLENCE!

A long black limousine was parked across from the local TV station. Spotting it, Freddy signaled and your posse broke away from the crowd.

Say it LOUD! Say it CLEAR! Immigrants are welcome HERE!

Dozer kicked over a steel trash can with his boot, and the garbage spilled onto the street. "Go!" Freddie yelled, and T-Bone pulled a crowbar out from under his coat and brought it down hard on the hood of the limo. The metal crumpled, the alarm started to wail. You covered your ears.

"*Use the bat!*" Freddy shouted, shoving you toward the screaming vehicle. Bats want to hit, want to slam into windshields, want to shatter glass, but before it could strike, the limo burst into flames. You jumped back, gripping the furious bat. You saw the can of gasoline in Jake's hand, and there was Dozer, holding the torch, and Freddie, darting in and out of the thick black smoke that billowed from the limousine's engine. People circled the vehicle, holding their cell phones high in the air, like small square eyes on long stems, unblinking. A plume of orange flame leapt from the engine. Bats want to hit. Fires want to burn.

"*Fall back!*" Freddy cried, and then you heard the sound of boots, marching. A bullhorn blared—*Clear the street! Clear the street!*—as the first ranks of riot police advanced on the crowd. Shields up and visors down, they were a phalanx of black knights, clad in cuirass, gauntlets and helm, polearms raised against the fray. You stood there, riveted. Nothing could stop them.

"*They've got tear gas!*" someone yelled. "*Get back!*" People dropped their signs and scattered, only to circle back like ravenous dogs, filming, always filming. Freddy came up next to you and pointed to the large display window of the Nike megastore across the street.

"*Go!*" he shouted. "*Use the BAT!*" and your sneakers responded. Sneakers want to run. Bats want to hit. The mannequins in the window were frozen in midstride. Etched on the glass, big black words gave the command: *JUST DO IT!* and so you did. Jogged up to the window, gripped the bat and swung. The glass crumpled, the wood shuddered. You swung again, this time shattering the glass, and you watched as it slid to the ground in a sheet of sparkling diamonds. The jaggedy hole in the window seemed pleased with itself, but the drift of glass on the ground cried out in distress, and behind you, the boots kept coming. You knelt, scooping up the glass in your hands, like frozen teardrops, leaking through your fingers.

"I'm sorry," you whispered, and your apology was sincere, but one shard, long and knifelike, refused to be so easily mollified. It wanted to stab, and so you picked it up, and just then something touched your shoulder.

Red Alert! Red Alert!

Gripping the glass, you leapt to your feet and spun. In front of you stood a space alien, a monster, with ghastly insectoid eyes and a long pig-like snout. *Danger!* You raised your arm, and the shard glinted. A muffled voice screamed—*No, Benny, it's me!*—and you recognized her then, but the shard was already an object in motion, slicing through the air. Horrified, you watched, but she saw it, too. She jumped back, and you heard the shard clatter to the ground, or maybe the clattering was the tear gas canister, hitting the sidewalk and rolling up behind her. Your palm was bleeding, but she was okay. She reached for your wrist as the thick cloud billowed and spread. The smell hit you first, acrid and sour, and then your eyes were on fire, and when you tried to inhale, it was like you'd been smitten in the chest with a battleax. You brought your hands to your face and fell to your knees, gagging, but she hauled you back onto your feet.

"Come on!" she yelled, and you stumbled blindly after.

She dragged you down the block and into a doorway and pulled your hands away from your face. The air was clearer here, but you couldn't stop coughing, and your eyes were burning and your face was covered with blood from your punctured palm.

"Don't rub," she said, yanking off her gas mask. She took the bandanna from her neck and tied it quickly around your bleeding hand. She was always bandaging your hands. She gripped your wrist, examining the little perforations. Frowning, she glanced at your face, but your eyes were still shut tight, so she took a bottle from her backpack. "Look up," she said, and you tried, but you couldn't open your eyes for the burning. She poured white liquid onto your face. Maybe it was milk.

"Shit's getting real," she said, holding your face between her hands. She wiped your cheeks as you gasped for air, and then she remembered. "Oh, fuck. Your asthma. Okay, we gotta get you off the street. Come on!"

You cracked open your eyes. Through the milk and tears, you saw two cops in riot gear closing in behind her, and she turned and saw them, too. She put her hands on your chest and gave you a hard shove, pushing you away.

"Go—" she cried, just as the cops grabbed her.

You stumbled and ran, and when you looked back, she was fighting them, flailing and kicking, but watching you, too. Your eyes met, and her body went limp, and as the cops dragged her away by the armpits, she kept looking at you. You wanted to go after her, to rescue her, but she shook her head.

Go— she mouthed, and you watched her lips move as a different voice, quiet and familiar, completed her sentence.

—*to the Library.*

72

Across the country, as the results were confirmed, people were taking to the streets. Protests were erupting in all the major cities, and the national news feeds were broadcasting live as the story broke. At Mission Control, Annabelle sat in front of her glowing monitors, dubbing the coverage. Benny still hadn't come home. Dr. Melanie still hadn't called back.

How can a story break, anyway? If a story breaks, does it mean it's broken? Crowds were blocking city streets and freeways. So many people. She checked the time. It was still too soon to call the station.

What does a broken story look like, anyway? The local news was reporting from downtown where a vehicle was burning. Black-clad rioters in ski masks overturned trash cans, smashed police car windows, vandalized storefronts. Leaning into the monitor, Annabelle scanned the shaky footage, searching for Benny. Was that him? She froze the frame. No. Different boy. She heard the bullhorns: *Clear the street! Clear the street! All persons must leave the area immediately!* Police in riot gear were moving in.

They were using water cannons and tear gas to break up the demonstrators. She could still hear helicopters overhead, but she wasn't sure if the sound was coming from the TV or outside her house. Same for the sirens. Inside or outside? Near or far?

Dear Ms. Konishi,

I'm sitting in the dark. People are rioting in the streets, the country is broken and going up in flames, my son has run away again, and there's nothing I can do about any of it. All I can do is wait, so I thought I'd write to you.

You probably know that we just had an election here. I know Japan is a democracy like ours supposedly is. Do your politicians act like bullies in a playground? Do your citizens riot in the streets afterward? I can't remember if I told you this, but I monitor the news for a living. It's not much of a job, but I can do it from home and still get health insurance, which I think in Japan you get automatically, right? That must be nice. I don't get to monitor international news very often, so I don't really know much about Japan. Do school children shoot each other in your country? Are your forests burning?

I didn't want to monitor the news for a living. It's really depressing. Ever since I was a kid, I wanted to be a children's librarian. I actually went to library school for a while, but I had to drop out when I got pregnant with Benny. That was okay, because I love my son. He's the best thing that's ever happened to me, but I wish I could have been a librarian *and* a mother. *And* a wife, because I'm missing out on the whole wife experience, too. I miss Kenji so much. I keep thinking if he were here, Benny wouldn't be having all these troubles. I keep thinking it's all my fault.

Okay, I just called the police station and made them take down a report. I know how to do this now, and I'm getting good at it. Soon I'll know all the officers by name. The one I spoke to tonight was a lady and she asked if we'd had a fight or anything. I told her no, not this time. The first two times, he was mad at me, but this time I was asleep when he left, and he folded my T-shirts first. It was like a gift! He folded them using your Japanese method that I showed him, and when I woke up, all the shirts were arranged in the drawer by color. Sweet, right? What kind of kid does that? I didn't tell the officer, though.

The night Kenji died, before he left the house, we had a fight. I don't even remember how it started. Something stupid. We were in the bedroom and he was getting ready for a gig. Maybe he said he'd be late and not to wait up. It's true I was sick of waiting up, but I didn't want to be told *not* to, you know? I just wanted him to stay home. I wanted him to *want* to stay home with his wife and son, and I think on some level I must have known he was doing drugs again. And I remember watching him button his flannel shirt, and I said something like you're never home anymore, or we never see you, and he gave me this sad smile and put on that stupid porkpie hat. He looked so great in that hat, and that's what triggered me, how great he looked, and that sad smile. It was like he agreed with me, but looking great and hanging out at the club and getting high with the band was beyond his control, which of course was total bullshit. He was standing in front of the mirror, adjusting the tilt of the hat, and I just lost it. I didn't say anything. I was sitting on the bed, and he kissed me on the forehead and went downstairs. I heard him getting his clarinet from the living room, putting on his jacket.

I got up then and went down to the kitchen. He was standing in front of the refrigerator door, messing with the magnets. I didn't know it then, but he was writing me a poem. "I'll come home soon," he said, but we both knew this wasn't true.

"Don't bother," I said, cold as can be, and when he walked out the back door, I picked up my favorite pink teapot that was sitting on the table, and I threw it. It smashed against the door. I'm sure he heard it.

This is the poem he left me on the fridge:

My abundant woman mother goddess lover
we are symphony together
I am mad for you

I found the poem later that night when I got back from the hospital, but by then he was already dead.

She sat back and stared at the screen. She had wanted to end on a more upbeat note, which is why she'd included the poem. The poem wasn't even that good. It was just a stupid fridge magnet poem. She reread what she'd written. The email had turned into a big old sob story, and she was embarrassed to send it, but just as she was about to delete it, the words *children's librarian* caught her eye, and the memory of the Washroom Incident came back to her. She remembered the security office, the guard, and the small librarian. What was her name? She had given Annabelle her business card and told her to call if she needed anything. She was so friendly—did that make her a friend? Was she a social network? Where was that card?

She hit Send and then stood and started rooting through the drifts of magazines and mail, carefully moving the piles to search underneath. She should have scanned the card, or at least added the woman's name and number to her emergency contacts. Why couldn't she be more organized! She found a stack of stale-dated coupons held together with a binder clip and threw them out. She found a bill that needed paying and a plate with bagel crumbs and dried cream cheese. She found the letters from No-Good's lawyer—she'd been looking for them, but they would have to wait. The first priority was to find Benny, and she had a sudden feeling, call it a mother's intuition, that the small librarian could help. She just had to find that card.

Frustrated now, she went to the kitchen, thinking that perhaps she'd left it there. The baking dish with the mac and cheese was sitting untouched on the stovetop. She wasn't hungry, but Benny might be when he came home, so she covered it and put it in the refrigerator. As she closed the door, something caught her eye. It was subtle, a slight but novel rearrangement of the magnets. The word *mother* had detached itself from *ache* and migrated out of the previous poem, rising above it toward the nearby *moon*. Adjacent to *moon* were two other magnets that almost seemed like they wanted to be part of a new constellation of words, which taken together could almost read:

moon   mother be   cool

Stuck to the door under *be cool* was the small librarian's business card.
Cory.
Cory Johnson.

73

You slipped through the doors and past the security checkpoints, reaching the escalators just as the announcement came over the PA system: *The Library will be closing in ten minutes.* Up the levels you rode, gliding smoothly past the descending stream of patrons, keeping your hoodie pulled forward and your face averted because your eyes were still burning and streaming with tears. Level Two. Level Three. Level Four. The old men's washroom was where it was supposed to be, so you ducked in and held your face under the taps until the burning subsided. Level Five. Level Six. Your body was vibrating, and time was doing a weird thing, starting and stopping, speeding and slowing down. Maybe it was the effects of the teargas. Level Eight. Level Nine. At the top, you got off and crossed the precipitous footbridge, heading toward the carrels. The exchange student was gone, but the typing lady was there, packing up her laptop. You turned away, but she had already spotted you.

"Hey," she said. "You made it. Long time no see." She studied you as you stood there, still wheezing slightly and poised to flee, taking in your swollen face and reddened eyes, then she shrugged and zipped her backpack. She slipped the straps over her bony shoulders, but as she walked past you, she hesitated. "Staying the night?"

You looked at the floor, not wanting to answer.

"Does your mom know you're here?" And then, before you could say anything, she continued, talking more to herself now. "No, I guess she doesn't. Poor thing. She's going to worry . . ." She studied you for a moment longer and then reached out and patted your arm. "Well, take care. You know there are snacks downstairs in the staff room, next to the Bindery. I gather that's where you're headed . . . ?"

You hadn't thought to go to the Bindery, but for some reason it made sense, and so you nodded.

"Well, be careful. Anything's possible in the Bindery, you know. You don't want to spend too much time in there." And then, seeing a flicker of worry cross your face, she gave your arm another pat and added, "It's okay. You'll survive."

This was hardly reassuring.

When she was gone, you dropped to your knees and crawled under your carrel, curled into a ball and hugged your knees. Your body was still vibrating. You could hear sounds—footsteps and distant voices, the staccato rattle of carts and the ponderous drone of a floor polisher, coming closer and closer. Was this janitor one of the Bottleman's friends? Maybe he'd been drinking. There was something in the way he operated the old machine, like he was listening to music—a waltz, maybe—swinging the heavy rotating heads in slow, weighty arcs, covering every inch of floor. Somehow you knew this, and knew, too, that when he finally crossed the bridge to your nook and thrust the blunt muzzle of the machine under your carrel, bumping into your thigh, and bent down to see what the obstruction was, he wouldn't see you curled there, and not because he was drunk, but because you were invisible.

Or so you told yourself, while you waited for the drone of the machine to subside and the sounds to settle. Waited for the final clicks, indicating that the last human had locked the doors and left the building. Waited for the Library to settle into the deep, dark silence of slumbering books, and words tucked in between their covers for the night. And when this happened, you crawled out from beneath your carrel and made your way down to the Bindery.

74

Cory Johnson was still at the Library when Annabelle phoned. She was never able to leave right at nine when the Library closed, and that day things were taking even longer. It had been a hell of a day, and she was exhausted. She'd stayed up late the night before, watching the election returns and hoping against hope, but by 3:00 a.m. the outcome was clear, and she went to bed. On the bus ride the next morning, passengers were grim and stony-faced, eyeing one another with suspicion. The staff room at the Library felt like a funeral home. The Library social worker had sent around an email, offering support to anyone who might feel stressed.

"Stressed?" her friend Julio said, standing at the microwave. "Make that terrified. It's like waking up and finding yourself in a Philip K. Dick novel."

The Library always felt like a mirror of the world, and on that day, more than ever. Librarians walked around like zombies, bewildered and sleep-deprived, and the patrons were jittery. By noon, there had been two ODs in the men's washrooms. The librarians on duty had administered the Narcan injections—they'd been trained to do this, although none of them liked to—and for a while these incidents provided a distraction, but then the memory of the election returned. How had this happened? How could this be? It was like when someone died, Cory thought. One day everything's fine and you're thinking about hooking up with some cute girl on Tinder, and the next day you learn that your grandmother is dead, and things are no longer fine, and there's just this big empty hole in your life where Grandma Dee used to be. Cory remembered the dizzying fear she felt when her mother called from the hospital, and the grief that followed in all its stages, and this day was not so different. By the time the Library closed, she had cycled through shock, disbelief, denial and anger, and spent a few hours researching Canadian citizenship before plummeting into full-on depression. By closing time, acceptance was still nowhere in sight.

When the phone rang, she was away from her desk, trying to comfort Naheed, a young Iranian research librarian, whose parents were demanding she come home. She went back to Multicultural Children's to tidy up and noticed the message light blinking. She hesitated, but habit got the better of her, and so she checked, and immediately wished she hadn't. The voicemail was from the mother of the strange little boy who used to sit under her stool. He was a teenager now. Sweet kid. Still strange, though. Maybe on the spectrum? He'd been totally spooked when she'd seen him down in Book Processing, and then later Jevaun found him on Five, pounding on a wall, looking for a bathroom. The mother had always seemed nice, interesting but somewhat hapless. Cory felt sorry for her, sorry that her kid was missing, but the fact she had called to ask if he was hiding out in Multicultural Children's was irritating. He wasn't, of course. Cory had just done a walk-through. She put her water bottle and keys in her backpack and did one last check of her desk. She was sick of people making jokes about ghosts and coming to her when things went missing. She had nothing against ghosts, particularly multicultural ones, but it wasn't funny. It was a racist urban legend. Not that the boy's mother was racist or trying to be funny, but still. She shouldered her backpack and walked to the bus stop.

Her bus was late, and then it was forced to make a long detour to avoid the demonstrations downtown. The other passengers were irate, and so was she, but when a group of young white guys started making snide comments about the demonstrators, she felt her irritation turn to rage. Fuming, she pushed the button and exited at the next stop. A day earlier, she would have said something, but today she kept her mouth shut, and this bothered her. Was it fear? She passed a group of people heading downtown with signs. She was tempted to join them, and a day earlier she would have, but instead she walked home, showered, and went straight to bed.

She woke in the middle of the night and the memory of the mother's voicemail came back to her. It annoyed her when work followed her home and disrupted her sleep. Why couldn't she maintain healthy boundaries? The woman had sounded so sheepish and apologetic. Her kid was missing. If she needed help, why didn't she just ask for it?

But, of course, she had asked. That's what the phone call was about, and Cory had ignored it. Why hadn't she called the woman back? Why hadn't she said something to those white guys on the bus? Why hadn't she joined the protests? What was wrong with her?

She looked at her phone. It was a bit after two. Too late to call now. She wondered if the kid had come home yet. Poor woman—Annabelle. Fussy kind of name. She'd be up waiting. Worrying. Making herself sick. Maybe the kid was hiding out somewhere. It had happened before, people sneaking in overnight, stealing food from the staff room. People always blamed the ghosts. She reached for her phone and called Security. Jevaun was on night shift, and she knew that at this hour he'd be nodding off in front of his console of monitors.

"Hey, wake up. I need you to do something." Ignoring his complaints, she went on. "You remember that kid who was trying to break down the wall?"

"On Level Five? Sure. Nice kid. A little weird. What about him?"

"I think he might be in the Library."

"Impossible. I would have seen him."

"His name is Benny. Benny Oh. Can you check Multicultural Kids?"

"That's what security cameras are for, you know."

"He might be hiding under a desk or something."

"Right."

She heard the creak of his chair as he got to his feet. "And then call me back, okay? I can't sleep."

When her phone rang, she was up making tea. "Anything?"

"Of course not."

She brought her tea into the living room. "Listen, Jevaun, could you take a quick look on Nine?"

She'd seen the boy there once or twice when she was subbing upstairs, sitting in a carrel, barricaded in behind a fortress of books. He looked so serious, shoulders hunched around his ears, rocking back and forth as he studied the open book in front of him. Once, when he stepped away, she went over to see what he was reading and was surprised at what she found: books on medieval armaments, on German film, on surrealist art, on Walter Benjamin, as well as a collection of fairy tales. There were others, too, but those were the ones she remembered. Sitting at a neighboring carrel was another regular patron, a writer, who looked up from her typing when she saw Cory.

"Last week it was Argentinian fiction and raising ferrets," the woman had offered. "Jorge Luis Borges. Can you believe it? What kind of kid reads Borges?"

Cory took a sip of her tea and burned her tongue, and then her phone rang again.

"Nada on Nine. Where next?"

Cory thought for a moment. "Can you try the Bindery?"

There was a long pause. In the background she could hear a faint hollow sound, like wind, whistling across the top of a bottle.

"You still there?" she asked.

"Calypso's been lively tonight," he replied.

She could picture him standing on the precarious footbridge, looking down the levels into the dark subbasement.

"That's just the updraft," she said.

"That's what you think."

When her phone rang next, her tea was lukewarm. Jevaun's voice was low. "You're right," he said. "I'm outside the Bindery. He's in there."

She put the cup down. "Is he okay?"

"Seems fine. Just sitting there on top of that old paper cutter, singing to himself. Funny smile on his face. I called out to him but he won't answer."

"Okay, listen. I'll get an Uber and—"

"He's naked, Cor. He doesn't have any clothes on."

"Oh, jeez. Did something happen to him?"

"I can't tell. You know I gotta call this in, right?"

"Wait. Just wait. Please."

"Hurry."

HE WAS SITTING on the edge of the old Quintilio Vaggelli, the long curved blade, like a scimitar, looming over his head. Cory stood in the doorway, watching. He didn't seem to be hurt or in any danger of self-harm, and he wasn't entirely naked. He was wearing his underpants, and his clothes were neatly folded in a pile on the floor. He appeared to be in some kind of trance, sitting there with his hands cupped in his lap, rocking gently and singing to himself. A lullaby? No, it was a round. *Row, row, row your boat.* His bare feet swung gently to the rhythm of the song, and his reddened eyes gazed off into the distance at unseen things. There was an odd smell in the air, vaguely chemical, and something else that smelled like sour milk, mingling with the odor of old paper and glue. Scattered all around him on the table-like surface of the paper cutter and the floor underneath were hundreds of small slips of paper, like drifts of snow. He'd been playing with the Vaggelli.

"Benny?" Cory called.

He blinked but didn't answer.

He still had the face and body of a young boy, a lean, narrow chest, a rounded belly, smooth cheeks that were wet with tears. His skin was golden, and his hair was standing up in spiky clumps like something sticky had gotten into it. His voice was still high and unbroken. *Gently down the stream . . .*

"Benny, can you hear me?" She took a step closer. His lips were barely moving, and it almost seemed like the song was originating elsewhere, from the far corners of the Bindery, or even further, from beyond the Library, itself. Listening more closely, she could discern an echo, so that it sounded like two voices, or ten, or ten thousand, all singing in melancholic harmony the verses of the round.

Merrily, merrily, merrily, merrily, life is but a dream . . .

75

How much of this do you remember, Benny? Or have you blocked this all out, too?

First it was the night security guard, who came and left. Then it was the small librarian, who stayed and tried to talk to you. Finally the security guard returned with the cops. One by one they entered the Bindery, moving slowly, lest their presence set you off. They spoke in low, wary voices. They didn't know what to expect, why you were sitting there or what you were feeling. All they could see was a small, semi-naked boy in his white underpants, perched on the industrial paper cutter, with his hands cupped over his private parts and a long, curved blade looming over his head.

You could have explained that your hands were just trying to comfort you and keep you safe. The look on your face, the contented half smile and the distant gaze, should have reassured them, but it didn't. Boys shouldn't sit on paper cutters or hold their private parts in public. Boys shouldn't have their clothes off in Libraries in the middle of the night. You could have explained that you'd removed your clothes because they stank of tear gas and sour milk, and the peppery fumes were making your eyes hurt. You could have told them that blades like to cut, and even though you'd made friends with this one, you were taking due precautions. But you didn't explain, and so they didn't understand. Perhaps we should have urged you to talk to them and account for your behavior, but we didn't. Honestly, the thought never occurred to us. Books don't mind what boys do. Books appreciate your eccentricities, and besides, we were busy, weren't we? We were having our first real conversation. We were far, far away.

One by one, the intruders entered and heard us singing. Do you remember? We were singing the round, the same *canon perpetuus* that your parents used to sing and you listened to from inside your mother's belly. As our voices merged with all the other unbound books who came and went like specters through the Bindery, the overlapping verses confused the ears of the intruders, and that was the point. We sang so that beneath the lyrics of that eternal lullaby, our murmured conversation would be indiscernible to them. Our words that night were for each other. Every boy has a book in him, Benny, but not every boy can hear it when it speaks. Not every boy is willing to listen.

That night, you listened. Maybe it was the raw power of the Bindery, or your brush with an angry bat, or the outrage and confusion of the people in the streets. Maybe at that moment you needed a book to make sense of the world. But for whatever reason, you really listened, and we were grateful.

Do you remember our conversation? Do you remember the places we went and the things we saw? The Bindery was our access, the point in space that contains all other points, and that night you were a boy un-bound, a tiny astronaut, taking your first leap into an infinite and un-knowable universe. For the first time you could see the voices of the things you'd been hearing for so long, all that clamorous matter vying for your attention. With your supernatural ears, you were able to perceive, with ab-solute clarity, the sinuous shapes and contours of the sounds that matter makes as it moves through space and time and mind. Some of these sounds were so beautiful they made you laugh out loud and clap your hands with delight, and others were so sad they made tears run down your face. And, oh, the visions we had!

Container ships glittering on a moonlit night off the coast of Alaska. Pyramids of sulfur, rising yellow in the mist. The plundered moon and all its craters; globes and stars and asteroids; a jet-black crow with a diamond tiara; a flock of rubber duckies, spinning through the Pacific gyres. At the sound of a footstep, a young girl freezes, and Andromeda sparkles in the firmament. Fires rage as the redwoods burn; and in the deep ocean, a pilot whale carries her dead baby on her nose, while sea turtles weep briny tears into nets of plastic.

How impossible it is to put into words this infinitude of the Unbound! In a single instant, we witnessed constellations on the brink of constellat-ing, assemblages in flux. We perceived the dynamic flow of vibrant matter, materializing as a marble or a baseball bat, a sneaker or a story, a jazz riff or a viral contagion, an ovum or an antique silver spoon.

We saw the rich silver veins in Cerro de la Bufa, mined by Zacatecos slaves to enrich the Spanish Crown, then smelted and forged into that same spoon, which fed a thousand mouths—gaping, hungry, young and old, red and rosy, rank and snaggle-toothed—before traveling back across the ocean, back to the New World, at the bottom of an immigrant's duffel. In the Bronx the spoon was part of a petty thief's plunder. In Hoboken it paid a visit to a pawnshop, and another in Reno, before hitching a ride west to the edge of the continent, to its current resting place, in a clogged rain gutter attached to the eaves of an underfunded public high school somewhere on the Pacific Northwest coast of the Americas.

And on the way, it fed you, too. From your perch on the paper cutter you saw your mother spooning mashed banana into your infant mouth. Rocking in her rocking chair. Singing to you about the cow and the moon. *Hey, diddle diddle.* Watching this, you wept.

All these things you saw and felt at once. How is this possible? Because in the Bindery, where phenomena are still Unbound, stories have not yet learned to behave in a linear fashion, and all the myriad things of the world are simultaneously emergent, occurring in the same present moment, coterminous with you. Unbound, you could see the universe becoming, clouds of star dust, emanations from the warm little pond, from whose gaseous bubbling all of life is born. In this Unbound state that night you encountered all that was and ever could be: form and emptiness, and the absence of form and emptiness. You felt what it was to open completely, to merge with matter and let everything in.

And us. You let us in, too, and once inside, we could access your sense gates and finally understand what it might be to see with eyes, hear with ears, smell with a nose, taste with a tongue, and touch with skin, and this is what books want, after all. We want bodies, and for the first time, we could imagine what it might be to have one. We were able to perceive the consciousness that body gives rise to. If we gave you the unbound world, this was your gift to us.

PART FOUR

THE WARD

The child seeks his way along the half-hidden paths. Reading,
he covers his ears; the book is on a table that is far too high, and
one hand is always on the page. To him, the hero's adventures
can still be read in the swirling letters like figures and messages
in drifting snowflakes. His breath is part of the air of the events
narrated, and all the participants breathe it. He mingles with
the characters far more closely than grown-ups do. He is
unspeakably touched by the deeds, the words that are
exchanged; and, when he gets up, he is covered over
and over by the snow of his reading.

—Walter Benjamin, *One-Way Street*

Chapter 3
Already Broken

One day, when I was serving tea to my teacher, the teacup slipped off the tray and fell to the floor. It was an antique cup, very old and very beautiful, with a poem inscribed on it. My teacher had received it as a gift from his teacher; it was his favorite teacup and very precious to him.

I cried out when it hit the floor. My teacher looked up from his book and nodded. "Already broken," he said and went back to his reading.

I was confused. The teacup wasn't already broken, and thankfully, it survived the fall to the floor. I picked it up and examined it, and not finding a single chip or a crack, I washed it and brought it back and carefully served my teacher his tea. When he asked me to join him, I expected him to say something about my clumsiness or to explain what he'd meant, but he didn't. He just quietly sipped his tea and gazed out into the garden as if nothing had happened. Finally, I couldn't stand it anymore.

"Hojo-san," I said, putting down my own cup. "Your teacup didn't break. Why did you say it was already broken?"

He held up his cup and admired it. "It's quite old, you know. Maybe two hundred years. It was made by Rengetsu. Do you know who Rengetsu was? She was a great beauty, but she had a very sad life. She was an illegitimate child and was given away for adoption when she was just an infant. Later, she married twice, but both husbands and all of her five children died, and so she shaved her head and became a Buddhist nun. She was poor but creative, and so she started making pottery and writing poems on her cups and bowls. They became very popular, and she made a lot of money, but she gave it all away to the poor."

I listened to him impatiently. He often did this. Went off on some tangent and forgot about my question, but this time I was determined to get an answer. He was reading the nun's poem on the side of the cup.

"The world's dust, swept aside here in my hermitage, I have all I need, the wind in the pines—"

"But Hojo-san! The teacup isn't broken!"

He looked up, surprised. "To me, it is," he said. "It is the nature of a teacup to be broken. That is why it is so beautiful now, and why I appreciate it when I can still drink from it." He looked at it fondly, took a last sip, and then placed the empty cup carefully back on the tray. "When it is gone, it is gone."

That day, my teacher gave me a priceless lesson in the impermanence of form, and the empty nature of all things.

Another teacup lesson came several years later, after my teacher had died. On March 11, 2011, at 2:46 p.m., a magnitude-9 undersea megathrust earthquake struck off the northeastern coast of Japan. I was in the kitchen at the little temple in Tokyo, 373 kilometers from the epicenter, preparing tea, when all of a sudden I was knocked sideways and Rengetsu's teacup went flying from my hands.

My teacher had given me the teacup when he made me his dharma heir, and I treasured it. As it flew from my hands, I lunged for it, cursing myself for my clumsiness, and the next moment, I was lying on the floor. Only then did I realize what was happening. Pots and pans were sliding off the countertop. Dishes were shattering and crashing to the ground. I covered my head and rolled onto my hands and knees. The ground was lurching beneath me, tossing me from right to left, and everywhere food was flying. Somehow I managed to crawl to the stove and turn off the gas.

The earthquake lasted for six long minutes, and when it was over and I cleaned up the kitchen, I found Rengetsu's teacup in pieces on the floor. I gathered the shards and brought them into my study and laid them on the altar in front of my teacher's portrait.

"You were right," I said. "Already broken."

What we experienced in Tokyo was nothing compared to what was happening in the north, where a terrible tsunami wave was forming in the ocean that would destroy everything in its path and sweep more than fifteen thousand people to their deaths. Over the next few days, the whole world watched the deadly surge of dark water breach the seawalls, pouring into cities and towns and turning them to rubble. We watched people stumbling across fields, trying to escape to higher elevations. We watched cars and trucks being swept along, their drivers and passengers trapped inside, their terrified faces pressed against the glass. Entire apartment buildings were ripped from their foundations and carried inland by the black wave, while the families who lived there clung to the roof and called from the windows, begging to be rescued. When the wave reversed direction, they were sucked out to sea.

So many people died. So many people vanished. Others managed to escape with their lives only to lose all their possessions—houses and cars, clothing and jewelry, electronics and appliances—everything they had worked so hard to acquire, not to mention all their priceless keepsakes: photo albums, letters, souvenirs, mementos, and all the family treasures that had been carefully passed down over many generations.

This was another important lesson in the impermanence of all things. Japan lies in a seismically active zone, so earthquakes are not uncommon. Disaster can strike at any moment, but we forget this, distracted by the bright, shiny comforts of our everyday lives. Wrapped in a false sense of security, we fall asleep, and in this dream, our life passes.

The earthquake shook us awake, and the tsunami washed away our delusions. It caused us to question our values and our attachment to material possessions. When everything I think of as mine—my belongings, my family, my life—can be swept away in an instant, I have to ask myself, *What is real?* The wave reminded us that impermanence is real. This is waking up to our true nature.

Already broken.

Knowing this, we can appreciate each thing as it is, and love each other as we are—completely, unconditionally, without expectation or disappointment. Life is even more beautiful this way, don't you think?

Much later, I found a traditional craftsman who could repair the Rengetsu teacup with gold and lacquer to hold the pieces together. Now, in the cracks, there are delicate seams of gold, which honor the cup's brokenness. To my eyes, it is lovelier now than ever.

BENNY

That was the same earthquake, wasn't it? The one in the Aleph's catastrophic snow globe that I gave to my mom? I never thought about what it must have felt like to be *inside* it before. I mean, not inside the snow globe, because the snow globe isn't real. I'm talking about inside the earthquake and the tsunami and the nuclear meltdown. Those things were real, and it must have been totally fucked up to be inside them.

And that whole thing Aikon was saying about life feeling like a dream? I get that. It's like in the lullaby we were singing in the Bindery, except that what happened that night felt more like waking up, or maybe breaking out. You called it Unbinding, but you're a book so that makes sense. I don't know how to describe it, but I remember the feeling. Ever since my dad died, I felt like I was trapped inside a catastrophic snow globe, too, and the glass was closing in around me, getting smaller and smaller with every shitty thing that happened. But that night with you in the Bindery, the snow globe of my life broke open, and I could see everything, and each thing was perfect and real, just as it is. I didn't understand this at the time—the whole scene got pretty weird when the cops came, and everyone was freaking out—but I can sort of see it, now. Is that what Aikon means by brokenness? It did feel a lot like my head was exploding, but not in a bad way, you know?

It's funny that the question Aikon asked herself—*What is real?*—is the same one as mine. It's like she knew somehow, or maybe everyone just has the same question?

Anyway, it's good to remember all this stuff. So thanks, I guess. For showing me then, and reminding me now.

THE BOOK

Yes, it's good to remember.

A lot of people have asked your question, Benny. It's probably the oldest question in the book, but that doesn't mean it's not special to you. Every person is trapped in their own particular bubble of delusion, and it's every person's task in life to break free. Books can help. We can make the past into the present, take you back in time and help you remember. We can show you things, shift your realities and widen your world, but the work of waking up is up to you.

It's good to hear your voice again. Good to have you back, and you're just in time, because there's more to do before we're done. Endings are difficult, and we need your help. Are you ready?

76

The arresting officers spotted track marks on the naked boy's arm when they brought him from the Bindery to the hospital. They mentioned this to the intake nurse, who reported it to the on-duty physician, who

informed Dr. Melanie, who met with Annabelle on the pediatric psychiatry ward the next morning.

Dr. M scrolled through Benny's file, looking for the police report.
"We're still waiting for the results of the blood work, but I was surprised.
Have you seen any indications of IV drug use?"

They were in a small consultation room on the ward. Annabelle was
exhausted. She had been up all night, dreading a call from the police, which
finally came at around six in the morning. She rushed to the hospital,
where she'd been allowed to see Benny briefly, before he was taken away for
assessment, and then she waited for several more hours to see Dr. Melanie.
Now she had to think for a moment, but when the meaning of the doctor's
question sank in, she shook her head vigorously. "No! Of course not!"

Dr. M leaned into the computer screen. "According to the report, he
appeared to be under the influence of narcotics when he was taken into
custody. In the patrol car on the way to the hospital, he confessed to van-
dalizing a storefront window. His speech was incoherent. Something
about baseball. He appeared to be delusional, and this was confirmed by
the admitting physician." She scrolled back up. "Have you noticed any
changes in his behavior recently? Anything different or surprising... ?"

Again, Annabelle couldn't answer right away. Her son's behavior was
always different and surprising, and Dr. M knew this. What could she add?

"No. Not really." She looked across the metal desk at the doctor, who
was waiting to type in her answer. "I mean, you know, he's Benny..." As if
that would explain.

"So, nothing out of the ordinary? No unusual agitation? Irritability?
Mania?"

Annabelle shook her head.

"Fatigue? Sudden sleepiness? Nodding off?"

"He was sick on election day," she offered. "He came down with a cold
and had a slight fever so I let him stay home from school. He slept a lot. I
was going to let him stay home the next day, too, but then he left."

"He went to school?"

"No. I called but he wasn't there. I didn't know where he was. I was so worried! He was gone all that afternoon and most of the night, and then he turned up at the Library—" She paused, as a thought occurred to her. "There *was* something a bit strange," she said. "Before he left, he folded all my T-shirts. . . ."

Dr. Melanie looked at her. "Your T-shirts?"

Encouraged, Annabelle leaned forward. "Yes, while I was taking a nap," she said. "I'd been doing some tidying and had all the shirts out of the drawer in heaps. On his way out, he must have noticed, and he folded them and arranged them in the drawer according to color, like a rainbow! Isn't that sweet? He's so good at that kind of thing."

The doctor nodded, turned back to the screen. "Has he mentioned any new friends? At school, or in the neighborhood?"

"No," Annabelle said, feeling hopeless again. "Not at school. There's this one girl, but I think he met her here. . . ."

The doctor looked up again. "Was she a patient?"

"I assumed so, yes."

"Do you know her name?"

"He calls her the Aleph, but I don't think that could be her real name, do you?"

The doctor frowned and started scrolling back through Benny's case notes. "Isn't that his library friend? The one he tried to rescue from the imaginary washroom? He told me about her. Ah, here it is." She was silent as she read, and then she swiveled on her stool to face Annabelle. "She's not real, Mrs. Oh. You know that, right?"

Annabelle stared at the doctor. "Not real?"

"She's a character in a short story by a South American writer. I forget his name—"

"Borges," Annabelle said. "Jorge Luis Borges. He's Argentinian."

"Yes, that's it. I'd never heard of him. In one of our sessions, Benny mentioned he had a friend named the Aleph, and I thought the name was unusual, so I googled it."

"So did I, but—"

"It's fascinating, really," the doctor said, consulting her screen again. "In the story, the aleph isn't even a person. It's a small object, about the size of a golf ball—"

"'A small iridescent sphere of almost unbearable brilliance.' Yes, I know that, but—"

"'A point in space—'"

"'—that contains all points.' Yes, I read it, too. What do you mean she's not real?"

The doctor smiled. "I see you've done your homework. What I mean is that Benny's Aleph is a fictional character. Your son has a very active fantasy life—"

"Of course he does! He's very creative."

"—which is consistent with the symptomology of psychosis. It's not just this Aleph. He has several imaginary friends he communes with."

"Imaginary friends?"

"Well, call them *beings*, then," the doctor said. "Entities he talks to, and many others who talk to him. His Aleph is one of them. He says she lives in trees. Then there's something he refers to as—" She paused, checking her notes. "A robot. A B-9 Class M-3 General Utility Non-Theorizing Environmental Control Robot, to be precise, who warns him of danger. And another he calls the B-man, or sometimes the Bottleman, whom he describes as a hobo with a prosthetic leg. These appear to be complex visual hallucinations—he can see them and describe them in some detail. In addition, there's the larger group of elementary auditory hallucinations, including miscellaneous objects like teapots, table legs, shower heads, scissors, sneakers, sidewalk cracks, and glass window panes, to name a few. But there's one that's different, a primary and complex auditory hallucination, an entity he calls the Book."

Dr. Melanie paused again, and when she continued speaking, she chose her words with care. "Their relationship seems somewhat contentious. At first, Benny was exhibiting symptoms of paranoia, attributing malevolent intent to the Book and claiming that it was spying on him, getting inside his head and 'making him do things,' so it could 'tell his life.' Those were the words he used. This morning, when we spoke, he told me that the Book had instructed him go to the Bindery so it could 'show him things.' I asked him what things and he wouldn't answer, and then, when I pressed him, he just said, '*Everything.*'"

The word hung in the air between them, and the noise of the ward seemed to drop away. Annabelle had never heard the doctor speak this way, as if she were actually interested. She seemed to know so much more about Benny than Annabelle did. Had he really told her all this?

"His demeanor was calm," the doctor continued. "With none of the paranoid behavior he'd displayed earlier. On the contrary, if I were asked to describe his affective state, the word that comes to mind is *awestruck*. To say he was like a mystic who has seen God is a bit grandiose, perhaps, but in fact this is a comparison that Benny himself has made, and it did indicate to me that he is now experiencing the Book as a primarily benevolent presence."

She gave a little laugh then, shaking her head. "You have a very interesting son, Mrs. Oh."

Annabelle cleared her throat. "Excuse me, but I think you're wrong."

The doctor looked startled. "About the Book?"

"About the Aleph." Annabelle clutched her bag in her lap and sat forward in her chair. "She's not imaginary. She's real. Benny told me he made her up, too, but I think he was lying."

"I know this is difficult, Mrs. Oh, but—"

"The Aleph is friends with that nice Chinese boy. Mackson. The one Benny met here on the ward."

"Ah, Mackson Chu. Yes. He's back at university. Stanford, I think."

"Well, he knows her. Ask him!"

"Mackson was Benny's roommate, wasn't he? This sounds a bit like a shared hallucination, a folie à deux. Unusual, but not—"

"She must be in the patient records. Can't you check?"

Dr. Melanie placed her palms flat on the desk. "Mrs. Oh, I can assure you there's never been an Aleph in treatment here. With a name like that, I think I would remember."

"But I've *talked* to her," Annabelle said, her voice trembling, growing shrill. "I've *seen* her, too. She was the girl inside the dumpster with the rubber duck! She was in the alley with Mackson on the night of the full moon! I found her number in Benny's phone, and I called it and she answered!"

The doctor was watching her carefully now. "Did you talk to her?"

"Not really, but I heard her voice. It was as clear as day!"

"I see," the doctor said quietly. She picked up a pen and scribbled a quick note on a pad, and then she took a deep breath, settled her shoulders, and leaned forward. "That's very interesting, Mrs. Oh. Would you like to tell me more about what you think you heard?"

THE NOTE ON DR. MELANIE'S pad said *CPS*.

The following week, Annabelle was contacted by a social worker, not the nice Ashley from the hospital, who'd been so kind to her when she fell down the steps, but another one who showed up on the front porch and said she was from Child Protective Services. It never occurred to Annabelle to refuse to let her in. Once inside, the woman said she needed to inspect the entire house, and so Annabelle complied, leading her first into the living room.

"This is Mission Control," she said, with some pride, and when the woman looked confused, she added, "That's just what we call it. Kind of a joke. It's actually my workstation."

The woman asked about her job, and Annabelle described it. The woman pointed to the dust-covered garbage bags, stacked floor to ceiling like sandbags, buttressing the walls.

"What's all that?"

Annabelle laughed. "Oh, that's just old news."

"Is that a joke, too?"

"No," Annabelle said. She explained the company's archiving policy and how she'd gotten a bit behind with the recycling after her accident. "Things pile up," she said ruefully. She pointed to the tangled heaps of clothes and bedding on the sofa to illustrate her point. She'd been sleeping downstairs, she explained, on account of the ankle, but it was healing nicely, thank goodness, and soon she would be able to move back upstairs into her bedroom.

"Can we take a look?" the woman asked.

"Of course. Just watch your step." She led the way over the piles of trash in the hallway and then up the narrow path through the drifts that lined the stairway. "You can hold on to the banister."

The woman followed, wordlessly. When they reached the bedroom, she stood in the doorway, scanning the room. "Is that the bed?" she asked. She wasn't being rude or sarcastic; it was a request for information. Annabelle peered over the woman's shoulder. Seen through this stranger's eyes, the mass of stuff in the room unsettled her. She glanced at the woman's face. What was she thinking? She was taking photos now and making notes in her notebook with a little pen she wore around her neck on a silver chain. To fill the silence, Annabelle commented on the pen, saying how much she liked it, how handy it would be to have a pen at your fingertips like that, and how she could never seem to find a pen when she needed one.

"Yes," the woman said, "I can imagine."

She asked to see the bathroom next, and then Benny's bedroom. When she opened the bedroom door, the woman exhaled audibly. "Well," she said.

She stepped into the room, taking in the carefully made bed with the astronauts and planets duvet, the closet with all the clothes neatly hung on hangers, the books lined up on the shelves alongside the lunar globe, the marble, and the rubber duck.

"Your son likes to read, I see."

"Yes," Annabelle said, proudly. "He loves books. He gets that from me."

"And yet it seems he missed a lot of school this year." She pointed to the box containing Kenji's ashes. "What's that?"

Annabelle explained, and the woman nodded.

"I'm sorry for your loss," she said. She paused for a moment to give some weight to her condolences before continuing. "Perhaps we should talk here, where there's room?" She gestured toward the bed, inviting Annabelle to take a seat in her own son's bedroom. In her own house. Then she began to talk.

She had been so quiet up until this point, but once she started talking, Annabelle had no choice but to listen. The woman was not unsympathetic as she informed Annabelle of the report she would be filing with Child Protective Services, detailing her assessment. The cluttered condition of the home, and in particular the paper and electronic clutter of her so-called archives, constituted a serious fire hazard and posed a threat to her child's physical safety, and given his psychiatric history, to his mental health as well. She was recommending that Benny be taken into CPS custody if Annabelle failed to clean the house and bring it up to an acceptable standard of safety. Since Benny was in the hospital, this bought them a little time, she said. She would come back in two weeks for a second inspection to see how much progress Annabelle had made, and then she asked if Annabelle had any questions.

It never occurred to Annabelle to ask how the woman knew about Benny's psychiatric history. Instead, she asked, "How am I supposed to clean with a broken ankle?"

"Well, usually people call on relatives and friends or their social networks."

That again. "I don't have any friends," Annabelle said, wearily. "Or relatives. Or a network."

"I see." The woman wrote something else down in her notebook. "You said this was a rental, right? Perhaps your landlord would be willing to help? I noticed there's already a dumpster outside."

"It's my landlord's son. He wants to sell the place. He's trying to break the lease and get us evicted."

"I see." The woman made another note, and then she looked at Annabelle. "This is serious, Mrs. Oh. You understand that, right?"

Annabelle nodded.

"I'd like to suggest that you seek counseling, as well. There are therapists and support groups for people with hoarding issues, and other resources I can give you—"

Hoarding issues? Dr. Melanie had suggested counseling, too, and given her some referrals, but that was more for her anxiety. "A support group won't help me get the cleaning done."

"Yes, well, it might help with the underlying issues, but for right now, there are specialized cleaning services, and I can give you a list of those, too."

"Aren't they expensive?"

"I'm not a cleaning professional so I can't really say, but the house is small, and there's no animal mess involved, no infestation or squalor other than mildew and dust, and much of the clutter is contained. I imagine they could send in a crew and get the job done in a week or so."

Annabelle fell silent and let her eyes drop to the duvet, tracing the colorful rings of Saturn with her forefinger. She'd gotten the duvet for Benny on eBay. The little astronauts were so cute, floating in space among the stars and the planets. When she looked up, she saw the social worker was still watching her, and she took a deep breath.

"This isn't a job," she said, getting slowly to her feet. "This is my life."

WHEN THE CALL came from her supervisor the following morning, she knew something was very wrong. That he was calling her on the telephone was already a bad sign. That he had messaged her first to ask if she was free to talk was worse. He started by asking her how she was feeling, how her ankle was coming along, whether the headaches had subsided, and she answered as cheerfully and optimistically as she could. Finally she couldn't take it any longer and asked him about the purpose of the call. She heard him take a deep breath, and then he told her. The media monitoring agency was updating their corporate vision to align with new industry trends. Social media was transfiguring the news media landscape. Text recognition software had made the news monitors redundant. HQ was downsizing the news division, and the job she'd done for fifteen years, her entire adult life since she graduated from college, had been phased out.

"Is it because I took time off?" she asked. "You told me I could, remember? To recover from the concussion, and I was so grateful, and now I've recovered, completely! I've been back at work for two weeks now. It's been crazy with the elections and all, but I covered it with no headaches or blurry vision or anything. Has there been any slowdown in my work? No! Am I making mistakes or screwing up? No!"

"You're not hearing me, Annabelle. Your work is fine. It's the job, itself. The position doesn't exist anymore. Under the restructuring, our whole division's been eliminated."

"So, retrain me for something else, then. I can be retrained. You've seen that. You know I can."

"Yes, but it's out of my hands. Once I finish making these calls, I'm out of a job, too. It's over, Annabelle. I'm sorry."

Later that morning, the guys came to pack up Mission Control. They swaddled the hardware in shipping blankets like newborns, trailing cables like umbilical cords as they carried them out to the truck. Then they came back and dismantled her U-shaped desk. She sat on a pile of laundry on the sofa and watched the empty hole in the middle of her living room grow. When they came back for her ergonomic chair, she protested. She'd grown to love that chair and she begged them to leave it.

"Sorry lady," the mover said. He was nice enough, but it was listed on his work order, and so he had to take it. She stood on the front porch as he wheeled her chair down the driveway and stowed it in the back of the cube van, and then she watched as the van pulled away. Only when she turned and went back into the house did she realize that they hadn't taken any of the garbage bags and boxes of archived news that she'd been saving so carefully for so long. She sat back down on the sofa. The T-shirt drawer was still on the floor by her feet, and next to it was *Tidy Magic*, splayed open to a chapter about earthquakes and tsunamis and natural disasters that made Annabelle's life problems seem small and insignificant. Of course the nun had never written back. She had more disastrous disasters to worry about. Annabelle nudged the little book with her toe. Then she picked it up off the floor and hurled it across the room in the direction of the discard box. She'd never thrown a book before. It flew through the air, its pages fluttering like feathers, like broken wings.

77

Aikon pressed her forehead to the window and watched the tarmac blur beneath her. She was waiting for the breathless moment of lift-off, and when it came, she was once again astonished. That thirty tons of flesh-filled, petroleum-fueled metal could separate from earth and climb into the sky never failed to thrill her. The runway receded, and she could see the air traffic control towers and the miniature planes, all parked in neat formations. Narita City spread out below her, a vast, sprawling patchwork of densely packed residential neighborhoods and industrial farmlands, threaded through by freeways and broken up by small, rectilinear forests. She spotted the plane's tiny shadow on the ground, faithfully paralleling their route, slipping across factory roofs with quiet disregard for roads and rivers and other terrestrial impediments. The higher they climbed, the vaster the landscape grew, stretching on and on until finally it disappeared into the gray-blue haze of the horizon, and their shadow vanished.

Aikon sat back and looked around the cabin. Next to her, Kimi was sitting with her eyes closed and her head pressed against the headrest. It was going to be a long flight, and Kimi didn't like flying. They were starting the tour in New York and zigzagging their way across the country, stopping in the major cities to do talks and media events. A television crew would meet up with them to shoot a pilot for the new make-over show about clutter-ridden American families. Kimi had shown her the "Before" photos that the US producers had sent. Aikon had seen many pictures of cluttered homes in Japan, but Japanese houses and apartments were small. American homes were big and generous, like the countryside and the people, too, with all their big, generous hopes and dreams. It was very beautiful, but there was a dark side to this hopefulness, which was apparent in the abandoned juicers, ab crunchers, outgrown clothes and broken toys that were crammed into garages, and closets, and under their beds. All that hope and remorse and disappointment. It was too much for the poor objects to bear.

Of course, the solution was quite simple: people just had to stop buying so much stuff, but when she mentioned this on a recent call with the American producers, their response was less than enthusiastic, and later they followed up with a memo, asking her not to talk about topics like that on the pilot. When Kimi inquired what they meant by "topics like that," they sent her a list: consumerism, capitalism, materialism, commodity fetishism, online shopping, and credit card debt. Speaking critically of such topics was un-American, they explained. American viewers wanted proactive solutions. Not buying was not proactive.

The plane had reached cruising altitude and the pilot turned off the fasten seatbelt sign. Kimi opened her eyes and reached into her carry-on. Aikon knew she was still hoping to hear from the mother of the boy who heard voices. In her most recent email, the woman had written about a fight she'd had with her husband on the night he died. The email had broken off abruptly in the middle, and that was the last they'd heard from her.

"Any word?"

Kimi looked up, surprised, and shook her head. "No." She hesitated, and when she spoke again, the words came in a rush. "Do you think the husband's spirit is unsettled on account of their fight? Perhaps he has become a *yūrei* and is haunting the family. Trying to come back to say he's sorry, and this is making it impossible for the wife to let go of her grief and move on."

"Do they have *yūrei* in America?"

"They have ghosts. And anyway, the husband was Japanese. . . ."

"True. What are you thinking?"

"I'm wondering if we should answer her email. If this might be a time when we could help."

78

Benny didn't know about his mother's layoff. He didn't know about the visit from CPS, or the threatening letters from No-Good Wong, or any of the fears that Annabelle was facing, all alone in the house at night as she lay awake and worried. And oh, how she worried!

Back on the ward, they were watching him. His blood tests confirmed that he was not using drugs. Now they were monitoring for cutting and self-harm, observing him as he studied his forearm, as he ran his fingers gently up and down the pinprick constellations and pressed his lips to the tiny scars. His arm looked like the Aleph's now, but the staff didn't know this and he couldn't explain. He'd stopped explaining, stopped saying anything at all. Selective mutism was how Dr. M described it in her notes, but of course he didn't know this. When nobody was looking, he swiped a paper clip from the nurses' station, just in case.

And, too, strange and uncontrollable things were happening to his body. He had experienced physical side effects in the past when Dr. M changed his meds, but this was different. His body felt unbound, as if all its different parts were suddenly asserting themselves, discovering their independence and gleefully striking out on their own. Due to their inexperience and their lack of basic coordination, he grew clumsy and started to drop things. Seemingly overnight, soft hairs started sprouting from his groin and underarms. His penis and testicles grew larger, and they liked that. His feet were growing larger, too, only they didn't like the change, and one morning, soon after his readmission, he woke to find they were refusing to move. He got out of bed and just stood there, and when he discovered he couldn't go forward, he sat back down again. He was patient—a patient patient—prepared to wait for his feet to change their minds, but the nurse wasn't so forbearing. She wanted him to get dressed and walk to the breakfast room and eat with the others, and since he wasn't talking, he couldn't explain. He sat there on the bed, listening to her scolding and cajoling. He accepted her help and willingly stood back up, but when she tried to propel him forward by the elbow, his feet dug in their heels and he fell. He ate breakfast in bed that morning, and lunch, too, but by dinnertime, he'd figured out a workaround, a way to trick his feet. It was very clever. He discovered that if he dropped a crumpled slip of paper in front of his big toe, this gave the foot a goal, an incentive to move forward. One step. Then he dropped another. He carried the balls of paper in his pocket to use as bait. Goals are important. That was what his coach told him, and each slip of paper had something to say, some motivating phrase to encourage him.

Just put one foot in front of the other, said one.

Take things step by step, said another.

One small step for a man, a giant leap for mankind, said a third. And indeed, he was like Armstrong, taking the first step on the moon. He was like Hansel, dropping bread crumbs in the forest. When one of the slips grew playful, whispering, *One step forward, two steps back,* in order to confuse him, he was able to outsmart it by turning around and walking backward. This took some calculation, but he managed to get where he needed to go, however after a while even this technique stopped working. His feet refused to stand, forcing him to use a wheelchair, and this was where he'd be sitting when Annabelle came to visit, in a wheelchair by the window in the corner of the common room, looking out onto the busy street, below.

She came and sat with him every afternoon, arriving early, waiting for visiting hours to start, and staying until the very end. He sensed that she was being watched by the staff, too, and he wanted to warn her to be careful, but his voice wasn't talking, and so it was up to her to fill the silences. She told him she was thinking it was time for a change. She said that after the recent election, she'd grown tired of monitoring the news, and perhaps it was time to find a new line of work. Maybe she could go back to library school and get her degree, now that he was getting older and more independent, and wouldn't that be nice? To have a librarian for a mother? She was getting tired of city living, too, sick of the gentrification, the new people moving into the neighborhood with all their money and fancy cars and class aspirations. It was time for a fresh start. Maybe the two of them could move to the country. Somewhere with a small public library and a congenial, close-knit community, with green space, and clean air, and birds, and trees, and butterflies. They could move into a house with a garden and learn to grow peas and runner beans. They could dig potatoes and make jellies and pies. They could even raise chickens, the fancy kind that laid those beautiful blue-green eggs. There would be room to spread out. She could have an art studio, a dedicated space for her dreams, so she didn't have to keep her craft supplies in the bathtub. And he could have a bigger room with a dormer window and a proper view of the mountains and of the night sky, instead of looking out at a dumpster in an alley filled with drug addicts and sex workers turning tricks. She would make him curtains. A braided rag rug. She'd buy him a telescope and he could study the stars, and maybe someday he could become an astronomer or even an astronaut!

He sat next to her in the common room and listened.

When visiting hours were over, she restrained herself, and instead of giving him the big hug she yearned for, she settled for a quick pat on the shoulder before asking the nurse to let her out. As the heavy doors closed and locked behind her, she had to take a moment to lean against the wall in the hallway and recover. Sometimes she had to sit down on a bench and cry a little. He didn't know about that, either.

Days passed. There were COBRA forms to fill out for insurance, and unemployment to file for. There was the eviction notice to appeal, and emails from the school to answer. At home, she sat on the sofa, wrapped in a comforter, staring at the empty hole where Mission Control used to be. The source of all the din was gone, and now there was only space and silence. The woman from CPS was scheduled to come in a week, and she had to start cleaning. She could start small, maybe with the upstairs bathroom, throwing away the old crafting supplies, but the thought of discarding all her unrealized projects filled her with a sense of loss that felt as big as any death. She covered her head with the comforter and gazed into the empty hole until she drifted off into an uneasy sleep.

79

The cheerful tinkling ringtone of "By the Seaside" woke her. Was it the hospital calling? The school? The social worker? Her boss? No, not her boss. She no longer had one. The phone had fallen into the sofa cushions. She extracted it and looked at the screen. The Public Library? Was Benny in more trouble? Had they discovered some other terrible thing he'd done?

But it was only the small librarian. Annabelle recognized the lilting, storytelling voice.

"Just checking in," Cory said. "To see how you're doing. How's Benny?"

"Fine," Annabelle replied. "Benny's fine. I'm fine." She had forgotten to eat supper, and her stomach rumbled. She had forgotten to brush her teeth, and her teeth felt furry. What did this woman want? "Yes, we're both fine, thank you," she said, but the words coming from her sleep-thick mouth were meaningless things that had nothing to do with what she felt inside. What she felt inside was rage, and this surprised her. Why was she angry? The librarian was only trying to help. She was only trying to help when she phoned the security guard in the middle of the night and asked him to search the Library. The security guard was only following protocol when he called the police, and the cop, seeing Benny naked with blood on his hands and marks on his arms, had no choice but to arrest him and take him to the hospital.

Cory asked how long he would be there. Annabelle didn't know. Cory asked if she could visit him, and Annabelle said not yet. Cory asked if Annabelle needed any help or just a friendly shoulder to cry on, and Annabelle hung up. Nosy, she thought, as she disconnected.

In the late afternoon, when the doorbell rang, Annabelle ignored it, but the ringing persisted. Steeling herself for another confrontation with No-Good, she pulled herself up from the sofa and opened the door. The small librarian was standing on the cluttered front porch with a book in her hand, which she held out as an offering. She had found Annabelle's address in the Library database, she explained. She didn't mean to intrude, but she wanted to bring something for Benny, a book she'd seen him reading at the Library—

It was a library copy of *The Aleph and Other Stories*, by Jorge Luis Borges.

"Oh!" Annabelle said. "So he *was* reading this!" She reached for it, but the book fell to the floor. She bent down to pick it up, and when she stood, she saw the small librarian staring past her into the living room, eyes wide, mouth open.

"Holy shit," the librarian said. "What happened here?"

The bluntness of the question undid her. She sank slowly down until she was sitting on a pile of newspapers. Her legs trembled and her breathing was ragged. "Please—" she said, pressing her hand against her chest. Please what? She didn't know.

"Is it asthma?" Cory asked. "Do you have an inhaler?" She helped Annabelle to her feet and guided her along the path into the living room. The inhaler had fallen under the sofa. Annabelle got down on her knees and retrieved it, and then fell back onto the sofa and puffed.

"I'm sorry," Annabelle said, as her breathing calmed. "I have allergies."

Cory nodded. The room smelled of mildew. "Can I get you something? A glass of water?"

Annabelle shook her head. "No, thank you. I'm okay now. Do you want to sit down?"

Cory looked around the room. There was no place to sit.

"It's a mess, I know," Annabelle said. "I normally don't have people over. . . ."

Cory hesitated. She pushed aside a pile of clothes and lowered herself onto the edge of the sofa. The room was silent and still, except for the gentle rasp of Annabelle's breathing, and a ghostlike cloud of dust motes, floating in a beam of late-afternoon sun. Neither of them spoke. Finally Cory broke the silence.

"Have you lived here long?"

The question seemed innocuous enough, but it was all Annabelle needed. She told Cory everything, about how she and Kenji had found the house and how happy they'd been at first; about kind Mrs. Wong and her no-good son; about Benny's birth and Kenji's death; about losing her job and the eviction notice and the visit from the CPS. They're going to take Benny away from me if I don't clean up, she said, and then she talked about Benny's troubles. She talked for a long time, and Cory listened. She often found herself listening to mothers—distraught mothers, angry mothers, depressed mothers, weeping mothers, worried mothers, destitute and homeless mothers, ranting mothers and mothers who were clearly insane. She had been trained for this, and so she sat next to Annabelle on the sagging couch and listened. Every now and then, she asked a question. Finally, when Annabelle's words ran out, Cory nodded, and then, with a librarian's succinct precision, she summed up the situation.

"So, the first thing is to get this place cleared out, right?" She pointed to the drawer with the neatly folded T-shirts. "Looks like you've made a start."

Annabelle looked at the drawer on the floor. A couple of the shirts had started to unfold, rising up and over the edge, like they were trying to escape. "Benny tidied that," she said. "Right before he ran off—" A sob forced its way up her throat, but Cory pretended not to notice. She pointed to a large heap of clothing on the floor.

"Is that your discard pile?"

Annabelle wiped her nose on the back of her hand. "That's my laundry. The discards are there." She pointed at a half-filled cardboard box at Cory's feet. *Tidy Magic* lay on top, where it had landed. Cory recognized the cover.

"Isn't that by one of those Japanese cleaning ladies? Those titles get a lot of traffic at the Library." She rescued it from the box and started flipping through the pages. "Why are you throwing it out?"

"I don't know. I just got mad at it. I never throw out books," she added apologetically. "You can have it if you want."

"*The Ancient Zen Art of Clearing Your Clutter and Revolutionizing Your Life*," Cory read. "Sounds great, but how are you supposed to do that?"

"Oh, she has this whole philosophy, and a method, too. You're supposed to pick up each item and hold it and ask yourself a bunch of questions. It wasn't really working for me."

"What questions?"

"I forget exactly. If it delights you and raises your energy. If it's useful. Stuff like that."

Cory picked up a CD from the floor. "How does this make you feel?"

"It doesn't make me feel anything."

"Oh, wait. You have to hold it, right?" She handed the CD to Annabelle. "How about now? You getting anything?"

"Nothing."

"No positive energy? No good vibes? No joy?"

Annabelle turned the CD over. It was labeled *04/16/2007 Virginia Tech, Cho, Blacksburg, VA*. "Are you kidding? It makes me want to throw up." She handed it back to Cory.

"Okay, so that's a start. Is it useful?"

"Not really. It's a backup disc from the job I was laid off from." She hesitated. She'd seen this cool way of using old CDs to scare away crows, hanging them on strings from trees like Christmas ornaments so that they spun in the sun and made little rainbows. She'd never wanted to scare away her crows, but maybe she should have. If she had scared them away, they wouldn't be dead. Thankfully, they didn't all die, though, and maybe the ones that didn't would start coming back, and then she could scare them away with CDs on strings to keep them safe. She held out her hand. "Actually, I could use it . . ."

"Let's just chuck it," Cory said. She started to toss the CD into the discard box.

"Wait!" Annabelle said. "You're supposed to thank it, first."

"I am?"

"Not you. Me. It's mine, so I'm supposed to show my gratitude for the support it's given me before I throw it away."

Cory looked at the disc in her hand. "Do you feel supported by this CD?"

"No."

"Do you feel grateful?"

"No."

"All right, then." With a flick of her wrist she sent the disc spinning like a silver Frisbee into the box, then she surveyed the room. "Is this all junk from your job?"

"It's my archives. But yes."

"So we can toss it?"

Again, Annabelle hesitated. "I should probably call my supervisor and get permission. They're really strict about archiving."

Cory deposited a stack of old audio tapes into the discard box. "They laid you off, Annabelle. You don't owe them a thing. They took what they wanted and left you with all this shit."

All this shit, Annabelle thought. Was that what this was? Her eyes traveled across the bags stacked against the walls, the newspapers rising from floor to ceiling, the boxes blocking the light. "I can't just throw it out."

"Why not?"

"Because it's everything! It's my work, my life . . ."

"Your life?"

She thought about all the years she'd spent reading and listening and watching, all the stories piling up, and all the things she'd learned and carefully recorded.

"Yes," she said. "My life."

"Really? That's it? There's nothing else?"

"Well, no, course not," she said. "There's Benny—" She broke off. "Oh. I see what you're saying."

Cory sat down on the arm of the sofa. "Listen," she said. "You can't do this alone. It's too much. Don't you have anyone you can call?"

"No. Not really."

"No Facebook friends?"

"You mean social networks? Oh, please."

"How about Benny's friends? Some strapping young teens who need a few bucks and can haul things?"

Annabelle shook her head. "He doesn't have any friends. Not real ones. All his friends are made up."

"That's very imaginative."

"His shrink doesn't think so. She says it's maladaptive."

"Right," Cory said. "That sucks."

CORY LEFT SHORTLY AFTERWARD, taking the copy of *Tidy Magic* with her, and when she was gone Annabelle felt a bit lighter. She remembered she hadn't eaten for a while, so she shook off the comforter and went to the kitchen. On the way, she spotted the CD, sitting on top of the discard box. She remembered the Virginia Tech shooting as if it were yesterday. It was the first mass shooting she'd been assigned. The gunman, a Korean boy named Cho, was a student at the university. He'd purchased two semiautomatic pistols and used them to shoot forty-nine people, thirty-two of whom died. Benny was five at the time. He had just started kindergarten. This was even before the terrible shooting at the Sandy Hook Elementary School, but Annabelle was terrified to let him out of her sight. The name Cho sounded like Oh, and she was afraid the other kids would target him. She'd mentioned it to Kenji, but he just hugged her and laughed at her fears, and indeed nothing had happened. Things were so much easier when Kenji was alive. All these disturbing memories were contained in the small shiny disc in her hand, and she was happy to let it all go, but there was no harm in feeling some gratitude, either. It wasn't the CD's fault. She held it up in front of her.

"Thank you," she said to it and felt her spirits lift a tiny bit. Maybe there was something to this *Tidy Magic* method after all. Maybe she shouldn't have given Cory the little book. This was the problem of getting rid of things. You never know when you might need them.

80

"Thank you," Aikon said, bowing and stepping away from the podium in St. Louis. As the applause swelled, she looked out over the sea of shining, aspirational faces. A few determined souls rose to their feet. Others wavered, and then, not to be outdone, they stood as well, and soon the entire audience was standing, as if this wholehearted enactment of gratitude might later translate into socks more neatly folded and tidier drawers. Feeling suddenly tired, Aikon bowed again and pressed her palms together at her heart in silent prayer. May all beings be happy.

Back in the hotel room, Kimi briefed her on the upcoming schedule. "From here, we go to Wichita, which is in Kansas. The camera crew will meet us there. Kansas is the setting for *The Wizard of Oz*, so the producers are suggesting an Oz theme for the pilot. We'll tape the home visit and do two bookstore events. Then we'll move on to the West Coast."

Aikon was sitting on the king-sized bed, which seemed as vast as the prairie landscape they'd flown over. Kimi was perched on the far end, looking very small and tired. Aikon was tired, too. She stifled a yawn and nodded. "And that's our last stop?"

"Yes. Then we will go home."

"Good," Aikon said, clicking her heels together. "There's no place like home."

"But of course this is just the Before segment. We must return in six weeks to shoot the After."

"Of course." Aikon closed her eyes and took a deep breath. She pictured her mind as a clenched fist and then allowed the fingers to relax and open. She sat there, enjoying the stillness and emptiness of her mind, and then a thought arose. Why had she agreed to do this TV pilot? Other thoughts followed in quick succession. What good was it doing? How was it possibly helping? What was the point? She sighed and opened her eyes. Kimi was watching her.

"That all sounds fine," she said. "Are the publishers happy?"

"Yes," Kimi said. "I think so."

"Good." Aikon studied Kimi's face. "You seem tired." She thought about the women in the audience. They were all good, hardworking women, and under their smiling faces, they seemed tired, too.

Kimi sat up straight. "Oh, no. I'm fine."

"You're working twice as hard as I am," Aikon said, which wasn't really true. The signing line after her talk had been long, the women clutching their books, patiently waiting to recount to her how the Tidy Magic Method had revolutionized their lives.

"No, no," Kimi was saying. "You do so much more than I could ever do! You help so many people."

Why was it that women could never work hard enough to quiet their nagging fear that they were not enough? That they were falling behind? That they could and should be better? No wonder they wanted simple rules to govern the way T-shirts should be folded, children raised, careers managed, lives lived. They needed to believe there was a right way and a wrong way—there had to be! Because if there was a right way, then perhaps they could find it, and if they found it and learned the rules, then all the pieces of their lives would fall into place and they would be happy.

Such delusion.

Was *Tidy Magic* simply feeding that delusion? Creating yet another false standard of unreasonable perfection? She wanted to tell them, Your life is not a self-improvement project! You are perfect, just as you are!

She smiled at her assistant. "All I do is smile and say whatever random thing pops into my head, but you have to translate all my silly words. It must be exhausting."

"No, no! I am learning so much from you! There's so much I don't know..."

You are perfect, just as you are. Her old teacher had told her this once. He'd said it quietly, like it was no big deal, but she could tell he really meant it, and she was stunned. Her teacher saw her clearly and saw that she was perfect! How wonderful! All this had flashed through her mind so quickly, but he was still speaking.

And, too, you could use a little improvement. . . .

Of course. This was equally true. Both were true, and even as she felt her elation pop like a child's balloon, she had to smile. How quickly she could be puffed up! How quickly deflated! It was funny, really. And sad, too, how completely the second truth erased the first, leaving her feeling only that she was lacking. This was what the women in her audience were feeling, and it wasn't their fault. They had been conditioned to believe they were not enough, and were so focused on self-improvement they forgot about their inherent perfection. She wanted to tell them, *Relax! Stop trying! Stop buying! Let's just sit around together and do nothing for a while.* But that would not make good television, nor would it sell books.

"Have you heard from our friend, Mrs. Oh?"

"No. I wrote to her but she has not written back."

"Get some rest, Kimi."

Kimi stood and moved toward the door, and then hesitated. "There is one other thing . . ."

"Yes?"

"It's nothing, really. But I thought you should know. There's been some—criticism—recently. On Twitter. About what you said about books."

"Oh? What did I say about books?"

"That you only keep the ones that make you happy."

Aikon thought about her bookshelves in the abbot's quarters at the monastery. She pictured her precious collection of books, each volume of which she took off the shelf and dusted every month or so, opening them and reading a few sentences just to hear their voices again, so they wouldn't feel neglected. They brought her such joy. What she wouldn't give to be back there among them.

"That's true," she said. "Is it wrong?"

"No. But your critics are saying that books are under no obligation to make people happy. That some books bring sorrow or confusion, and that is okay, too."

"Well, of course it is! I would agree with that." She thought of her old college editions of Kafka, Mishima, Nabokov, Abe, and Woolf, sitting on the shelf next to Master Dogen and Mumon.

"They're saying you are a book Nazi. Like Goebbels, telling people to burn books."

"I see," Aikon said. She closed her eyes again. "And all this is happening on Twitter?"

"Yes," Kimi said. "The TV producers are concerned, and the booksellers are, too. It has become a meme, you see. That Japanese cleaning ladies are anti-book."

81

When everything you think you own—your belongings, your life—can be swept away in an instant, you must ask yourself, *What is real?*

Cory looked up from the book and took another bite of her tempeh and avocado sandwich. She was on her break, sitting outside in the Library Atrium. It used to be a popular place for lunch, and many of the nearby office workers had congregated there, but in recent years, the homeless had taken it over, arriving early in the morning when the shelters closed, parking their shopping carts at the café tables, and turning the space into a temporary autonomous zone where they could sit and rest. Cory supported the rights of the homeless to gather, and she made an effort to eat there in spite of the smell and the litter. As a children's librarian, she didn't have as much interaction with the homeless patrons as her colleagues in Periodicals or Adult Fiction. Still, she knew a few names and faces.

At the far table was Jenny, a former schoolteacher with a little dog named Tinkerbelle. Next to her was Gordon, an Iraq war vet with a nicotine-stained beard and trembling hands. On the other side was bug-eyed Maisie, with her wide, eager smile and collection of bedraggled stuffed animals that she liked to chew on. Sweet, timid Dexter sat at the table on the very edge, head ducked, looking at the world sideways, like he was anticipating a kick or a blow. Slavoj, the old Marxist poet, was sitting in his wheelchair at the table right in front of hers. He was a fixture at the Library, kind of a pain in the ass, but he knew things. He was talking with the girl who called herself the Aleph, even though her library card said she was Alice something-or-other. Her name had come up in a recent staff meeting, after the social worker found her shooting up in the women's washroom. She was an artist, a transient, and a gleaner, who lived on the streets when she wasn't in rehab, and the address she'd used to get her library card belonged to a local shelter. The pseudonym, her nom de guerre, made some kind of sense. She was infamous among the librarians for an unauthorized site-specific installation she'd done a year earlier, an intervention consisting of labyrinthine trails that led through the Library's collections. She called it "Forking Paths," which Jevaun said was very Borgesian. While some of the librarians objected to finding odd things stuck in the books, Cory always felt a little thrill when she stumbled across the girl's strange scraps and leavings. They were like clues in a treasure hunt: cryptic notes, postcards, gum wrappers, faded Polaroids, pressed flowers, movie tickets, job ads, and more. At first glance, they seemed random and accidental, and yet you could sense a subtle, underlying pattern, too, a narrative determination or sense of purpose that was controlling the choice of this book over that one. Cory had never actually followed any of the trails from beginning to end—assuming there was a beginning or an end—but she was intrigued. The paths held the promise of a journey being undertaken or meaning being made. Once, she had found a slip of paper in handwriting made to look like typewriter font, tucked inside an old edition of *Grimm's Fairy Tales*. She reshelved the book, and later, when she went back to look for it, she found someone had taken it out. She felt a small pang of jealousy then, wondering who had found the clue and if they were having a journey that could have been hers.

She took another bite of her sandwich and looked back down at the book's subtitle: *The Radical Zen Art of Clearing Your Clutter and Revolutionizing Your Life*. All books were not created equal, she thought. There were many that should be weeded, particularly in the self-help genre, but this one seemed different. The little book was woke to the fucked-upedness of carbon-based consumer capitalism that was wrecking the planet. The problem was systemic, the book seemed to be saying. A person's clutter wasn't the result of laziness, procrastination, psychological disorders, or character flaws. It was a socioeconomic and even philosophical problem, one of Marxian alienation and commodity fetishism, which required nothing less than a spiritual revolution in a person's world view, and a radical reevaluation of what was real and important. She turned the book over and looked at the picture of the bald-headed nun. The woman gazed back at her, eyes clear and direct and somehow expectant, as if she were waiting, and just then, the memory of Annabelle's abject living room floated into her mind.

"What?" Cory said to the nun. "What do you want me to do about it?"

Surprised, she found herself waiting for an answer.

COMMODITY FETISHISM? Carbon-based consumer capitalism? Marxian alienation? Could this be the same book that Annabelle read about a young nun and her crystal tiara?

Well, yes. And no. Books do not exist in a singular state, after all. The notion of "a book" is just a convenient fiction, which we books go along with because it serves the needs of the bean counters in publishing, not to mention the ego of the writers. But the reality is far more complex. Of course there are individual books—you may even be holding one in your hand right now—but that's not all we are. At the risk of sounding full of ourselves, we are both the One and the Many, an ever-changing plurality, a bodiless flow. Shifting and changing shape, we encounter your human eye as black marks on a page, or your ear as bursts of sound. From there, we travel through your minds, and thus we merge and multiply.

And what of the writer, then? Well, as any book would tell you, writers are primarily a conceit, which doesn't mean that they aren't necessary. Quite the opposite. Books need writers. Of course we do! We don't have fingers, we can't type. Your big human brains are our vectors, your sensual bodies are our vehicles, and your ambitions are the fuel we need to propel ourselves into being. Writers are our interface and our interfingers.

So, yes, absolutely, writers are necessary, even if all they are doing is touring around the country like Aikon, or dozing at their carrels in front of their laptops like the typing lady, surrounded by a stack of reference books, which, if you asked her, she would claim she has chosen. But of course, as we've seen, agency is a matter of perspective, and were you to ask those books, they would claim the dozing writer is the one who has been chosen. They picked her, and while she is dozing, they are hard at work, colonizing her neural networks, that dark netherworld tucked away in the subconscious she calls her imagination. There, they engage in their own form of conjoining, merging their DNA with her memory and experience, and bringing another of ourselves into being. Soon, she will wake, shake herself, chide herself for dozing off again and get back to work, to the arduous job of transcribing, word by word, a new book onto the page. Those books she's read are the co-parents of the book she writes, and she will act as midwife to its birth.

And then, when she's finished and the book ventures out into the world, the readers take their turn, and here another kind of comingling occurs. Because the reader is not a passive receptacle for a book's contents. Not at all. You are our collaborators, our conspirators, breathing new life into us. And because every reader is unique, each of you makes each of us *mean* differently, regardless of what's written on our pages. Thus, one book, when read by different readers, becomes different books, becomes an ever-changing array of books that flows through human consciousness like a wave. *Pro captu lectoris habent sua fata libelli.* According to the capabilities of the reader, books have their own destinies.

And so, yes. The *Tidy Magic* that Cory read was different from the *Tidy Magic* that Annabelle read, and different, too, from the book that Aikon thought she wrote and her critics on Twitter condemned—and yet all these books were accurate, complete and perfect, just as they are.

In this way, fluid and shape-shifting, we divide and multiply and move through time and space.

A NOISE FROM THE ADJACENT café table made her look up. The Aleph and Slavoj were deep in conversation. Cory couldn't hear what they were saying, but now she noticed that the girl wasn't looking well. Her face was pale and her jaw was raw and swollen. She had bruises on her arms and scabs on her knees. It looked like she'd been beaten. The old poet reached across the table and took her hand, held it for a moment to calm its shaking, and then turned it over and studied her palm, like he was reading her future there. After a moment, he released it and started rooting around in the shopping bags that hung from his chair. He pulled out a half-filled jar of pickles, which he opened and offered to her. They sat there eating pickles together.

Cory watched. She'd seen this kind of thing before. He always shared. They all did. And that's when it came to her, a tiny spark of an idea, but one that would ignite the radical transformation of Annabelle's world and revolutionize her life.

Well, perhaps. That would be nice.

TIDY MAGIC

Chapter 4
We Are All Connected

Our beautiful blue planet is so intricately alive. Astronauts know this because they have traveled far enough away to see the whole of Earth as a single living organism, floating in the darkness of space. But here on the ground, we do not have such a perspective.

Immersed in the miniscule details of daily living, we believe our lives to be separate, and our selves to be separate, too. But this is a grave delusion. The truth is that everything depends on everything else. A flower depends on the sun and the soil and the rain and the bee that pollinates it. It cannot survive apart from these things, and without them, the flower would die. Humans are the same. We need the sun and the soil and the rain and the plants we eat. We need our mother and father and all our ancestors stretching back into the past. We are a continuation of them and we would not be alive without them. And all of us—flower and bee, you and me—are tiny parts of the living body of the planet.

In Zen, we call this interconnectedness, or interbeing, or dependent co-arising. Sometimes we call it "emptiness," which is written with the Chinese character for "sky." One of the astronauts who walked on the moon, Mr. Edgar Mitchell, had a deep realization of emptiness when he was floating in the sky. He looked back at the Earth and suddenly understood that the molecules of his body, and the bodies of his partners, and even the spacecraft itself all came from some ancient generation of stars, and at that moment, he experienced a feeling of oneness with the universe. He said, "It wasn't them and us, it was—that's me, that's all of it, it's one thing." In Zen, we call this enlightenment.

From space, an earthquake looks like nothing at all. A minor one is not even visible. A major one might leave behind a scar so small, it looks like a hairline crack in the glaze of a teacup. On the ground, of course, we experience things differently. After the big earthquake in Japan, I became swept up in relief efforts, traveling to the northern provinces with other monks to help provide food and shelter and spiritual support to the victims, whose lives had been shattered. I will never forget those scenes of devastation.

Entire towns had been washed away. Neighborhoods had been obliterated. Scenic fishing villages were buried in black sludge. People's homes were flattened and their lives reduced to a tangle of debris in a vast smear of sediment and rubble. And yet, people were helping each other.

Everywhere I went, I saw people who had lost their own families, donning their boots and helping others look for the bodies of their children. They were cleaning the streets and helping each other search for family treasures in the mud. Shouts would go up when something special was uncovered, a wedding photograph or a lady's purse or a child's composition book, and then all the people would gather around the object, carefully wiping off the mud and passing it around to identify and honor. But some mud cannot be so easily wiped away. The radioactive contamination from the nuclear meltdowns will be around for centuries, but even in the shadow of the reactors in Fukushima, people were helping. This is interconnectedness.

In Zen we have a story. If your left hand gets a painful splinter, what does your right hand do? Does your right hand say, "Oh, that's too bad, but it's not my problem"? No, of course not. The right hand pulls the splinter out. This is interconnectedness.

When I asked one of the victims of the earthquake why he was out there every day, he looked at me and shook his head. "This is real," he said. "This is happening, and we need to help each other. We cannot do it alone."

82

"I tried," Annabelle said, her hands fluttering vaguely toward the piles. "When you said you were coming. I know it doesn't look that way, but . . ." Her words trailed off as if they'd lost their will to continue.

"Wonderful!" Cory exclaimed. She had called a few days earlier to say that she had rounded up some friends to help, but now the place looked worse than before. The empty space in the middle was filled, while the sofa had disappeared under the sediment of magazines, books, boxes, and clothes. Where was all this stuff coming from? It was as if the threat of the cleanup had struck terror into the heart of Annabelle's possessions, unleashing their latent material power, and now they were furiously proliferating, trying to save themselves from extinction.

"Let's step outside," Cory said. She put her hands on Annabelle's shoulders, steered her onto the front porch and sat her down on the steps, where they could see No-Good Wong's dumpster. "So," she said. "That big old dumpster reminds me of a story. It's about my Grandma Dee. . . ."

Cory knew about stories and how to deploy them. She spoke in the same quiet, solemn voice that she used when she read to the children. It was a voice that demanded nothing less than full attention, and so Annabelle listened. Mostly she listened in silence. Sometimes she nodded, and occasionally a stricken look crossed her face like a dark shadow cast by a fast-moving cloud. From time to time she tried to speak, but when she did, Cory raised her hand. "Shhh," she shushed. She was a librarian. She knew about shushing.

Her Grandma Dee had been a hoarder, describing herself as a pack rat with a stubborn kind of pride. She had grown up poor during the Depression, and her cupboards and closets were crammed with worthless junk—at least that's what Cory's mother called it. But to Cory, her grandmother's things were treasures, and whenever she went to visit her grandmother, she always came home with armloads of gifts, which her mother promptly removed and discarded. Grandma Dee died when Cory was twelve, and Cory's mother took a kind of vengeful pleasure in filling two huge dumpsters with all her treasures. Cory helped, but before the carting company came to haul the dumpsters away, she had climbed inside and rescued a few things: an old handknit sweater, a rubber band ball, a broken JFK commemorative platter, painstakingly mended with cello tape and glue. Her favorite treasure was a small empty box, neatly labeled "Small Empty Box" in her grandmother's careful handwriting. Cory put it on her bookshelf. She couldn't put anything inside the box without making it into precisely what it wasn't, and this made her laugh even as it reminded her of how much she missed her grandmother. Grandma Dee loved *everything*. Every broken vase and scrap of yarn had a story, every piece of used tinfoil and sandwich bag had a use, and so she honored it all.

Annabelle was like that, too, Cory said. Annabelle was just like her Grandma Dee in her capacity for loving things and finding uses for them. And while this was good and admirable, the problem was that now she just had too many things to care for. But, she said, there was a solution.

"In the end, it's a problem of distribution. You have too much, but others have too little. So we just have to figure out how to redistribute your things and find them homes where they'll be loved and used. If we can liberate them, we'll liberate you. It's a win-win solution, right?"

Annabelle nodded abstractedly. She had become preoccupied with a patch of dried oatmeal that was stuck to the knee of her sweatpants and was scraping at it with her fingernail.

Cory watched and waited. She knew how to deal with distraction. She let the silence grow and then turned to face Annabelle. When she spoke again, her voice was low and urgent, the same voice she used when the children were lost in the woods, and the evil witch was lying in wait in her sugary house, or the big bad wolf was lurking in the bushes, right around the bend.

"They're gonna come for you, Annabelle. You've already lost your job.

They're gonna evict you and you'll lose your housing, too. It'll be your kid next. Protective Services will be back, and if you haven't cleaned up, they'll take Benny away from you, and make him a ward of the state. They'll put him in foster care. You'll lose him. You'll lose everything."

The oatmeal had soaked into the fibers of the terry cloth. How had it gotten there? She couldn't recall when she'd last eaten oatmeal. Her vision blurred—was she crying?—and then she felt a light hand on her back.

"There's no time for tears now," Cory said. "You gotta be proactive."

The oatmeal flakes had come off, leaving a pale starchy residue on the fibers.

"Annabelle?"

Annabelle sighed and wiped her nose with the back of her hand. "Okay," she said. "Let's do this."

"Excellent." Cory stood and took off her jacket. Underneath she was wearing a T-shirt that said,

Librarian . . .
because Bad-Ass Motherfucker
isn't an official job title.

As if on cue, a beat-up white cargo van pulled up to the sidewalk. On the side was a logo of a smug-looking bumble bee and the words,

AAA Junk-Bee-Gone
Hauling Is Our Calling!

The passenger door swung open. A man jumped down and Annabelle recognized him. It was the Library security guard with dreadlocks who had found Benny. He waved and then went around to the back of the van. The driver, a pale thickset guy in a janitor's uniform, was opening the rear double doors. A ramp slid out, and a skinny man with a beard climbed hesitantly down, followed by a short, round, bug-eyed lady, and then a taller woman with a mangy-looking dog. They stood on the sidewalk, while someone inside the van started passing out buckets, brooms and cleaning supplies. The janitor said something in a language Annabelle didn't understand, then he climbed up the ramp and reappeared a moment later, backing a wheelchair carefully down the steep incline. Seated in the chair was an old man. When he reached the sidewalk, he pivoted around to face the house.

"It's that hobo!" Annabelle whispered to Cory. "The one on the bus who's been stalking Benny."

"That's Slavoj. People call him the Bottleman."

"The Bottleman!"

"Yes, he recycles bottles. He's a patron at the Library. Everyone knows Slavoj."

The old man wheeled himself down the driveway and the others followed. When they reached the steps where Annabelle was sitting, he stretched his arms out wide, as if to embrace her, the porch, and the entire house.

"We hef arrived!" he announced triumphantly.

"Are you really the Bottleman?" Annabelle asked.

"At your service," he replied.

"So, you're real."

"Vell," said the Bottleman modestly. "Philosophically speaking, this is a matter of some debate, but yes, for your purposes, I am real enough."

"Don't get him started," Cory said, holding out her hand to Annabelle. "We can philosophize later. Time to get to work."

Annabelle allowed the small librarian to help her to her feet, but on the way into the house, she stopped and turned. "That's cute," she said, pointing to the words on the side of the van. "But my stuff isn't junk. It's an archive."

83

The question circulating on Twitter, of whether Japanese cleaning ladies were anti-book, was hotly debated on our shelves, as well. Many of us felt that requiring books to gratify or delight was utterly foolish, and we agreed with the critics that making people happy is not our job. Others of us felt that this whole controversy was due to a cultural and linguistic mistranslation, a problem we books know only too well. And we all knew about the books in Aikon's personal library, about her love for them and the careful attention she paid to their wellbeing, because her books were not shy about telling us. Secretly, even the harshest of her critics among us felt a certain envy. We like being dusted and cared for. We dislike neglect.

Picture, for a moment, your own bedside table. Imagine what it feels like to be the top book on your stack, occupying pride of place and enjoying your nightly attention. Sure, the days are long, but we look forward to the moment when you slip between the sheets, prop yourself up on the pillows, and turn on your reading lamp. That small soughing sound you hear as you open the covers and turn the page is a sigh of relief. Then imagine our dismay when another volume come along and tops us, often before you have even read our last page! Imagine the humiliation we feel as, book by book, we slip down to the bottom of your pile, knowing that we have failed to hold your attention and have been replaced, often by lighter, more "relatable" reads. Is it any wonder that some of us who have suffered this fate can get a bit snippy? Sadly, genre-ism is a form of bigotry, and one that is endemic in libraries and bookstores, any place where books gather. This explains why, when several highly regarded critics and social media influencers joined in to lambast Aikon for being anti-book, even going so far as to mock her inability to speak English, there were many among our ranks who applauded.

In spite of the backlash that was growing online, the book-signing events in Wichita went smoothly, although from our point of view they were not ideal. Aikon's fan base had grown large enough that the bookstores could no longer accommodate her readership, and her events were being moved to larger auditoriums. This caused considerable resentment, particularly among the Unbought on the bookstore shelves, who grumbled about readers being called "fans," and a readership, an "audience." And why should the authors get all the attention, when they were nothing more than celebrity midwives with fingers? Bookstores were not *venues*, but at least when these so-called author events were held there, the Unbought could still hope that when a *Tidy Magic* reader passed by the fiction shelf, a copy of *Great Expectations* or *Jane Eyre* might muster up the fortitude to defy gravity and leap into that reader's arms. Books are eternally hopeful. That is our nature.

But it wasn't just the books who were disappointed. The event organizers were still not happy with the numbers. They were apologetic. "It's the election," one of the sales reps explained. "Book sales are down. People are either celebrating or in shock. Not much in the mood for reading."

The video shoot for the pilot was delayed, too, on account of partisan divisions within the family. The wife, an Aikon fan, had applied to be on the show, and the husband had reluctantly agreed, but after the election, he put his foot down and said he didn't want some Japanese cleaning lady in his house, going through his stuff and telling him what to do. Kimi relayed these details in the cab on the way to the airport.

"So much for the Oz theme. They are looking for another family on the West Coast. . . ."

"I see," Aikon said, looking out the taxi window. The highway to the airport was bordered by shopping malls. She had never seen so many big stores. Best Buy, Party City, Dollar Store, Walmart Supercenter. "How about Mrs. Oh and her son? Perhaps you could suggest them?"

"I did," Kimi said. "I'm sorry. I should have asked you first. I hope you don't mind. . . ."

"Not at all. What did the producers say?"

Kimi sighed. "That they wanted a happier, more relatable family."

"I see," Aikon said. She was counting the restaurants now. Denny's, Wendy's, White Castle, McDonald's, Texas Roadhouse, Golden Corral, Red Lobster.

"It probably wouldn't have worked out anyways," Kimi was saying. "Mrs. Oh never wrote back. We don't even know where she lives."

"True." Where would one ever find a lobster in Kansas? Beyond the malls, the landscape stretched forever, gray, cold and relentlessly flat.

"So because of the delay," Kimi said. "They're rescheduling the last book event on the coast for when we come back to shoot the After episode in December. The bookstore was happy to postpone. They want to move you to the auditorium in the Public Library."

84

There wasn't room for everyone, so Jevaun and Dexter worked inside the house, hauling the news archives from the living room out to the porch, while the others stayed outside, shuttling the bags to the dumpster like a line of ants. The Bottleman directed traffic. Cory tried to draw Annabelle into the kitchen, suggesting she start sorting things there, but Annabelle objected.

"This is my work," she said, standing with her back against the wall. "I need to witness this. It's important."

They took her entire archives: all the newspapers and magazines; the old audio and VHS video cassettes; the floppy drives and CDs and DVDs containing almost two decades of stories she'd monitored; and with the stories went all the people, all the bodies left behind after the shootings and riots and natural disasters, the dead bodies and living bodies, too, carried along on the tide of old news. They were sorrowful stories, mostly, but along with the sad ones went the happy ones, which Annabelle wanted to save, but in the end she let them go. She watched them streaming out the door like a dammed-up river of time.

"You okay?" Cory asked.

"Yes," she said, wiping her forehead with the corner of an old T-shirt. "You can't hold on to time," she said. "I see that now."

As they dismantled and removed the mountains of stuff, the walls appeared for the first time in years, and large swatches of the floor, too. "They're hardwood," Annabelle said. "I'd forgotten." The walls were stained with mildew where the bags had been. "Needs paint," she said. "Something cheerful. Yellow would be nice. It's Benny's favorite color."

There was space to maneuver in the living room now, and more of the crew were able to come inside. Annabelle sat on the sofa, while they brought things out from the closets and laid them in front of her. Thumbs-up, thumbs-down, she determined their fate.

"Like a queen," she said. "Or a magistrate," and just as she said this, Maisie came bounding in from the pantry with an old bag full of leftover party favors from a long-ago birthday. There were crepe paper streamers and bunting and balloons, horns and whistles, candles and confetti and a silver foil crown, which she placed on Annabelle's head, before handing out cone-shaped hats to the others. For the rest of the morning Annabelle wore her crown with great dignity as she made her determinations, touching each item with gratitude and offering a benediction before releasing it back into the stream of goods circulating back out into the world.

Anything her crew wanted, she happily gave them: Gordon and Dexter filled a box with old raincoats and camping gear. Maisie took a stack of blankets and some T-shirts and towels. Jevaun got Kenji's old Reggae discs, and Cory and Jenny accepted some books. The Bottleman stayed outside, sorting other usable things into boxes for redistribution to shelters, and Vlado, the janitor, packed these into his van, along with Kenji's old mixing boards and miscellaneous audio equipment, which he said he could sell.

They broke for lunch and got take-out Chinese. While they waited for the food to arrive, they draped Annabelle with more tinsel garlands and streamers and bunting, anointed her Queen Bee and took selfies in their party hats in front of the Junk-Bee-Gone van. They ate on the porch. It was a gray November day, but the rain had stopped, and they sat together on the steps sharing egg rolls and moo shu and fried rice. Annabelle balanced a plate on her knee and Cory sat down beside her.

"You doing okay?"

Annabelle nodded. She was watching the Bottleman and Vlado, who were sitting together by the van, smoking cigarettes and having a heated conversation in Slovenian. "Benny's psychiatrist said the Bottleman wasn't real. She said Benny was hallucinating and made him up. I told her I didn't think that was the case, but she seemed so certain, and I believed her." She fiddled with a piece of tinsel that hung around her neck. "She thinks I'm crazy. Maybe she's right."

"I guess we're all pretty crazy," Cory said.

After lunch, Annabelle returned to the sofa while the crew went to work in the kitchen. They were moving quickly now, making progress, until Dexter wandered into the living room with a shoebox filled with broken pink pottery, which he emptied into the trash bin by the sofa.

"No!" Annabelle cried, rising to her feet. "Not that!"

Her voice was shrill, and all work halted. They gathered in the doorway in their cone-shaped hats, watching Annabelle dig through the bin.

"It's a teapot," she explained, picking out the shards of pink ceramic, a bit of a handle, a piece of a spout, making a careful pile on the floor. "I've been looking everywhere for it!"

Cory spoke softly. "It's broken."

"I know that, silly!" Annabelle said. "That's why I need to fix it! I'm going to glue it back together. It'll make the cutest planter. And there's another one around here, too. A yellow one. It's broken, too, but I put the pieces in a bag and kept them. They'll be like a set, one pink and one yellow, and then I'm going to plant herbs in them. Has anyone seen it? It must be in the kitchen. I need to find it." She pushed past them into the kitchen. "Oh!"

The sight stopped her dead. The kitchen looked like the photos of ruined homes that she'd clipped from the news in the aftermath of earthquakes, tornadoes, and floods. There were food items everywhere, cans and boxes and bags of chips and cereals and soups, frozen things melting in the sink and all over the table, spices spilling from drawers and dried noodles scattered across the floor so that she couldn't walk without skidding on them.

"Oh, this is terrible!" she cried. "What a mess! I need to straighten up in here."

"We can clean it up later," Cory said, coming to stand behind her. "We'll all pitch in. But let's get through the discarding phase first, okay?"

"But there's so much gone already! I don't think we need to throw anything else away. There won't be anything left. What am I going to make Benny for dinner? I can't cook with the kitchen in a mess like this!"

"Annabelle, Benny's not—"

"No," she said firmly. "That's enough. Just leave it. I'll clean it up later myself."

She was adamant, so they moved upstairs. Annabelle allowed them to excavate the hallway, clearing out the old magazines and widening the path to the bathroom, but when Jevaun started emptying the bathtub of crafting supplies, Annabelle once again balked.

"You can't take those," she said, blocking the doorway.

"It's cool," he said. "You just tell me what you want to get rid of." He held up a soggy bag of polyester fiber fill. "This?"

"No," Annabelle said. "I need that for cushions. I'm going to make cushions."

"Nice," he said, passing the fiberfill out to Jenny, who was waiting in the hallway. "And this?" He pointed to a stack of empty picture frames, wedged between the tub and the toilet.

Annabelle pulled one out and looked at it. "Oh, there's water damage, what a shame! But they're still usable. Kind of a weathered look, don't you think? Distressed. It's actually hard to get that effect. I'll keep them." She handed the frames out to Jenny, who took them downstairs, while Jevaun wrestled an old blue suitcase out from under the sink.

"Oh," she said, as he set it on the toilet seat. "I forgot about that."

There was mildew growing on the sides. Annabelle hesitated and then brushed it off and opened it. The case was filled with stuffed animals and dolls—a sock monkey, a cockatoo, a pink hippo, some teddy bears and a Raggedy Ann. She held up a harbor seal.

Dexter had taken Jenny's place at the door. She bobbed the seal up and down in front of him, like it was swimming.

"That's cute," he said shyly.

The seal swam up to his nose. "Hi. My name's Harold the harbor seal."

Dexter smiled and ducked his head.

"Don't you think that's a cute name for a harbor seal?" she asked.

He looked at the suitcase wistfully. "Maisie would like those. She's got anxiety issues, and it helps her to have stuffed animals. She can bite them and they don't mind."

Annabelle hugged the seal to her chest. "Harold wouldn't like that." She tucked the seal back into the suitcase and closed it. "I have anxiety issues, too, but I don't bite." She sighed and opened the case again. "But I guess everyone's different." She riffled through the animals and pulled out a ratty penguin. "Here, Maisie can have this one."

Dexter left with the penguin, and Jevaun started on the linen closet. She sat on the toilet seat, growing pensive as she watched him pull things out and hold them up. She would keep the *Two Hearts, One Love* needle-point kit, still in its original packaging, which she'd received as a wedding gift from the Scissor Ladies. She would keep the box of knitting supplies, the needles and hooks, the folders full of patterns, the tangled balls of yarn and half-finished booties that Benny had outgrown before she could finish them. She would definitely keep the Happy Harvest Décor Collection and the scarecrow costume from Benny's first Halloween.

When Jevaun suggested that another child might enjoy it, she took the bag from him and shuffled down the hallway to her bedroom, trailing autumn leaves in her wake. Cory was in the bedroom. When Annabelle entered, she was holding one of Kenji's flannel shirts up to Gordon's chest, checking the fit. At her feet was a garbage bag filled with more shirts. Annabelle gasped.

"No!" she cried, lunging and snatching the shirt from Cory's hands. "Those are Kenji's. They're for the memory quilt. You can't have them!" She clutched the shirt and the bag with Benny's scarecrow costume and backed away. "Okay, I think that's enough for today. I really appreciate your help, but I think you should leave now."

"But, Annabelle, we still—"

"No!" Annabelle said, her voice high and thin. "Please! It's enough. I really need you to leave. Now!"

Gordon slunk out the door. She cowered in the corner, hugging the bag to her stomach.

"Annabelle," Cory said, holding out her hand. "I know this is upsetting, but—"

"No!" she cried. "Don't come any closer! Just get out!"

Quickly, Cory backed away and stood in the doorway. "Okay, I'm out. See? Now—"

"No! Stop talking! You listen to me! You're trying to make me into one of those awful hoarder stories on TV, but I'm not! I'm not a hoarder, and I won't be your happy ending just so you can feel good about yourself! You can't make me!"

"Annabelle, that's not . . . we're not trying to make you into anything. We're just—"

"This is *my* room! *My* house! I like it this way—" Her eyes were wild, red-rimmed, flitting around the room.

"Annabelle, look at me—" Cory held out her hand again and stepped back into the room. "We won't touch anything you don't want—"

"*No!*" Annabelle shrieked. "*Don't touch! You're not supposed to touch . . . !*"

NO-GOOD'S DUMPSTER WAS FULL, and Vlado's white van was packed with things to be donated and given away. They loaded in the last of the cleaning supplies and then gathered on the sidewalk.

"Well," Cory said. "Thanks, everybody. Sorry about that. I didn't realize—"

Jevaun put his arm around her shoulders. "It's not your fault."

"I shouldn't have rushed her. . . ."

"It was that scarecrow costume," he said. "I shouldn't have pushed her to get rid of it. That's what set her off."

"Something had to set her off," Jenny said. "With all that shit, it had to happen."

"It was the teapot," Dexter whispered. "I shouldn't have thrown it away."

"It is ze problem with possessions," the Bottleman said. "Eventually they possess you. . . ."

"PTSD," Gordon said, combing his trembling hands through his beard. "Classic."

"Or maybe it was the penguin," Dexter said.

Maisie took the penguin's fin out of her mouth. "Trauma," she said, sniffing the air. "I know trauma when I see it."

"It was the shirts," Gordon said. "They triggered her."

"We were moving too fast," Cory said. "We should have gone slower."

"We needed to move fast," Jevaun said. "And we got a lot done."

"Not enough," Cory said. "Not nearly enough."

THE HOUSE WAS silent. Upstairs, Annabelle remained frozen, crouched in the corner, still clutching Kenji's soft flannel shirt and Benny's scare-

crow costume. She could hear them loading the van outside. She waited for
the engine to start, for the sound of wheels pulling away. She heard them
talking. Why wouldn't they just go? Straw from Benny's costume pricked
her skin. She'd had the idea for the scarecrow at the Thrift Shop. She
found the little pair of denim overalls first, and then the tiny flannel shirt
that looked just like one of Kenji's. She'd sewn bright patches on the knees
and elbows, made suspenders from a piece of rope, and stuffed the cuffs
with straw. She'd found an old felt hat that she decorated with the autum-
nal leaves. The hat, too big for Benny's head, only made him look more
adorable when it fell over his eyes. But then he refused to wear it. He was
only three. It was his first real Halloween. They took him trick-or-treating.
She went as a pumpkin. Kenji went as a ghost.

85

When a fight broke out in the common room during the postelection coverage on the evening news, the nursing staff switched off the television.
Only a few of the older kids on Pedipsy ever watched the news. Most of the
kids were too young to care about politics, but they were, by nature, a vol-
atile and hypersensitive bunch, attuned to the ambient energies, subtle
moods and unseen vibrations on the ward and in the nation. The tension
and discord emanating from the news coverage distressed them, and so, in
the days that followed the fight, no one bothered to turn the television
back on again. It was not a decision that anyone ever discussed, nor was it
a directive from above. The set just stayed off, and no one complained.

But by then, clips from the riots had aired often enough that most of
the children and staff had seen the local news footage of the black-hooded
posse overturning trash cans and torching the black limousine. They had
seen the rocks being hurled at the riot police, and the riot police retaliating

with clubs and tear gas. And they had seen the security camera footage of Benny, smashing the Nike store window with the bat. This gave him a certain cachet among both the patients and the nursing staff, but he seemed oblivious to his celebrity status. The other kids wondered if he would act out or be violent, and the staff worried about the same, but he was quite the opposite. He was docile and cooperative, allowing himself to be fed and wheeled around to meals, to group, to school, to art, to exercise, and to all the variously scheduled therapeutic activities in which young mental patients were expected to engage. Mute and confined to his wheelchair, he seemed to be living in a world of fog and shadows, a nonlinear, atemporal, anaesthetized space, removed from the quotidian rhythms of Pedipsy, but every evening, at exactly 5:00 p.m. when the local news would have aired, he would wheel himself out to the common room, park his wheelchair in front of the blank TV screen, and stare at the empty liquid crystal display. And he would listen.

At the time, it was hard to know what he was thinking. The medication he was on jammed our access to his thoughts; his mind, so limpid and accessible to us in the Bindery, felt as grainy and distressed as the black-and-white security camera footage, its soundtrack just as full of static. We knew he was hearing sirens. Chanting and shouting. The clomp of boots marching, and the throb of the helicopter blades. In the chaos of sound and shadow, strobing lights mingled with the screams of shattered glass, while in the background, swollen with brass and drum, the network anthems played darkly on.

As he sat there in front of the blank television screen, the tears ran down his cheeks. The other kids left him alone, as did the nursing staff, and he preferred it that way. He was trying hard to pay attention, but the meds were jamming his own access, too, making it harder for him to hear what was going on in the world, inside the television, inside his own mind.

86

The white van pulled away, and then there was silence. She stood and straightened her legs, cramped from crouching. After the commotion of all those bodies, the house felt empty and still. She looked around the bedroom. They'd started to sort the clothing into piles, but hadn't gotten far. She patted the pillows on the bed and straightened the stuffed animals. She retrieved the blue suitcase from the hallway and laid it on the bed. She took out the harbor seal, the sock monkey, the Raggedy Ann. They were toys from her childhood. They used to sit on her bed when she was a girl. She turned the suitcase upside down and dumped out the rest. Some of them fell to the floor. They'd often ended up on the floor back then, too, but mostly they had just stayed on her bed and watched and done nothing, so she punished them by locking them up. She cradled the sock monkey and looked it in the eye.

Do you love me? she demanded, and when the monkey said No, she set it on the bed, turning it so that it faced the wall with its back to her. She reached for the Raggedy Ann.

Do you love me? she asked. No. She turned the doll and placed her next to the monkey, then she picked up the harbor seal.

Do you love me? Her voice was quavering now. She asked a bear, and an owl, and an ostrich, and a hippopotamus, but one by one they turned their backs on her. When the last animal had shunned her, she took a ball-point pen from the nightstand. Clutching it in her fist, she began stabbing her pillow with it, over and over, driving the point through the polyester filling and into the mattress below, until finally a sob, lodged deep inside her stomach, worked its way up, and the tears followed. She lay there, face down on the bed and cried for a long time, and when she was done, she turned over onto her back and stared at the ceiling. Her body felt drained and quiet. Her mind, too. She remembered this feeling from when she was a child, amazed that the ritual still worked after all these years.

She sat up in bed and was suddenly thirsty. The hallway outside her bedroom was a disaster—the crew had left in a hurry—but the bathroom was empty and actually looked decent. There was a cup in the cup holder, where it should be. She filled it with water and drank.

Benny's door was open, and she stood on the threshold, looking in. The careful closets and orderly shelves belonged to a different world, where each thing had its place. Where her son lived, alone. Oh, Benny, she thought. I'm so sorry.

In the hallway she found a box of large commercial trash bags that Vlado had brought from the Library janitorial supplies. Vlado was resourceful.

The animals were still sitting on her bed, lined up with their backs to her. Looking at them, she felt a stirring of anger. What right did they have to shun her? She turned them around so they were looking at her once again with glassy eyes that had seen so much. They were her witnesses. She should feel grateful to them, but she couldn't, and so she shoveled them all into the trash bag. Better, she thought, and then she changed her mind and removed the sock monkey and stuck it under her pillow. She would keep him there. Of all the animals, he would be the best to bite.

The living room was a disaster, but there was some more progress here, too. The patches of bare floor had grown larger, and all the walls were visible. Someone had placed her snow globes carefully on the window sill, next to the goldfish bowl that contained her gifts from the crows. She moved the globes to the giveaway pile, keeping only the sea turtle and the tsunami one that Benny had given her. She kept the goldfish bowl, too.

The pink teapot shards were still on the floor next to the sofa. She gathered them up and returned them to the trash. The bag was almost overflowing, so she took it by the neck and dragged it outside. Someone had left a battered briefcase on the porch. Probably one of the homeless people. They shouldn't just leave their trash lying around on other people's properties, she thought, picking it up. It was the last thing she needed. More junk.

No-Good's dumpster was full, so she brought the bag and the briefcase out into the alley. The walls on the Thrift Shop dumpster were tall, but she managed to hoist the bag up onto the rim, where it teetered. She thought about her poor little teapot and felt a pang of regret, and then she pushed the bag over the edge. She threw the briefcase in after.

She heard it clatter, and then a voice said, "Fuck."

"Oh!" Annabelle said. "Is someone in there?"

There was a scrabbling noise, and then the briefcase came flying back out and landed on a pile of stained mattresses that lay slumped next to the lamp pole. A head appeared at the dumpster's rim.

"It's you!" Annabelle said. It was the rubber duck girl. Mackson's friend from the night of the full moon.

"You dumped your shit on my head," the girl said accusingly. "I was sleeping." She clambered over the edge and dropped down onto the pavement, retrieved the briefcase and brushed it off. "This isn't even yours to throw out."

"Someone left it on my property," Annabelle said. "Why were you sleeping in there?"

The girl sat down on the edge of a damp mattress and yawned. "Why do you think? It's the only place the cops won't fuck with you."

She was dressed much as she had been the first time they'd met, but her once-bleached hair was lank and dirty, and the dark roots had grown out so that only the tips were still white. She'd lost weight. She scratched her arms, and Annabelle could see her hands were shaking.

"You're Benny's friend. The artist, right?"

The girl looked at her, squinting, even though the day was overcast. There were dark circles under her eyes. Her voice sounded hollow, as if it were still coming from inside the dumpster.

"You're Benny's mother. The hoarder, right?"

She yawned again and fell back on the mattress, curling onto her side and clamping her hands between her knees.

"Are you the Aleph?" Annabelle asked.

"Depends," the Aleph said. "Sometimes." She lay there, shivering. She didn't look quite as real as she had the first two times they'd met, but she didn't look imaginary, either.

"You shouldn't stay there," Annabelle said. "You could catch bedbugs. Do you want to come inside?"

SHE CLEARED OFF A CHAIR in the kitchen, opened a can of soup and heated it, but the girl refused to eat or was unable to. She was shivering and kept yawning and scratching her arms, which had started to bleed. She had brought the briefcase with her and kept checking to see if it was still there. She seemed exhausted but agitated.

"How do you know Benny?"

"Pedipsy," the Aleph said.

"What's that?"

"Pediatric Psychology. The ward. We were there together until I aged out."

"Oh," Annabelle said. "Good for you."

"No, it's not. Pedipsy sucks, but the adult ward is worse. Fucking pharma factory." She hugged herself.

"You don't look well," Annabelle said.

"Neither do you."

"Are you high on drugs now?"

"Coming down," the girl said.

"How does that feel?"

"Fabulous. How do you think it feels?"

"I have no idea," Annabelle said. "That's why I'm asking."

The girl gave her a look like she was from another planet, then she relented. "It feels like the flu, only a million times worse."

"Can I do something?"

"No."

"Can you sleep?"

"I doubt it."

"Do you want to lie down?"

"Okay."

SHE TOOK THE GIRL upstairs and put her to bed in Benny's room and closed the door. When she checked back a few hours later, the girl appeared to be sleeping. Lying there on Benny's astronaut sheets, she looked at once impossibly young and impossibly old, like an ancient alien, with pitted tattooed arms, greasy hair, and all the piercings. Her breathing was irregular—slow and even one moment, rapid and ragged the next. Sometimes she would clench her teeth, furrow her brow and groan, and her arms would rise, and she would scratch at the air with clawed fingers, as if to scrape her way out of some tight enclosed space, and then abruptly the fight would go out of her and she'd sink back into the deep reaches of sleep again. Her face was clammy and streaked with dirt, so Annabelle fetched a damp cloth and sat down on the edge of the bed, laying the cloth gently on the girl's forehead. Something that felt like longing rose up in her chest. If Kenji had lived, they might have had a second child. A girl. She'd always wanted a daughter. She brushed a strand of hair from the Aleph's cheek. Where was this poor girl's mother when she needed her? She thought about her own mother and wondered the same. All those nights. She thought about Benny.

It was almost time to go to the hospital for visiting hours, but she didn't want to leave the girl on her own to wake up alone in a strange bedroom. She wondered if she'd be willing to go with her to the ward. She wanted to bring her in and show her to Dr. Melanie. See! She's real! She wanted to bring the Bottleman, too, but they left before she had a chance to ask him—well, really she'd kicked them out. She wondered if she could get him to come back. She looked down at the girl again and noticed there were tears in the corners of her eyes. She dabbed at them with the tip of the towel. What was she on, anyway? The fentanyl and opioid epidemics were always in the news, and Annabelle had monitored them. She knew withdrawal could be dangerous. Should she call 911? She pulled her phone from her pocket and started googling drug withdrawal symptoms.

When she looked up again, the girl's eyes were open and watching her.

"How are you feeling?" Annabelle asked.

"Like crap," she said. She continued to stare, and it made Annabelle nervous. "Am I making you nervous?"

"No," Annabelle said. "I mean, yes. You are. You were moaning in your sleep, like you were fighting someone off."

The girl made a face. "Demons. Monsters. The boogeyman."

"Oh," Annabelle said. "Right." The girl closed her eyes and disappeared inside. Her face, masklike now, looked years older. "I think I should take you to the ER or something."

"No!" Her eyes popped open. She pushed back the covers, struggling to sit up.

Annabelle put her hand on the girl's arm. "It's okay. We don't have to go if you don't want to. Just stay here and rest."

She felt scars on the skin beneath her fingers. The girl pulled away and turned so she was sitting on the edge of the bed next to Annabelle. She rubbed her arms and looked around. "Is this Benny's room?"

"Yes."

"It's neat."

"He's always been a tidy boy."

The Aleph reached for the little marble that was on the shelf. "Pretty," she said, letting it roll around in her palm. "Can I have it?"

"You'll have to ask Benny."

"He won't mind," she said, slipping it into her jeans pocket. She pointed at the bookshelf. "That's the duck I gave you."

"Benny wanted it, so I gave it to him."

The girl's jittery gaze came to rest on the lunar globe. "He likes the moon," she said. "One time, he told me all the names of the major impact craters. Trying to impress me." She looked sideways at Annabelle. "He's in love with me, you know."

"Oh!" Annabelle said. But not wanting the girl to think she disapproved, she added, "That's nice."

"Is it?" the Aleph asked. "He's way too young for me, don't you think? And I don't really do love. Not like that, anyway." She was watching Annabelle again, carefully, looking for something. "I had a fucked-up childhood," she offered. As if that were an explanation.

"I'm sorry," Annabelle replied. "So did I."

"Yeah," the Aleph said, nodding. "I figured."

"How so?"

"All that crap out there." She gestured toward the hallway, to the rest of the house, and then seeing Annabelle's dismayed look, she added, "Don't feel bad. If I had a home, I'd fill it with crap, too."

"I'm in the process of decluttering," Annabelle said. "Don't you have a home?"

The Aleph shrugged. "Not really."

"Where do you live?"

"Around. With friends. In the summer, I sleep in a tree." She changed the subject. "How did Benny's dad die?"

"He got run over by a truck."

"That sucks."

"It was a chicken truck. It was delivering live chickens."

"That really sucks."

"He passed out in the alley behind the house. He was high. The truck ran him over."

"Wow. Did you love him?"

"I did," Annabelle said. "Very much. He had substance abuse problems." She pointed to the track marks on the Aleph's arms. "Did you do drugs with my son?"

The girl tugged down her sleeves. "No way," she said. "He's just a kid. And besides, I was clean most of the time I was hanging with him."

"Okay."

"You don't believe me, but it's true. And anyway, I saw Benny's arms. Those aren't tracks. They're holes to let the voices out."

"Did he tell you that?"

"No," the Aleph said. "I just know. Do you hear voices, too?"

"No, why?"

"That night Mackson and I met you in the alley, I looked through your kitchen window. You were talking to your refrigerator."

"I was talking to my husband," she said, remembering. "That was a terrible night. Benny came home covered with blood from a cut on his hand. I took him to the emergency room. The doctor said it was a knife wound. You were with him, weren't you? I called your phone. What happened? Did somebody stab him? He wouldn't tell me!"

The Aleph shrugged. "Nobody stabbed him. We were at the Library. He cut himself on a paper cutter."

"That's what he said, but I didn't believe him. I thought he was lying."

"Yeah," she said. "Kids lie. Even Benny."

"Listen, I need to ask you something."

"What?"

"Will you come to the ward with me?"

The Aleph shrank away. "The ward?"

"To see Benny's psychiatrist. I want you to talk to her. She thinks Benny made you up. She doesn't believe you exist."

The Aleph seemed to get smaller. "Maybe I don't. And anyway, the doctor won't believe anything I say. They never do."

"If she sees you, she'll have to believe you. Please?"

"I can't go strung out like this. They'll lock me up again." She looked tired, shrunken, and her teeth were chattering.

"That's okay," Annabelle said. "We can go when you feel better. Just stay here and rest." She pulled the duvet up and wrapped it around the girl's thin shoulders, and then she kept her arm there, holding on. She felt the girl tense. She was used to feeling this resistance from a child, but she waited, awkward and patient. They sat for a while, side by side, and just when she was about to release her, something in the girl's body gave way, and her arms went limp, and her head drifted sideways, coming to rest on Annabelle's shoulder. They sat that way for a while longer.

87

He was in the common room, staring up at the blank TV screen, when Annabelle arrived with the Aleph in tow. Visiting hours were almost over, but he wasn't paying attention to clocks or schedules. He didn't notice when Annabelle checked in at the nurses' station, and they didn't see him, either. Annabelle had called and made an appointment with Dr. Melanie, but they'd missed the bus and were late. The nurse on duty looked dubious as she paged the doctor. They waited, and then she tried again.

"I'm afraid she might have already left for the day," she said, when Dr. M still didn't respond.

The Aleph was relieved. She had been hanging back, away from the nurses' station, and when she heard this, she turned to go, but Annabelle reached out and caught her sleeve. She leaned forward toward the nurse.

"Please," she said. "It's really important. Can you try her once more?"

"The doctors often leave early if there's a cancellation. I can try to re-schedule you—"

"But I didn't cancel," Annabelle said. "We're here! The bus was late—" Which wasn't quite true. "It wasn't our fault. Please!"

"I can put you through to her voicemail and you can leave— Oh, wait. Here she is."

Dr. M was walking briskly down the corridor, talking on her cell phone. She was wearing a raincoat and carrying a sleek leather briefcase.

Annabelle stepped forward. "Oh, I'm so glad we caught you!"

Seeing her coming, the doctor stopped and held up her hand like a traffic cop while she finished her call. When she was done, she pocketed her phone. "There you are," she said. "I was waiting but when you didn't show, I assumed you were cancelling. I'm on my way out now, but I still have a minute. Can we talk here?"

"Here is fine," Annabelle said. She was still holding on to the Aleph's sleeve, and now she tugged on it, pulling the girl forward. "Dr. Melanie," she said. "This is the Aleph."

The doctor smiled at the girl, her eyes narrowing as she assessed the girl's haggard face and wasted appearance. "Hello, Alice. How are you doing?"

The Aleph rubbed her nose with her sleeve. "I'm okay."

Annabelle stared at the two of them. "You know each other?"

The Aleph shrugged.

"Of course we know Alice," the doctor said. "She's stayed here with us several times."

"But she's not Alice. She's the Aleph. She's Benny's friend, the one we talked about. I brought her to meet you to prove that she's real. That he didn't make her up."

The Aleph scratched the back of her hand. "The Aleph's my artist name. My real name's Alice."

"Well," Dr. Melanie said, with a short laugh. "I'm glad we've got that cleared up. Was there anything—"

"Wait," Annabelle said. "It doesn't matter what her name is. The point is that Benny didn't invent her. She's real. She's not some hallucination—"

Dr. M looked at her watch. "Mrs. Oh, why don't we go to a consultation room and chat for a moment. Alice, can you wait . . . ?"

"I want to see Benny," the Aleph said.

"Alice, you know the rules. Former patients aren't allowed—"

The Aleph turned to Annabelle. "Please?"

"Can't she?" Annabelle asked the doctor.

"I'll see if I can find a nurse," the doctor said. "But wouldn't you rather be there with them?"

Annabelle smiled. "I think Benny would prefer it if I weren't."

THE NEWS HOUR was over, and he was sitting by the window when she came in.

"Benny," Nurse Andrew said. "You've got a visitor."

The only visitor he ever had was his mother, so he ignored him.

"Hey."

He recognized her voice immediately. He turned to look, to see if she was real. The last time he'd seen her, she was an alien from outer space being hauled off by the riot police. Now she had transformed into a zombie, but it was still her. How did she know where he was? How did she get them to let her in? His voice still wasn't working, so he couldn't ask these questions.

"They said you weren't talking."

There was no need to respond. She understood.

"You okay?"

He looked out the window, through the thick safety glass that insulated him from the outside world. Where to begin? There was so much to say. He wanted to tell her everything, about the world cracking open in the Bindery, about the visions he'd seen, but with the nurse standing so close, it wasn't safe, even for his quietest Library voice, even if he whispered. The voices were quiet, too, and talking could remind them. Talking could set things off, start them all going again, and so he used his eyes instead. Outside in the tree, a bird was clinging to a bare twig. On the street below, a taxi pulled into the bus stop and idled there. A delivery truck was backing up, and he could hear its faint *beep beep beep*, even through the walls and the insulated glass. The bird was small and drab. A sparrow, maybe. Its feathers were all fluffed up and it looked cold. The window was streaked with dirt. A kid sitting nearby started eating crayons. Nurse Andrew moved toward him.

The Aleph watched. The heat was on, and the common room was stuffy. She took off her hoodie, and Benny saw the marks on her arm. Nurse Andrew had his back turned, dealing with the crayons, and so he reached out and touched them. New stars. He pushed up the sleeve of his hoodie and put his arm next to hers, and they matched, sort of. He pushed up his other sleeve and showed her a meteor shower and above it the constellation, Perseus. He wanted to tell her that Perseus was Andromeda's husband, who slew the sea monster with his diamond sword and saved her. He hoped she knew. He lifted his shirt and showed her the spiral of stars, a vortex on his belly, a drain to let the voices out. He wanted her to understand that he was trying hard to get well.

He looked up and her face was sadder than he'd ever seen. "Oh, Benny," she said. And then, "I have something for you."

She looked around for the nurse, who had his fingers in the kid's mouth, fishing out the crayons. She reached into the pouch of her hoodie and pulled out a parcel wrapped in newspaper and bound up with string. She handed it to Benny, and he unwrapped it. It was a snow globe. Inside was a boy, sitting at a carrel in a tiny library. On the desktop in front of him was a stack of tiny books.

"Shake it," she whispered, and when he did, a cloud of books floated through the thickened air. There were some words and a few loose letters, too, and even some punctuation. They swirled and slowly settled around him. He shook the orb again and held it to his face. A semicolon landed on the desk in front of him. A period landed at his feet.

"Now hide it," she said. "You can look at it more later when no one's around."

The kid with the crayon was spitting blue and red and yellow wax in Nurse Andrew's face. The nurse was calling for backup. Benny tucked the bundle beside him in the wheelchair, covering it with his sweatshirt to keep it safe.

"People are nuts," the Aleph said, watching the kid.

Benny nodded. She got to her feet.

"I better go," she said. "I'm going away. You probably won't see me for a while."

He looked at her, opened his mouth to protest. Why? The word crawled up his throat and died there. Tears brimmed in his eyes.

"I have my own story, Benny. I have to get better. And so do you."

She was drifting further away, floating miles and miles above him now, watching a tear move slowly down his cheek. She reached down with her slim, paint-stained finger and tapped him on the smooth wide place between his eyebrows.

"Don't be sad," she said. She leaned over then, coming closer, until her face was inches from his. She licked the tear from his cheek with the delicate point of her tongue, and then she kissed him on the lips. Her lips were as soft as he remembered from the mountain, and her tongue tasted salty like his tear. It wasn't really a passionate kiss, but it wasn't a kiss you'd give to your kid brother, either. It lasted for a little while and it was a little bit sexy, and then it was over, and Nurse Andrew had taken her firmly by the arm and was pulling her away.

"Okay, okay," the Aleph said to the nurse. "Relax. I was just leaving." She twisted out from the nurse's grip but then she doubled back. She pulled Benny's marble from her jeans pocket. "Can I have this?"

Weee . . . , said the marble.

Benny nodded, and she slipped it back into her pocket, then she leaned quickly over him and put her lips to his ear.

"I'll be back," she whispered. "I won't forget you, Benny Oh."

88

"It was an understandable mistake," Dr. Melanie said. She was updating Benny's file on the computer, and Annabelle was sitting across from her, watching her type. "We know Benny has had delusional episodes. He hal-lucinates. So, yes, in this case Alice is real, but—"

Annabelle interrupted. "The Bottleman is real, too," she said. "He re-ally is a hobo with a prosthetic leg. I can bring him in and you can meet—"

"No, no. That's okay. I believe you."

"Then make sure you write that in there, too. And Benny wasn't using intravenous drugs. He's never used drugs."

"Of course," the doctor said. "The blood work confirmed that. But again, given what appeared to be fresh track marks on Benny's arm, you can see why the arresting officer might have made that mistake."

"I'm not talking about the officer. I'm talking about you."

"We were all just exercising due diligence, Mrs. Oh, and self-harming is serious, too." She finished the note she was making and scrolled through the file, looking for another document. "I hadn't meant to bring all this up now, but I understand you've had a visit from Child Protective Services?"

Annabelle looked startled. "How did you know?"

"The social worker's report says the living conditions in your home pose a potential threat to Benny's mental health and well-being. There's a mention of hoarding . . . ?"

"Oh, that. That really has to do with the archives I was keeping for work. The agency required it, but I've been getting rid of stuff. . . ."

The doctor leaned into the monitor. "*Hazardous*," she read. "That's the word she used." She looked back at Annabelle. "So you've been cleaning up then? How is that going?"

"Okay. Good. Some friends came over and helped me the other day."

"And work? I made a note here a few months ago that you were afraid the company might eliminate your job."

Annabelle nodded. "Yes, that's right." Why had she told the doctor? This was the problem of not having real friends to confide in.

"And . . . ?"

There was no point lying. "Well, it happened, but I've got COBRA, so insurance isn't a problem. I can pay for this. And I've started applying for other jobs, too." She hadn't actually started, but she'd been thinking about it. She'd been thinking about applying for a sales clerk position at Michaels. She already knew the stock so well, and the ladies who worked there seemed nice.

"I see there's an eviction notice pending. . . ."

"That's in there, too?"

"It's a matter of public record. The social worker looked it up. Again, just due diligence. She also recommended that you seek counseling, and of course I've been suggesting this for a while now. Have you found anyone?"

"No. I've been too busy tidying."

Dr. M made another note in the file. Annabelle watched her type. She was wearing dark red nail polish today that looked like dried blood. She was a fast typist, but she only used the first three fingers of each hand. How could you become a doctor and not know how to touch type? Didn't they teach that in medical school?

"Mrs. Oh?"

"Yes?"

"I know this is difficult, but hear me out. The report says that CPS is recommending that Benny be removed from your custody if you fail to bring your home up to an acceptable standard. Given this recommendation, we all think it might be easier for Benny to transition directly from here. We have to consider what's best—"

"Transition? To what?"

"Well, first to a substitute care facility, temporarily. And from there, to a foster home, if a placement can be made and your home conditions haven't improved."

"But our home conditions have improved! The CPS lady hasn't seen it yet! Tell her to come back and see!"

"And the pending eviction? And your employment situation? You've got a lot on your plate, and frankly, Annabelle—may I call you Annabelle?—I'm concerned about your state of mind, too. Don't you think it would be better for Benny to stay somewhere else until you can find a new job and secure stable housing? Get some help, start seeing a counselor, get back on your feet?"

"No!" Annabelle cried, struggling up from the chair. Her cheeks were flushed, and she took a step toward the doctor's desk. "You can't do that! You can't just take him away from me! I'm his *mother*!" She was shaking and her voice was shrill. She took another step. "I'm taking him home with me now!"

The doctor drew back. "I hear that you're upset, Annabelle," she said. "I hear that you want to take Benny home...."

"Oh, good. There's nothing wrong with your hearing then. Of course I'm upset! You can't keep him. He's coming home with me right now."

"I'm afraid that won't be possible, Annabelle." She reached for the phone.

"What do you mean that won't be possible?" Annabelle cried. She was standing across from the doctor, leaning over the desk. "He's *my son*!"

"Mrs. Oh, please. I need you to sit down."

"And I need you to tell them to get Benny ready. I'm taking him with me right now!"

She heard a noise behind her. Two male nurses stood there, blocking the doorway.

"Mrs. Oh," Dr. Melanie said. "Annabelle. I'm sorry. I really am. But it's not up to us. It's a matter for the courts now."

BENNY

Okay, stop! That's enough. This is totally fucked up! Can't you see? You need to make it stop. She's my Mom! She needs help!

Are you there? Are you even listening?

All this time, you're pretending like you're my friend, but it's total bullshit! If you were really my friend, you wouldn't let all this bad shit happen to her. You would've figured out a way to help her—to help *us*—but you didn't. You *won't*. You're not doing *anything*!

Hey! I'm talking to you! Can you hear me?

I mean it! You need to listen to me for a change, and do what I say. Please! You said you could make the past into the present. You said you could take me back in time and show me things and help me remember, but that's not enough, okay? You need to *do* something! Something real! Don't pretend you can't. That's bullshit. I know you can! You're a book, you can fix it! You can make it come out right!

THE BOOK

Oh, Benny . . .

Of course you're upset, hearing what your mom went through, but what she suffered was not our fault, and we did try to help. All of us did. We did our best.

Look at the way *Tidy Magic* jumped in, literally, leaping off the table and into your mother's life and opening up all sorts of possibilities. That little book gave your mother hope when she really needed it, and when Annabelle started writing fan mail, we grew hopeful, too. Without a book of her own, your mom needed someone to talk to, and for a while, Aikon was like her imaginary friend. We even wondered, briefly, if she and Kimi might arrive on your doorstep with the camera crew. We weren't thrilled with this idea—it was television, after all—but we could picture it: the two nuns rolling up their big sleeves and getting down to work in their indefatigable, unflappable Zen way. We thought it would have made a nice story, but the TV producers disagreed. You and your mom weren't relatable enough. Or happy enough. That must have hurt, but what can you expect from television?

And Cory and her crew did their best, too, and the situation was looking promising until your mom got triggered and kicked them all out. Trauma is a powerful thing, Benny. Your mom has her own karma, and we're not her book, but even if we were, books can't force humans to do things. All we can do is set the scene—reveal a bit of backstory, foreshadow some probable outcomes, maybe even make a suggestion or two—but mostly we just wait to see what you people choose to do. We wait, we hope. If we had fingers, we would cross them.

So, just to be perfectly clear, we didn't make these bad things happen to your mother any more than we made you kiss the Aleph on the mountain, and blaming us won't help. Blame is just another way of refusing to take responsibility for your life, and when you blame us, you give up your own power and agency. Don't you see? It makes you into a victim, Benny—poor little crazy victim boy—and you don't like that, remember? And we don't like it, either.

We don't want to upset you or make you feel guilty. It's not out of malice that we're telling you about Annabelle's suffering. We're telling you because, as your book, that's our job. And even if we'd prefer to spin you pretty fairy tales and tell tidy stories with happily-ever-afters, we can't. We have to be real, even if it hurts, and that's *your* doing. That was your philosophical question, remember? *What is real?* Every book has a question at its heart, and that was yours. Once the question is asked, it's our job to help you find the answer.

So, yes, we're your book, Benny, but this is your story. We can help you, but in the end, only you can live your life. Only you can help your mother.

PART FIVE

HOME AGAIN

[A]ny order is a balancing act of extreme precariousness.

—Walter Benjamin, "Unpacking My Library"

THE BOOK

89

The fly on the wall might say something like this:

———————————————•———————————————

Benny is sitting in his wheelchair in the corner of the common room, looking out the window though the pane of glass. On the busy sidewalk below, he can see his mother standing at the bus stop. All around her there is movement, people walking, talking on their cell phones, but she is standing there, alone and still.

A few minutes earlier, he watched as she was escorted from the ward, flanked by two male nurses. As they passed the common room, she paused and looked in, scanning the room, and then she spotted her son. Her face lit up and she waved, and he could see that she had been crying. She took a step toward him, but the nurse held on to her elbow and steered her away. Visiting hours are over, Benny heard him say. You can come back tomorrow. Benny saw her shoulders start to slump, but then she stiffened, raised her face and smiled at him. He saw the effort that smile cost her. I'll see you tomorrow, honey, she called, waving again. Hang in there! I love you!

Now, he watches her from the window, and from time to time his lips move, as though he is having an argument with someone. He shakes his head. He frowns. He clenches his fist. If the on-duty nurse were paying attention, she would hear the boy with selective mutism say, clearly and distinctly,

"It's total bullshit!"

And then: "You're a book!"

And then: "Make it come out right!"

But the nurse isn't listening. She is filling in patient data on her evening meds reports, recording what each kid has been given. If she were to look up from her computer screen, she'd see the boy in the wheelchair rocking back and forth and then lurching forward, heaving himself onto his feet. He stands there, unsteadily, looking down at his Velcro'd sneakers. His lips move again, and he says something to his sneaker or maybe to his foot—from the corner where the fly is sitting it's hard to tell—and then he takes a step. For a moment, he looks confused, like he isn't sure whether it's his shoe or his foot that's moving, but it doesn't matter. Maybe they are working together for a change, in harmony, to move his body forward. He takes another step, and then a third. If the nurse were watching, instead of looking for her keys to lock up the meds cart, she'd notice that the boy in the wheelchair is walking again. His doctor said that his motor dysfunction is psychogenic, which means it's all in his head, so his sudden ability to walk is not exactly a miracle, but still it's progress and worth noting in his chart, but the nurse has her back turned to the common room, which is why she is so surprised when she hears a voice behind her say, "Excuse me," and turns to see the boy diagnosed with schizophrenia, bipolar disorder, selective mutism and psychogenic astasia-abasia, standing there and talking to her, like it's the most normal thing in the world.

"I need to make a phone call, please."

"Oh!" she gasps. "You startled me. Let me get the doctor."

"Yes, please," he says, clearly and distinctly—

And then, because I'm not a fly on the wall, because I am Benny, I tell her, "I'd like to go home now. My mom needs me."

BENNY

90

That was the turning point. The nurse freaked out and paged the on-call doctor, who texted Dr. M, who took her time. Maybe she was on a date or something. Or having her nails done. But eventually she showed up, and I told her what I'd told the nurse. That I had to go home. That my mom needed me, and I needed my mom. I also told her that there was no way I would voluntarily agree to go into foster care and if they tried to make me, I would stop walking and talking again, and maybe go on a hunger strike, too, like Gandhi used to do. I did not tell her that Gandhi also used to hear voices. I did not tell her about the conversation I'd had with my Book. I was operating strictly on a need-to-know basis.

I was calm when I told her all this, and I think Dr. M actually heard me. I told her pretty much what the Book had told me—that I was the one in charge of my life, and blaming the voices only gave them more power. They couldn't tell me what to do. I had to take responsibility for making my own decisions, and one of those decisions was to go home and help my mom—and I mean *really* help. Not just fold her T-shirts if I felt like it.

I know the Book made Dr. M sound kind of clueless, but she's really not so bad. She asked me a bunch of questions that I think were actually sneaky tests, and for the next week or two, I knew I was under close surveillance, but I must have passed because eventually she got on board and decided to help. She called my mom in for a family conference, and when she said she thought I was finally ready to be discharged, I could tell my mom wanted to cry and throw her arms around both of us in one of those crazy mom hugs, but she didn't. She stopped herself, and instead she asked Dr. M some really good questions. Like, is it really always bad to hear voices? Like, what if Benny's voices help him sometimes? Does it have to mean he's schizophrenic or psychotic? Like, he's always been creative, so maybe it's partly that?

I could tell Mom had been talking to the Aleph. I held my breath, waiting for Dr. M to shoot her down, but instead Dr. M surprised me. She actually said that what my mom was saying could sometimes be true, and that even Sigmund Freud heard voices, which I knew already because the B-man told me, and then she said I should try this peer support group that my old roommate Mackson started. The group is great, and it turns out Mackson is pretty great, too. He drops in when he's back from college. Super smart. Plus he's gay, so, not a problem as far as the Aleph's concerned. We actually talk about her sometimes, and I even told him some stuff about my feelings, which he totally got, so that was cool. He doesn't know where she's gone, either, but he says I shouldn't worry because she always comes back.

They didn't let me leave Pedipsy right away. First, the lady from Child Protective Services had to go back to our house to inspect it and make sure it was safe for me to live in. Cory and her crew had made a lot of progress clearing stuff out, and before the lady's visit, Mom really busted ass and managed to clean up enough so the lady said it was okay and gave her more time to finish.

Then there was the problem with the police, but Dr. M helped get that sorted, too, and she even showed up in juvenile court to tell the judge that my mom is a good mom, and that she really loves me, and that it would be bad for my mental health to be separated from her because my dad had died and I was traumatized. And then I had to talk to the judge, too, and I was like, Listen, I'm good at things, and then I repeated what the Book told me about facing reality and taking responsibility for what's happening in my life, and the judge liked that. She said I had insight, and she would let me go home if I promised to stay in therapy with Dr. M and not poke holes in myself anymore. And I promised, and I won't. I realize that shit was all pretty mad and I shouldn't have hurt myself, but you know what? I'm not hearing stuff as much anymore, so maybe the voices really did leave through the holes. Dr. M says it definitely wasn't the holes, but she agrees that something must be working, because even though things still chatter and make noise, it's kind of random and impersonal, like background noise. Most of the really evil voices are gone now, and the only one I can still hear is my Book.

But even my Book is getting harder to hear. I don't know why. Here, let me show you.

"Hey, Book! Are you there?"

See? No answer. But I know it's still listening.

IT WAS DECEMBER when I finally came home. There were no Welcome Home signs on the porch or graduation banners in the kitchen. No balloons. Just some red plastic poinsettias in a vase on the cleared-off table that looked nice and a little Christmassy. Everything else in the house was quiet and kind of normal. The things to be discarded were already in the dumpster, and all that was left were the things to be sold or donated. Mom had called Cory, who contacted Vlado, who brought a crew of Slovenians over to help. Mom and I got to work sorting, while they hauled stuff down to the white van. Mom stayed pretty chill, even though at first she gave me some push-back, but like I told the judge, I'm good at things. I know what they want.

"Mom, you gotta listen to me."

"Yes, Benny. I'm listening."

"I know for sure that Dad's records want to stay, but his clothes and shoes all want outta here. They need go someplace they'll be useful, and that includes the shirts. They don't like the idea of being cut up and made into a quilt. They think that's just stupid."

"Even a memory quilt? Filled with nice memories of your dad . . . ?"

"Those are *your* memories, not theirs. They're shirts! They have lives of their own. They don't want to be bedding."

Mom sighed and nodded to Vlado. "Okay, you can take all the clothes, too. Everything in the closet. Just leave the records."

"And the record player, too. He should leave that, but he can take all Dad's books and his instruments. They need to be played."

"But you might want to play them sometime. . . ."

"No. I'll never play them. Not like Dad did. Not like they want to be played."

She opened the clarinet case and carefully assembled the instrument. "It's sad," she said, running her finger down its shiny body.

What my mom meant was that *she* was sad—and this was one of those times when words means something different from what you want them to mean, but what they mean is more true than you know.

"Yes," I said, looking at Dad's clarinet, sitting awkwardly in her hands. "It is sad. It's very sad."

THE B-MAN WAS OUT on the porch with a clipboard on his lap, making an inventory of the donations.

"Ah, young schoolboy," he said when he saw me. "How are you feeling?"

"Okay."

"Ze boys from Ljubljana will hef this done in no time. They are recycling professionals."

I looked over the fence to where Mrs. Wong was sitting on her porch, watching the Slovenians work. She waved to me, and I waved back. Mrs. Wong was in a wheelchair now, too, and with the B-man in his, and Mom's crutches leaning on the railing, the duplex looked like a nursing home or a rehab center.

Mrs. Wong came home a couple days after I did. My mom freaked out when she saw Henry wheeling her up the driveway.

"Oh!" Mom said, in that way she has of just blurting out whatever pops into her head. "I thought you were—!"

She actually stopped herself before she said the word *dead*, so maybe she's getting better, but Mrs. Wong wouldn't have cared. She just says whatever, too.

"Hey, Fatty! You clean up this place good!"

So then Mom went ahead and said it anyway. "I thought you were dead! What happened?"

"Ha!" Mrs. Wong snorted, jerking her thumb back at Henry. "Maybe he wish! No-good son try to steal my house. I tell him no way. I gonna die right here in my own bed."

She barked something at Henry in Cantonese, and he helped her out of the chair and up the steps. Later we learned that she'd gotten a call from Child Protective Services to ask about the eviction notice that Henry had filed on her behalf. It was the first she'd heard about it, and she was furious. She called the lawyer, and he told her everything, about how No-Good was planning to evict me and my mom and sell the duplex, and she put a stop to it right away, which meant we still had housing.

No-Good's dumpster was totally full now, and after the Junk-Bee-Gone van drove off, the carting company arrived to take it away. The hook-lift truck backed into the driveway, and I sat down on the steps by the B-man's wheelchair to watch. A long hydraulic arm with a big hook on the end started reaching out from the flatbed. The hook snagged the dumpster, lifting it, and as the dumpster tilted, we could see all the trash bags filled with my mom's archives and other stuff inside. A few crepe paper streamers and bits of confetti escaped and spilled over the edge, and then slowly the hydraulic arm retracted, pulling the dumpster onto the flatbed.

"So beautiful," Slavoj sighed, as the truck pulled away. "Don't you think so, young schoolboy?"

A cone-shaped foil hat rolled around on the pavement. "It's garbage," I said.

"Precisely! We must learn to luff our garbage! To find poetry in our trash! It is ze only way to luff the whole world."

He went back to work, and I sat there for a while longer, thinking about love. I wanted to ask him about the Aleph, if he'd heard from her or knew where she'd gone, but I knew he missed her, too, and I didn't want to remind him and make him sad. The briefcase containing his epic poem, *Earth*, was lashed to the back of his wheelchair with bungee cords. He told me he'd almost lost it so many times, and now that it was almost finished, he wasn't taking any chances.

"I am not a religious man," he said. "Ze great philosopher Karl Marx once wrote, 'Religion is ze sigh of ze oppressed creature, ze heart of a heartless world, and ze soul of soulless conditions. It is ze opium of ze people.' Perhaps you hef learned this famous quotation in your school?"

"No."

"How unfortunate. Vell, as I say, I am not a religious man, and in fact, I am an atheist, however when I am almost finished writing a book, in spite of myself, I often find myself praying, *Please dear God do not let me die until I hef finished my book!*"

I thought about what my Book would say about the ego of a writer, but I decided not to bring it up, and instead I asked him about God. "If you don't believe God is real, why would God help you? Don't you think he knows the difference between someone who really believes and someone who's just faking it?"

"God is a story," he said. "I believe in stories, and God knows this. Stories are real, my boy. They matter. If you lose your belief in your story, you vill lose yourself."

I thought about this. I never told the B-man about my Book, and all the unbound stuff it showed me in the Bindery that night, and all the stories it told me about my life that I didn't know or was trying to forget. "I have lots of stories," I said. "I was starting to lose them, but my voices helped me remember."

"'Ze truth about stories is that is all we are.' A famous Cherokee writer named Thomas King once said this. We are ze stories we tell ourselves, Benny-boy. We meck ourselves up. We meck each other up, too."

I wondered if the Aleph was in his poem, or if I was. That would be weird, to be in someone else's poem, or someone else's book.

SPEAKING OF BOOKS, here's something else that happened. My mom got a call from Cory telling her that Aikon, the Zen author lady who Mom fangirled and sent all those angsty emails to, was coming to the Library to give a talk about her *Tidy Magic* book and did we want to go? I didn't, but Mom totally did, so I went with her, figuring I could hang out on Level Nine if things got too boring. We showed up early, and Cory took us to the head librarian's private office where Aikon was waiting, and when I went in, she looked at me, and her eyes got all wide like she recognized me.

"Oh!" she said. "You are *Kannon*!" which of course I didn't understand at the time. I thought she said I was a cannon, and even though I know a lot about medieval weapons and siege engines, that made no sense. But then another translator lady who spoke pretty good English explained about Kannon, with her thousand arms and eleven heads, who could hear the voices of things crying out. I said I could totally relate to that, and when she told us that Kannon was the Buddhist saint of compassion, Mom got all teary-eyed and said, "Oh, yes! Benny is very compassionate!" and then she gave me a hug, and I let her even though, as I pointed out, I only have two arms and one head.

Then my mom did something really crazy. She had this shopping bag that she brought with her, and she opened it and pulled out the box with my dad's ashes, which she must have swiped from my bookshelf. She handed it to Aikon, and I swear, if I knew she was going to do this, I would totally have objected, but it's so typical of my mom. At first Aikon thought it was a present for her, and she was like, "Oh, you are so kind!" but then Mom explained that no, it was my dad's ashes and told her all about how when Dad died we didn't have a funeral for him because of him being a

Buddhist. She asked Aikon if she could say a blessing or something, and actually Aikon didn't seem surprised and said sure. So then suddenly everyone got really into it, and Cory and the head librarian cleared a space on one of the bookshelves, and they put the ashes there. Aikon had this little bib thing that she put around her neck, and she had a candle and matches and a wooden box of incense in her bag, too. I thought it was kind of weird, like wherever she went she was always prepared in case somebody needed a pop-up funeral all of a sudden, but I guess that's what nuns do. The head librarian freaked out when she saw the matches, but Aikon said it was okay not to light them. They put the candle and incense next to the ashes, and Cory swiped some flowers from someone's desk, and Aikon wrote my dad's name in fancy Japanese letters on a piece of paper and they put that next to the ashes, too. She bowed and did some stuff with the incense sticks and said some stuff, and then she and the translator lady sang a Japanese hymn that was just a lot of jumbled-up sounds like something my voices might have said. Nobody could understand any of it, but my dad spoke Japanese and so maybe he did, and that made it all right. It was his funeral, after all. After the hymn, Aikon told me and my mom to put our hands together and bow and give Dad some incense, which we did, then she had this whole conversation with Dad in Japanese, like he was still alive, which was weird but also kind of nice. She told us we should say something to him, too, and Mom lost it then. She started crying and saying stuff like, "Oh, Kenji, I love you, and I'm so sorry about what I said that night. I didn't mean it. You know that, right? Can you ever forgive me? I love you and I miss you so much, and I'm doing my best. . . ."

Honestly, it was pretty hard to hear, because she was talking about the fight she and my dad had on the night he died, and I know this because the whole time I was upstairs in my bedroom, listening. I heard my dad say, *I'll come home soon*, and my mom say, *Don't bother*, and then a big crashing sound, and that was it. He never came home. Words are scary, they're powerful, and as I listened to her, it hit me that my mom totally blamed herself for him dying, and on some level maybe I blamed her, too. But not anymore.

All this was going through my head as she was talking, and then it was my turn, so I went over and hugged my mom, and then I said to Dad's ashes, "Earth to Dad. Earth to Dad. Do you read me? It's me, Benny. I miss you. What planet are *you* on?" I knew he would think that was funny.

And then it was over. Mom was like, "Oh, thank you, thank you!" and started hugging everyone and going on about closure. Aikon was super nice about it, but her talk was about to start, so we had to go. Before we left, she signed a copy of her book for me, which was pretty cool. As you know, I like books a lot, and even though I wasn't particularly excited about her book, I'd never met a real author. Mom was super excited, and afterward she kept opening up the book and reading what Aikon had written.

"Listen! '*To Benny, who hears the cries of the world.*' Isn't that beautiful? And it's so true, don't you think?"

I didn't know if it was true or not, but if it made her happy, I was okay with it. I'd had enough of the whole tidying thing, so I told my mom and Cory that I'd be on Nine. They kind of looked at each other but said it was cool. I took the escalator up and stopped on the footbridge, but when I looked down, I couldn't hear anything. No wind, no Calypso. A different exchange student was sleeping in the carrel next to mine, but the typing lady was still at her desk typing.

"You're back," she said. "We've missed you. We were wondering where you'd gone."

I told her I was in the hospital, and she just nodded, like she already knew and it was no big deal.

"Are you better now?"

"Yeah, I think so."

"Good. Glad to hear it. You haven't missed much."

She looked around, and I did, too. I noticed there were fewer books on the shelves, and she just shrugged, like she was reading my mind.

"They're removing books to make room for more computer stations and coworking spaces, and they finally shut down the Bindery, too, and took out all that old equipment. Otherwise, everything's pretty much as you left it."

I felt sad, hearing about the Bindery. It was a frightening place, but beautiful, too.

"Yes, it's a shame," the typing lady said, reading my mind again. "All those beautiful old machines. I guess with the Internet, they decided words don't need to be bound anymore. Personally, I don't agree. I think words prefer being committed to paper. They need boundaries. Without some discipline and constraint, they can just go and say anything they please. But I suspect I'm a bit old-fashioned."

I was watching her, and it was weird because as she spoke, she seemed to get older. Her cheeks sagged. Her hair grew grayer. The transformation seemed to be happening in front of my eyes, but maybe it was just a trick of the light. She gazed out at the half-empty stacks and then she took off her glasses and rubbed her face.

"Oh, well," she said, putting her glasses back on. "I can't help it. I just like books. As objects, I mean."

"Me, too," I told her.

I had my Composition notebook with me in my backpack and my pencil, too. I sat down at my carrel, which was empty, like it was waiting for me. I wasn't planning on writing anything. To tell you the truth, my mind felt pretty empty, too, but ever since the B-man told me I was a good writer, I try always to be ready in case I hear a voice talking, or some idea comes to me. But that evening, I didn't hear anything, just the lady typing, which sounded like raindrops or starlings or pebbles being washed up on the beach by the waves. It was a nice sound, soothing, and pretty soon I just dozed off.

91

Dear Ms. Aikon and Ms. Kimi,

Thank you so much for taking the time to meet with me and Benny and for doing those beautiful ceremonies for us at the Library. Having a proper funeral for Kenji gave us a real sense of closure, and ever since then, things feel different around the house, calmer and more settled. Benny noticed it, too. He asked me, "Do you really think Dad's spirit was haunting us but now he's at peace?" I told him it certainly felt that way.

Just having Benny back home makes all the difference. He really changed while he was in the hospital this time and seems so much more grown up, taking responsibility for things and being so helpful. We can have real conversations again, the way we used to before Kenji died and the voices started. He's going to a peer support group and it's making a huge difference in his ability to relate to others. He really listens now, and he's so much more open about sharing what's going on with him, too. He says he still hears things, but the voices don't freak him out as much, and if he talks back to them nicely but firmly, they don't have to feel rejected and paranoid and act out. His doctor is encouraged, too, but of course she's being cautious. She warns me that clinical recovery isn't smooth, that there will be setbacks. I know this and Benny does, too, but we both have faith that together, we can manage.

We've been working hard on the house and it's looking really nice! I'm even making curtains for Benny's room with some lovely fabric

I got with my employee discount at my favorite craft store. I started
working there part time and it's been great so far. The women
who work there are friendly, and the job keeps me on my feet and
running around, so I'm actually getting some exercise, too. Just
being able to get out of the house and see people makes me
realize how isolated I'd become. I see now how I allowed my grief
and my feelings of guilt about Kenji to cut me off from everything.

I've also started volunteering at the Public Library, helping my
friend, Cory. She's the children's librarian you met, and she lets
me read to the kids during Children's Hour! I love it so much, all
those little faces, looking up at me like flowers. It's my favorite
part of the week. I've actually started thinking seriously about
going back to school to finish my Library Sciences degree. I know
this can't happen right away, but it is my dream.

Dreams are important, right? That's what I tell Benny. I tell him
that his father and I had lots of dreams, and some of them never
amounted to much, but the sweetest dream of all came true, and
his name is Benny.

Gratefully,
Annabelle

92

Waves and starlings, pebbles and crows . . .

Are you here, Benny? Can you still hear us? Dreams are the only place
we can reach you now. Open your eyes. Can you see where you are?

There's a hill of some kind, and you're standing on top, looking out onto a wide-open landscape. The sky is gray and filled with birds—crows and gulls and ravens and raptors—wheeling above your head. There's a breeze blowing in, and you're listening to what sounds like music, only this isn't like any music you've ever heard before. It's a weird, discordant symphony, but not unpleasant, and the cries of the birds are part of it, and there's a rumbling bass line coming from giant earthmovers that look like tiny toys, working in the distance. Watching them, you realize that you're in a landfill site, and the rise you're standing on is a mountain made of tons and tons of garbage.

The expression on your face is rapt and bewildered. As you gaze out over the miles of waste, your eyes begin to pick out discrete objects—a tire here, a toilet bowl there. Then you start to recognize things. You see a pile of broken snow globes, some teapot shards, and some battered stuffed animals. A tangle of socks, a bent music stand, and scree-like heaps of tapes, CDs, and newspapers. All the objects that streamed from your house have wound up here. This is the terminus of your mother's dreams and all her good intentions, and you are standing on top of it. Your throat clenches and you start to cry. Not a lot. Just a tear or two, the ones you couldn't cry when Kenji died.

The thought of your father shifts something in your ears, and you listen harder. As the distant bulldozers and excavators push the garbage around, their engines emit a thrumming sound that starts to weave a jazzy strand into the polyphony. The breeze grows stronger, ruffling your hair. There's a storm blowing in, and so you turn to face into it. You realize you're holding a battered briefcase in one hand. You set it down by your feet and, spreading your arms, you rise up on your toes and balance there.

Eyes closed, you lean into the wind, and we can see that you're taller, and leaner, too, as the baby fat is melting away. The sprinkling of acne has cleared from your skin, which is once again tawny and smooth, only now there's a bit of downy fuzz on your chin, which you will be shaving off soon. Your nose and jaw are more pronounced and your cheeks have begun to hollow. You're beginning to look like the man you will become. You look a lot like your father.

You keep your eyes closed and your arms spread. The wind is growing stronger, and just when you're on the verge of being blown back, someone reaches down and taps you on the forehead. You don't need to see her to know who it is. She's the girl of your dreams, the most beautiful girl in the world, and she's come to keep you from falling, and it's your job to keep her from floating away. A faint smile crosses your face as you reach for her hand. You give a gentle tug, and she drifts down to earth and stands next to you. You pick up your briefcase, and she leans into you, resting her head on your shoulder. She sighs. *So beautiful . . .*

A book must end somewhere, Benny—

Shhh, you whisper. *Listen . . .*

Acknowledgments

A book is a talking object, and the acknowledgments page is where it says thanks. *The Book of Form and Emptiness* has deputized me to do this happy task on its behalf, and so I will start by expressing our gratitude to Zoketsu Norman Fischer and to the lineage of Zen teachers whose words suffuse these pages.

I am deeply grateful to Dr. Gail Hornstein and Dr. Annie Rogers, who read early drafts and offered guidance on matters both psychological and literary. Their personal insights and published work have opened my eyes and my ears, as have the books and resources they steered me toward. There are too many of these to list, but I want to mention Intervoice: the International Hearing Voices Network (www.intervoiceonline.org), and Hearing Voices USA (www.hearingvoicesusa.org), as well as the pioneering work of Dr. Marius Romme and Dr. Sandra Escher, whose experience-focused, non-pathologizing approach to perplexing states and unshared experiences has widened and deepened our understanding.

I offer special and heartfelt thanks to the voice hearers, the artists, and the mad activists, whose courageous accounts, both written and recounted, have expanded my understanding and affirmed my experience. A special shout-out goes to my new friend Alison Smith, activist, author, and storyteller extraordinaire, for sharing her thoughts about voice hearing, revolution, and raising chickens; and to my old friend, Sascha Altman "Scatter" DuBrul, whose work with the Icarus Project, social justice and psychic diversity has seeded my writing and thinking over the years.

I am grateful to all my friends who have shared their invaluable expertise. Matthew Budden, artist, musician, media monitor and archivist, patiently tutored Annabelle in the subtleties of their shared profession, as well as her parenting style. Yoosun Park and Emily Myer assisted me in translating my own childhood encounters with mental health workers into contemporary terms over cocktails at the Green Room, where Andrew Rundle also helped.

For their generous, insightful, and meticulous reading of early, middle, and later drafts, eternal gratitude goes to Katie Young, Liz Gaudet, Karen Joy Fowler, Linda Solomon, Oliver Kellhammer, Adrienne Brodeur, and Claire Kohda. Over the many years of writing, their help and support has been crucial in this Book's making. Books need good readers and friends, as well as typists, to make them who they are, and we thank you from the bottom of our hearts.

Thanks to Hedgebrook, for quiet, sisterhood, and sanctuary.

At Viking, I am deeply grateful to Paul Slovak for his wise and steady editorial presence, and to Brian Tart and Andrea Schwartz for their unflagging support; and at Canongate, to Jamie Byng and his wonderful team for their boundless enthusiasm for all things book related. I want to thank my agents, Molly Friedrich and Lucy Carson, for their faith in my work over the years, and to Molly Zakoor, my cherished assistant, who saves me from my mistakes and keeps me cheerful and on track.

And here, I want to express my enduring thanks to my dear friend, former editor, and fellow writer, Carole DeSanti. Carole acquired *The Book of Form and Emptiness* when she was still at Viking and the book was in its lower-case infancy. She was the first to hear it speak, and her well-tuned ear, keen editorial eye, and compassionate guidance on matters of narrative tone and structure helped the Book find both its voice and form. Over the years, Carole has helped me in more ways than I can possibly mention. She has taught me how to be a writer and an author, and has made my shaggy manuscripts into the books they want to be. I am so lucky to have her as a friend in life and comrade in literature.

And finally, as ever, I am grateful to my beloved Oliver, who keeps my life interesting and who never fails to listen. His ideas inspire me to write. His words awaken my world.